Cousin Bette

HONORÉ DE BALZAC

COUSIN BETTE

Translated by Kathleen Raine

Introduction by Francine Prose

Notes by James Madden

THE MODERN LIBRARY

NEW YORK

1847

2002 Modern Library Edition
 Published in the United States by Modern Library, an imprint of The Random House Publishing Group, a division of Random House, Inc., New York, and simultaneously in Canada by Random House of Canada Limited, Toronto.

LIBRARY OF CONGRESS CATALOGING-IN-PUBLICATION DATA
Balzac, Honoré de, 1799–1850.
[Cousine Bette. English]
Cousin Bette / Honoré de Balzac; translated by Kathleen Raine;
introduction by Francine Prose; notes by James Madden.
p. cm.—(Modern Library classics)
ISBN 0-375-75907-7 (trade pbk. : alk. paper)
1. Paris (France)—Social life and customs—19th century—Fiction.
I. Raine, Kathleen, 1908– II. Title. III. Series.
PQ2165.C5 E5 2002
843'.7—dc21 2001051209
Modern Library website address:
www.modernlibrary.com

Printed in the United States of America

4 6 8 9 7 5 3

Honoré de Balzac

Honoré de Balzac, often said to be the greatest of French novelists, was born in Tours on May 20, 1799. His father was a civil servant who had survived the Revolution and prospered under Napoleon; his mother came from a middle-class Parisian family. Raised by a wet nurse until the age of four, he was later sent to study at the Oratorian college in Vendôme. In 1814 the family moved to the Marais district of Paris, where Balzac attended the Lycée Charlemagne. Following three years as a legal clerk he earned a Bachelor of Law degree in 1819, but soon decided to pursue a literary career. His first effort, *Cromwell,* a verse tragedy, was a complete failure. During the 1820s Balzac supported himself as a hack journalist, turning out sensational novels and potboilers under various pseudonyms. He also tried to make money in several publishing ventures, all of which failed and left him saddled with debt. The appearance in 1829 of *Les Chouans,* the first work published under his own name, along with *La Physiologie du mariage,* marked the beginning of Balzac's success as a novelist. *Scènes de la vie privée* (1830), a collection of short stories, quickly enhanced his reputation.

"Salute me for at this very moment I am in the throes of becoming a genius," Balzac announced to his sister in 1833, when he conceived the idea of pouring all his creativity into writing one great chronicle of the age, *La Comédie Humaine.* "[It] was at first as a dream to me," he later explained. "French society would be the real author; I should only be the secretary. By drawing up an inventory of vices and virtues, by collecting the chief facts of the passions, by depicting characters, by choosing the principal incidents of social life, by composing types out of a combination of homogeneous characteristics, I might perhaps succeed in writing the history which so many historians have neglected: that of Manners. By patience and perseverance I might produce for France in the nineteenth century the book which we must all regret that Rome, Athens, Tyre, Memphis, Persia, and India have not bequeathed to us: a history of their social life."

Balzac devoted the rest of his life to this monumental task. Clothed in a white dressing gown that resembled a monk's robe and imbibing huge quantities of strong black coffee, he began writing at midnight and continued until midday. Famous for composing an entire work on successive galley proofs instead of submitting a finished manuscript to printers, Balzac published five or six books a year, with as many others in various stages of completion. Over a period of two decades he produced ninety-two novels filled with some two thousand characters. Among the most outstanding are *Eugénie Grandet* (1833), *Le Père Goriot* (1835), *César Birotteau* (1837), *Illusions perdues* (1837–1843), *Ursule Mirouët* (1842), *La Cousine Bette* (1846), and *Le Cousin Pons* (1847).

Yet in many ways Balzac's own life became his most extraordinary creation. An exuberant, flamboyant man who pursued married women and unsuccessful business schemes with equal ardor, he was constantly in debt, forever unable to control the follies of his own passionate impulses. In *Story of My Life,* George Sand offered this telling remembrance of him: "One evening, when we had dined on a strange assortment of food at Balzac's—I believe we had boiled beef, a melon, and whipped champagne—he tried on a brand-new dressing gown, showing it off to us with girlish joy, and wanted, thus appareled, to accompany us, candle in hand, up to the Luxembourg gate. It was late, the place was deserted, and I pointed out to him that he would get murdered going back home. 'Not at all,' he told me. 'If I meet some thieves, they'll take me for a madman and will be afraid of me. Either that, or they'll take me for a prince, and pay me homage.' It was a calm, beautiful night. He accompanied us thus, carrying his lighted candle in its pretty holder of chased vermeil, speaking of the four Arabian horses he did not yet have, that he should have soon, that he never did get, and yet firmly believing he sooner or later would have. He would have walked us to the other end of Paris, if we had let him."

During the last years of his life Balzac traveled throughout Europe, often in the company of Madame Eveline Hanska, his longtime mistress. The two married on March 14, 1850, in the parish church near her vast estate in the Ukraine. Honoré de Balzac died just five months later in Paris on August 18, 1850. "Balzac [was] the master unequalled in the art of painting humanity as it exists in modern society," judged George Sand. "He searched and dared everything.... Childlike and great; always envious of trifles and never jealous of true glory; sincere to the point of modesty, proud to the point of braggadocio; trusting himself and others; very generous, very kind, and very crazy, with an inner reserve of reason which controlled all aspects of his work; brazen yet celibate; drunk on water; intemperate regarding work, but sober in the other passions; materialistic and romantic to equal excess; credulous and skeptical; filled with inconsistencies and mysteries—that was Balzac."

Contents

Introduction

Francine Prose

To read the first chapter of *Cousin Bette* is like entering a foreign city that seems eerily like our own—and turning a corner and coming upon a brutal mugging in progress. Few novels have more violent beginnings, though the violence is all psychological, and, seen from a distance, might even pass for polite conversation. The fierceness of Balzac's courage and his reckless determination to portray the Human Comedy precisely as he saw it becomes clear when we consider how few contemporary writers would risk beginning a work of fiction with a scene so repulsive, and so brave in its refusal to hint or promise that, by the novel's conclusion, sin will be punished, virtue rewarded, and redemption freely offered to the wicked and innocent alike. *Cousin Bette* portrays a world in which almost everyone will do anything to anyone if sex and money are at stake, a milieu in which sex is routinely traded for money, in which friendships and alliances are forged to advance the most immoral motives, and in which only fools and martyrs are deluded enough to follow the outmoded promptings of honor, loyalty, and conscience.

Published in 1847, *Cousin Bette* was composed (as always, at breakneck speed) near the end of a prodigiously prolific career that produced nearly a hundred novels, novellas, and short stories. By then, Balzac had mastered the seemingly effortless technical skill and the brilliant, gleeful assurance with which, at the start of *Cousin Bette,* he portrays the meeting between Monsieur Crevel and the Baroness Adeline Hulot—two Parisians with little in common except for the speed at which their social status has changed, and the not unrelated fact that their grown children are married.

The former owner of a perfume shop, Celestin Crevel is a vulgar opportunist and libertine who has manipulated the fluid political climate to propel his rise along the somewhat shady margins of Paris society. By the time the novel opens, in 1838, Crevel is already an ex–deputy mayor, and wears the ribbon of a Chevalier of the Legion of Honor. At once more dramatic and more deserved, Adeline Hulot's ascent has, alas, proved more temporary. For some years after her beauty and dignity persuaded the Baron Hulot to marry her despite her lowly Alsatian-peasant origins, she enjoyed a brief interlude of marital bliss. But now, her beloved husband has succumbed to a tragic flaw that today—when practically every child is conversant with the latest psychological syndromes—would doubtless be diagnosed as a world-class case of sexual addiction.

The Baron's obsessive tendency to fall madly in love with, and subsequently enslave himself to, paradoxically cheap and expensive women has brought his family to near-ruin. And though Adeline is aware that "for twenty years Baron Hulot had been unfaithful," she "kept a leaden screen in front of her eyes" and has chosen not to know the details until Crevel visits her at home and puts his terms very plainly: Unless Adeline (who, at forty-eight, is still a beauty) agrees to sleep with him, her adored daughter, Hortense, will never marry, because Crevel will let everyone know that the once-distinguished, once-prosperous Hulots cannot afford to provide her with a dowry. And in case the faithful, long-suffering Adeline (also diagnosable, in this case, as one of literature's great enablers) wonders how this dire situation came about, the ever-thoughtful Monsieur Crevel has come to explain: Having tired of his lover, Jenny Cadine, whom he corrupted when she was thirteen, the Baron has stolen Monsieur Crevel's own mistress, Josépha, the "queen of the demimonde," an insatiably avaricious "Jewess" who has not merely "fleeced" the Baron but, in Kathleen Raine's deft translation, "skinned" him to the tune of over a hundred thousand francs. But all is not lost. If Adeline agrees to become his lover—for ten years!—Crevel will give her the money for Hortense's dowry.

This scene of breathtaking cruelty and sexual blackmail—essentially, a rape in which both parties remain fully clothed—introduces and prefigures the themes that Balzac will develop throughout the novel: heartlessness, self-interest, meretriciousness, greed, revenge, bloodthirsty sexual competition. The unnerving conversation between Crevel and the Baroness will resonate later in the book, its echo amplified by a series of events that parallel and outdo this one in their sheer awfulness—most notably, another meeting between Adeline and Crevel, three years after the opening scene. In this variation on the introductory chapter, the now desperate Adeline can no longer afford the luxury of virtue. She tearfully agrees to accept Monsieur Crevel's proposition, only to learn that what had originally inspired the former perfumer was not in fact love or lust (motives for which there is much to be said, though perhaps not in this instance) but rather, the darker, less affirmative and sympathetic desire for revenge: specifically, revenge on her husband for having stolen Josépha. And now that Crevel has liberally helped himself to the favors of the Baron's newest obsession—the scheming, ambitious, and apparently irresistible Madame Marneffe, a civil servant's wife who turns out to be more skillful and greedier than the most successful courtesans—Crevel no longer feels the compulsion to possess the Baron's wife.

Such summaries omit the telling details, the razor-sharp observations, the nearly unbearable exchanges, the sudden switches in argument and reasoning that portray precisely the characters of both participants, and the clever parallels (having earlier observed Madame Marneffe completing her calculatedly seductive toilette, we now watch Adeline attempt something similar, only to ruin it when she reddens her nose by crying a torrent of real tears as opposed to the few attractive droplets that Madame Marneffe would have shed) that serve as cornerstones in the novel's satisfying and (given its interest in the consequences of uncontrolled lust and passion) surprisingly orderly formal structure.

But summarizing the two scenes suffices to illustrate what underlies the construction and the spirit of the novel: the resolve, and again, the sheer bravery required to begin a book with an example of truly repugnant behavior and then have the general tone of events and the prevailing standards of conduct go pretty much straight down from there. As the plot progresses, vengefulness, greed, and unfeeling ambition are passed, like some sort of evil baton, between the small but successful group of schemers and villains, both minor and major, that populate the novel.

—

Lurking on the edges of the Hulot family parlor, a room that clings so stubbornly to gentility despite the frayed upholstery that Crevel so helpfully points out, is the book's title character, Cousin Bette, a vengeful and resentful relative of Adeline's. Ironically, regardless of the sexual, marital, and financial humiliations to which her cousin is at the moment being subjected, the poor relation is utterly consumed by envy of Adeline and her wonderful life. Balzac dispatches Cousin Bette in a few swift, brutal strokes: "Lisbeth Fischer ... was far from being a beauty like her cousin; for which reason she had been tremendously jealous of her. Jealousy formed the basis of her character, with all its eccentricities.... A Vosges peasant woman in all senses of the word—thin, dark, her hair black and stringy, with thick eyebrows meeting in a tuft, long, strong arms, flat feet, with several moles on her long simian face—such, in brief, was the appearance of this old maid." Though she long ago "gave up all idea of competing with or rivaling her cousin ... envy remained hidden in her secret heart, like the germ of a disease that is liable to break out and ravage a city if the fatal bale of wool in which it is hidden is ever opened."

In fact, Bette proves capable of one of the book's few acts of generosity and devotion: her support of, and attachment to, the gifted and impecunious Polish sculptor Wenceslas Steinbock. Thus she shows herself to be, like so many of Balzac's most memorable characters, full of contradictions, immensely complex, and capable of great extremes—that is to say, to be a recognizable, plausible human, whose humanity we must acknowledge, however much we might wish to disown it.

In any case, when Bette's outwardly disinterested but, at heart, possessive love for Wenceslas is thwarted, the "germ" does eventually break out, and the scorned Cousin Bette unleashes a fury that indeed outdoes hell's. Bette sets in motion her evil plans for the unfortunate Hulot family—a campaign whose chances for success are dramatically improved when Bette's neighbor, Madame Marneffe, realizes that the erotomaniacal Hulot is the perfect stepping-stone to aid her on her way to great wealth and social position, at least in the demimonde. Thus Balzac demonstrates that greed and wickedness are, as it were, equal opportunity employers, willing to use the services of a pretty married woman, an ugly unmarried one, and an assortment of male characters, from the insufferable Crevel to the pathetic Monsieur Marneffe, who readily prostitutes his wife in the hopes of a modest career advancement.

From various motives, none of them good, these men and women conspire to impoverish and destroy Baron Hulot and his family. Of course, none of their schemes could succeed were it not for the Baron's own weakness. Yet Balzac seems to display a certain sympathy for (or at least, a reluctance to condemn as harshly as he condemns the rest) a lover whose taste runs the gamut from hardened courtesans to preadolescent girls. Or perhaps the scene in which we watch Madame Marneffe prepare to make her conquests, and the rapidity with which even the uxorious Wenceslas succumbs to her charms, is meant to imply that no male (least of all one like Hulot) can hope to resist the meticulously constructed, perfectly aimed sexual allure of certain women. One almost suspects that Balzac can't help admiring a man who, like himself, possesses monumental appetites and energies, however misdirected; this suspicion reminds us, in turn, of the profound ambivalence that drove Balzac, who may have been the most obsessive shopper, collector, speculator—and serious debtor—in the history of world literature, to condemn, in novel after novel, a society that overvalues and worships the power of money. Balzac's personal familiarity with the vice he railed against most vehemently cannot help but add to the reader's impression that the failings of his most unforgivable characters are, finally, only human.

—

Ultimately, what's most shocking and inspiring about *Cousin Bette* is its sheer relentlessness, a steely mercilessness on the part of the author that echoes and at moments even exceeds the pitiless schadenfreude of its title character. What hope does the novel offer? Not much, at least not for this world. Throughout the book, women steal each other's husbands, men steal each other's mistresses, and everyone—male and female alike—conspire to steal one another's money. Generosity and virtue are repaid with humiliation, betrayal, and the opportunity to discover some devastating piece of personal information. Certainly that is Adeline's fate, from that first interview with Crevel to the book's conclusion, when—having devoted herself to a form of charitable social work that furthers the institution of marriage, an institution which has ruined her life—she receives, as her earthly reward, the chance to see, for herself, the nearly unimaginable depths to which her husband has descended.

Nowadays, when critics make sure that the novelist understands the crucial importance of creating characters with whom the reader can sympathize and identify, approve of and like, when the book-buying public insists upon plots in which obstacles are overcome and hardships prove instructive, in which goodness and kindness are recognized and rewarded—given these fashions and prevailing pressures, few novelists would have the nerve to author a book as unsparing (and for that reason, as exalting) as *Cousin Bette.* Reading Balzac's masterpiece reminds us of the reasons why we need great literature: for aesthetic pleasure and enjoyment, for beauty and truth, for the opportunity to enter the mind of another, for information about the temporal and the eternal. So much of what Balzac tells us has by now become much more difficult, indeed practically impossible (or impermissible) for us to admit to ourselves, or to say: the fact that the poor and the ugly might envy the beautiful and the rich, that our craving for sex and money is so powerful and so anarchic that it can defeat, with hardly a struggle, our better instincts and good judgment. Balzac, who knew about all these things (firsthand, as it were), continues to remind us, in novels such as *Cousin Bette,* what we humans are capable of—which is to say, what we are.

—

FRANCINE PROSE's most recent novel, *Blue Angel,* was a finalist for the 2000 National Book Award. A contributing editor at *Harper's* magazine and a former Director's Fellow at the New York Public Library Center for Scholars and Writers, she writes regularly for numerous publications, including *The New York Times* and *The Wall Street Journal.*

Cousin Bette

Chapter I

Toward the middle of the month of July, in the year 1838, one of those vehicles called milords[1] that had lately made their appearance in Paris drove along the Rue de l'Université, carrying a heavily built man of middle height in the uniform of a captain of the National Guard.[2]

Among Parisians, of whose intelligence we hear so much, there are some who think themselves infinitely better men in uniform than in their ordinary clothes, and who imagine that the taste of women is so depraved that they will be favorably impressed—so they fancy—by the sight of a busby and military trappings.

The features of this captain of the second company expressed a self-satisfaction that gave a positive radiance to his ruddy complexion and his rather chubby face. This halo, bestowed upon the brows of retired tradesmen by money made in business, marked him out as one of the elect of Paris—an ex–deputy mayor of his district at least. And, needless to say, the ribbon of the Legion of Honor adorned his chest, which was dashingly padded out in the Prussian style.

Proudly ensconced in the corner of the milord, this decorated gentleman allowed his attention to stray over the passers-by—who, in Paris, often in this way come in for pleasant smiles meant for beautiful eyes that are not present.

The milord stopped in the part of the road between the Rue de Bellechasse and the Rue de Bourgogne,[3] at the door of a large house that had recently been built on part of the court of an old mansion standing in its own garden.[4] The mansion had been preserved, and remained in its original condition at the end of the court, whose size had been reduced by half.

The way in which the captain accepted the help of the driver as he got down from the milord was enough in itself to betray a man in his fifties. There are certain movements whose manifest heaviness is as indiscreet as a birth certificate.

The captain drew his yellow glove on to his right hand again, and without consulting the concierge, made his way toward the flight of steps leading to the ground floor of the mansion, with an air that meant "She is mine!"

Paris porters take things in at a glance; they never stop decorated gentlemen of heavy gait who wear blue uniforms. In other words, they recognize money when they see it.

This whole ground floor was occupied by the Baron Hulot d'Ervy, Commissary-General under the Republic, late officer-in-charge of the Army Commissariat, and now head of one of the principal departments of the War Ministry, Councilor of State, a senior officer of the Legion of Honor, and so on and so forth.

Baron Hulot had himself taken the name of d'Ervy, his birthplace, in order to distinguish himself from his brother, the celebrated General Hulot,[5] colonel of the grenadiers of the Imperial Guard, created Count de Forzheim by the Emperor after the campaign of 1809.

The elder brother, the Count, to whose charge the younger brother had been committed, had, with paternal prudence, placed him in military administration, in which, thanks to the services of both brothers, the Baron had won, and indeed deserved, the favor of Napoleon. From the year 1807 Baron Hulot had been Commissary General of the armies in Spain.

After ringing, the bourgeois captain made desperate efforts to straighten his coat, which had wrinkled up both in front and behind—the result of a prominent corporation. Admitted on sight by a manservant in uniform, this important and imposing man followed the maid, who announced, as she opened the door of the drawing room, "Monsieur Crevel!"

On hearing this name, so admirably suited to the figure[6] of its bearer, a tall, fair, well-preserved woman rose as if she had received an electric shock.

"Hortense, my angel, go into the garden with your cousin Bette," she said quietly to her daughter, who was working at her embroidery a little distance away.

After making a gracious bow to the captain, Mademoiselle Hortense Hulot went out by a French window, taking with her a dried-up spinster who looked older than the Baroness, although she was five years younger.

"It is about your marriage," Cousin Bette whispered in the ear of her young cousin Hortense, without seeming to be in the least offended by the way in which the Baroness had sent them away, treating her as of almost no consequence.

This cousin's style of dress would, if need be, have accounted for this lack of ceremony.

The old maid was dressed in a maroon-colored merino dress, whose cut and trimmings suggested the Restoration,[7] an embroidered collar worth about three francs, and a stitched straw hat with blue satin bows edged with straw, of the kind worn by old-clothes women in the market. At the sight of her kid slippers, whose style suggested a fourth-rate shoe shop, a stranger would have hesitated before greeting Cousin Bette as a relation of the family, for she looked just like a daily sewing woman. Nevertheless, the old maid gave a little friendly nod to Monsieur Crevel as she went out, a greeting to which that personage replied with a look of mutual understanding.

"You are coming tomorrow, aren't you, Mademoiselle Fischer?" he said.

"There won't be company?" asked Cousin Bette.

"Only yourself and my children."

"Very well," she replied, "you can count on me."

"I am at your service, Madame," said the bourgeois captain of the militia, turning again to Baroness Hulot, and giving her a look of the kind that Tartuffe casts upon Elmire,[8] when a provincial actor thinks it necessary to stress the intentions of that character.

"If you will come this way, we can discuss things much better than in the drawing room," said Madame Hulot, leading the way to an adjoining room, which, as the flat was planned, was used as a card room.

This room was divided off only by a thin partition from a boudoir, whose window opened upon the garden, and Madame Hulot left Monsieur Crevel alone for a moment, for she thought it necessary to close the window and the door of the boudoir, so that nobody could listen there. She even took the precaution of closing the French window of the drawing room as well, smiling as she did so at her daughter and cousin whom she saw sitting in an old summerhouse at the end of the garden. She came back, leaving the door of the card room open, so that she would be able to hear the drawing-room door open if anyone were to come in.

As she came and went, the Baroness, being unobserved, allowed her thoughts to express themselves in her face; and if anyone had seen her, they would have been alarmed by her agitation. But as she returned from the communicating door of the drawing room to the card room, her face was veiled with that impenetrable reserve that all women, even the most open, seem able to assume at will.

During these preparations, singular to say the least, the national guardsman examined the furniture of the room in which he found himself.

As he scrutinized the silk curtains, once red, but faded violet by the sunlight, and frayed along their folds with long use, a carpet whose colors had disappeared, furniture whose gilt was worn and whose silk, marbled with stains, was worn to shreds, expressions of disdain, satisfaction, and hope naïvely succeeded one another on his stupid shopkeeper's face. He was looking at himself in the mirror behind an old Empire clock, taking stock of himself, when the rustle of a silk dress announced the entry of the Baroness.

He immediately struck an attitude.

After seating herself on a little sofa that must certainly have been very pretty in 1809, the Baroness motioned Crevel to a chair whose arms ended in bronze sphynx heads, and from which the paint was flaking off, leaving patches of bare wood, and signed to him to sit down.

"These precautions of yours, Madame, might be taken as a good sign for a—"

"A lover," she replied, interrupting the national guardsman.

"The word is weak," he said, placing his right hand over his heart, and rolling his eyes in a way that nearly always makes a woman laugh when she sees such an expression in cold blood. "Lover! Lover! Say, rather, one bewitched . . ."

Chapter II

"Listen, Monsieur Crevel," the Baroness went on, too anxious to be able to laugh. "You are fifty—ten years younger than Monsieur Hulot, I know; but at my age a woman's folly would have to be justified by good looks, or youth or celebrity, or by distinction, by one or the other of those splendors that dazzle us to the point of quite forgetting ourselves, and even our age. Even if you have fifty thousand a year, your age counterbalances your fortune; therefore you possess none of the qualifications that a woman requires . . ."

"And love?" said the national guardsman, rising and coming toward her. "A love that—"

"No, infatuation," said the Baroness, interrupting him to put an end to this absurdity.

"Yes, infatuation, and love," he went on, "but also something better, the right—"

"The right?" Madame Hulot exclaimed, and she became exalted in her scorn, defiance, and indignation. "But on this subject we shall never reach the end of a futile discussion, and I did not ask you to come here to talk about the reason for which I forbade you the house, in spite of the connection between our two families."

"I thought you had."

"Not again!" she replied. "Don't you see, from the free and detached manner in which I speak of lovers, love, of everything that is most scandalous for a woman, that I am absolutely sure of remaining virtuous? I am not afraid of anything, even of incurring suspicion by being alone with you. Would a frail woman behave in such a way? You know very well why I asked you to come."

"No, Madame," Crevel replied, assuming a cold manner. He pursed his lips and struck his attitude again.

"Very well, I will be brief and bring our mutual embarrassment to an end," said the Baroness Hulot, looking at Crevel.

Crevel made an ironical bow, in which a tradesman would have recognized the gesture of a one-time commercial traveler.

"Our son has married your daughter."

"And if that were to be done over again . . ." said Crevel.

"The marriage would not take place," replied the Baroness quickly. "No doubt. All the same, you have nothing to complain of. My son is not only one of the leading lawyers of Paris, but he has been a deputy for a year, and his debut in the Chamber has been brilliant enough to give us reason to believe that he may be in the Government before long. Victorin has twice been nominated as official spokesman for important debates, and he could have the post of attorney-general in the Court of Appeal today if he wanted to. If you are trying to tell me that you have a son-in-law without a fortune—"

"A son-in-law whom I am obliged to keep," Crevel replied, "which seems to me worse, Madame. Of the five hundred thousand francs of my daughter's dowry, two hundred thousand have gone heaven knows where . . . in paying your son's debts, in furnishing his house in style, a house worth five hundred thousand francs, which is bringing in only fifteen thousand, because he occupies the best part[1] of it, and on which he still owes two hundred and sixty thousand francs—the rent he gets barely covers the interest on the debt. This year I have had to give my daughter something like twenty thousand francs to help her to make ends meet. And my son-in-law, who was making thirty thousand francs at the Assizes,[2] they say, is now going to throw that up for the Chamber."

"Even that, Monsieur Crevel, is a mere trifle, and we are getting away from the point. But, since we are discussing the subject, if my son gets into office, and if he has you made an officer of the Legion of Honor, and a municipal councilor of Paris, you, as a retired perfumer, will have nothing to complain of. . . ."

"Ah, there we have it! I am a tradesman, a shopkeeper, an ex-salesman of almond paste, eau-de-Portugal, and hair oil! I ought to be highly honored to have married my only daughter to the son of the Baron Hulot d'Ervy! My daughter will be a baroness. Regency! Louis XV![3] Period! Fine! I love Célestine as one does love an only child. I love her so much that, rather than give her brothers or sisters, I have put up with all the inconvenience of being a widower in Paris—and in my prime, Madame—but let it be understood that in spite of my love for my daughter, I am not going to ruin myself for your son, whose expenses do not seem very clear to an old shopkeeper like me."

"At this very moment Monsieur Popinot, who was a chemist in the Rue des Lombards, is Minister of Commerce!"

"A friend of mine, Madame," said the retired perfumer, "for I, Celestin Crevel, old César Birotteau's ex–head salesman, bought the business of the said Birotteau, Popinot's father-in-law,[4] when Popinot was just an ordinary salesman in the business, and he remembers me, because he is not proud—I will say that for him—when it comes to remembering men in good positions, who have incomes of sixty thousand francs."

"Very well, sir, the ideas that you describe as 'Regency' no longer apply in a period when men are accepted for their personal qualities; and that is what you did when you married your daughter to my son."

"You don't know how that marriage came about!" exclaimed Crevel. "Ah! wretched bachelor life! But for my bad ways, my Célestine would have been Viscountess Popinot today!"

"But in any case, do not let us indulge in recriminations over what is done," said the Baroness eagerly. "Let us discuss the reasons for my complaints over your strange conduct. My daughter Hortense might have married, the marriage depended entirely upon you, and I expected generosity on your part. I thought that you would behave fairly toward a woman whose heart has never held any other image than that of her husband, that you would have recognized that it was necessary for her not to receive any man who might compromise her, and that you would have been eager, out of respect for the family to which you are allied, to help toward establishing Hortense with the Councilor, Monsieur Lebas.... And instead, sir, you have wrecked the marriage."

"Madame," replied the ex-perfumer, "I acted as an honest man. I was asked whether the two hundred thousand francs of Mademoiselle Hortense's dowry would be paid. These were my actual words: 'I cannot answer for it. My son-in-law, to whom the Hulot family promised that sum on his marriage, was in debt; and I believe that if Monsieur Hulot d'Ervy were to die tomorrow his widow would be penniless.' There you are, dear Madame."

"Would you have said the same, sir," asked Madame Hulot, looking straight at Crevel, "if I had forgotten my duties for your sake?"

"I would not have had the right to say it, dear Adeline," exclaimed this singular lover, interrupting the Baroness, "for you would have found the dowry in my note-case."

And in proof of his words, the stout Crevel, seeing her plunged by these words into a silent horror that he mistook for hesitation, went down on one knee and kissed Madame Hulot's hand.

"Buy my daughter's happiness at the price of— Please get up, or I shall ring."

The ex-perfumer got up with considerable difficulty. This circumstance made him so angry that he struck his attitude again. Nearly all men affect some posture that they believe brings out all the advantages with which nature has blessed them. For Crevel, this attitude consisted in crossing his arms like Napoleon, turning three-quarter face, and looking in the direction that the painter had made him look for his portrait—that is, toward the horizon.

"Be faithful," he said, with well-feigned rage, "be faithful to a libert—"

"To a husband, sir, which is only right," replied Madame Hulot, interrupting Crevel, in order to prevent him from pronouncing a word that she did not wish to hear.

"Well, Madame, you wrote asking me to come; you wish to know the reasons for my conduct; you repulse me with your queenly airs, your scorn and your contempt! Anyone would think I was a slave! I repeat, upon my word! I have the right to—to pay court to you, because ... But no, I love you enough to hold my tongue...."

"Speak, sir! In a few days I shall be forty-eight, and I am not absurdly prudish; I can hear anything ..."

"Very well, will you give me your word as an honest woman—for you are an honest woman, worse luck for me—never to mention my name, never to say that I let you into the secret?"

"If that is the condition of your telling me, I promise you that I shall not tell anyone who it was that told me whatever enormities you are going to confide in me—not even my husband."

"That I can well believe, because it concerns no one but him and yourself."

Madame Hulot turned pale.

"Oh, if you still love Hulot, it will hurt you! Would you rather I said nothing?"

"Speak, sir, because according to you it is a question of justifying in my eyes the strange declarations that you have made to me, and your persistence in tormenting a woman of my age whose only wish was to marry her daughter, and afterwards ... die in peace!"

"You see, you are unhappy."

"I, sir?"

"Yes, beautiful and noble creature," cried Crevel, "you have suffered all too much!"

"Sir, say no more and go! Or speak to me as you should."

"Do you know, Madame, how Hulot and I became acquainted? Through our mistresses, Madame!"

"Oh, sir!"

"Through our mistresses, Madame!" Crevel repeated, in a melodramatic tone, breaking his pose in order to gesticulate with his right hand.

"Well, sir?" said the Baroness calmly, to the great amazement of Crevel.

Seducers, with their petty motives, can never understand noble minds.

"I, having been a widower for five years," Crevel went on, in the manner of a man who is going to tell a story, "not wishing to remarry, in the interest of my daughter whom I adore, and not wishing either to carry on any intrigues in my house, although at the time I had a very pretty cashier, I set up house, as the saying goes, for a little working-girl of fifteen, whose beauty was really astonishing, and with whom, I must admit, I had fallen head over ears in love. And, Madame, I even asked my own aunt, whom I brought up from the country—my mother's sister!—to live with this charming creature, and to look after her, and see that she remained as well behaved as was possible in a situation that was what one might call... dubious ... no, compromising! This little girl, who had a decided talent for music, had masters and got some education—it kept her out of mischief! And besides, I wanted to be at the same time her father, her benefactor, and—to put it bluntly—her lover; to kill two birds with one stone, to do a good deed as well as having a good time. I had five years of happiness. The child had one of those voices that is worth a fortune in the theater, and I can only say of her that she was a Duprez in petticoats.[5] It cost me two thousand francs a year, simply to give her her talent as a singer. She made me crazy about music, and I took a box at the Italian Opera for her and for my daughter. I went with them on alternate evenings, one night with Célestine, and the next with Josépha."

"What, the famous singer?"

"Yes, Madame," Crevel continued with pride, "the famous Josépha owes everything to me.... Well, when the girl was twenty, in eighteen thirty-four, thinking that I had attached her to me for life, and having become very soft with her, I wanted her to have some amusement, and I allowed her to meet a pretty little actress called Jenny Cadine, whose circumstances were not unlike her own. That actress also owed everything to a protector, who had brought her up in the lap of luxury. This protector was the Baron Hulot—"

"I know, sir," said the Baroness in a calm voice that did not show the least alteration.

"Oh! Indeed!" cried Crevel, more and more put out. "All right! But do you know that your monster of a husband was protecting Jenny Cadine when she was thirteen years old?"

"Well, sir, go on!" said the Baroness.

"As Jenny Cadine was twenty, the same age as Josépha," went on the ex-shopkeeper, "when they got to know each other, the Baron had been playing the part of Louis XV to her Mademoiselle de Romans[6] ever since eighteen twenty-six, and you were twelve years younger then...."

"I had reasons for allowing Monsieur Hulot his freedom."

"That lie, Madame, will no doubt suffice to wipe out all the sins that you have ever committed, and will open for you the gate of Paradise," replied Crevel, with a knowing air that made the Baroness turn crimson. "Tell that to others, sublime and adorable woman, but not to old Crevel, who, you must know, has dined too often as one of four with your rake of a husband not to know your worth! Sometimes he used to reproach himself when he was a little tipsy, and expatiate on your perfections. . . . Oh, I know you well: you are an angel. A libertine might hesitate between a young girl of twenty and yourself.... For me, there is no hesitation."

"Sir!"

"Very well, not another word.... But you must know, saintly and noble woman, that husbands, when they are fuddled, tell their mistresses a great many things about their wives."

The tears of shame that rolled from under Madame Hulot's lovely eyelids made the national guardsman stop short, and he quite forgot to strike his attitude.

"To proceed," he said, "we became acquainted, the Baron and I, through our mistresses. The Baron, like all bad characters, is very likable and a thoroughly good sort. Did I like the fellow? You bet I did! But no more of these reminiscences. . . . We became like two brothers. The scoundrel, quite in the Regency style, did his best to corrupt me, preached Saint Simonism[7] on the subject of women, tried to give me lordly ideas and whatnot; but, you see, I loved my little girl enough to have married her. Only I was afraid of having children. Between two old papas, friends as we were, naturally the idea of marrying our children came up. Three months after the marriage of his son with my Célestine, Hulot—I can hardly bear to speak his name, for he has deceived both of us, Madame—very well, the scoundrel went off with my little Josépha. The villain knew that he had been supplanted by a young Councilor of State and by an artist—if you please!—in the heart of Jenny Cadine, whose success was becoming more and more smashing, and he took away my poor little mistress, a love of a girl! But you must have seen her at the Italian Opera, because he got her in there through his influence. Your husband isn't as careful as I am; I am as orderly as a page of music paper—he had been badly stung already over Jenny Cadine, who must have cost him pretty nearly thirty thousand francs a year. Well, you may as well know that he is completely ruining himself for Josépha. Josépha, Madame, is a Jewess;[8] her name is Mirah—the anagram of Hiram—an Israelitish label to identify her, because she is a foundling who was abandoned in Germany. I made some inquiries and discovered that she is the illegitimate child of a rich Jewish banker. The theater, and above all the education she received from Jenny Cadine, Madame Schontz, Malaga, and Carabine[9] on the subject of how to treat old men, brought out in the little girl that I kept in an honest and economical way the instinct of the ancient Hebrews for gold and jewels, for the Golden Calf! The celebrated singer, who is now hot on the scent, wants to be rich, very rich! And she doesn't waste any of the money that is wasted on her! She has tried it out on old Hulot and fleeced him. Oh! fleeced is not the word—skinned him, I should say! This wretched man, after bidding for her against one of the Kellers, and with the Marquis d'Esgrignon[10]—both of them mad about Josépha—not to mention unknown adorers, is about to see her carried off by that duke who is so mighty rich and who patronizes the arts . . . what's his name? . . . a dwarf . . . oh, yes, the Duc d'Hérouville. This great man wants Josépha to himself; all the courtesan world is talking about it, and the Baron doesn't know a thing; because it's just the same in the Thirteenth District[11] as it is in all the others: the lover, like the husband, is the last to hear. Now do you understand my right? Your husband, dear lady, robbed me of my happiness, the only pleasure I have known since I became a widower. Yes, if I had not had the misfortune to meet that old charmer, I should still have had Josépha. Because I, mind you, would never have let her go into the theater, she should have remained obscure and well behaved, and my property. Oh, if you had seen her eight years ago! Slim and highly strung, a golden Andalusian, as they say, with her hair black and shining like satin, her eyes with long brown lashes, flashing fire, the distinction of a duchess in every movement, the modesty of poverty, real grace, and as pretty in her ways as a wild deer. And now, thanks to Hulot, her charm and purity have become a mantrap, a money-box for hundred-sou pieces.[12] The girl is the queen of the demimonde, as they say. And how she can put it across nowadays, she who used to know nothing about anything, not even that expression."

Here the ex-perfumer wiped his eyes, from which some tears had trickled. The sincerity of this grief touched Madame Hulot, who emerged from the reverie into which she had fallen.

"Well, Madame, am I going to find a treasure like that at fifty-two? At that age love costs thirty thousand francs a year; I know the figure through your husband, and I, for my part, am too fond of Célestine to ruin her. When I saw you, on the first evening that you received us, I could not understand how that scoundrel Hulot could keep a Jenny Cadine... you looked like a queen. You are not thirty," he went on; "you are young to me, you are beautiful. My word of honor, that day I was touched to the heart, and I said to myself: 'If I had not my Josépha, since old Hulot neglects his wife, she would suit me like a glove.' Oh! pardon me, that is an expression from the old days![13] The perfumer comes out every now and then, that is what prevents me from aspiring to be a deputy. So, when I was so badly served by the Baron, because, between old rakes like ourselves, our friends' mistresses should be sacred—I made up my mind to take his wife. It's only fair. The Baron could say nothing, so that we would be safe. You showed me the door like a mangy dog at the first words I spoke on the state of my heart; by that you redoubled my love, or my infatuation, if you like, and you shall be mine!"

"Really? How?"

"I don't know, but it shall be so. You see, Madame, an idiot of a perfumer—retired!—who has only one idea in his head, is worth more than an intelligent man who has thousands. I am mad about you, and you are my revenge! And that makes it as if I loved twice over. I am speaking frankly to you, as a man who has made up his mind. I am being plain with you, just as you are with me when you say: 'I will not be yours.' So, my cards are on the table, as the saying is. Yes, you shall be mine, when the time comes. Oh! if you were fifty, you should still be my mistress! It will happen, because, between ourselves, nothing would surprise me where your husband is concerned."

Madame Hulot turned on this calculating tradesman such a look of terror that he thought that she had become demented, and stopped short.

"You asked for it; you covered me with your contempt. You have defied me, and I have spoken out!" he said, feeling in himself the need to justify the brutality of his last words.

"Oh! my daughter, my daughter!" exclaimed the Baroness in a despairing voice.

"Oh, I have lost my senses!" Crevel went on again. "The day that

I lost Josépha, I was like a tigress whose cubs have been taken from her . . . in fact, I was like you at this moment. Your daughter! For me, she is the means of obtaining you. Yes, I have wrecked your daughter's marriage. . . . And without my help you won't marry her at all! However beautiful Mademoiselle Hortense may be, she must have a dowry."

"Yes, alas!" said the Baroness, drying her eyes.

"Very well, try asking the Baron for ten thousand francs," went on Crevel, who had struck his pose again.

He paused for a moment, like an actor who has made his point.

"If he had them, he would give them to Josépha's successor!" he said with emphasis. "Where will he stop in the way he is going? He was always too fond of women—there is moderation in all things, as our King has said[14]—and now his vanity is involved. He's a fine husband! He will have you all sleeping on straw, for the sake of his pleasure. You are halfway to the workhouse already. Look here, since I first set foot in your house you have not even been able to do up your drawing-room furniture. 'Hard up' is written in every slit in these chair covers. What son-in-law would not back out, and take fright at the ill-disguised evidence of the cruelest kind of poverty, that of families of good class? I have been a shopkeeper. I know. There is nothing like the eye of a Paris tradesman for knowing real wealth from apparent. You haven't got a sou," he said, lowering his voice; "that is evident in everything, even in the uniform of your manservant. Would you like me to let you into the fearful mysteries that are concealed from you?"

"Oh, sir!" said Madame Hulot, who was weeping until her handkerchief was wet through, "don't say any more!"

"Well, my son-in-law gives money to his father, and that is what I was going to tell you when I started on the subject of your son. But I watch over my daughter's interests, don't you worry!"

"Oh, if only I could marry my daughter and die!" cried the unhappy woman, beginning to lose control.

"Very well, here is the means!" said the ex-perfumer.

Madame Hulot looked at Crevel with an expression of hope that changed the aspect of her face so quickly that this one gesture ought surely to have touched the man and made him give up his ridiculous project.

Chapter III

"You will still be beautiful in ten years' time," Crevel went on, striking his attitude again. "Be kind to me, and Mademoiselle Hortense's marriage is made. Hulot has given me the right, as I have explained, to propose the deal—to put it crudely—and he won't distress himself. I have increased my investments during the last three years, because my amusements have been cut down. I have three hundred thousand francs lying idle over and above my capital, and it is yours."

"Go, sir," said Madame Hulot, "go and do not ever let me see you again! If you had not made it necessary for me to ask you the secret of your mean conduct in the affairs of Hortense's proposed marriage—yes, mean!" she repeated, in answer to a gesture from Crevel. "How could you allow enmities of that kind to affect a poor girl, a lovely and innocent creature?— If it had not been for that necessity, that goaded my mother's heart, you would never have spoken to me again, you would never have set foot again in my house. Thirty-two years of honor, of a wife's loyalty, are not going to be swept away by the assaults of Monsieur Crevel."

"Retired perfumer, successor to César Birotteau at *La Reine des Roses,* Rue Saint-Honoré," said Crevel ironically, "late Deputy Mayor, Captain of the National Guard, Chevalier of the Legion of Honor, exactly like my predecessor."

"Sir," said the Baroness, "if Monsieur Hulot, after twenty years' fidelity, has deserted his wife, that concerns no one but myself; but, you see, sir, that he does not advertise his infidelities, for I did not know that he had succeeded you in the favors of Mademoiselle Josépha."

"Oh," exclaimed Crevel, "at a price, Madame! His songstress has cost him more than a hundred thousand francs in two years. Oh, no! you have not seen the worst yet!"

"Can't we stop this futile discussion, Monsieur Crevel! I will not give up for your sake the pleasure that a mother has in being able to embrace her children without any sense of guilt in her heart, in knowing herself respected and loved by her family, and I will give back my soul to God without stain."

"Amen," said Crevel, with that diabolical bitterness that one may see in the faces of pretenders who fail, and not for the first time, in an attempt of this kind. "You don't know the extremes of poverty yet, the shame, the dishonor. I have tried to warn you. I wanted to save you, you and your daughter. Very well, you will have to spell out the modern parable of the Prodigal Father, from A to Z. Your tears and your pride touch me; it is terrible to see the woman one loves in tears," said Crevel, sitting down. "I can only promise you, dear Adeline, not to do anything to injure you, or your husband, but don't ever ask me for information. That is all!"

"Oh, what shall I do?" cried Madame Hulot.

Until now the Baroness had borne up bravely under the threefold torture that this interview had inflicted on her heart, for she had suffered as a woman, as a mother, and as a wife. As a matter of fact, the more red and aggressive her son's father-in-law had become, the more she had found strength to resist the shopkeeper's brutality; but the good nature that he showed, along with the exasperation of a rejected lover, and a humiliated gallant of the National Guard, broke down her nerves, strung to breaking point; she clasped her hands and burst into tears, and she was in such a state of stupefied exhaustion that she allowed Crevel, on his knees again, to kiss her hands.

"Oh dear, what will happen?" she went on, drying her eyes. "How can a mother look on coldly while her daughter pines away under her eyes? What will become of such a splendid girl, doubly endowed by her pure, good upbringing under her mother's care, and by her own fine nature? Sometimes she walks in the garden, melancholy, without knowing why; I find her with tears in her eyes."

"She is twenty-one," said Crevel.

"Must she go into a convent?" asked the Baroness. "In situations of this kind religion is often powerless against nature, and even girls whose upbringing has been most religious lose their heads!"

"Heads!" said Crevel jokingly, "you call that the head!"

"But do get up, sir. Surely you see that everything is over between us now; that you are hateful to me, that you have wrecked a mother's last hope!"

"And if I were to revive it?" he said.

Madame Hulot looked at Crevel with an expression of rapture that touched him; but he drove pity back into his heart, because of those words "you are hateful to me." Virtue is always a little too much all of a piece and disregards those fine shades and modulations with which one can maneuver one's way out of a false position.

"No one nowadays can afford to marry a girl as beautiful as Mademoiselle Hortense without a dowry," Monsieur Crevel observed, resuming his stiff manner. "Your daughter's beauty is of the kind that frightens husbands off, like a highbred horse that calls for too much trouble and expense to find many purchasers. Just imagine walking along with a girl like that on your arm! Why, everybody would look at you, and follow you, and covet your wife. That kind of success scares plenty of men who don't want to have to kill lovers; for after all, one kills only one of them. In your situation, you can marry your daughter in only one of three ways: with my help—which you don't want—that is one; by finding an old man of sixty, very rich, with no children, but who would like to have some, which is difficult, but it does happen; there are plenty of old men who take up with Josépha and Jenny Cadines; you might find one who would commit the same folly legitimately—if I had not Célestine and our two grandchildren I would marry Hortense myself. That is two! The third way is the easiest."

Madame Hulot looked up and watched the ex-perfumer anxiously.

"Paris is a city where all those energetic men who grow up like saplings all over France tend to collect, and it is swarming with talent without heart or home, but with courage equal to anything—even to making a fortune. Well, these youngsters—your humble servant was one of them in his day, he knows all about it!—what was du Tillet,[1] what was Popinot, at twenty? They were both in old Birotteau's shop, with no other capital than their own determination to get on, which to my mind is worth more than capital! You can run through capital, but you can't run through stamina. What had I? The wish to get on, and guts. Du Tillet today hobnobs with all the great. Little Popinot, the richest chemist in the Rue des Lombards, became a deputy, and now he's a minister. Well, one of these free lances,[2] as they say, of business, or the pen, or the brush, is your only chance in Paris of marrying a beautiful girl who hasn't a sou; because they have courage enough for anything. Monsieur Popinot married Mademoiselle Birotteau without asking for a farthing in dowry. These chaps are all crazy! They believe in love just as they believe in their fortunes and their talents! Find a man with enterprise who will fall in love with your daughter, and he will marry her without giving a thought to the money. You must admit that for an enemy I'm generous, because this advice is against my interest."

"Oh, Monsieur Crevel, if you want to be my friend, give up your absurd ideas!"

"Absurd? Madame, don't run yourself down like that. Look at yourself! I love you, and you will turn to me! I want to say one day to Hulot: you took Josépha from me, I have taken your wife! That is the old *lex talionis*.[3] And I shall persevere so long as you do not become excessively ugly. I shall succeed, and I'll tell you why," he said, striking his attitude and looking at Madame Hulot.

"You will never find either an old man or a young lover," he resumed after a pause, "because you love your daughter too much to expose her to the maneuvers of an old libertine, and you would never consent, you, Baroness Hulot, sister of the old lieutenant-general who commanded the veteran grenadiers of the Old Guard, to look for a man of enterprise where he is to be found, for he might be a simple workingman, like many a man who is a millionaire today, and who was a common workman ten years ago, just an overseer, or a simple foreman in a factory. And then, when you look at your daughter, with the instincts of a girl of twenty, who might disgrace you, you will say to yourself, 'Better that I should dishonor myself than that she should. And if Monsieur Crevel will keep a secret, I can earn my daughter's dowry, two hundred thousand francs, for ten years of attachment to that ex-haberdasher, old Crevel.' I am boring you, and what I say is awfully immoral, isn't it? But if you were the victim of an irresistible passion you would be able to find plenty of reasons for yielding to me, those reasons that women always do find when they are in love. Very well, Hortense's interests will put these reasons into your head, these capitulations of conscience!"

"Hortense still has an uncle."

"Who? Old Fischer? He is winding up his business; and that is the Baron's fault, too, because he has his rake-off on all the cash that passes through his hands."

"Count Hulot."

"Oh! Your husband has already squandered the old lieutenant-general's savings; he used them to furnish the house of his opera singer. Come, are you going to send me away without any hope?"

"Goodbye, sir. One soon gets over a passion for a woman of my age, and you will think better of it. God protects the unfortunate!"

The Baroness rose, forcing the captain to withdraw, and she drove him back into the drawing room.

"Should the beautiful Madame Hulot be living among old junk?" he said.

And he pointed to an old lamp, a sconce with its gilt falling away, the threadbare carpet, the tatters of opulence that conspired to make the great room in white, red, and gold look like a corpse of Empire festivities.

"Virtue makes all this radiant, sir. I have no wish to purchase magnificent furnishings by using the beauty that you say is mine as a *mantrap, a money-box for hundred-sou pieces.*"

The captain bit his lip as he recognized the expressions that he had used to castigate Josépha's avarice.

"And to whom are you so faithful?" he said.

The Baroness had by now maneuvered the ex-perfumer to the door.

"To a libertine!" he said, with all the contempt of a virtuous man and a millionaire.

"If you are right, sir, my constancy deserves a little credit, that is all."

And she took leave of the captain as one gets rid of some importunate creature, and turned away too quickly to see him strike his attitude for the last time.

She went to reopen the doors that she had closed and did not see Crevel's threatening farewell gesture. She walked with the proud nobility of a martyr in the Colosseum. All the same, she had spent her strength, for she collapsed on the divan of her blue boudoir like a woman ready to faint, and looked with fond eyes toward the little ruined summerhouse where her daughter was chattering to Cousin Bette.

From the day of her marriage until now the Baroness had loved her husband, as Joséphine came to love Napoleon, with an admiring, maternal, but abject love. She might not have been aware of the details that Crevel had just given her, but all the same she knew very well that for twenty years Baron Hulot had been unfaithful; but she had kept a leaden screen in front of her eyes; she had wept in silence, and never had a word of reproach escaped her. In return for this angelic sweetness she had gained her husband's veneration, a sort of cult of worship with which he surrounded her.

A woman's affection for her husband, and the respect in which she holds him, are contagious in a family. Hortense regarded her father as the perfect model of conjugal love. And Hulot's son, brought up to admire the Baron, whom everyone regarded as one of the giants who had seconded Napoleon, knew that he owed his position to his father's name and standing and the respect in which he was held. What is more, the impressions of childhood are lasting; he still feared his father; and even if he had suspected the irregularities revealed by Crevel he was even now too deferential to have made any protest to him, and would have excused them by those arguments that men commonly employ in such matters.

But it is necessary to give some explanation of the extraordinary devotion of this beautiful and noble woman, and this, in a few words, is her story.

From a village situated on the extreme frontiers of Lorraine, at the foot of the Vosges, three brothers of the name of Fischer, simple peasants, set out, following the call-up of the Republic, to join the so-called Army of the Rhine.[4]

In 1799 the second of these brothers, a widower, and Madame Hulot's father, left his daughter in the care of his eldest brother, Pierre Fischer, who had been disabled by a wound that he had received in 1797, and had undertaken some small-scale contracting for the Military Transport, an employment which he owed to the favor of the ordnance officer, Hulot d'Ervy.

It so happened that Hulot, on his way to Strasbourg, saw the Fischer family. Adeline's father and his younger brother were at that time employed as contractors for forage in Alsace.

Adeline at sixteen might be compared to the famous Madame du Barry, who like herself was a daughter of Lorraine. She was one of these perfect, dazzling beauties, one of those women like Madame Tallien, whom nature has fashioned with a special care; on such she bestows her finest gifts—distinction, dignity, grace, refinement, elegance, and an incomparable complexion of a color compounded in the mysterious workshop of chance. These beautiful women are all rather alike. Bianca Capella, whose portrait is one of Bronzino's masterpieces; the Venus of Jean Goujon, whose original was the famous Diane de Poitiers; that Signora Olympia whose portrait is in the Doria gallery; Ninon, Madame du Barry, Madame Tallien, Mademoiselle Georges, Madame Récamier—all these women who remained beautiful in spite of the years, their passions, or their lives of excess, are strikingly similar in their build, their figure, in the style of their beauty, as if there were some aphrodisian current from which all these Venuses had emerged from the ocean of generation, all daughters of the same salt wave.[5]

Adeline Fischer, one of the most beautiful of that divine race, possessed the distinguished features, the flowing lines, the veined flesh of these women born to be queens. The golden hair that Mother Eve received from the hand of God, her queenly stature, her air of dignity, the august contours of her profile, and her rustic modesty made men stop to look at her as they passed, like amateurs before a Raphael. And so, when he saw her, the ordnance officer forthwith made Mademoiselle Adeline Fischer his wife, to the great astonishment of the Fischers, who had all been brought up to look up to their betters.

The eldest, the soldier of 1792, who was severely wounded in the attack on Wissembourg, adored the Emperor Napoleon, and everything that had to do with the *Grande Armée.* André and Johann spoke with respect of Ordnance Officer Hulot, the Emperor's protégé, to whom, besides, they owed their positions, for Hulot d'Ervy, finding them honest and intelligent, had promoted them from the army forage wagons and placed them in charge of an important contract. The brothers Fischer had done good service during the 1804 campaign. And Hulot, after the peace, had obtained for them their contract for forage in Alsace, without knowing that he would later be sent to Strasbourg to make preparations there for the campaign of 1806.

For the young peasant girl, this marriage was like an Assumption. The lovely Adeline went straight from the mud of her village to the paradise of the Imperial Court. For it was at that time that the ordnance officer, one of the most trustworthy, active, and hardworking members of his corps, was made a baron, given a place near the Emperor, and attached to the Imperial Guard. The lovely peasant girl had spirit enough to educate herself, out of love for her husband, with whom she was quite madly in love. The ordnance officer-in-chief was, besides, a masculine replica of Adeline. He belonged to the elect number of handsome men. Tall, well-built, fair, with blue eyes, full of fire and animation; his graceful and elegant figure was irresistible; he was outstanding among men like d'Orsay, Forbin, and Ouvrard[6]—in short, among the ranks of the beaux of the Empire.

Although a man of many conquests, and holding the ideas of the *Directoire*[7] on the subject of women, his career of gallantry was interrupted for a considerable time by his attachment to his wife.

For Adeline, the Baron was therefore from the first a kind of god, who could do no wrong. She owed everything to him: fortune, for she had her carriage, her house, and all the luxury of the time; happiness, for she was openly loved; a title, for she was a baroness; celebrity, for was she not called the beautiful Madame Hulot, and in Paris? She even had the honor of refusing the advances of the Emperor, who presented her with a diamond necklace, and who always remembered her, for he used to ask from time to time, "And is beautiful Madame Hulot still as virtuous as ever?" in the tones of a man prepared to avenge himself on any man who should triumph where he had failed.

It is not therefore very difficult to understand the causes that produced an element of fanaticism in the love of the simple, naïve, and lovely soul of Madame Hulot. Having persuaded herself that her husband could never do her any wrong, she made herself, in her inmost being, the humble, devoted, and blind servant of the man who had made her what she was.

It must be said, besides, that she was gifted with great good sense, that peasant common sense that gave a solidity to her education. In society she spoke little, never said anything against anyone, and did not attempt to shine; she thought everything over, listened, and modeled herself on the most respectable and well-bred women.

In 1815 Hulot followed the example of the Prince de Wissembourg,[8] one of his closest friends, and became one of the organizers of that improvised army whose defeat brought the Napoleonic era to an end at Waterloo. In 1816 the Baron was one of the most hated men of Feltre's Ministry, and was not reappointed in the Commissariat, until 1823, when he was needed on account of the war with Spain.[9] In 1830 he reappeared in the administration as deputy minister, as a result of Louis-Philippe's policy of calling up the old Napoleonic officials.

Since the younger branch, whom he had actively supported, had succeeded to the throne, he had remained in this post, an indispensable director of the Ministry of War. He had already obtained his marshal's baton, and short of making him a minister or a peer of the realm the King could do no more for him.

During the years between 1818 and 1823, being otherwise unoccupied, Baron Hulot occupied himself with women, and Madame Hulot attributed the first infidelities of her Hector to the downfall of the Empire. The Baroness, then, had held undisputed sway as *prima donna assoluta* in her married life for twelve years. She continued to enjoy that old inveterate affection that husbands feel for their wives when they have been relegated to the role of good, gentle companions; and she knew that no rival would last for two hours against one word of reproach from herself; but she shut her eyes, and stopped her ears, and refused to know anything about her husband's conduct outside his marriage. And finally she came to treat her Hector as a mother treats a spoiled child. Three years before the conversation that has just taken place Hortense had recognized her father at the *Variétés* in a box in the middle of the first tier, with Jenny Cadine, and exclaimed, "There's Papa!"

"You must be mistaken, my angel; he is with the Marshal," the Baroness had replied.

She had, of course, seen Jenny Cadine, but instead of feeling her heart contract when she saw how pretty she was she had said to herself, "That naughty Hector must be enjoying himself." All the same she suffered, and in secret she endured raging torments; but as soon as she set eyes on her Hector again she remembered her twelve years of happiness and could not find it in herself to utter one word of complaint. She would have liked the Baron to confide in her; but she never dared to let him suspect that she knew of his escapades, out of respect for him. This excess of delicacy is only to be met with among beautiful women of the people, who know how to receive blows without giving them in return; they have some of the blood of the first martyrs in their veins. Well-born girls, being the equals of their husbands, find it necessary to torment them and to score up, as in billiards, their acts of tolerance, with cutting remarks, in a spirit of malicious vengeance, in order to ensure either their superiority or their right to take their revenge.

The Baroness had an ardent admirer in her brother-in-law, Lieutenant-General Hulot, the venerable colonel of the Infantry Grenadiers of the Imperial Guard, who was awarded the marshal's baton in his later years. The old man, after commanding from 1830 to 1834 the military division that included the Department of Brittany, the scene of his exploits in 1799 and 1800,[10] came to live in Paris, near his brother, for whom he still felt a fatherly affection.

His old soldier's heart sympathized with that of his sister-in-law; he admired her as the noblest and best of her sex. He had not married, because he hoped to find a second Adeline, looking in vain for such a one through twenty countries and as many campaigns. Rather than lose the esteem of the irreproachable and faultless old Republican, of whom Napoleon had said, "That brave Hulot is the most stubborn Republican, but he will never betray me," Adeline would have endured far worse sufferings than those that she had just undergone. But the old man of seventy-two, broken by thirty campaigns, wounded for the twenty-seventh time at Waterloo, offered Adeline admiration rather than protection. The poor Count, among other infirmities, was unable to hear without the help of an ear-trumpet.

While the Baron Hulot d'Ervy was a handsome man, his love affairs did no damage to his fortune, but at fifty he had to bargain with the Graces. At that age love, in old men, turns to vice; it becomes involved with outrageous vanities. And at about this time

Adeline watched her husband becoming excessively preoccupied with his toilet, dyeing his hair and mustache, wearing waistbands and corsets. He must remain handsome at all costs. This cult of his appearance, a fault which in the old days he used to make fun of, he now carried to all extremes. And at last Adeline began to realize that the source of the wealth that was poured out on the Baron's mistresses was her own home. In eight years a large fortune had disappeared so completely that when, two years previously, young Hulot had set up house, the Baron had been forced to admit to his wife that his salary was his whole fortune.

"What will that bring us to?" had been Adeline's comment.

"Don't worry," the Councilor of State had replied, "I shall leave you my salary and I shall see about a settlement for Hortense, and our future, by doing some business."

His wife's profound faith in the ability and outstanding talents, the capacities and the character of her husband, had calmed that momentary anxiety.

Chapter IV

It is not difficult, then, to understand the Baroness's thoughts and her tears after the departure of Crevel. The poor woman had realized for two years past that she herself was living in the depths, but imagined that she alone was involved. She had not known how her son's marriage had come about; she had not known of her husband's liaison with the grasping Josépha; and she had hoped that nobody in the world knew of her troubles. Now, if Crevel could speak so lightly of the Baron's dissipations, Hector's reputation would suffer. She could glimpse through the irritated ex-perfumer's vulgar outpourings, the kind of base familiarity of which the marriage of the young lawyer was the outcome. Two depraved girls had been the priestesses of that marriage, proposed during some orgy, in a setting of degrading intimacy, between two tipsy old men.

"He is forgetting Hortense altogether," she thought, "although he sees her every day. Will he try to find her a husband among his worthless set?"

At that moment she was more mother than wife, for she could see Hortense with her cousin Bette, laughing with that wild laugh of reckless youth, and she knew that this nervous laughter was a symptom no less alarming than those tearful moods of her solitary walks in the garden.

Hortense was like her mother, but she had red-gold hair, naturally wavy and astonishingly thick. Her complexion was like mother-of-pearl. In her one could recognize the child of a real marriage, in the prime of a pure and noble love. From her eagerly expressive face, her gay gestures, her youthful abandon, her freshness and vitality, vigor and good health seemed to radiate in electric waves. Hortense drew all eyes. When her sea-blue gaze, in all its limpid innocence, fell on some young passer-by he would thrill involuntarily. Nor did any trace of that redness which is often the price of the white skins of these golden blondes mar her complexion. Tall, rounded, but not heavily built, her handsome, graceful figure rivaled her mother's in nobility; so that she deserved the epithet of goddess that the authors of antiquity used so freely. Indeed, no one, seeing Hortense in the street, could help exclaiming, "Heavens! What a lovely girl!"

She was so utterly innocent that she would say when she returned home, "But why, Mamma, do they all say 'Lovely girl!' when you are with me? Aren't you much more beautiful than I am?"

And, indeed, at forty-seven the Baroness might well have been preferred to her daughter by lovers of sunset beauty; for by one of those rare chances—rare in Paris especially—for which Ninon,[1] who so long continued to eclipse the glory of the plainer ladies of the seventeenth century, was so notorious, she had lost none of what women call their "good points."

Thinking of her daughter reminded the Baroness of the father; she imagined him falling from day to day, by degrees, into the dregs of social disrepute, perhaps being dismissed from the Ministry. The thought of the fall of her idol, accompanied by an indistinct picture of the troubles that Crevel had foretold, was so agonizing to the poor woman that she lost consciousness in a sort of trance.

Cousin Bette, with whom Hortense was talking, looked up from time to time to see whether they could go back into the drawing room, but her young cousin was so teasing her with questions just when the Baroness was reopening the French window that she did not notice her.

Lisbeth Fischer, five years younger than Madame Hulot, although she was the daughter of the eldest of the Fischer brothers, was far from being a beauty like her cousin; for which reason she had been tremendously jealous of her. Jealousy formed the basis of her character, with all its eccentricities—a word invented by the English to describe the follies of distinguished families. A Vosges peasant woman in all senses of the word—thin, dark, her hair black and stringy, with thick eyebrows meeting in a tuft, long, strong arms, flat feet, with several moles on her long simian face—such, in brief, was the appearance of this old maid.

The family, who all lived as one household, had neglected the plain girl for the beautiful one: the harsh fruit for the dazzling flower. Lisbeth worked in the fields while her cousin was spoiled, and on one occasion, finding Adeline alone, the impulse came over her to pull her cousin's nose—a true Grecian nose that all the old ladies admired. Although she was beaten for this misdeed, she continued all the same to tear the favorite's dresses and spoil her collars.

At the time of her cousin's fantastic marriage Lisbeth had bowed to fate, as Napoleon's brothers and sisters bowed before the splendor of the throne and the power of authority. Adeline, who was kind and sweet-natured to a degree, remembered Lisbeth when she was in Paris, and sent for her, in about 1809, with the intention of rescuing her from poverty and finding her a husband. Seeing that it would be impossible to marry this girl, with her dark eyes and black brows, who could neither read nor write, straight away, the Baron began by finding her a trade; he apprenticed Lisbeth to the embroiderers to the Imperial Court, the well-known Pons Brothers.[2]

This cousin, called Bette[3] for short, now a worker in gold and silver embroidery, with all her mountain-bred energy, was enterprising enough to learn reading, writing, and arithmetic; for her cousin the Baron had demonstrated to her the necessity of possessing such knowledge if she was to run an embroidery establishment of her own. She was determined to get on; in two years she had transformed herself. By 1811 the peasant girl had become a well-mannered, skilled, and intelligent forewoman.

The profession of gold and silver braiding included the working of epaulettes, sword knots, aiguillettes, and, in short, all the countless brilliant decorations that used to glitter on the rich uniforms of the French Army and on civil dress clothes. The Emperor, who had a true Italian love of finery, had adorned all the uniforms of those in his service with gold and silver, and his Empire comprised a hundred and thirty-three Departments. The making of these trimmings, usually supplied to well-established and sound tailoring establishments, or direct to important officials, was a safe profession.

Just when Cousin Bette, the best workwoman in the Pons establishment, where she was in charge of the workroom, might have set up her own business, the Empire collapsed. The olive branch of the Bourbons alarmed Lisbeth, and she was afraid of a decline in a trade that would now have only eighty-six instead of a hundred and thirty-three Departments to exploit, let alone the enormous reductions in the Army. Taking fright at the prospect of the various risks of the trade, she refused the propositions of the Baron who thought her mad. She justified this opinion by quarreling with Monsieur Rivet, who bought the Pons establishment, with whom the Baron had proposed to set her up in partnership, and she went back to being a simple workwoman.

The Fischer family meanwhile had relapsed into the precarious situation from which the Baron had raised them.

Ruined by the disaster of Fontainebleau,[4] the three Fischer brothers in desperation joined the Volunteer Corps of 1815.[5] The eldest, Lisbeth's father, was killed. Adeline's father, condemned to death by court-martial, fled to Germany and died at Trèves in 1820. The youngest, Johann, came to Paris to implore the help of the queen of the family, who, it was said, ate from gold and silver dishes, never appeared on public occasions without tiaras and necklaces of diamonds as large as hazelnuts, the gifts of the Emperor. Johann Fischer, then forty-three, was given a sum of ten thousand francs by Baron Hulot to set him up in a small foraging business[6] at Versailles, obtained from the Ministry of War through the private influence of friends with whom the late officer-in-chief of the Commissariat still kept in touch.

These family misfortunes, Baron Hulot's fall from favor, and the sense of how little she mattered in that great struggle for existence of people and parties and projects that makes Paris at once an inferno and a paradise, discouraged Bette. The girl gave up all idea of competing with or rivaling her cousin, having experienced the effects of her superior qualities; but envy remained hidden in her secret heart, like the germ of a disease that is liable to break out and ravage a city if the fatal bale of wool in which it is hidden is ever opened.

From time to time she would say to herself, "Adeline and I are of the same blood—our fathers were brothers—she lives in a mansion and I live in an attic." But every year, on her birthday and on New Year's Day, Lisbeth received presents from the Baroness and the Baron. The Baron, who was very good to her, paid for her wood in the winter. She was invited to dinner one day a week by old General Hulot, and there was always a place laid for her at her cousin's table. They made fun of her, but they were never ashamed to acknowledge her. In fact, they enabled her to live independently in Paris the life that she herself had chosen.

She had, as a matter of fact, a great dislike of being dictated to in any way. If her cousin suggested that she should live with her, she at once flinched from the curb of domesticity; on several occasions the Baron had solved the difficult problem of finding a husband for her, but although the idea would please her to begin with, she would presently shy off, taking fright at the prospect of being criticized on account of her want of education, her ignorance, or her lack of fortune; if, however, the Baroness suggested her keeping house for their uncle, instead of his having an expensive housekeeper, she would reply that she would be able to marry even less well in those circumstances.

In these notions Cousin Bette showed all the oddity that one finds in characters that have developed late in life, and among savages, who think much and say little. Her peasant shrewdness had, however, through her conversation with the employees, both men and women, of the workrooms, acquired a Parisian sharpness. This girl whose character was very much like that of the Corsicans,[7] vainly tormented by the instincts of a strong nature, would have liked to look after a man of weak character; but, living in the capital, she was changed superficially. The Parisian veneer left her strongly tempered spirit to rust. Gifted, like all those who live a life of real celibacy, with penetrating insight, and with the original turn that she gave to all her ideas, she would have been formidable in any other situation. With ill will, she could have broken up the most united family.

In the early days, when she still nursed certain hopes, whose secret she confided to no one, she decided to wear corsets and follow the fashion, and she had a moment of splendor during which the Baron considered her marriageable. Lisbeth at that time was the attractive brunette of old French novels. Her piercing look, her olive complexion, and her slim figure might well have attracted a major on half pay; but she was satisfied, she said, laughing, with her own admiration. And besides, she found her life pleasant enough, once she had solved her financial problems, for she dined in town every evening, after a day's work that began at the crack of dawn. Therefore she had only her rent and her lunches to pay for; besides that, she was given most of her clothes, as well as all sorts of useful extras such as sugar, coffee, wine, and so forth.

In 1837, after twenty-seven years of life largely paid for by the Hulot family and by her uncle Fischer, Bette had resigned herself to being a nobody, and allowed herself to be treated without much ceremony. She herself refused to go to large dinner parties, preferring the intimacy of the family, in which she could hold her own and in which she was spared injuries to her pride. She seemed to be at home everywhere, with General Hulot, with Crevel, with the young Hulots, with Rivet (successor to the Pons Brothers, with whom she had made up her differences, and who made much of her), and with the Baroness.

Wherever she went, moreover, she knew how to get on to friendly terms with the servants, by giving them small tips from time to time, and by talking to them always for a moment or two before going in to the drawing room. This familiarity, in which she placed herself frankly on their own level, assured her their servile good will, highly necessary to parasites. "She is a really good sort!" was everyone's opinion of her. Her endless willingness to oblige (when this was not asked of her!) and her affectation of good nature were, to be sure, made necessary by her position. She had come at last to learn her lesson in life through being at everybody's mercy; and in the desire to appease everybody she laughed with the young people, who liked her on account of her flattering ways which always took them in; she learned and championed their wishes, she became their go-between, she seemed to them the best possible confidante, for she had no right to criticize them. Her absolute discretion earned for her the confidence also of the older ones, for, like Ninon, she possessed some of the masculine qualities. As a rule, our confidences are made to those below us rather than to those above us. Our inferiors are employed much more often than our superiors in secret affairs; and they thereby become the recipients of our hidden thoughts, they share in our private deliberations; Richelieu[8] considered that he had won success when he had the right to take part in privy councils. Everyone imagined that this poor spinster was in such a state of dependence on everybody as to be forced to absolute silence. The cousin referred to herself as the family confessional. Only the Baroness, by reason of the bad treatment that she had received during her childhood from her cousin, stronger although younger than herself, maintained a certain reserve. Besides, out of shame, she would not have confided her domestic troubles to anyone but God.

It is perhaps necessary to say here that the Baroness's house still preserved all its former splendor in the eyes of Cousin Bette, who had not, like the ex-perfumer, noticed the signs of distress written on the worn armchairs, the discolored hangings, and the tattered silk. As with oneself so with one's furniture; looking at ourselves every day, we come, like the Baron, to think ourselves very little changed, still young, when other people can see our hair turning to chinchilla, the V-shaped furrows on our brows, and our figures like pumpkins. These rooms, for Bette, were forever lit up with the Bengal lights of Imperial receptions, perennially resplendent.

With the years Cousin Bette had acquired some curious old maid's fads. For instance, instead of following the fashion, she tried to make the fashion fit her habits and fall in with her ideas, which were always behind the times. If the Baroness gave her a pretty new hat, or a dress cut in the style of the moment, Cousin Bette would forthwith take it home and alter it, according to her own ideas, in every particular, and spoil it in the process of transforming it into a garment after the style of the First Empire, and the dresses of her early days in Lorraine. The thirty-franc hat would be turned into a dowdy shapeless object, and the dress into a rag-bag. In these matters Bette was as stubborn as a mule; she insisted on pleasing herself and thought herself charming as she was; whereas these assimilations, that suited her only insofar as they made her look an old maid from head to foot, turned her into such a fright that with all the good will in the world nobody could invite her on smart occasions.

This stubborn, capricious, independent strain, and the inexplicable unsociableness of the girl for whom the Baron had, on four different occasions, found a match (a civil servant, a major, an army contractor, and a retired captain), and who had refused an embroiderer (who afterwards became rich), earned for her the nickname of the Nanny,[9] which the Baron jokingly gave her. But this nickname was applicable only to her superficial eccentricities, those distinguishing traits that we all display to one another in society. This spinster, closely observed, would have been seen to possess the brutal side of the peasant character, and was still the child who wanted to pull her cousin's nose, and who might perhaps, had not wisdom prevailed, have killed her in a paroxysm of jealousy. She only held in check that natural impulsiveness with which country people, like savages, translate their feelings into actions, because of her knowledge of the law and of the world. Herein, perhaps, lies the only difference between primitive and civilized man. The savage has only feelings; the civilized man has both feelings and ideas. With savages, besides, the brain receives, so to speak, but few imprints, and is therefore entirely swayed by the particular feeling with which it is carried away; whereas in the case of civilized man ideas act upon the feelings and modify them; he has any number of interests, and many emotions, while the savage entertains only one at a time. This is the reason for that momentary supremacy of a child over its parents, which ceases when its wish is satisfied; but with primitive people this cause operates all the time. Cousin Bette, a primitive peasant of Lorraine, and not without a streak of treachery, was a character of this type, a type that is more common among the peasantry than one might suppose, and that may perhaps explain their behavior during revolutions.

At the time at which this narrative opens, if Cousin Bette had wished to be well dressed, if she had, like the women of Paris, learned to follow the fashion, she would have been presentable and acceptable; but she remained as stiff as a post. And without some degree of charm no woman can exist in Paris. Therefore her black hair, her hard fine eyes, the rigid lines of her face, and the dusky Spanish complexion that made her look like a figure by Giotto, and which a real Parisienne would have used to good advantage, and above all her odd clothes made her appearance so freakish that she sometimes looked like nothing so much as one of those dressed-up monkeys that Swiss children lead about. As she was well known in the various households, united by family ties, among whom she moved, and as she restricted her social movements to that circle, and as she liked to keep to herself, her oddities no longer surprised anyone; and they were merged, out-of-doors, in the great throng of the Paris streets, where only beautiful women are looked at.

Hortense's laughter at that moment was occasioned by a triumph achieved over the obstinacy of Cousin Bette, from whom she had just wrung an admission for which she had been angling for three years. However guarded an old maid may be, there is one emotion that will always make her break a vow of silence, and that is vanity! For three years Hortense had been very inquisitive about a certain topic and had been besieging her cousin with questions that to all appearances were perfectly innocent. She wanted to know why her cousin had never married. Hortense, who knew the story of the five rejected suitors, had built up her own little romance, and believed that Cousin Bette cherished a secret passion, and from this a warfare of banter had begun. "We young girls," Hortense would say, referring to herself and her cousin. Cousin Bette had on several occasions replied with perfect good humor, "How do you know that I haven't a sweetheart?" Cousin Bette's sweetheart, real or imaginary, became finally the subject of good-natured teasing. Finally, after three years of this little campaign, on the last occasion when Cousin Bette had come, Hortense's first words had been, "And how is your sweetheart?"

"So-so," she had replied; "he is not very well, poor young man."

"Oh, is he delicate?" the Baroness had asked, laughing.

"Yes, indeed; he is so fair.... Coal-black girls like me always fall in love with fair men, as pale as moonlight."

"But who is he? What does he do?" said Hortense. "Is he a prince?"

"A prince of tools, just as I am a queen of bobbins. Do you expect a poor girl like me to be loved by a rich man with a house of his own and an income from the State, or a duke or peer or some Prince Charming out of a fairy-tale?"

"Oh, I should love to see him!" Hortense had exclaimed, smiling.

"To see what a man who can love an old nanny looks like?" Cousin Bette had replied.

"He must be some frightful old clerk with a goatee beard!" Hortense had said, looking at her mother.

"Well, that is just where you are wrong, Miss!"

"But have you really a sweetheart?" Hortense had asked, with an air of triumph.

"Just as surely as you have not!" her cousin had replied, piqued.

"Well, if you have a sweetheart, Bette, why don't you marry him?" the Baroness had said, exchanging a look with her daughter. "It is three years now since we first heard of him; you have had time to get to know him, and if he has remained faithful to you, you ought not to prolong a situation that he must find a little wearisome. Besides, it is a question of conscience; and what is more, if he is young, it is time to acquire a prop for your old age."

Cousin Bette had looked hard at the Baroness, and seeing that she was laughing, she had replied, "It would be marrying hunger and thirst; he has to work and so have I; if we had children, they would have to work.... No, no, it will have to be a love of the soul ... it costs less!"

"Why do you hide him?" Hortense had asked.

"He's a failure!" the old maid had answered, smiling.

"Do you love him?" the Baroness had asked.

"Oh, to be sure! I love him for himself alone, the angel! For years now I have carried his image in my heart!"

"Well, if you love him for himself," the Baroness had said seriously, "and if he exists, you are treating him shamefully. You don't know what it is to love!"

"We all know that trade from birth!" said the cousin.

"No, some women love and still remain egoists, which is what you are doing."

The cousin had bowed her head; her glance would have made anyone who had seen it tremble, but she was looking only at her cotton-reels.

"If you will introduce your sweetheart to us, Hector will be able to find him a place, and put him in the way of making his fortune."

"That is impossible," Cousin Bette had said.

"And why?"

"He is a sort of Pole, a refugee."

"A conspirator?" exclaimed Hortense. "Aren't you lucky! Has he had adventures?"

"He has fought for Poland![10] He was a teacher in the school whose students started the revolt, and as he was placed there by the Grand Duke Constantine,[11] he cannot expect to be pardoned."

"Teacher of what?"

"Art."

"And he came to Paris after the defeat?"

"In eighteen thirty-three he crossed Germany on foot."

"Poor young man! And how old is he?"

"He was not quite twenty-four at the time of the insurrection, and he is twenty-nine now."

"Fifteen years younger than you are?" the Baroness had said.

"How does he live?" Hortense had asked.

"By his talent."

"Oh! He gives lessons?"

"No," Bette had answered, "he receives them, and hard ones at that!"

"Has he a nice Christian name?"

"Wenceslas!"

"What imaginations old maids have!" the Baroness had exclaimed. "From the way you talk anyone would think it was true, Lisbeth!"

"Don't you see, Mamma, that this Pole was brought up on the knout,[12] and Bette reminds him of that little luxury of his native country?"

All three had burst out laughing, and Hortense had sung "Wenceslas! *idole de mon âme!*"[13] instead of "*O Mathilde!*"[14] And there had been something like an armistice for a few moments.

Chapter V

"These young girls!" Cousin Bette had said, looking at Hortense when she was next to her. "One would think that no one could have lovers but themselves."

"Well," Hortense had replied, finding herself once more alone with her cousin, "prove to me that Wenceslas is not an invention and I will give you my yellow cashmere shawl."

"But he is a count!"

"All Poles are counts!"

"But he is not a Pole; he is a Li . . . va . . . Lith . . ."

"Lithuanian?"

"No."

"Livonian?"

"That's it!"

"But what is his name?"

"Listen, can you keep a secret?"

"Oh, Cousin, I shall be mute!"

"As a fish?"

"As a fish!"

"On your eternal salvation?"

"On my eternal salvation!"

"No, on your happiness on earth?"

"Yes!"

"Very well; his name is Wenceslas Steinbock!"

"There was a general of that name in the time of Charles XII."[1]

"That was his great-uncle. His father settled in Livonia after the death of the King of Sweden; but he lost everything in the eighteen-twelve campaign,[2] and died, leaving the poor child, who was only eight years old, without a penny. The Grand Duke Constantine, for the sake of the name of Steinbock, took him under his protection and sent him to school."

"I have not lost my forfeit yet," Hortense had replied. "Give me a proof of his existence and my yellow shawl is yours! That color is as good as make-up with a dark complexion, you know!"

"You will keep my secret?"

"You shall have all mine!"

"Very well; next time I come, I will bring the proof!"

"But the proof is the lover!" Hortense had said.

Cousin Bette, who ever since she had come to Paris had had a great fancy for shawls, was fascinated by the idea of possessing this yellow cashmere that the Baron had given his wife in 1808, and which, according to the habits of some families, had passed from the mother to the daughter in 1830. The shawl had been constantly in use for ten years, but in the eyes of the old maid this precious object, always kept in a sandalwood box, remained, like the Baroness's furniture, still new.

She had therefore brought in her bag a present that she intended to give the Baroness on her birthday, and which, as she thought, was conclusive proof of the existence of the fantastic sweetheart.

This present consisted of a silver seal composed of three figures back to back, wreathed in leaves, and holding up the globe. These three personages represented Faith, Hope, and Charity, their feet on monsters that struggled with each other, among which twined the symbolic serpent. In 1846, after the great innovations in the art of Benvenuto Cellini made by Mademoiselle Fauveau, Wagner, Jeanest, Froment, Meurice, and others, and wood-carvers like Lienard, this masterpiece would not have surprised anyone; but at that time a young girl with a taste for jewelry could scarcely have failed to be astonished as she examined the seal that Cousin Bette had given her, saying, "Well, what do you think of this?"

The figures, in their composition, their draperies, and their rhythm were in the style of Raphael; in execution they suggested the Florentine School of bronzes, that of Donatello, Brunelleschi, Ghiberti, Benvenuto Cellini, Jean de Bologna, and the rest. The

French Renaissance contorted no stranger monsters than those that symbolized the evil passions. The palms, ferns, reeds, and rushes that enveloped the Virtues showed a sense of style and taste, and a technique that might well have made other craftsmen despair. A ribbon twined about the three heads, and in the ribbon, in the spaces between the heads, there was a W, a chamois, and the word "*Fecit.*"[3]

"Whoever made this?" asked Hortense.

"My sweetheart, to be sure," replied Cousin Bette. "There are months of work in it. And I earn more by making sword knots. He told me that Steinbock in German means 'animal of the rocks,' or chamois. He intends to sign all his work like that. Ah! I shall have your shawl!"

"And why?"

"Could I buy a thing like this? Or order it? It would be impossible; therefore it must have been given to me. Who would give such a present? Obviously a sweetheart!"

Hortense, with a dissimulation that would have alarmed Lisbeth Fischer if she had noticed it, took care not to show how much she was impressed, although in fact she experienced the enchantment that those whose minds are sensitive to beauty experience in the presence of a faultless masterpiece, perfect and unexpected.

"Upon my word," she said, "it really is pretty."

"Yes, it is pretty," the old maid repeated, "but I would rather have a yellow shawl. Well, my dear, my sweetheart spends his time making things like that. Since coming to Paris he has made three or four little pieces of nonsense, of the same kind, and that is the only fruit of four years of work and study. He has been apprenticed to bronze-founders, molders, and jewelers—well, so have hundreds and thousands of others. But he now tells me that in a few months he will be famous and rich."

"And you really know him?"

"Really! Do you think I am inventing it? I told you the truth in joke!"

"And he loves you?" Hortense asked quickly.

"Adores me!" replied the cousin, becoming serious. "Listen, my dear, he has never known any women who are not pale and colorless, as they all are in the North. A dark girl, slim, young like me, has warmed his heart. But not a word! You promised me!"

"He will fare like the five others," said the young girl mockingly, looking at the seal.

"Six, Miss! I left one in Lorraine who would have fetched down the moon for my sake, and would to this day."

"This one will do better. He will bring you the sun."

"What money is there in that?" Cousin Bette asked. "One must have a lot of earth before the sun can do any good."

These pleasantries, coming in rapid succession, and leading up to the kind of nonsense that one can imagine, were the cause of the laughter that had increased the anxiety of the Baroness, by forcing her to compare her daughter's future with her present, in which she saw her full of the gaiety of her youth.

"But surely he would not give you jewels that take six months to make unless he owed you a great deal?" asked Hortense, for the little object had made her think very hard.

"Ah, you want to know too much all at once!" Cousin Bette replied. "But listen—wait. I'm going to let you into a secret."

"Is your sweetheart in it, too?"

"Ah! you want to see him, don't you? But, you know, an old maid like your friend Bette who has managed to keep her sweetheart for five years knows how to hide him! So just leave me alone. You know I have neither a cat nor a canary nowadays, nor a parrot. An old nanny-goat like me needs some little thing to love and to fuss over. Well, I have found a Pole."

"Has he a mustache?"

"As long as that," said Bette, indicating a skein of gold threads. She always brought her embroidery out with her and worked while waiting for dinner.

"If you keep worrying me with questions, you won't be told anything," she went on; "you are only twenty-two[4] and you chatter more than I do at forty-two, nearly forty-three."

"I am listening. I am as dumb as a doorpost," said Hortense.

"My admirer has made a bronze group ten inches high," Cousin Bette continued. "It represents Samson slaying a lion, and he has buried it and made it rusty, so that now anyone would think it was as old as Samson himself. This fine piece of work is on sale in one of those antique shops in the Place de Carrousel, near my house. If only your father, who knows Monsieur Popinot, the Minister of Trade and Agriculture, and Count de Rastignac,[5] could speak to them about this group as a fine antique that he had noticed in passing! If only some of these great ones would spend their money on that object instead of giving all their thought to our sword knots, my sweetheart's fortune would be made. If only they would buy it, or even only go and look at the wretched lump of bronze! The poor fellow thinks that the thing can be passed off as an antique, and that it might bring a high price in that way. And then, if it was bought by one of these ministers, he would go and present himself, prove that he was the author, and his fortune would be made! Oh, he thinks highly of himself, and he is proud enough for two newly created counts, that young man!"

"Michelangelo over again! But for a lover, he has kept his wits," said Hortense. "And how much does he want for it?"

"Fifteen hundred francs ... the dealer cannot sell it for less, because he must have his commission."

"Papa," said Hortense, "is the King's Commissioner just now; he sees the two Ministers every day at the Chamber, and he will manage it for you. Just leave it to me. You shall be rich, Madame the Countess Steinbock!"

"No, my young man is too lazy; he spends whole weeks fiddling with red wax and does nothing. Bah! he spends his whole life in the Louvre, or in the library, looking at engravings and making drawings. He's an idler."

And the two cousins chattered on. Hortense forced herself to laugh, because she was overcome by a love that all young girls have experienced, love of the unknown, love of a vague kind, whose thoughts crystallize around some figure heard of by chance, just as frost crystals form around dry stalks of grass blown into a windowpane. For ten months she had made a real figure of her cousin's imaginary lover (for she believed, as her mother also did, in her cousin's perpetual celibacy) and for eight days now this phantom had become Count Wenceslas Steinbock; the dream had materialized, the mist had solidified into a young man of thirty. The seal that she was holding, like an Annunciation in which genius shone like light, had the power of a talisman. Hortense felt so happy that she began to doubt whether the story could be true. Her blood was on fire, and she laughed wildly, to put her cousin off the scent.

"I believe that the drawing-room door is open," said Cousin Bette. "Let us go and see whether Monsieur Crevel has gone."

"Mamma has been very worried for the last two days; the marriage they were talking about must have fallen through."

"Oh! that can be put right; it is a question—I can tell you that much—of a Councilor of the Supreme Court. How would you like to be *Madame la Présidente*?[6] Why, if it depends on Monsieur Crevel, he is sure to say something to me, and I shall hear tomorrow if there is any hope...."

"Cousin, leave the seal with me," said Hortense. "I won't show it to anyone. Mamma's birthday is not for another month, and I will give it back to you in the morning."

"No, give it to me ... it must have a case."

"But I want to show it to Papa, so that he can speak to the Minister with some idea of what it is all about, because men in authority must not compromise themselves," she said.

"Very well. I only ask you not to show it to your mother, because if she knew I had a sweetheart she would laugh at me."

"I promise."

The two cousins reached the door of the boudoir just as the Baroness had fainted; Hortense's cry was enough to revive her. Bette went in search of smelling salts. When she returned she found mother and daughter in each other's arms, the mother quieting the fears of her daughter and saying, "It is nothing; it was just nerves. Here is your father," she added, recognizing the Baron's ring. "Whatever you do, don't mention it to him."

Adeline rose to go and meet her husband, intending to lead him out into the garden until dinner, and to speak to him about the broken marriage, discuss the future, and try to give him some advice.

Baron Hector Hulot[7] appeared in a dress at once parliamentary and Napoleonic, for it is easy to distinguish the Imperials (men attached to the Empire) by their military stoop, their blue uniforms with gold buttons, buttoned high, their black silk cravats, and the air of authority that they contracted from the habits of command acquired when the rapidly changing circumstances of their career made despotism a necessity. Nothing about the Baron, to be sure, suggested an old man. His sight was still so good that he read without glasses; his handsome oval face, framed in side whiskers that were, alas! all too black, was ruddy, and marked with those little veins that indicate a sanguine temperament; and his figure, supported by a corset, was still what Brillat-Savarin[8] would describe as majestic. A fine aristocratic air and abundant affability served to conceal the libertine with whom Crevel had been on so many fine sprees. He was one of those men whose eye lights up at the sight of a pretty woman, and who smile at every beauty, even those who pass by and whom they will never see again.

"Did you speak, my dear?" said Adeline, seeing that he looked grave.

"No," replied Hector, "but I was bored by having to listen to speeches for two hours before they put it to the vote. They carry on a war of words, with speeches like cavalry charges that don't scatter the enemy! They talk instead of acting, which is small consolation to men who are used to marching. As I said to the Marshal as I left him. But it is quite bad enough to be bored on the benches of the Ministry—let us amuse ourselves here. How do you do, old nanny, and how are you, young kid?"

He put his arm around his daughter's neck and kissed her, teased her, and drew her on to his knee, resting his head on her shoulder to feel her lovely golden hair on his face.

He is worried and tired, Madame Hulot thought to herself, and now I am going to worry him still more. "Are you going to spend the evening with us?" she said aloud.

"No, my children. After dinner I must leave you and, if it had not been the Nanny's day, and my children's, and my brother's, you would not have seen me at all."

The Baroness picked up the newspaper, looked at the theaters, and put down the sheet in which she read the notice that *Robert le Diable*[9] was at the Opera. Josépha, whom the Italian Opera had lent for six months to the French, was singing the part of Alice. This dumb show did not escape the notice of the Baron, who looked attentively at his wife. Adeline lowered her eyes, and went out into the garden, where he followed her.

"What is it, Adeline?" he said, putting his arm around her and drawing her to him. "Surely you know that I love you more than . . . ?"

"More than Jenny Cadine or Josépha!" she dared to say, interrupting him.

"And who told you that?" asked the Baron, letting his wife go and taking two steps back.

"Someone wrote me an anonymous letter which I burned, my dear, saying that Hortense's marriage had fallen through because of the financial difficulties that we are in. As your wife I would never have said a word, Hector; I have known of your liaison with Jenny Cadine, and have I ever complained? But as Hortense's mother, you must be frank with me."

Hulot, after a moment of silence, terrible for his wife, whose heart was beating loudly, uncrossed his arms, took her, pressed her to his heart, kissed her forehead, and said with all the emphasis of strong emotion, "Adeline, you are an angel, and I am a wretch."

"No, no," answered the Baroness, quickly laying her fingers on his lips to prevent him from speaking ill of himself.

"Yes, I haven't a sou at the present moment to give to Hortense, and I am very much worried, but since you have opened your heart to me in this way I can confess to you the troubles that are preying on me. If your uncle Fischer is in difficulties, it is on my account; he has lent me twenty-five thousand francs in bills of exchange![10] And all that for a woman who deceives me, who makes fun of me behind my back, who calls me an old *dyed tomcat*! Oh, it is terrible to think that it costs more to satisfy a vice than to keep a family.... And it is irresistible—I might promise you now never to go near that abominable Jewess, and yet if she were to write me two lines I would go, as one goes into battle under the Emperor!"

"Don't distress yourself, Hector," said the poor woman, in despair, and forgetting her daughter at the sight of the tears that fell from the eyes of her husband. "After all, there are my diamonds; above all, you must save my uncle."

"Your diamonds are hardly worth twenty thousand today. That would not be enough for old Fischer. So keep them for Hortense. I shall see the Marshal tomorrow."

"Poor darling!" exclaimed the Baroness, taking her Hector's hands and kissing them.

And that was the whole extent of her rebuke. Adeline offered her diamonds, the father gave them to Hortense; this gesture seemed to her sublime, and she had no more strength left.

"He is the master—he has the right to take everything here, and he leaves me my diamonds! How noble he is!"

Such were the thoughts of this woman who had certainly obtained more by her sweetness than another woman would have gained by jealous anger.

No moralist can deny that, in general, well-bred and thoroughly vicious people are much more attractive than the virtuous; having crimes to make up for, they take care to ensure their own indulgence by showing themselves lenient with the faults of their judges, and they pass as charming people. Although there are delightful characters among the virtuous, virtue regards itself as sufficiently fair-seeming in itself, without going out of its way to take special pains; besides, really virtuous people (for one must except hypocrites) are nearly always a little unsure of their ground; they feel that they have in some way been cheated in the great market of life, and they are a little querulous, like people who feel themselves misunderstood. Therefore the Baron, knowing that he was to blame for ruining his family, exerted all the resources of his wit and his seductive graces for the benefit of his wife, his children, and Cousin Bette. As soon as he saw his son and Célestine Crevel, who was nursing a young Hulot, arriving, he was charming to his daughter-in-law, loading her with compliments, a diet to which Célestine's vanity was not accustomed, for no daughter of money was ever more common or more completely insignificant. The grandfather took the baby, kissed it, and said that it was delightful and charming; he talked baby talk to it, prophesied that his grandson would be taller than himself, slipped in some flattering references to the younger Hulot's good judgment, and returned the child to the fat Normandy nurse in charge. And Célestine exchanged with the Baroness a look that said: "What an adorable man!" Need it be added that she always stood up for her father-in-law against her own father's attacks upon him?

Having played the agreeable father-in-law and the indulgent grandfather, the Baron led his son into the garden in order to give him some very sensible advice on the line to take in the Chamber over a delicate issue that had arisen that morning. He filled the young lawyer with admiration for the profundity of his views, won his sympathy by his friendly attitude, and even more by the almost respectful way in which he seemed nowadays to wish to treat his son as an equal.

The younger Hulot was a typical young man of the 1830 revolution. His mind wholly absorbed with politics, taking his ambitions very seriously, concealing them under an assumed gravity, very envious of established reputations, he expressed himself in sententious phrases instead of those incisive sallies that are the diamonds of French conversation; very correct, he mistook haughtiness for dignity. Such men are walking coffins of an older France; the Frenchman stirs at times and struggles against his English envelope, but ambition restrains him, and he consents to stifle in it. These coffins are always draped in black.

"Ah! here is my brother!" said Baron Hulot, advancing to receive the Count at the door of the drawing room.

Having greeted the probable successor of the late Marshal Montcornet, he led him forward, taking his arm with every mark of affection and respect.

This peer of France, excused on account of his deafness from attending public functions, had a handsome head, frosted by the years with gray hair, still abundant enough to be flattened, as it seemed, by the pressure of his hat. Small, thick-set, dried-up, he carried his green old age with liveliness; and as he still possessed immense energy, condemned to idleness, he divided his time between reading and walking. His gentle habits were reflected in his pale face, in his bearing, and in the seemliness and good sense of his conversation. He never spoke of war and campaigns; he was too sure of himself to have any need to assume greatness. In a drawing room he confined himself to showing himself constantly attentive to the wishes of the ladies.

"You are all very gay," he said, seeing the animation that the Baron had infused into this little family gathering. "Hortense is not yet married, however," he added, recognizing traces of melancholy in the face of his sister-in-law.

"All in good time," Bette shouted in his ear in a formidable voice.

"That is what you think, you bad seed that refused to flower!" he replied, laughing.

The hero of Forzheim was quite fond of Cousin Bette, for in some ways they had much in common. Without education, a man of the people, his courage alone had raised him to his military eminence, and he had more common sense than brilliance. Full of honors, and with clean hands, he was ending, radiantly, his good life, surrounded by the family in which all his affections were centered. From time to time, however, the good little Count Hulot asked why old Crevel was not present. "My father is in the country!" Célestine would shout to him. On this occasion they told him that the ex-perfumer was on a journey.

This gathering of her family, in such real sympathy, made Madame Hulot say to herself: "This is the surest kind of happiness, and what, after all, can take it from us?"

Seeing his favorite Adeline the object of the Baron's attentions, the General teased him about it so much that the Baron, afraid of being made to look ridiculous, transferred his gallantry to his daughter-in-law, who, in the course of these family dinner parties, was always the object of his flattery and attention, because through her he hoped to induce old Crevel to set aside his resentment.

Anyone who had seen that intimate family scene would have found it difficult to believe that the father was on the verge of ruin, the mother of despair, the son anxious to the last degree about the future of his father, and the daughter planning to steal a sweetheart from her cousin.

Chapter VI

At seven o'clock, seeing his brother, his son, the Baroness, and Hortense all settled at whist, the Baron left to go and applaud his mistress at the opera, taking with him Cousin Bette, who lived in the Rue du Doyenné, and who used the loneliness of the quarter as a pretext for always leaving soon after dinner. Any Parisian will readily admit that the old maid's prudence was reasonable enough.

The existence of the block of houses running the length of the old Louvre is one of those protests that the French like to make against common sense, in order that the rest of Europe may be reassured on the subject of their supposed intelligence, and have no fears on that account. Perhaps we have here lighted unawares upon an important political idea.

There is nothing for it, indeed, but to begin by describing this corner of present-day Paris, for in the future it will be impossible to imagine it; and our nephews, who will no doubt see the Louvre[1] completed, will refuse to believe that such a slum should have existed for thirty-six years in the heart of Paris, opposite the Palace in which three dynasties[2] have received, during the same thirty-six years, the elite of France and of Europe.

Beyond the little gate that leads from the Carrousel bridge to the Rue du Musée, anyone visiting Paris, even for only a few days, is bound to notice a dozen houses with dilapidated façades, whose discouraged landlords have not troubled to repair them, and which are the remnant of an old quarter that has gradually been in the process of demolition ever since Napoleon's decision to complete the Louvre. The Rue du Doyenné and the blind alley called the Impasse du Doyenné are the only passages that penetrate this dismal and deserted block, whose inhabitants are presumably ghosts, for one never sees anybody there. The footway, much lower than the level of the pavement of the Rue du Musée, comes out on a level with the Rue Froidmanteau. Already buried by the raising of the square, these houses are enveloped in the perpetual shadow cast by the high galleries of the Louvre, blackened on that side by the north wind. The darkness, the silence, the cold air, the cavernous depth of the ground level, combine to make these houses into crypts, living tombs. In passing this dead wedge and happening to notice the Impasse du Doyenné, one experiences a chilling of the soul, and wonders who could possibly live in such a place, and what goes on there at night, when the alley becomes an ambush, and where the vices of Paris, wrapped in the mantle of night, are given full scope.

This question, alarming in itself, becomes still more frightful when one observes that these so-called houses are bounded by a swamp on the Rue de Richelieu side, an ocean of tumbled pavement on the side of the Tuileries, little plots and sinister hovels on the side facing the galleries, and steep stone steps and demolitions on the side toward the old Louvre. Henry III and his minions, looking for their breeches, and Marguerite's lovers,[3] in search of their heads, might dance sarabands by moonlight in these deserted spots, dominated by the vault of a chapel, still standing, as if to prove that the Catholic religion, so deeply rooted in France, survives everything. For nearly forty years the Louvre has been crying out through every aperture in these broken walls, through every yawning window: "Get rid of these blemishes on my face!" No doubt the utility of this ambush has been recognized, and the necessity of symbolizing, in the very heart of Paris, that intimate alliance of squalor and splendor so characteristic of the queen of capitals.

These cold ruins, moreover, in whose heart the legitimist newspaper[4] contracted the disease from which it is perishing, the shameful hovels of the Rue du Musée, the wooden circumference of street stalls that adorn it today, may perhaps have a longer and more prosperous life than three dynasties!

In 1823 the cheapness of rooms in condemned houses had intrigued Bette into living there, in spite of the necessity that living in such a quarter imposed on her of getting home before nightfall. This necessity was in accord, however, with the habit that she had kept of going to bed at sunset, a habit that represents such a notable saving of light and fuel among country people. She lived, then, in one of the houses that, thanks to the demolition of the famous house formerly occupied by Cambacérès,[5] now had a view of the square.

Just as Baron Hulot had seen his wife's cousin to the door of this house, and said, "Good night, Cousin," a young woman, small, slight, pretty, dressed with great elegance and exhaling an expensive perfume, passed between the cab and the wall in order to enter the same house. This woman, without any kind of premeditation, exchanged a glance with the Baron, simply in order to see the cousin of the tenant; but the libertine received the lively impression that all Parisians recognize when they encounter a pretty woman who complies with what the entomologists would describe as their *desiderata;*[6] and he put on one of his gloves with a studied slowness before once again getting into the cab, in order to make a good impression, and in order to allow his eye to follow the young woman, whose dress was agreeably balanced by something better than those horrible and deceptive crinoline bustles.

"There," he said to himself, "is a charming little woman whose happiness I would be glad to ensure, for she would ensure mine!"

When the unknown woman reached the turn of the staircase that served the main part of the building overlooking the street, she looked back at the carriage entrance, out of the corner of her eye, without actually turning round, and saw the Baron rooted to the spot with admiration, devoured with desire and curiosity. This is a kind of flower whose fragrance all Parisian women breathe with pleasure when they chance to find it in their way. There are women, devoted to their duties, both pretty and virtuous, who go home out of humor if they have not received some such small bouquet during their walk.

The young woman hurried up the staircase. Presently a window of the second-floor flat was opened and she appeared there, but accompanied by a bald man, whose rather ill-tempered look declared him to be her husband.

"How knowing and clever they are!" said the Baron to himself. "She did that to show me where she lives. That is going a bit too fast, especially in a quarter like this. Better take care!"

The Director looked up as he got into the milord, and the woman and the husband hastily withdrew, as if the Baron's face had produced on them the effect of the mythological head of Medusa.

"They seem to know who I am," thought the Baron. "That would explain the whole thing."

As the cab reascended the slope of the Rue du Musée he leaned out to look at the unknown woman, and saw that she had returned to the window. Ashamed of having been caught looking at the hood that covered her admirer, the young woman quickly withdrew again.

"I shall find out who she is from the Nanny," the Baron thought to himself.

The appearance of the Councilor of State had produced, as we shall see, a deep impression on the couple.

"But that is Baron Hulot, the head of my department!" exclaimed the husband, as he left the window balcony.

"In that case, Marneffe, the old maid on the third floor at the end of the court, who lives with that young man, must be his cousin! How odd that we should only have found that out today, and by accident!"

"Miss Fischer lives with a young man?" repeated the civil servant. "That is just the porters' gossip. We must not speak so lightly of the cousin of a Councilor of State who makes the weather at the Ministry! Come along, let us dine now; I have been waiting for you since four."

Pretty Madame Marneffe, natural daughter of Count de Montcornet, one of Napoleon's most famous lieutenants, had been married, with the help of a dowry of twenty thousand francs, to a minor official in the Ministry of War. Through the influence of the illustrious Lieutenant-General, Marshal of France for the last six months of his life, this scribe reached the unlooked-for position of head clerk in his office; but, just as he had been appointed head clerk, the Marshal's death had cut short the hopes of Marneffe and his wife. The humble salary of Monsieur Marneffe (for Mademoiselle Valérie Fortin's dowry had already melted away, partly in paying the official's debts, partly in buying the necessities of an ex-bachelor setting up house, but chiefly by the demands of a pretty woman, accustomed, while living with her mother, to pleasures that she was unwilling to forgo) had obliged the family to economize in rent. The situation of the Rue du Doyenné, not far from the Ministry of War and from the center of Paris, appealed to Monsieur and Madame Marneffe, who had been living in the same building as Miss Fischer for nearly four years.

Monsieur Jean Paul Stanilas Marneffe belonged to the class of petty officials who hold out against becoming completely brutalized by means of a kind of strength that depravity imparts. This little thin man with wispy hair and beard, a palish face, not so much wrinkled as worn, eyes with rather reddish pupils, rigged out with spectacles, of shabby appearance and even more shabby bearing, was the personification of the type that everyone imagines being brought before the police courts for offenses of indecency.

The flat occupied by this couple presented, like many Parisian homes, the deceptive appearance of a kind of sham luxury that characterizes many interiors. In the drawing room, the furniture was upholstered in shabby cotton velvet, plaster statuettes masquerading as Florentine bronzes, a badly carved sconce, merely painted, with molded glass candle-rings, carpet whose cheapness was belatedly explaining itself in the quantity of cotton used in its manufacture, which had become visible to the naked eye, everything—even to the curtains, that declared to you that woolen damask has only three years of splendor—everything cried out poverty as loudly as a ragged beggar at a church door.

The dining room, badly kept by a single maid, had the nauseating atmosphere of the dining rooms of provincial hotels; everything was dirty and ill-kempt.

The master's room, not unlike the room of a student, was furnished with his single bed, the furniture of his bachelor days, faded and shabby like himself, and cleaned once a week. That horrible room, where everything sagged, where dirty socks hung on the chairs stuffed with horsehair, whose brown flowers reappeared outlined in dust, clearly announced the man who is indifferent to his home, who spends his time out, playing cards in the cafés or elsewhere. The mistress's room was the exception to the degrading neglect that dishonored the common living rooms, whose curtains were everywhere yellowed with smoke and dust, and where the child, obviously abandoned to his own devices, left his toys lying about. Situated in the angle that joined on one side the part of the house looking on to the street with the main body of the building looking on to the end of the court of the adjoining property, Valérie's room and dressing room, elegantly furnished with chintz and rosewood furniture, and a pile carpet, proclaimed the pretty woman, almost, one might say, the kept woman. Above the velvet hangings of the mantelpiece stood a clock in the style then fashionable. There was a little Dunkirk cabinet quite well fitted, and jardinières of chinese porcelain, with expensive stands. The bed, the dressing table, the wardrobe with a mirror, the small sofa, and all the trifles strewn about, were in the style of the latest novelties of the moment.

Although everything was of a third-rate order of luxury and elegance, and at least three years old, a dandy would have found nothing in this room to complain of, except perhaps that the luxury was in rather middle-class taste. Art, and the distinction that arises from things that taste knows how to select, was totally absent here. A doctor of social sciences would have detected the existence of a lover, by some of these futilities in expensive jewelry that can only come to a married woman from that ever-absent but ever-present demigod.

The dinner set before the husband, wife, and child, the dinner that had waited since four o'clock, would have revealed the financial crisis that this family was going through, for the table is the most reliable thermometer of the fortunes of Parisian households. A soup made of vegetables and bean stock, a piece of veal with potatoes, saturated in brownish water, instead of gravy, a dish of beans, and some cherries of inferior quality, all served and eaten from chipped plates and dishes, with silver with the heavy ring of cheap plate—was this a menu worthy of a pretty woman? The Baron would have wept to see it! The dark decanters could not redeem the bad color of the wine, bought by the liter at the wine merchant's on the corner. The napkins had to last a week.

In a word, everything betrayed an undignified poverty, the indifference of both husband and wife to the family. The most obtuse observer would have said to himself, on seeing them, that these two had arrived at that dismal moment when the necessity to live called for some well-planned dishonesty.

Valérie's first words to her husband will therefore explain the dinner's long delay, due probably to the self-regarding devotion of the cook: "Samanon would only take your bills of exchange at fifty per cent and asked for a guarantee in the form of an assignment of your salary."

Poverty, still hidden in the household of the head of the department in the Ministry of War, where it was still held off by a salary of twenty-four thousand francs, besides bonuses, had reached its last stage with his employee.

"You have *made*[7] my chief," said the husband, looking at his wife.

"I thought so, too," she replied, without shrinking from a phrase borrowed from the slang of the gutters.

"What can we do?" went on Marneffe. "The landlord will take our furniture tomorrow. And your father went and died without making a will! My word, these Empire chaps think themselves as immortal as their Emperor."

"Poor Father," said she, "I was his only child and he was very fond of me! The Countess[8] must have burned the will. How could he possibly have forgotten me, when he used to give us three or four thousand-franc notes at a time?"

"We owe four quarters' rent, fifteen hundred francs! Is our furniture worth that amount? *That is the question!* as Shakespeare says."

"All right, goodbye, duckie," said Valérie, who had eaten only a few mouthfuls of the veal whose gravy the maid had extracted for a brave soldier back from Algiers. "Desperate situations call for desperate remedies!"

"Valérie, where are you going?" Marneffe exclaimed, stepping between his wife and the door.

"I am going to see our landlord," she replied, arranging her ringlets under her pretty hat. "As for you, you had better try to get on to good terms with that old spinster, if she is really the Director's cousin."

The mutual ignorance of tenants of the same building about one another's social positions is a constantly recurring fact that serves to explain the course of Parisian life; but it is easy to understand that an official who leaves every day early in the morning for his office, who returns home for dinner, and who goes out every evening, and a wife addicted to the pleasures of Paris, might very well know nothing of the life of an old maid living on the third floor at the end of the court of their block, particularly when the old maid in question has habits like those of Miss Fischer.

Lisbeth was the first in the house to take in her bread, milk, and charcoal, speaking to no one, and going to bed at sundown; she never received letters or visits, or got on to speaking terms with her neighbors. She led an anonymous, insectlike existence, the kind one comes across in certain houses, in which one discovers after four years that there is an old gentleman living on the fourth floor who knew Voltaire, Pilâtre de Rozier, Beaujon, Marcel, Molé, Sophie Arnould, Franklin, and Robespierre.[9]

What Monsieur and Madame Marneffe had just said about Lisbeth Fischer they had come to know by reason of the isolation of the locality, and the intimate terms that they were on with the porters, for their financial distress, and their consequent dependence on the good will of the porters, had made such an intimacy much too necessary not to be cultivated assiduously. As it happened, the spinster's pride, silence, and reserve had given rise, among the porters, to that exaggerated respect and cold relations that are the mark of the unavowed dissatisfaction of inferiors. The porters, moreover, thought themselves of equal rank (as they say at the Palace) with a tenant paying a rent of two hundred and fifty francs. Cousin Bette's confidences to her second cousin, Hortense, were in fact, true; so that anyone will understand how the porter had, in some intimate conversation with Madame Marneffe, libeled her, thinking that he was merely passing on scandal.

As soon as the spinster had taken her candlestick from the hands of the respectable Madame Olivier, the portress, she went on to see whether there was light in the windows of the attic above her flat. At that hour, and in July, it was already so dark at the end of the court that the old maid could not go to bed without a light.

"Oh, Monsieur Steinbock is in, don't you worry; he hasn't even been out," Madame Olivier said maliciously to Miss Fischer. The spinster did not answer. She was still a peasant in her indifference to what people said who were not closely connected with her, and just as peasants care only for their own village, she paid no attention to opinions outside the little circle in whose midst she lived. Therefore she firmly went up not to her own flat but to the attic. For at dessert she had put into her bag fruit and sweets for her sweetheart; and she was going to give them to him, for all the world like an old maid taking a titbit to her dog.

She found the hero of Hortense's dreams working by the light of a little lamp, whose light was increased by passing through a globe filled with water—a pale, fair young man, sitting at a sort of bench covered with a sculptor's tools—red wax, chisels, roughly shaped bases, bronzes copied from models; he wore a blouse, and was holding a little group in modeling wax that he was scrutinizing with the attention of a poet at work.

"Look what I have brought you, Wenceslas," she said, spreading her handkerchief on a corner of the bench. Then she carefully took from her bag the confections and fruit. "You are most kind, Mademoiselle," replied the poor exile sadly.

"They will refresh you, my poor child. You heat your blood working like this; you were not born for this hard existence."

Wenceslas Steinbock looked at the spinster with an expression of surprise.

"Eat them," she repeated sharply, "instead of looking at me as if I were a model you are pleased with."

On receiving this verbal prod, the young man ceased to be surprised, recognizing again his female mentor, whose acts of tenderness always took him by surprise, so accustomed was he to being abused. Although Steinbock was twenty-nine, he might have passed, like many fair men, for five or six years less; and looking at that youth, whose freshness had succumbed to fatigue and distress, side by side with the hard, dry face of his companion, one might have thought that nature had made a mistake in allotting them their sexes. He got up and flung himself into an old Louis XV armchair covered with yellow Utrecht velvet, as if his one desire was to relax. The spinster thereupon took a *reine-claude* plum and gently offered it to her friend.

"Thank you," he said, taking the fruit.

"Are you tired?" she asked, giving him another.

"I am not tired with work; I am tired of life," he replied.

"Good gracious, what an idea!" she said rather sharply. "Haven't you got a good angel to look after you?" she went on, handing him the sweetmeats, and watching him with pleasure as he ate them all. "You see, I thought of you while I was dining with my cousin."

"I know," he said, directing on Lisbeth a look at once caressing and plaintive. "Without you I would have been dead long ago; but you know, my dear friend, artists need some distractions!"

"Oh, so that's it!" she exclaimed, interrupting him, putting her hands on her hips and turning with flaming eyes. "You want to lose your health in the vices of Paris, like so many artists who end by dying in the hospital![10] No, no, make your fortune first, and when you have an income you can amuse yourself, my child, for then you will have the money to pay for the doctors as well as the pleasures."

Wenceslas Steinbock bowed his head before this tirade, delivered with looks that pierced him with their magnetic fire. If her most scathing detractor could have witnessed the beginning of this scene, he would already have realized the falsehood of the calumnies uttered by the Oliviers, man and wife, against Mademoiselle Fischer. Everything in the tones, the gestures, and the glances of these two bespoke the purity of their relationship. The spinster manifested the tenderness of a harsh but real maternal regard. The young man submitted like a respectful son to the tyranny of a mother. This odd relationship seemed to be the product of a strong will constantly exerted upon a weak character, upon that instability peculiar to Slavs, who, while they can rise to heroic courage on the field of battle, reveal an extraordinary incoherence in their conduct, a moral weakness whose causes are for the physiologists to discover—for physiologists are to politics what entomologists are to agriculture.

"What if I die before I become rich?" Wenceslas asked laconically.

"Die?" exclaimed the spinster. "Oh, I will never let you die! I have life enough for two and I would give you my blood, if it came to that!"

On hearing that violent and naïve exclamation, Steinbock's eyes filled with tears.

"Don't you worry, my little Wenceslas," Lisbeth went on, deeply moved. "Listen, I think my cousin Hortense liked your seal very much! Now I'm going to manage to sell your bronze for you; then you will be out of my debt, and able to do what you like—you will be free! Come now, smile!"

"I shall never be out of your debt, Mademoiselle," replied the poor exile.

"And why not?" asked the Vosges peasant, taking the Livonian's part against herself.

"Because you have not only fed me, housed me, cared for me in my distress: you have put strength into me, you have made me what I am. You have often been hard; you have often made me suffer."

"I?" said the spinster. "Are you going to start your nonsense again about poetry and the arts, and crack your fingers and wave your arms, talking about ideal beauty and all your Nordic nonsense? The beautiful is nothing to the real, and I'm reality! You have ideas in your head? Very fine! I have ideas, too. What you have in your head is of no use if you don't turn it to any advantage! People with ideas aren't as well off as those who have none, but who know how to get on with things. Instead of thinking about your daydreams, you must work. What have you been doing since I left?"

"What did your pretty cousin say?"

"Who told you she was pretty?" Lisbeth asked sharply, in a tone in which raged the jealousy of a tiger.

"Why, you did."

"That was to see how you would take it. Do you want to go running after petticoats? You love women? Very well, make one, put your desires into bronze, for you will have to do without love affairs for some time—and especially with my cousin. She is not a goose for your den—that girl needs a husband with an income of sixty thousand francs—and he has been found. Look, the bed is not made!" she said, looking through into the other room. "Oh, my poor dear, how I have been neglecting you!"

Whereupon the energetic spinster took off her gloves, her cape, and her hat, and, like a maid, she briskly set to work to make the little camp bed on which the artist slept. This mixture of brusqueness, even of downright rudeness, with kindness, accounts for the power that Lisbeth had gained over this man, of whom she had taken complete possession. Does not life bind us by its opposites, good and evil? Had the Livonian encountered Madame Marneffe instead of Lisbeth Fischer, he would have found in his protectress a complaisance that would have led him into some shady and dishonorable course, in which he would have been lost. He would certainly not have worked, and the artist in him would not have developed. Moreover, even while he lamented the spinster's hard-hearted ways, his good sense told him that her rule of iron was better than the idle and precarious existence led by some of his compatriots.

Here is the story of the events to which the marriage of this feminine energy with that masculine weakness was due—a kind of reversal of roles said to be not uncommon in Poland.

Chapter VII

In 1833, Mademoiselle Fischer, who sometimes worked at night when she had a great deal on hand, noticed, at about 1:00 A.M., a strong smell of carbonic acid, and heard the groans of a dying man. The smell of gas and the death rattle proceeded from an attic situated immediately above the two rooms of her flat. She guessed that a young man who had recently come to the house and taken this attic, which had been to let for three years, must be attempting suicide. She hurried upstairs and forced the door, flinging herself against it with all her peasant strength, and found the tenant rolling on his camp bed in the convulsions of agony. She put out the charcoal stove. The door being open, fresh air streamed in and the exile was saved;[1] later, when Lisbeth had put him to bed like an invalid, and he had gone to sleep, she was able to recognize the cause of his suicide in the absolute bareness of the two rooms of this attic, in which there was nothing but an old table, the camp bed, and two chairs.

On the table was the following letter, which she read:

> I am Count Wenceslas Steinbock, born at Prelia in Livonia.
>
> No one is to blame for my death; the reasons for my suicide are, in the words of Kosciusko: *"Finis Poloniae!"*[2]
>
> The great-nephew of a brave general of Charles XII did not wish to beg. My delicate health prevented me from entering military service, and yesterday saw the end of the hundred thalers with which I came from Dresden to Paris. I leave twenty-five francs in the drawer of the table to pay the rent that I owe the landlord.
>
> Having no longer any relations living, my death affects nobody. I beg my compatriots not to blame the French government. I have not made myself known as a refugee, nor have I asked for any help; I have not met even a single exile. Nobody in Paris knows of my existence.
>
> I shall die as a Christian. May God forgive the last of the Steinbocks!
>
> WENCESLAS.

Mademoiselle Fischer, profoundly touched by the honesty of a dying man who paid his rent, opened the drawer, and found, in fact, five hundred-sou pieces.

"Poor young man!" she exclaimed. "And with no one in the world to care for him!"

She went down to her own room, fetched her needlework, and settled down to work in the attic, while keeping watch over the

Livonian gentleman. Imagine the exile's astonishment when he awoke and saw a woman sitting by his bed; he thought himself still dreaming. While she sat stitching gold aiguillettes for a uniform, the spinster had made up her mind to look after this poor boy, whom she had admired as he lay sleeping. When the young Count was quite awake Lisbeth cheered him up and asked him questions with a view to finding out how to put him in the way of earning his living. Wenceslas, after telling his story, added that he had owed his profession to his acknowledged talent for art; he had always wanted to be a sculptor, but the time necessary for study had seemed too long for a man with no money, and he felt much too weak for the moment to take up manual work or to undertake large works of sculpture. All this was Greek to Lisbeth Fischer. She replied to this unfortunate young man that Paris offered many openings, and that a young man of determination could not fail to make a living there.

"I am only a poor woman myself, a peasant, and have managed very well to make a living," she added in conclusion. "Listen to me. If you will really work in earnest, I have some savings, and I will lend you month by month enough money to live on, but to live hardly, not to waste and squander! You can dine in Paris on twenty-five sous a day, and I will make your breakfast with mine, every morning. And I will furnish your rooms, and pay for whatever apprenticeship you think necessary. You shall give me a formal receipt for the money I lay out for you, and when you are rich you can pay it all back. But if you do not work, I shall not consider myself as bound to you in any way, and I will leave you to your fate."

"Ah!" exclaimed the unfortunate youth, who still felt the bitterness of his first encounter with death; "the exiles of all countries have good reason for stretching out their hands to France, like souls in Purgatory reaching toward Paradise. In what other country could one find help, and generous hearts everywhere, even in a garret like this! I place myself absolutely at your service, my dearest benefactress. I shall be your slave! Be my sweetheart!" he had said, in one of these demonstrative and caressing impulses so characteristic of Poles, and for which they are quite wrongly accused of servility.

"Oh, no! I am much too jealous—I would make you miserable; but I will gladly be a sort of comrade," Lisbeth replied.

"Oh, if you only knew how eagerly I longed for any human being, even a tyrant, who had any use for me, when I struggled in the loneliness of Paris!" Wenceslas went on. "I would rather have been in Siberia, where the Emperor would have sent me if I had returned! Be my providence! I will work; I will surpass myself, although, as a matter of fact, I'm not a bad fellow."

"Will you do everything that I tell you?" she asked.

"Yes!"

"Very well, I adopt you as my child," she said gaily. "Here I am with a son risen from the grave. Now, we will make a start. I am going down to do my marketing; you must dress, and you can come and share my breakfast when I rap on the ceiling with my broom handle."

The following day Mademoiselle Fischer collected, at the firm to which she took her work, information about the profession of sculpture. By a series of questions, she succeeded in finding out about the studios of Florent and Chanor, a firm specializing in founding, where rich bronzes and costly services of silverware were produced. There she presented Steinbock, in the capacity of an apprentice sculptor, a somewhat odd proposition, since the firm carried out the designs of all the most famous artists, but did not teach sculpture.

But, thanks to the old maid's persistence and stubbornness, her protégé was at last taken on as a designer of ornaments. Steinbock soon learned to model ornaments, and invented new ones, for he had real talent. Five months after completing his apprenticeship as a sculptor he made the acquaintance of the famous Stidmann, the leading sculptor of the house of Florent. By the end of twenty months Wenceslas knew more of the art than his master; but in thirty months the savings amassed by the old maid in the course of seventeen years, bit by bit, had all gone. Two thousand five hundred francs in gold! A sum that she had intended to invest in an annuity—and what was there to show for it? A receipt from a Pole! And Lisbeth was now working as she had worked in her youth, in order to meet the expenses of the Livonian. When she found herself in possession of a piece of paper instead of her gold pieces she lost her head and went to consult Monsieur Rivet, who had for fifteen years been the friend and adviser of his able forewoman. On hearing of this adventure, Monsieur and Madame Rivet scolded Lisbeth, told her she was mad, abused all refugees, whose schemes for national independence were a threat to trade and peace at any price, and urged the old maid to obtain what in commerce are known as securities.

"The only security that this fellow has to offer is his liberty," Monsieur Rivet concluded.

Monsieur Achille Rivet was a magistrate in the Tribunal of Commerce.

"And that is no joke for foreigners," he went on. "A Frenchman spends five years in prison, and afterwards he comes out again, without having paid his debts, it is true, for only his conscience can force him to do so, which it never does; but a foreigner is never released from prison. Give me your bill of exchange. You must have it made out in the name of my bookkeeper; he will contest it, prosecute you both, and obtain a judgment against you with a penalty of imprisonment, and when everything is well on its way he will sign a defeasance. In acting in this way your interest will be growing, and you will always have a loaded pistol to point at your Pole!"

The old maid followed this advice, telling her protégé not to be alarmed at this procedure, taken merely in order to give guarantees to a moneylender, who would then consent to advance her some money. This subterfuge was the product of the inventive genius of the magistrate of the Tribunal of Commerce. The innocent artist, blind in his faith in his benefactress, lit his pipe with the stamped receipts, for, like all men who have worries to quiet or an excess of energy, he smoked. One fine day Monsieur Rivet showed Mademoiselle Fischer a dossier and said, "You have Wenceslas Steinbock bound hand and foot so thoroughly that within twenty-four hours you could have him in Clichy[3] for the rest of his days."

This worthy and honest magistrate of the Tribunal of Commerce experienced, on that day, the satisfaction that comes from the knowledge of having performed a bad good deed. Good will takes so many forms in Paris, and this singular instance corresponds to one of its variations. The Livonian being now snared in the toils of commercial procedure, the question was how to get the payment, for the eminent businessman regarded Wenceslas Steinbock as a swindler. The heart, honor, and poetry were, in his eyes, bad things in affairs of business. In the interests of poor Mademoiselle Fischer, who, to use his expression, had been "taken in" by a Pole, Rivet went to see the wealthy manufacturers whom Steinbock had recently left. There, assisted by the distinguished gold- and silversmiths already named, Stidmann, who was bringing French art to the perfection which it has now reached, a perfection which challenges comparison with that of the Florentines and the Renaissance, was in Chanor's office, when the embroiderer arrived to ask for information about "one Steinbock, a Polish refugee."

"Whom do you mean by 'one Steinbock'?" Stidmann exclaimed gaily. "Not by any chance a young Livonian who was a pupil of mine? You must know, sir, that he is a great artist. They say that I think myself the devil; very well, that poor boy does not realize that he might become a god!"

"Ah!" said Rivet, with satisfaction. Then he went on, "All the same, you speak very casually to a man who has the honor to be a magistrate in the Department of the Seine."

"Your pardon, Consul!" Stidmann interrupted, raising the back of his hand to his brow in salute.

"I am very glad of what you tell me," continued the magistrate. "So this young man could make money?"

"To be sure," said old Chanor; "but he will have to work hard; he would have made some already if he had stayed with us. But there you are! Artists cannot bear to give up their independence."

"They have a sense of their worth and their dignity," Stidmann replied. "I don't blame Wenceslas for going off on his own and trying to make his name and become a great man; he has a perfect right to do so. But it was a great loss to me, all the same, when he left."

"There you are!" exclaimed Rivet. "That is the conceit of these green young men just down from the university! Make sure of a good salary first, and go for glory afterwards, I say."

"The hand loses its virtue picking up money," replied Stidmann. "It is for glory to bring us fortune."

"What do you expect?" Chanor said to Rivet. "You can't tie them."

"They would eat the halter," Stidmann put in.

"All these young men," Chanor said, looking at Stidmann, "have more daydreams than talent. They are wildly extravagant, have their mistresses, throw their money out of the window, and have no time left to work; then they neglect their commissions; so we go to the workers who don't think highly of themselves, and who get rich. Then they complain of hard times, although, in fact, if they had given their minds to it they could have made heaps of money."

"You remind me," said Stidmann, "of old Lumignon, in that bookshop before the Revolution, who used to say: 'Ah! If only I could keep Montesquieu, Voltaire, and Rousseau, very hard up, in my garret, and keep their trousers locked up, what good little books they would write for me—I would make a fortune out of them!' If you could manufacture works of art like nails, every porter would make them—give me a thousand francs and say no more!"

The good Rivet returned, delighted on behalf of poor Mademoiselle Fischer, who dined at his house every Monday, where he now found her.

"If you can make him work hard," he said, "you will be luckier than you were wise; you will get your money back, interest, outlay, and capital. This Pole has talent; he could earn his living; but lock up his trousers and his shoes, prevent him from going to the Chaumière[4] or into the Notre Dame de Lorette quarter, keep him on the halter. Without these precautions your sculptor will idle his time away, and you know what artists call idling! Disgraceful, upon my word! I have just learned that they think nothing of spending a thousand-franc note in a single day!"

This episode had a disastrous effect upon the relationship of Wenceslas and Lisbeth. The benefactress had steeped the bread of exile in the bitterness of reproaches ever since she had seen her savings endangered, and she very often believed them lost. The good mother became a harsh stepmother; she lectured the poor boy, pestered him, and scolded him for not getting on with his work quickly enough, and for having chosen a difficult profession. She could not see that the models in red wax, the figurines, designs for ornaments, and sketches, had any use. Then these reproaches having spent themselves, she would try to wipe out their traces, by services, kindnesses, and attentions. The poor young man, after having groaned at finding himself dependent on this shrew, under the domination of a Vosges peasant, was again seduced by the caresses of that maternal solicitude, whose whole basis was the physical, the material aspect of life. He was like a wife who forgives ill-treatment that has lasted a week, for the sake of a fleeting reconciliation. Mademoiselle Fischer thus gained complete power over his mind. Love of power, whose germ had been latent in her spinster heart, was developing rapidly. She was able to satisfy her pride and her desire to play an active part. Had she not a human being all to herself, to scold, manage, and spoil, to make happy, without the fear of any rivalry? The good and the bad in her character were equally called into play. If at times she martyred the wretched artist, she showed, at others, a delicacy toward him as gracious as wild flowers; it was her pleasure to see that he lacked nothing, she would have given her life for him; of that Wenceslas was sure. Like all fine souls, the poor boy forgot the evil, the old maid's faults, and besides, she had told him the story of her life in order to excuse her roughness, and so he remembered only her kindnesses. One day, exasperated because Wenceslas had been out idling instead of working, the old maid made a scene.

"You belong to me!" she told him. "If you were an honest man, you ought to try to pay back what you owe me as quickly as possible."

The blood of the Steinbocks kindled in the veins of the young aristocrat, and he turned pale.

"Good heavens," she said, "soon we will have nothing to live on except the few pennies that I earn—I, a working woman."

The two, both irritated by their poverty, and aroused by argument, attacked one another; and for the first time the poor artist reproached his benefactress for having rescued him from death in order to compel him to live the life of a galley slave, worse than death, in which at least one is at peace, he said. And he spoke of running away.

"Run away!" exclaimed the spinster. "Ah! Monsieur Rivet was right!"

And she explained categorically to the Pole how within twenty-four hours he could be clapped into prison for the rest of his days. This was a crushing blow. Steinbock fell into a black depression and absolute silence. Next day Lisbeth, having heard him making preparations for suicide during the night, went up to her pensioner and presented him with the schedule and a legal quittance.

"There, my child, forgive me!" she said, with tears in her eyes. "Be happy, leave me; I torment you too much. Only say that you will sometimes think of the poor girl who put you in the way of earning your living. But there you are! You are the cause of my harshness. I might die, and what would become of you without me? That is why I am so impatient to see you making objects that can be sold. I am not asking for the money for myself, I assure you! I am afraid of your idleness, that you call reveries, of those ideas of yours that take up all the hours during which you look at the sky, and I would like to see you form the habit of working."

This was said in accents, and with a look and tears and an emphasis that went to the high-minded artist's heart; he took his benefactress in his arms, pressed her to his bosom, and kissed her forehead.

"Keep these," he replied almost gaily. "Why should you send me to Clichy? Am I not imprisoned here by gratitude?"

This crisis in their common life, which had happened six months earlier, stimulated Wenceslas to complete three pieces of work: the seal that Hortense was keeping, the group at the antique dealer's, and a fine clock that he had almost finished, for he was now putting in the last screws of the model.

This clock represented the twelve Hours, admirably personified by twelve female figures linked in a dance so wild and swift that three *amoretti*, poised on a pile of flowers and fruit, could not catch one of them as they passed; only the torn chlamys[5] of the hour of midnight remained in the hands of the boldest of the *amoretti*. This composition was mounted on a round base, skillfully ornamented with fantastic beasts. The hour was indicated in a monstrous mouth, opened in a yawn. Each hour carried some appropriate symbol characterizing the common occupations of the day.

It is now easy to understand the nature of the strange attachment that Mademoiselle Fischer had come to feel for her Livonian: she wanted to see him happy, and she saw him wasting away, pining in his garret. The reason for this fearful state of affairs is easy to imagine. The peasant woman watched over this child of the North with the tenderness of a mother, the jealousy of a wife, and the energy of a dragon; she so arranged things as to make all kinds of folly or dissipation impossible for him, by never giving him any money. She would have liked to keep her victim and her companion entirely to herself, well behaved, as he was compelled to be, and she did not realize the barbarity of this absurd desire, for she herself had grown accustomed to every privation. She loved Steinbock enough not to marry him, but too much to give him up to another woman; she could not resign herself to being only his mother, although she saw the folly of contemplating the other alternative. These contradictions, this ferocious jealousy, the pleasure of having a man all to herself, disturbed the spinster's heart beyond all bounds. Having really been in love for four years, she cherished the fond hope of making this inconsequent and inconclusive life, in which her very persistence was to cause the loss of the man she thought of as her child, continue forever. The conflict between her instinct and her reason rendered her unjust and tyrannical. She wreaked on the young man her own grievance at being neither young, nor beautiful, nor rich; and then, after each act of vengeance, she proceeded, recognizing her own fault, to infinite humility and tenderness. She could not contemplate sacrificing to her idol until she had exercised her own power on it, by means of hatchet blows. In fact, it was Shakespeare's *Tempest* in reverse, with Caliban as master of Ariel and Prospero. As for the unfortunate young man with such high ideals, meditative, inclined to be lazy, his eyes revealed, like those of caged lions in the zoo, the desert that his benefactress had created in his heart. The penal servitude that Lisbeth imposed upon him did not satisfy the needs of his heart. His boredom became a physical malady, and he was literally dying without being able to ask for, without knowing how to procure, the money for the distraction he often needed. On certain energetic days, on which his sense of unhappiness increased his exasperation, he would look at Lisbeth, as a thirsty traveler, crossing a desert coast, must look at salt water. These bitter fruits of poverty, and this solitude in Paris, were savored as pleasures by Lisbeth. Moreover, she divined with terror that the first breath of passion would carry away her slave. Sometimes she blamed herself for having by her tyranny and her reproaches driven this poetic soul to become a great sculptor of little things, for having given him the means of escaping beyond her power.

The next day these three existences, so variously and so really unhappy, that of a desperate mother, that of the Marneffe home, and that of the unfortunate exile, were all to be affected by Hortense's naïve passion, and by the singular outcome of the Baron's unfortunate passion for Josépha.

Chapter VIII

As he entered the Opera the Councilor of State was struck by the dark aspect of the Rue le Peletier entrance hall, where he saw no gendarmes, no lights, no attendants, no barriers to hold back the crowd. He looked at the notice board and saw on it a white band, across which blazed these sinister words:

POSTPONED OWING TO INDISPOSITION.

Immediately he rushed off to Josépha's lodgings in the Rue Chauchat, for, like all the artists attached to the Opera, she lived nearby.

"Whom do you want, sir?" the porter said to him, to his great astonishment.

"Don't you recognize me?" the Baron asked, disturbed.

"On the contrary, sir, it is because I have the honor to remember Monsieur that I ask you where you are going."

A mortal chill seized the Baron.

"What has happened?" he asked.

"If Monsieur le Baron goes into Mademoiselle Mirah's flat, he will find Mademoiselle Héloise Brisetout, Monsieur Bixiou, Monsieur Léon de Lora, Monsieur Lousteau, Monsieur de Vernisset, Monsieur de Stidmann,[1] and various women reeking with patchouli, who are having a house-warming party."

"And where, then, is . . . ?"

"Mademoiselle Mirah? I don't really know whether I would be doing the right thing in telling you."

The Baron slipped two hundred-sou pieces into the porter's hand.

"Well, she's living now in the Rue de Ville d'Évêque, in a house they say the Duc d'Hérouville has given her," said the porter, in a stage whisper.

Having asked for the number of this house, the Baron took a milord and drew up outside one of those charming modern houses with double doors, where everything, down to the very gaslamp in the porch, proclaims luxury.

The Baron, dressed in his blue coat, white cravat, white waistcoat, nankeen breeches, shining patent-leather boots, and well-starched shirt frills, was taken by the porter of this new Eden for a belated guest. His haste, his bearing, and everything about him, seemed to justify this opinion.

At the sound of the bell rung by the porter a footman appeared in the hall. This footman, new, like the house, made way for the Baron, who said to him in imperial tones and with an imperial gesture, "Send in this card to Mademoiselle Josépha."

The *patito*[2] looked mechanically around the room in which he found himself, and discovered that he was in a hall filled with rare flowers, whose furnishing must have cost twenty thousand francs. The footman, returning, asked him to wait in the drawing room until the party came from the dining room to take their coffee.

Although the Baron had known the luxury of the Empire, which was prodigious, to be sure, and whose creations, although they may not have been durable, had nevertheless cost fantastic sums, he remained stunned, dumfounded, in this drawing room whose three windows opened on to a fairy garden—one of those gardens made in a month, with soil brought for the purpose and transplanted flowers, whose lawns seem to have been produced by some process of alchemy. Not only did he admire the taste, the gilding, the costly carvings in the Pompadour style, marvelous furnishing materials such as any tradesman could have bought for enormous sums of money, but also treasures of the kind that only princes have the gift of choosing, finding, paying for, and offering: two pictures by Greuze, two Watteaus, two heads by Van Dyck, two landscapes by

Ruysdael, two by Le Guaspre, a Rembrandt, a Holbein, a Murillo, and a Titian, two paintings by Teniers and two by Metzu, a Van Huysum and an Abraham Mignon—in fact, two hundred thousand francs' worth of pictures, superbly framed.[3] The mounts were worth almost as much as the canvases.

"Ah! Now you understand, old boy?" said Josépha.

Coming on tiptoe through a noiseless door on Persian carpets, she had taken her adorer by surprise in one of those states of stupefaction in which the blood rings so loudly in the ears that they hear nothing but that knell of disaster.

The words "old boy" spoken to a personage so highly placed in the government, and which so well reveal the boldness with which these women abase even the greatest, left the Baron rooted to the spot. Josépha, in yellow and white, was dressed so exquisitely for this festivity that she was still able to shine in the midst of this incredible luxury, like a rare jewel.

"Isn't it lovely?" she went on. "The Duke has spent on this all the proceeds of floating a company and then selling out at a big profit.[4] He is no fool, my little Duke. There is nobody like the great aristocrats of the old style for knowing how to change coal into gold. The lawyer brought me the title deeds to sign before dinner, and the bills receipted. All the smart set are in there: d'Esgrignon, Rastignac, Maxime, Lenoncourt, Verneuil, Laginski, Rochefide, La Palférine, and the bankers Nucingen and du Tillet, and Antonia, and Malaga, and Carabine, and la Schontz[5]—they all feel for you deeply. Yes, old dear, you are welcome to stay, on condition that you immediately drink two bottles of Hungarian wine, Champagne, and *Cap*, to catch up with them. My dear, we are all too tight to sober up for the Opera. My director is as drunk as a cornet player; he's reached the noisy stage."

"Oh! Josépha!" exclaimed the Baron.

"Scenes are so futile!" Josépha interrupted, smiling. "Listen, have you got the six hundred thousand francs that paid for this house and its furnishings? Could you bring me a deed of endowment[6] for thirty thousand francs a year like the one the Duke has just given me in a white paper bag of sugared almonds? That was a nice touch!"

"What an outrage!" said the Councilor of State, who, in that moment of rage, would have bartered his wife's diamonds in order to be in the Duc d'Hérouville's shoes only for twenty-four hours.

"Outrage is my profession!" she replied. "Ah! don't take it like this! Why did you not think of floating a company, then? Really, my poor dyed Tom, you ought to thank me: I have left you just when you were on the point of spending on me your wife's future, and your daughter's dowry, and ... oh, you are crying! The Empire has fallen ... I salute the Empire."

She took a tragic pose, and recited: *"On vous appelle Hulot! je ne vous connais plus!"*[7]—and she left him.

The half-open door allowed a gleam of light, like a flash of lightning, to pass through, accompanied by the crescendo peal of the party, and by the smells of a banquet of the first order. The singer turned to look back through the half-closed door, and seeing Hulot standing rooted there as if he were made of bronze, she advanced a step, and reappeared.

"Monsieur," she said, "I left the rubbish of the Rue Chauchat to little Héloise Brisetout; if you wish to collect your cotton nightcap, your shoehorn, your corset, and your mustache wax, I have stipulated that they are to be returned to you."

This terrible insult had the effect of making the Baron leave like Lot flying from Gomorrah, but without, like Lot's wife, looking back.

Hulot returned home, striding in a fury and talking to himself; he found his family still calmly playing the same game of whist for two-sou stakes that they had begun before he left them. On seeing her husband, poor Adeline guessed that some frightful disaster had happened, some disgrace; she gave her cards to Hortense, and led Hector into the same little room in which Crevel, five hours before had predicted to her the most shameful miseries of destitution.

"What is it?" she said fearfully.

"Oh! forgive me! But let me tell you the infamies."

And he poured out his wrath for ten minutes.

"But, my dear," the poor woman replied heroically, "creatures like that know nothing of love! Pure and devoted love such as you deserve. How can you, with your intelligence, hope to compete with millions?"

"Darling Adeline," exclaimed the Baron, and took his wife in his arms, pressing her to his heart.

For the Baroness had poured balm on the bleeding wounds of his self-esteem.

"Certainly, apart from the fortune of the Duc d'Hérouville, she would not hesitate!" said the Baron.

"My dear," said Adeline, making a final effort, "if you absolutely must have mistresses, why don't you, like Crevel, take women who are not too expensive, the kind that will be satisfied for a long time with very little? We should all be the better for it! I can understand the need, but I absolutely fail to understand vanity."

"Oh, what a good and wonderful wife you are!" he exclaimed. "I am an old fool; I don't deserve to have an angel like you for a companion."

"I am simply my Napoleon's Joséphine," she answered, with a touch of sadness.

"Joséphine could not touch you," he said. "Come, I will play whist with my brother and my children; I must attend to my duties as the father of a family, find Hortense a husband, and bury the libertine."

These pleasant words touched poor Adeline so deeply that she said, "That creature has very poor taste to prefer anyone at all to my Hector. Ah! I would not give you up for all the gold in the world. How could anyone desert you who has the good fortune to be loved by you?"

The look with which the Baron repaid his wife's fanatical devotion confirmed her in the opinion that sweetness and submission were a woman's most powerful weapons. But in this she was mistaken. Noble sentiments carried to extremes are as productive of evil as the worst of vices. Bonaparte became Emperor by firing on the crowds only two paces away from the spot where Louis XVI lost his crown and his head in the bargain because he had not allowed the blood of a certain Monsieur Sauce to be shed.[8]

The following day Hortense, who went to bed with Wenceslas's seal under her pillow so as not to be separated from it while she slept, was up early and sent a message asking her father to go into the garden with her as soon as he was dressed.

At about half-past nine the father, falling in with his daughter's request, gave her his arm, and they proceeded together along the quays by the Pont Royal to the Place du Carrousel.

"Look as if you are just strolling, Papa," Hortense said, as they came through the turnstile to cross that great square.

"Strolling here?" the father answered, teasing.

"We are supposed to be going to the Museum, and over there," she said, indicating the stalls backing on to the walls of some houses that stood at right angles to the Rue du Doyenné. "Why, there are some antique shops, picture dealers!"

"Your cousin lives there."

"I know, but she must not see us."

"And what do you want to do?" asked the Baron, finding himself only thirty yards away from the windows of Madame Marneffe, who suddenly came into his mind.

Hortense had led her father to the window of one of the shops on the corner of the block of houses that runs along the length of the galleries of the old Louvre and faces the Hôtel de Nantes. She went into the shop. Her father remained outside, passing the time looking at the window of the pretty little woman who, the previous evening, had left her image implanted in the old beau's heart, as if to console him for the wound that he had received; and he could not resist the idea of putting his wife's advice into practice.

"Let us fall back on the middle classes," he thought to himself, recalling the adorable perfections of Madame Marneffe. "That woman would soon make me forget the grasping Josépha."

This is what took place simultaneously inside and outside the shop.

As he watched the windows of his new flame, the Baron noticed the husband who, as he brushed his own overcoat, was evidently on the watch, and seemed to be waiting for someone. Afraid of being noticed, and later recognized, the amorous Baron turned his back on the Rue du Doyenné, but only three-quarters, so as to be able to glance in that direction from time to time. This movement brought him face to face with Madame Marneffe, who, coming from the embankment, was turning the corner of the block on her way home. Valérie seemed to be disconcerted on meeting the Baron's astonished look, and she countered it with a prudish downward glance.

"Pretty woman!" exclaimed the Baron, "for whom a man would do many foolish things!"

"Indeed, sir!" she replied, turning with a gesture of a woman who has taken her courage in both hands. "You are Monsieur le Baron Hulot, are you not?"

The Baron, more and more astonished, made a gesture of assent.

"Very well, since chance has twice allowed our eyes to meet, and if I have been fortunate enough to interest you, or arouse your curiosity, may I say that instead of committing follies, you could indeed do justice—my husband's fate depends on you!"

"In what way?" the Baron asked gallantly.

"He is employed in your department, in the Ministry of War, in Monsieur Lebrun's section, Monsieur Coquet's office," she replied, smiling.

"I am ready, Madame . . . Madame . . . ?"

"Madame Marneffe."

"My little Madame Marneffe, to commit injustices for your sake. A cousin of mine lives in your house, and I will visit her one of these days, as soon as possible, and you shall come and make your request to me."

"Forgive my boldness, Monsieur le Baron, but you must know that I only ventured to speak in this way because I have no protection."

"Ah ha!"

"Oh, sir, you misunderstand me," she said, lowering her eyes.

To the Baron it was as if the sun had gone out.

"I am dreadfully worried, but I am an honest woman," she continued. "Six months ago I lost my only protector, Marshal Montcornet."

"Oh! you are his daughter?"

"Yes, sir, but he never acknowledged me."

"So that he could leave you part of his fortune?"

"He left me nothing, Monsieur, for the will was never found."

"Indeed, poor little woman. The Marshal was carried off suddenly with apoplexy.... But cheer up, Madame. Something is due to the daughter of one of the Chevaliers of the Empire."

Madame Marneffe took her leave graciously, and was as proud of her success as the Baron was of his.

"Where the devil was she coming from so early?" he wondered, contemplating the undulations of her skirts, to which she imparted a grace that was perhaps a little exaggerated. "She looks too tired to be coming from the bath, and her husband is waiting for her. It is very odd, very curious altogether."

When Madame Marneffe had gone in the Baron began to wonder what his daughter was doing in the shop. As he went in, still gazing at Madame Marneffe's windows, he ran into a young man with a pale forehead, and gray sparkling eyes, dressed in a light coat of black merino, coarse dark trousers, and high-cut boots, who was dashing out like a lunatic; he saw him run toward Madame Marneffe's house, and enter it. On going into the shop Hortense had instantly recognized the famous group, prominently displayed on a table in the middle, in line with the door.

Even if she had known nothing of his work, it would certainly have impressed the young girl by what one can only describe as the *brio* of a great work of art—this girl who certainly might herself have posed, in Italy, as the model of Brio.

Not all works of genius have in an equal degree this brilliance, this splendor that is apparent to all eyes, even those of the most ignorant. Thus some of Raphael's paintings, such as the famous *Transfiguration,* the *Madonna of Foligno,* the frescoes of the *Stations* in the Vatican, do not instantly call forth our admiration in the same way as the *Violin Player* of the Sciarra Gallery, the portraits of the *Doni,* the *Vision of Ezekiel* in the Pitti Gallery, the *Christ carrying the Cross* at the Borghese, or the *Marriage of the Virgin* in the Brera in Milan. The *St. John the Baptist* of the Tribuna, *Saint Luke painting the Virgin* in the Academy at Rome, have not the charm of the portrait of *Leo X,* or the Dresden *Virgin.* They are, nevertheless, of equal merit; greater, indeed; the *Stations,* the *Transfiguration* and the three easel pictures in the Vatican are in the highest degree sublime and perfect. But these masterpieces demand from even the most expert critic a certain effort of attention, and some study, before they can be fully understood; whereas the *Violinist,* the *Marriage of the Virgin,* and the *Vision of Ezekiel* make their own way into our hearts by way of our eyes, and there take their place. It is pleasant to receive them in this way, with no effort; it is not the highest form of art appreciation, but it is the most enjoyable. This fact proves that in the production of works of art the same various chances hold good as in families, where there are fortunately gifted children, born easily, without causing suffering to their mothers, children on whom life smiles, and who are always successful. The fruits of genius are as various as the fruits of love.

This *brio,* an Italian word for which the French language has no equivalent, is the mark of works of youth. It is the product of the impulse and vitality of early talent, an impulse that may later return in certain happy hours, but then that *brio* no longer comes from the artist's heart, and instead of being flung into his works like fires from a volcano it comes to him from outside; he owes it to circumstances, to love, to rivalry, often to hatred, and still oftener to the necessity of living up to his reputation.

Wenceslas's group bore the same relation to his later works as did the *Marriage of the Virgin* to the total achievement of Raphael; it was the first expression of his talent, achieved with an inimitable grace, with the vitality of childhood, its charming abundance, that energy hidden under white and rosy skin, and those dimples that seem to echo a mother's laughter. Prince Eugène[9] is said to have paid four hundred thousand francs for this picture, worth a million in a country possessing few Raphaels, whereas the finest of the frescoes would never bring that sum, even though as works of art their value is much greater.

Hortense held her admiration in check as she thought of the sum of her young girl's savings, and put on an air of light indifference as she asked the dealer: "What is the price of that?"

"Fifteen hundred francs," replied the dealer, exchanging a glance with a young man sitting on a stool in a corner.

The young man was stunned as he looked at Baron Hulot's living masterpiece. Hortense, her attention thus attracted, recognized the artist by the flush that overspread his face, pale with suffering, and she saw his two gray eyes light up with a sparkle at her question; she looked at that face, thin and drawn like that of a monk worn with asceticism; she adored his red and well-shaped mouth, his small fine chin, and his chestnut hair with its fine Slavonic texture.

"If it was twelve hundred francs," she replied, "I would ask you to have it sent to me."

"It is antique, Mademoiselle," said the dealer, who, like all his kind, thought that in so saying he had uttered the last word on a piece of bric-à-brac.

"I beg your pardon, sir; it was made this year," she replied calmly, "and I have come particularly to ask you, if you will agree to that price, to send the artist to see us, because we may be able to find him commissions of considerable importance."

"If he gets the twelve hundred francs, what shall I get out of it? I am a dealer," said the shopkeeper good-humoredly.

"Ah, yes, of course," replied the young girl with a scornful look.

"Oh, please take it! I shall arrange things with the dealer!" exclaimed the Livonian, beside himself.

Fascinated by Hortense's sublime beauty and by her evident love of art, he added, "I am the sculptor of the group, and for ten days I have been coming three times a day to see if anyone would recognize its value and buy it. You are the first to admire my work. Take it!"

"Come an hour from now, with the dealer, sir—here is my father's card," replied Hortense.

Then, seeing the dealer go into another room to wrap the group in cloth, she added in a low voice, to the great astonishment of the artist, who thought he must be dreaming, "For the sake of your future, Monsieur Wenceslas, do not show that card or mention the name of your purchaser to Mademoiselle Fischer; she is our cousin."

The phrase "our cousin" produced an overwhelming effect on the artist, and paradise seemed to open before him for a moment at the sight of one of its fallen Eves. He had dreamed of the beautiful cousin of whom Lisbeth had spoken, just as Hortense had dreamed of her cousin's sweetheart, and, when she came in, he had thought: "Ah! If only she could be like that!"

One may imagine the look that these two lovers exchanged—a look of flame, for virtuous lovers have no trace of hypocrisy.

"Well, what the deuce are you doing in here?" the father asked his daughter.

"I have spent my twelve hundred francs of savings. Let us go."

She took her father's arm again.

"Twelve hundred francs?" he repeated.

"Actually, thirteen hundred. But you will have to lend me the difference."

"And on what, in that shop, did you manage to spend all that money?"

"Ah! you may well ask," replied the happy young girl. "If I have found a husband, it won't be dear at the price!"

"A husband, my child, in that shop?"

"Listen, Papa dear, would you forbid me to marry a great artist?"

"No, my child. A great artist nowadays is a prince without a title; it means distinction and wealth, those two greatest of all social advantages—after virtue," he added, in a rather hypocritical tone.

"Oh, of course," Hortense replied. "And what do you think about sculpture?"

"It is a very bad profession," said Hulot, shaking his head. "It needs powerful patronage, as well as great talent, for the government is the only purchaser. It is an art that leads nowhere nowadays, when there are no great families, no great private wealth, no entailed mansions or hereditary estates.[10] We have only room for small pictures, at small prices; and the consequence is that the arts are in danger of pettiness."

"But a great artist who could find a market?"

"That would solve the problem."

"And with influence?"

"Better still!"

"And titled?"

"Come, come!"

"A Count?"

"And a sculptor?"

"He has no money."

"And he is counting on Mademoiselle Hortense Hulot's?" said the Baron gaily, with a searching look into his daughter's eyes.

"This great artist, a Count and a sculptor, has just seen your daughter for the first time in his life, and for five minutes, Monsieur le Baron!" Hortense calmly replied. "Listen—yesterday, my dear, darling Papa, while you were at the Chamber, Mamma fainted. This fainting fit, which she put down to an attack of nerves, really had something to do with the trouble over my broken marriage, because she said that to get me off your hands..."

"She is too fond of you to have used any such..."

"Unparliamentary expression," Hortense went on, laughing. "No, she didn't use those exact words; but I know that a marriageable daughter who does not marry is a very heavy cross for good parents to bear. Well, she thinks that if we are to find a man of enterprise and talent, who would be satisfied with a dowry of thirty thousand francs, we should all be happy. In fact, she thought it best to prepare me for my modest future, and to stop me from indulging in wild dreams. That must mean that my marriage is called off, and that there is no dowry."

"Your mother is a very good, admirable, and wise woman," her father replied, deeply humiliated, although also somewhat relieved by this confidence.

"She told me yesterday that you would allow her to sell her diamonds in order to marry me, but I would like her to keep her diamonds, and to find a husband for myself. I think I have found the right man, the suitor who fits in with Mamma's program...."

"There!... in the Place du Carrousel!... and in a single morning?"

"Oh, Papa, there is more in this than meets the eye!" she replied archly.

"Very well, now, my little girl; just tell your old father all about it," he said in a persuasive tone, concealing his anxiety.

Chapter IX

Under promise of absolute secrecy, Hortense gave an outline of her conversations with Cousin Bette. Then, when they reached home, she showed her father the famous seal, in proof of the soundness of her conjectures. The father, in his heart of hearts, marveled at the deep subtlety of young girls when they act on instinct, and admired the simplicity of the plan that an ideal love had suggested overnight to an innocent girl.

"You shall see the masterpiece that I have just bought; they are bringing it, and dear Wenceslas is coming with the dealer. The sculptor of a group like that is bound to make a fortune. But if you can get him, by your influence, a commission for a statue, and then rooms at the Institute..."

"How you run on!" exclaimed the father. "If you had things your own way you would be married as soon as the law would let you, in eleven days!"

"What, eleven days?" she replied, laughing. "In five minutes, for I have fallen in love with him, just as you did with Mamma, at first sight! And he loves me just as if we had known one another for two years. Yes," she said, in answer to a look from her father, "I read volumes of love in his eyes, and won't you and Mamma accept him for my husband, when he has proved to you that he is a genius? Sculpture is the highest of the arts!" she cried, clapping her hands and jumping up. "Listen, I will tell you everything!"

"Is there more to tell, then?" her father asked, smiling.

Her complete, uninhibited innocence had completely reassured the Baron.

"A confession of the greatest importance," she replied. "I loved him before I saw him, but I have been madly in love since I saw him an hour ago."

"A little too madly," said the Baron, who was enchanted by the spectacle of this naïve passion.

"Don't punish me for what I have told you," she replied. "It is so lovely to be able to say to your father, 'I am in love; I am happy to be in love.' Wait until you see my Wenceslas! His brow is so full of melancholy. He has gray eyes bright with the sun of genius! And he is so distinguished! Is Livonia a beautiful country? What, my Cousin Bette marry that young man, when she is old enough to be his mother! It would be murder! How jealous I am of what she has done for him! But I rather think she will not be very pleased by my marriage."

"Listen, my angel; we must not conceal anything from your mother," said the Baron.

"I would have to show her the seal, and I promised not to give away my cousin, who is afraid of Mamma laughing at her, she says."

"You are scrupulous about the seal and yet you steal Cousin Bette's sweetheart!"

"I promised about the seal, but I made no promise about its maker!"

This adventure, patriarchal in its simplicity, fitted in remarkably well with the secret straits of the family, and the Baron, having listened to his daughter's confidences, told her that from now on she must once more leave matters to the prudence of her parents.

"You must realize, my little girl, that it is not for you to make sure that your cousin's sweetheart is a Count, and has his papers in order, and that his record is good. As to your cousin, she refused five offers when she was twenty years younger than she is now, and she will not be an obstacle, I give you my word."

"Listen, Papa dear, if you want to see me married, do not speak to my cousin about our love affair until the contract of marriage is signed. For six months I have been questioning her on the subject. Well, there is something about her that one cannot understand."

"What?" asked the father, intrigued.

"Well, her expression is not pleasant when I go too far, even in fun, on the subject of her sweetheart. Make your inquiries, but let me manage my own affairs. What I have told you ought to reassure you."

"The Lord said, 'Suffer the little children to come unto me'! You are one of those who have come back!" the Baron replied with a touch of irony.

After lunch the dealer, the artist, and the group were announced. Her daughter's sudden blush made the Baroness first anxious, then observant, and Hortense's confusion, the ardor of her look, soon solved for her the mystery so thinly disguised in that young heart.

Count Steinbock, dressed in black, looked, the Baron thought, a very distinguished young man.

"Would you undertake a statue in bronze?" he asked him, as he examined the group.

Having admired it sufficiently, he passed the bronze to his wife, who knew nothing about sculpture.

"Isn't it beautiful, Mamma?" Hortense whispered in her mother's ear.

"A statue, Monsieur le Baron, is not so difficult to make as a clock like the one that this gentleman has been kind enough to bring," the artist replied to the Baron's question.

The dealer was busy unpacking on the dining-room sideboard the wax model of the twelve Hours that the *amoretti* were trying to capture.

"Leave me that clock," said the Baron, astonished at the beauty of the work. "I would like to show it to the Minister of the Interior, and the Minister of Commerce."

"Who is this young man who interests you so much?" the Baroness asked her daughter.

"An artist rich enough to exploit this model could get a hundred thousand francs for it," said the antique dealer, putting on a knowing and mysterious air as he noticed the sympathy expressed in the eyes of the young girl and the artist. "It would be sufficient to sell twenty examples, at eight thousand francs, for each model would cost about a thousand francs to make. But by numbering the examples and destroying the model one could easily find twenty amateurs who would be only too pleased to possess replicas of the work."

"A hundred thousand francs!" exclaimed Steinbock, looking at the dealer, Hortense, the Baron, and the Baroness in turn.

"Yes, a hundred thousand francs!" the dealer repeated, "and if I were rich enough, I would buy it from you myself for twenty thousand francs; because if the model were destroyed it would become an investment. But one of the princes would certainly pay thirty or forty thousand francs for this masterpiece, to decorate his drawing room. A clock has never been made, sir, in the history of art, to please the connoisseur and the ordinary man at the same time, and this one, sir, solves the problem."

"This is for yourself," said Hortense, giving six gold pieces to the dealer, who now withdrew.

"Don't say a word to anyone about this visit," the artist said to the dealer, following him to the door. "If anyone asks where we have taken the group, mention the Duc d'Hérouville, the well-known collector, who lives in the Rue de Varennes."

The dealer nodded by way of assent.

"Your name is . . ." the Baron asked the artist when he returned.

"Count Steinbock."

"Have you papers that prove your identity?"

"Yes, Monsieur le Baron; they are in Russian and German, but not legalized."

"Do you feel you could undertake a statue nine feet high?"

"Yes, sir."

"Very well, if the persons that I am going to consult are satisfied with your work, I can obtain for you the commission for a statue of Marshal Montcornet that is to be erected at Père-Lachaise, on his monument. The Minister of War and his old officers of the Imperial Guard are giving a fairly considerable sum, so that we are in a position to choose the artist."

"Oh, that would make my fortune, sir!" said Steinbock, who was stunned by so much good luck all at once.

"Don't worry," the Baron replied graciously. "If the two Ministers, to whom I shall show your group, and this model, admire these two works, your fortune will be well on its way."

Hortense squeezed her father's arm until it hurt him.

"Bring me your papers, and say nothing of your hopes to anyone, not even to our old cousin Bette."

"Lisbeth?" exclaimed Madame Hulot, at last understanding the end, though without divining the means.

"I could give you proofs of my ability by making a bust of Madame," Wenceslas added.

Struck by Madame Hulot's beauty, the artist had just been comparing the mother and the daughter.

"Come, sir, life could go very well for you," said the Baron, altogether won over by the fine and distinguished appearance of Count Steinbock. "You will soon discover that in Paris talent is not long unrecognized and that hard work always brings its reward."

Hortense, blushing, handed the young man a pretty Algerian purse containing sixty gold pieces. The artist, still very much a gentleman, replied to Hortense's blush by a flush of shame easy enough to interpret.

"Is this, by any chance, the first money you have received for your work?" asked the Baroness.

"Yes, Madame, for a work of art, though not for my labor, for I have been a workman."

"Well, let us hope that my daughter's money will bring you good luck!" Madame Hulot replied.

"And don't hesitate to accept it," added the Baron, seeing that Wenceslas still held the purse in his hand without putting it away. "One could get back that sum from some great man, perhaps from a prince, who would certainly repay it to us with interest in order to possess such a fine work."

"Oh, I value it too much, Papa, to sell it to anyone, even a prince royal!"

"I could make Mademoiselle Hulot another group better than this."

"But it would not be this one!" she replied. And, as if ashamed of having said too much, she went out into the garden.

"Indeed, I will break up the mold and the model when I go home!" said Steinbock.

"Well now, bring me your papers, and you shall soon have word from me, sir, if you come up to my impression of you."

On hearing these words, the artist was obliged to leave. Having taken his leave of Madame Hulot and Hortense, who came in again from the garden for the express purpose of receiving that greeting, he went, and walked to the Tuileries, to go gack to his attic, where his tyrant would besiege him with questions and extract his secret from him.

Hortense's lover imagined groups and statues by the hundred; he felt in himself strength enough to hew the marble himself, like Canova, who, delicate like himself, had died in consequence. He was transfigured by Hortense, who had become, for him, his visible muse.

"Now," said the Baroness to her daughter, "what is all this about?"

"Well, Mamma dear, you have just seen Cousin Bette's sweetheart, who, I hope, is now mine. But shut your eyes, pretend to know nothing. Oh dear! I meant to hide it all from you, and here I am telling you everything!"

"Well, goodbye, my children," said the Baron, embracing his daughter and his wife. "I may perhaps go and see the Nanny, and I shall find out a number of things from her about the young man."

"Papa, be careful!" Hortense said again.

"Oh, little girl," the Baroness exclaimed when Hortense had finished the recital of her poem, whose last canto was the adventure of that morning, "my dear little girl, there is no guile in the world like simplicity!"

Real passions have an instinct all their own. Set a plate of fruit in front of a gourmet and he will unerringly select the best even without looking. In the same way, leave a well-bred young girl absolutely free to choose her own husband, and if she is in a position to have the man that she selects, she will rarely make a mistake. Virtue is infallible. The work of nature, in such cases, is called "love at first sight." In love, first sight is literally second sight.

The Baroness's satisfaction, although hidden beneath maternal dignity, was as great as her daughter's. For, of the three ways of marrying her daughter, of which Crevel had spoken, the best, as she saw it, seemed likely to succeed. In this adventure she saw the answer of Providence to her fervent prayers.

Mlle. Fischer's prisoner was obliged, all the same, to return to his rooms; he hit upon the idea of hiding his joy as a lover beneath the happiness of the artist, delighted with his first success.

"Victory! My group has been sold to the Duc d'Hérouville, who is going to get me some commissions!" he said, flinging down the twelve hundred francs in gold on the old maid's table.

He had, of course, hidden Hortense's purse; he was wearing it next his heart.

"Well," Lisbeth replied, "that's just as well, because I've been killing myself with work. You see, my child, money comes in very slowly in the profession you have chosen; this is the first you have received, and for nearly five years you have been plodding! This money is barely enough to repay me what you have cost me since I exchanged my savings for an IOU. But don't worry," she added, after counting it, "all this money shall be spent on you. There is enough here to last for a year. And by the end of a year you will be able to pay it back, and have a good sum over for yourself, if you go on like this."

Seeing the success of his ruse, Wenceslas told a long story about the Duc d'Hérouville.

"I want to buy you some proper clothes—black—and get you some new linen, because you must be well dressed to go and see your patrons," Bette continued. "And soon you will have to have larger and more comfortable rooms than your dreadful garret, and properly furnished.... How gay you are! You are altogether different," she added, scrutinizing Wenceslas.

"But they said that my group was a masterpiece."

"Well, so much the better. Produce others!" replied that dry spinster, always practical and unable to understand the joy of triumph or of artistic beauty. "Don't go on thinking about what is sold; make something else to sell. You have spent two hundred silver francs, without counting your labor and your time, on that wretched *Samson*. Your clock will cost you more than two thousand francs to carry out. Listen, if you will take my advice, you will finish those two little boys crowning the little girl with cornflowers. That will please the Parisians. I shall look in on Monsieur Graff, the tailor, on my way to Monsieur Crevel. Now go upstairs and leave me to dress."

Next day the Baron, who could think of nothing but Madame Marneffe, went to call on Cousin Bette, who was considerably surprised to see him there when she opened the door, for he had never been to visit her before. And she said to herself, "Is Hortense after my sweetheart?" For she had heard from Monsieur Crevel, the evening before, that the proposed marriage with the Councilor of the Supreme Court had fallen through.

"What, you here, Cousin? This is the first time in your life that you have come to see me, so it can't be for my beautiful eyes!"

"Beautiful! Quite true," replied the Baron. "You have the finest eyes I have ever seen."

"What have you come for? Really, I am quite ashamed to receive you in such a wretched hole."

The first of Cousin Bette's two rooms was sitting room, dining room, kitchen, and workroom all in one. The furniture was that of a comfortable artisan home: walnut chairs with straw seats, a little walnut dining table, a worktable, and some colored prints in dark stained wooden frames, little muslin curtains at the windows, a large walnut cupboard, the floor well polished and shining with care, with not a speck of dust anywhere, but utterly cold and drab, a complete Terborch[1] picture, even down to the gray tone produced by a paper once blue, but faded to straw color. As for the bedroom, no one had ever set foot inside it.

The Baron took it all in at a glance, observed the stamp of mediocrity on everything, from the cast-iron stove to the household utensils, and he shuddered as he said to himself, "And this is virtue!"

"Why have I come?" he said aloud. "You are much too clever not to guess, so I had better tell you," he continued, sitting down, drawing back the pleated muslin curtains a little way and looking across the court. "There is a very pretty woman in this house."

"Madame Marneffe! Oh! now I understand!" she said, grasping the situation. "What about Josépha?"

"Alas, Cousin, Josépha is all over.... I was dismissed like a footman!"

"And you want ...?" asked the cousin, looking at the Baron with the dignity of a prude taking offense a quarter of an hour too soon.

"As Madame Marneffe is a lady, the wife of an official, and as you can see her without compromising yourself," replied the Baron, "I would like you to make friends with her. Oh! don't be alarmed; she will have the greatest respect for the Director's cousin!"

At that moment the rustle of a dress was heard on the stairs, accompanied by the sound of footsteps, like those of a woman wearing tiny shoes. The sound stopped on the landing. After knocking twice on the door, Madame Marneffe came in.

"Forgive me, Mademoiselle Fischer, for bursting in on you like this; but I could not find you yesterday when I came to call on you; we are neighbors, and if I had known that you were the cousin of Monsieur le Directeur I would have asked you a long time ago to speak to him on my behalf. I saw Monsieur le Directeur go in, and so I took the liberty of coming, because my husband, Monsieur le Baron, has spoken to me of a report on the staff at the Ministry that is going before the Minister tomorrow."

She seemed disturbed, agitated; but actually she had only run up the stairs.

"It is not for you to ask favors, lovely lady," the Baron replied; "it is for me to beg for the favor of seeing you."

"Very well, if Mademoiselle Fischer does not mind, please do come!" said Madame Marneffe.

"Yes, do go, Cousin; I will join you presently," said Cousin Bette prudently.

The Parisienne had counted so confidently on the visit, and on the intelligence of Monsieur le Directeur, that she had not only dressed herself suitably for such an interview, but even tidied her flat. Since the morning, it had been decorated with flowers bought on credit. Marneffe had helped his wife to clean and rub up the furniture, down to the smallest objects, scrubbing, sweeping, and dusting everything. Valérie wished to appear in a setting breathing an air of freshness, in order to please Monsieur le Directeur, in order to please him enough to have the right to be cruel, to tantalize him, like a child who wants a sweet, with all the resources of modern tactics. She had summed up Hulot. Give a Parisienne at bay twenty-four hours, and she will wreck a Ministry.

A man of the Empire, used to the style of the Empire, could not be expected to know anything about the fashions of modern love, the new scruples, the new conversations invented since 1830, in which the "poor weak woman" succeeds in passing herself off as the victim of her lover's desires, a sort of Sister of Charity healing wounds, or an angel sacrificing herself. This new art of love uses a prodigious number of evangelical phrases in the devil's work. Passion is a martyrdom. One aspires toward the ideal, the infinite, both parties aim at becoming better through love. All these fine phrases are a pretext for increasing the ardor of the act, infusing more frenzy into the fall than formerly. This hypocrisy, the fashion of our time, has corrupted courtship. The lovers are two angels, who behave like two demons if occasion offers. Love had not time for all these subtleties between two campaigns, and in 1807 its successes were as rapid as those of the Empire itself. And during the Restoration the handsome Hulot, becoming a ladies' man once more, had begun by consoling certain old flames, who had at that time fallen like extinguished stars from the political firmament, and from this he had proceeded, as an old man, to allow himself to be captivated by the Jenny Cadines and Josépha s.

Madame Marneffe had placed her guns according to her knowledge of the Director's antecedents, which her husband had described to her at length, on the basis of various rumors picked up at the office. As the comedy of modern sentiment might well have the charm of novelty for the Baron, Valérie made her plan accordingly, and, to be sure, the trial of its effectiveness that she made that morning came up to her highest expectations.

Chapter X

Thanks to these high-flown sentimental and romantic maneuvers, Valérie obtained for her husband, without having promised anything, the place of deputy head clerk of his office and the Cross of the Legion of Honor. Naturally, this little campaign involved dinners at the Rocher de Cancale,[1] visits to the theater, and a number of presents in the form of mantillas, scarves, dresses, and jewelry.

The flat in the Rue du Doyenné was not satisfactory; the Baron proposed to furnish one in style in the Rue Vanneau, in a charming modern house.

Monsieur Marneffe had been granted fifteen days' leave (to be taken in a month's time, in order to go and attend to some affairs in the country) and a bonus. He promised himself a little trip to Switzerland, to study the fair sex there.

Although Baron Hulot was much taken up with the "protection" of the lady, he did not forget his other protégé. The Minister of Commerce, Count Popinot, was a patron of the arts; he gave two thousand francs for a replica of the *Samson* group, on condition that the mold should be broken, and that the only two examples in existence should be his own and Mademoiselle Hulot's. This group was admired by a prince, to whom the model of the clock was shown, and who ordered it, again on condition of its being unique; for this he offered thirty thousand francs. The artists consulted, including Stidmann, were satisfied that the author of these two groups could undertake a statue. And at once the Marshal Prince de Wissembourg, Minister of War, and president of the committee for subscriptions to the monument of Marshal Montcornet, called a meeting at which it was agreed that the commission for this work should be given to Steinbock. Count de Rastignac, at that time Under-Secretary of State, wished to buy a work from the artist whose fame was beginning to grow, amid the acclamations of his rivals. He bought from Steinbock the charming group of the two little boys crowning a little girl, and promised him a studio in the government marble depot, situated, as everyone knows, at Le Gros-Caillou.

This was success, success of the Parisian kind—that is, dazzling, the kind of success that crushes those whose shoulders and loins are not strong enough to carry it—which, by the way, often happens. The journals and the reviews were full of Count Wenceslas Steinbock, without either himself or Mademoiselle Fischer knowing anything about it. Every day, as soon as Mademoiselle Fischer had gone out to dinner, Wenceslas went to the Baroness's. There he spent an hour or two, except on the day when Bette dined with the Hulots. This state of affairs lasted for some days.

The Baron had satisfied himself as to the titles and social standing of Count Steinbock; the Baroness was delighted with his character and his manners; Hortense was proud of her approved love, and of her suitor's fame; and all of them no longer hesitated to speak of the projected marriage; in fact, the artist was at the height of happiness when an indiscretion on the part of Madame Marneffe threatened to spoil everything. It happened in this way. The Baron was anxious that Lisbeth should make friends with Madame Marneffe in order to keep watch over her household, and she had already dined with Valérie; Valérie on her side wished to have a source of information about the Hulot family, and made much of the old maid. Valérie now had the idea of inviting Mademoiselle Fischer to the housewarming of the new flat, into which she was moving. The spinster, glad to find one more house at which to dine, and greatly taken with Madame Marneffe, accepted with pleasure. Of all the people with whom she was connected, not one had ever put themselves out to such an extent on her account. In fact, Madame Marneffe, who loaded Mademoiselle Fischer with attentions, stood, so to speak, in the same relationship toward her as Cousin Bette toward the Baroness, Monsieur Rivet, Monsieur Crevel—in fact, toward all those with whom she was in the habit of dining. The Marneffes had, besides, aroused Cousin Bette's sympathy by allowing her to see their great poverty, painting it, as always, in the most favorable colors: ungrateful friends whom they had helped; illnesses; a mother, Madame Fortin, from whom they had hidden their distress, and who had died believing them still living in opulence thanks to their almost superhuman sacrifices; and so on.

"Poor souls!" she said to her cousin Hulot. "You are quite right to interest yourself in them; they really deserve it; they are so brave, so splendid! They can scarcely live on one thousand crowns,[2] the salary of a deputy head clerk, because they got into debt after the death of Marshal Montcornet! It is barbarous on the part of the government to suppose that an official with a wife and family can live, in Paris, on a salary of two thousand four hundred francs a year!"

A young woman who showed her so much friendship, who confided in her and consulted her over everything, flattered her, and appeared willing to follow her advice, became in a very short time more dear to the eccentric Cousin Bette than all her relations.

The Baron, for his part, admired in Madame Marneffe a standard of manners, education, and breeding that neither Jenny Cadine nor Josépha nor her friends had possessed, and was, within a month, burning with a senseless old man's passion for her—a passion that seemed to him perfectly reasonable. For here he found neither the vulgarity, nor the orgies, nor the wild extravagance, nor the depravity, nor the contempt for the social proprieties, nor that absolute independence that had been the cause of all his sufferings at the hands of the actress and the singer. That courtesan rapacity, like the thirst of the sands, he was likewise spared.

Madame Marneffe, who had become his friend and confidante, made the greatest difficulties over accepting the least thing from him.

"Promotions and bonuses, whatever you can obtain from the government, are all very well; but do not begin by insulting the woman whom you say you love," Valérie would say. "Otherwise I shall not believe you . . . and I would like to believe you," she would add, ogling him in the style of Saint Theresa casting her eyes up to heaven.

Every present meant a fortress to be stormed, a scruple of conscience to be overcome. The poor Baron adopted all kinds of stratagems in order to give even a trifle—expensive, however—congratulating himself on having at last encountered virtue, on having found the realization of his dreams. In this simple household (so he thought) the Baron was as much a god as in his own home. Monsieur Marneffe seemed to be a thousand miles from thinking that the Jupiter of his Ministry had any intention of descending on his wife in a shower of gold, and he treated his august chief with servile respect.

How could Madame Marneffe, twenty-three years of age, the pure and coy middle-class wife, the hidden flower of the Rue du Doyenné, know anything of the depravities and demoralization of courtesans, which now filled the Baron with disgust; he had never before enjoyed the pleasures of a resisting virtue, and the timid Valérie enabled him to enjoy them, as the song says, "all the way up the garden."

This being the state of affairs between Hector and Valérie, no one will be surprised to know that Valérie had learned from Hector the secret of the forthcoming marriage of the eminent artist Steinbock with Hortense. Between a lover with no rights and a woman who cannot easily bring herself to become his mistress, verbal and moral duels take place, in which words often betray thoughts, even when, in an assault, the fencing becomes as animated as a duel with swords. The most prudent of men will then follow the example of Monsieur de Turenne. The Baron had cited the liberty of action that his daughter's marriage would give him, in reply to a challenge that the loving Valérie had more than once thrown out, saying: "I cannot imagine how any woman could give herself to a man who did not belong to her altogether!"

Already the Baron had told her a thousand times that "for twenty-five years" there had been nothing between Madame Hulot and himself.

"They say she is so beautiful!" replied Madame Marneffe. "I must have proofs!"

"You shall have them," said the Baron, delighted at a request by which Valérie compromised herself.

"And how? You would never have to leave me," Valérie had replied.

Hector had then been forced to reveal the project he was putting into execution in the Rue Vanneau, in order to demonstrate to his Valérie that he meant to devote to her that part of life that belongs to a legitimate wife, if we suppose that day and night divide equally the lives of civilized people. He spoke of separating from his wife without any fuss, of leaving her alone once his daughter was married. The Baroness would then spend all her time with Hortense and the young Hulots; he was sure that his wife would consent to this.

"And from that time, my little angel, my real life, my real love, will be in the Rue Vanneau."

"Good gracious, how you dispose of me!" said Madame Marneffe. "And my husband?"

"That scarecrow!"

"I am afraid that, beside you, he is!" she replied, laughing.

After hearing the story Madame Marneffe very much wished to see the young Count Steinbock; perhaps she wanted to obtain some piece of jewelry from him while they lived under the same roof. This curiosity displeased the Baron so much that Valérie promised never even to look at Wenceslas. But, having been repaid for abandoning this fancy by a little old Sèvres tea service, of *pâte tendre* she kept her wish buried in her heart, written, as it were, on the agenda. So, one day when she had asked *her* cousin Bette to take coffee with her in her room, she tackled her on the subject of her sweetheart, in order to discover whether she could see him without danger.

"My dear," she said—for they called one another *my dear*—"why have you not introduced me yet to your sweetheart? Do you know that he has become famous overnight?"

"He, famous?"

"Why, everyone is talking about him."

"Oh, nonsense!" exclaimed Lisbeth.

"He is going to do my father's statue, and I could be very useful to him in his work, because Madame Montcornet cannot lend him, as I can, a miniature by Sain, a beautiful thing, done in 1809, before the Wagram campaign, that was given to my poor mother—in fact, Montcornet when he was young and handsome!"

Sain and Augustin between them had shared the honors of miniature painting under the Empire.

"He is going to make a statue, did you say, my dear?" Lisbeth asked.

"Nine feet high, commissioned by the Minister of War. Really, where have you been? Am I the first to tell you these things? But the government is going to give Count Steinbock rooms and a studio at Le Gros-Caillou, in the marble depot; perhaps your Pole will become the director, a position worth two thousand francs a year—a feather in his cap!"

"How do you come to know all this, when I know nothing about it?" said Lisbeth at last, recovering from her amazement.

"Listen, my dear little Cousin Bette," said Madame Marneffe graciously, "are you capable of a devoted friendship, proof against anything? Would you like us to be like two sisters? Will you promise me never to have any secrets from me, if I promise to have none from you, to be my spy if I am yours? Will you promise me, above all, that you will never give me away, either to my husband, or to Monsieur Hulot, and that you will never say that I told you ..."

Madame Marneffe interrupted this *picador* attack, for Cousin Bette's expression frightened her. The peasant woman's face had become terrible. Her black piercing eyes were glaring like those of a tiger. Her face looked as we imagine that of the Pythoness; she ground her teeth to stop them from chattering, and a terrible convulsion shook her. She had passed her clenched hand under her bonnet to clutch her hair and to hold up her head, that had become too heavy to sustain; she burned! The smoke of the fire that ravaged her seemed to issue through the wrinkles of her face as if they had been so many crevasses opened by a volcanic eruption. It was a sublime spectacle.

"Well, why have you stopped?" she said in a hollow voice. "I will be for you all that I was for him. Oh! I would have given my lifeblood!"

"You love him, then?"

"As if he was my own son!"

"Well," Madame Marneffe went on, breathing more easily, "if you love him in that way, you will be very happy—because you want to see him happy?"

Lisbeth replied by a rapid nod of her head, like that of a lunatic.

"In a month he is going to marry your little cousin."

"Hortense?" cried the old maid, beating her brow and jumping up.

"Oh, then you're really in love with him, this young man?" asked Madame Marneffe.

"My dear, it shall be life and death between us!" said Mademoiselle Fischer. "Yes, if you have attachments, they shall be sacred to me. Indeed, your vices shall be virtues in my eyes, because I need them; I need your vices!"

"You were living with him, then?" Valérie exclaimed.

"No, I wanted to be a mother to him!"

"In that case, I simply don't understand," replied Valérie, "because if you have not been jilted or deceived, then you ought to be very glad to see him make a good marriage, and—well, it has happened. Besides, in any case, it is all over for you. Our artist visits Madame Hulot every day, as soon as you have gone out to dinner."

"Adeline!" said Lisbeth to herself. "Oh, Adeline, you shall pay for this! I will make you uglier than I am!"

"But you are as pale as death!" cried Valérie. "Is there anything the matter? Oh, what a fool I am! The mother and daughter must have been afraid that you would raise objections to this match, as they hid it from you!" exclaimed Madame Marneffe. "But if you did not live with the young man, all this, my dear, is a greater mystery to me than my husband's heart."

"Oh, you—you don't understand," Lisbeth replied. "You don't know all her underhand dealings! It is the last blow that kills! And I have suffered from the wounds of the heart! You don't know how, ever since I can remember, I have been overshadowed by Adeline! I was dressed like a drudge and she was dressed like a lady. I dug in the garden, I cleaned the vegetables; and she, she never lifted a finger except to arrange her finery. She married a Baron, she went to shine at the Emperor's court, and I stayed in my village until eighteen hundred and nine, waiting for a suitable match, for four years;

to be sure they took me away, but only to make me a workwoman, and to offer me petty officials and captains that looked like porters! I have been given the scraps for twenty-six years! And now, like the poor man in the Old Testament who possessed one lamb that was all his happiness, the rich covet the poor man's lamb and steal it—without hesitation, without asking. Adeline has robbed me of my happiness. Adeline! Adeline! I will see you in the mud, lower than I am! Hortense, whom I loved, has deceived me! The Baron.... No, it is impossible. Listen, tell me again how much of all this is really true."

"Calm yourself, my dear."

"Valérie, my dear angel, I will be calm," replied that strange old maid, sitting down. "Only one thing can make me sane again. Give me a proof!"

"But your cousin Hortense has the *Samson* group; here is the lithograph published in a review; she bought it with her savings; and it is the Baron who is backing him, and getting all those commissions for him, in the interest of his future son-in-law."

"Water, water!" Lisbeth implored, having looked at the print, beneath which was written: *Group belonging to Mademoiselle Hulot d'Ervy.* "Water! My head is burning! I shall go mad!"

Madame Marneffe fetched some water; the old maid took off her bonnet, loosed her black hair, and dipped her head in the basin her new friend held for her; she wet her brows several times, to stop the inflammation that had begun. After this immersion, she completely regained her self-control.

"Not a word," she said to Madame Marneffe. "Not a word about this. Listen!... I am quite calm, and it is all forgotten; I have other things to think about!"

"She will be in Charenton[3] tomorrow, that is certain," Madame Marneffe thought to herself as she looked at the peasant woman.

"What is to be done?" Lisbeth went on. "Listen, my angel, they expect us to say nothing, bow our heads, and go to the grave like water flowing down a river. What am I to do? I would like to grind them all to dust—Adeline, her daughter, the Baron. . . . But what can a poor relation do against a whole rich family? It would be the story of the iron pot against the clay pot."

"Yes, you are right," Valérie replied; "one simply has to snatch whatever one can for oneself from the hayrack. That is life in Paris."

"And," said Lisbeth, "I shall die in no time if I lose that boy, whom I had counted on being a mother to, with whom I hoped to spend the rest of my life."

There were tears in her eyes, and she paused. So much feeling in this old maid of fire and brimstone made Madame Marneffe shudder.

"At least I have found you," she said, taking Valérie's hand. "That is one consolation in this terrible trouble. We must be real friends; and why should we ever leave each other? And I would not interfere with your affairs. No one will ever be in love with me. All the men who proposed to me only wanted the Baron Hulot's protection. . . . To have enough energy to take heaven by storm, and to have to spend it in earning bread and water, a few rags, and a garret! Ah, my dear, that is martyrdom! It has withered me up!"

She stopped and pierced Madame Marneffe's blue eyes with a black look that transfixed that pretty woman's soul, as if the blade of a dagger had passed through her heart.

"And what is the use of talking about it?" she exclaimed, addressing this reproach to herself. "Ah! I have never said so much about it before. But the chickens will come home to roost," she added, after a pause, using a nursery proverb. "As you say so wisely—let us sharpen our teeth, and pull as much hay out of the rack as we can!"

"You are right," said Madame Marneffe, who had been so alarmed by this scene that she no longer remembered having uttered that aphorism. "I think you are absolutely right, my dear. After all, life is not so long; one must take what one can get, and make use of the other people for one's own advantage. . . . I have discovered that for myself, even at my age. I was brought up a spoilt child, then my father made an ambitious marriage, and practically forgot about me, after having idolized me, after having brought me up like a queen's daughter! My poor mother, who had such high hopes for me, died of grief when she saw me married to a little official with a salary of twelve hundred francs, an old worn-out libertine of thirty-nine, as rotten as the hulks, who saw no more in me than they saw in you—a means of getting on! Well, in the end I have found that this contemptible man is the best kind of husband. By preferring the filthy whores at the street corners to me, he leaves me free. And if he spends all his money on himself, at least he never asks me where my money comes from."

She stopped in her turn, like a woman who finds herself being carried away by the torrent of her confidences; and struck by Lisbeth's attentiveness, she judged it prudent to make sure of her before telling her all her secrets.

"You see, my dear, what faith I have in you!" Madame Marneffe went on, to which Lisbeth replied by a gesture of supreme reassurance. Far more solemn oaths are often sworn with a look and a nod of the head than in a court of law.

Chapter XI

"I keep up appearances," Madame Marneffe went on, laying her hand on Lisbeth's as if to accept her pledge of faith. "I am a married woman, and I am so much my own mistress that when he leaves for the Ministry in the morning, if Marneffe takes it into his head to say goodbye to me and finds my door locked, he just goes away. He cares no more for his own child than I do for one of those marble children playing at the feet of the river gods in the Tuileries. If I don't come in to dinner, he is quite content to dine with the maid, who is devoted to the master; and he goes out every evening after dinner and does not come home until twelve or one. Unfortunately I have had no maid of my own for a year, which, of course, means that I have been a widow.... I have only been in love once—my only happiness... he was a rich Brazilian who went away a year ago—my only infidelity! He has gone away to sell his property and realize his whole estate, so as to be able to settle in France. What will he find left of his Valérie? A dunghill! Well, that will be his fault, not mine, for being so long in coming back! Perhaps he has been shipwrecked, too, like my virtue."

"Goodbye, my dear," Lisbeth said abruptly. "We will keep together for good. I love you, I admire you, and I am wholly yours. My cousin keeps plaguing me to go and live in your new house in the Rue Vanneau, but I did not want to, because I see very well the reason for that new piece of bounty."

"Of course, you were to keep an eye on me, that is obvious," said Madame Marneffe.

"That is certainly the motive of his generosity," Lisbeth replied. "In Paris most good turns are speculations, just as most acts of ingratitude are revenges! Poor relations are treated like rats, who are lured with scraps of fat. But now I will accept the Baron's offer, for this house has become hateful to me. Yes, indeed! We have enough brains between us to keep quiet about things that would damage us, and to say what ought to be said, so—not another word, and we are friends!"

"Through thick and thin!" exclaimed Madame Marneffe, delighted to have a chaperone, a confidante, a sort of respectable aunt. "Listen! The Baron is doing wonders in the Rue Vanneau."

"I can well believe it," Lisbeth replied. "He has spent thirty thousand francs. I really don't know where he has got the money from, because Josépha, his singer, bled him white. Oh! you are in luck's way," she added. "The Baron would steal for the woman who holds his heart between two little white hands like yours."

"Very well," went on Madame Marneffe, with that courtesan generosity that is really only carelessness, "my dear, really you must take anything from this flat that you would like for your new rooms—that chest of drawers, that wardrobe with the mirror, this carpet, the curtains."

Lisbeth's eyes dilated with pleasure, for such a present was beyond her wildest dreams. "You do more for me in a moment than my rich relations have done in thirty years!" she exclaimed. "They have never asked me whether I had any furniture! The first time he came to visit me, a few weeks ago, the Baron pulled a rich man's face at the sight of my poor room. Well, my dear, thank you. I will repay you for that, as you shall find out by and by."

Valérie saw *her* cousin Bette as far as the landing, where the two women kissed each other.

"She reeks of hard work!" the pretty woman thought to herself when she was alone. "I won't kiss *my* cousin very often! All the same, I must be careful, I must humor her, because she may be very useful to me; she will help me to make my fortune!"

Like the true Parisian Creole[1] that she was, Madame Marneffe hated trouble; she had all the indifference of a cat that will run or pounce only when forced by necessity to do so. For her, life must be all pleasure, and pleasure must come without any effort. She loved flowers, provided they were brought to her. She would only consider going to the theater if she had a good box at her disposal, and a carriage to go in. These courtesan tastes Valérie inherited from her mother, who had been loaded with attentions by Montcornet during his visits to Paris, and who had had the world at her feet for twenty years; who, being a spendthrift, had squandered all her wealth, run through it all in a life of that kind of luxury whose secret has been lost since the fall of Napoleon. For in their follies the great ones of the Empire were a match for the grandees of the Old Regime. Under the Restoration, the aristocracy still remembers having been persecuted and robbed; so that, with few exceptions, they have become economical, prudent, cautious—in fact, bourgeois and inglorious. Meanwhile, 1830 has completed the work of 1793. In France, from now on, there may be great names, but no more great houses, unless there are political changes that are difficult to foresee. Each is for himself. The wisest have all purchased life annuities. The family has been destroyed.

The sharp goad of poverty that had pricked Valérie to the quick on the day on which she had, to use Marneffe's expression, "made" Hulot, had decided that young woman to use her beauty to make her fortune. And for some time she had felt the need of having someone at hand in the relationship of her mother, a devoted friend in whom to confide things that must be concealed from a maid, and who could act and come and go and think for her—a lost soul,[2] in fact, who would consent to an unequal division of life. She had guessed, just as clearly as Lisbeth had, the Baron's reasons for wishing her to make friends with Cousin Bette. Inspired by the formidable intelligence of the Parisian Creole who spends her hours lying on a sofa, and shining the lantern of her observation into the dark corners of human souls, sentiments, and intrigues, she had lit upon the idea of making an accomplice of the spy. Probably her terrible indiscretion was premeditated; she had recognized the ardent spinster's true character, her wasted passion, and decided to attach her to herself. This conversation was like the stone that a traveler drops into a chasm to discover its depths. Madame Marneffe had been horrified to discover both an Iago and a Richard III in this old maid, apparently so harmless, so humble, and so utterly inoffensive.

In a moment, Cousin Bette had become her true self again; in a moment, her Corsican and savage nature, having broken the slender bonds that held it in check, had risen again to its full threatening stature, like the branch of a tree springing back from the hands of a child who has bent it down to steal its green fruit.

Any observer of the social world must always be astonished by the completeness, the perfection, and the rapidity with which ideas are formed in virgin natures.

Virginity, like all monstrosities, has its peculiar richness, its absorbing grandeur. A life whose energies are conserved, takes on in the persons of virgins an incalculable quality of endurance and strength; the reserved faculties of the brain are enriched in their entirety. When chaste people have occasion to exert their bodies or their minds, when they are required to act, or think, they have muscles of steel; their intelligence is reinforced by intuitive knowledge—diabolical energy, or the black magic of the will.

In this respect the Virgin Mary—regarding her for the moment only as a symbol—eclipses in her greatness all the Hindu, Greek, or Egyptian types. Virginity, mother of great things, *magna parens rerum,* holds in her fair white hands the key to higher worlds. And that great and awe-inspiring anomaly merits all the honors paid to her by the Catholic Church.

In a moment, then, Cousin Bette became a Mohican[3] whose snares cannot be eluded, whose dissimulation cannot be penetrated, whose rapid power of decision is based on an organic functioning of supreme perfection. She was made up of hate and revenge, unmitigated, as these passions are found in Italy, Spain, and the East. These two emotions, the reverse aspects of friendship and love, are only carried to their absolute extremes in countries where the sun pours down. But Lisbeth was also a daughter of Lorraine, bent on deceiving.

She did not accept this last part of her role willingly; indeed, she made a strange attempt, a result of her profound ignorance. She imagined that prison was what all children imagine it to be—solitary confinement, whereas solitary confinement is the superlative form of imprisonment, and this superlative is the prerogative of the criminal bench.

On leaving Madame Marneffe, Lisbeth rushed off to Monsieur Rivet, whom she found in his office.

"Well, my dear Monsieur Rivet," she said, having first locked the door of the office, "you were right! These Poles! They are beasts—they have neither law nor honor, any of them."

"A nation that is bent on setting Europe on fire," said the peace-loving Rivet, "ruining all trade, and all businessmen, for a country that, they say, is all swamps, full of frightful Jews, to say nothing of the Cossacks and the peasants, wild beasts that ought not to be classed as human beings at all. These Poles don't realize the times we live in. We are not barbarians nowadays. War is finished, my dear lady; it went out with the monarchy. We live in times when trade, industry, and middle-class common sense are supreme, the virtues that made Holland what she was. Yes," he went on, warming to his theme, "we have entered upon a period in which the nations must achieve everything by legitimate extension of their liberties, and by the *pacific* exertion of their constitutional institutions; that is what the Poles cannot realize, and I hope ... You were saying, my dear?" he added, interrupting himself on noticing from the manner of his forewoman that high politics were beyond her comprehension.

"Here is the dossier," Bette replied; "if I am to avoid losing my three thousand two hundred and ten francs, that scoundrel must go to prison."

"Ah! what did I tell you?" exclaimed the local oracle of Saint-Denis.

The Rivets, successors to the late Pons Brothers, had remained in the Rue des Mauvaises-Paroles, in the old Langeais mansion built by that illustrious family at a time when the nobility used to live in the neighborhood of the Louvre.

"Yes, and I have been blessing you for it on my way here!" Lisbeth replied.

"If he doesn't suspect anything, he can be locked up by four in the morning," said the magistrate, looking at his calendar to verify the time of sunrise, "but not until the day after tomorrow, because he cannot be imprisoned without being given notice of arrest, by means of a writ authorizing constraint of person. And so—"

"What a stupid law!" said Cousin Bette. "Why, the debtor can escape."

"He has every right to do so," replied the magistrate with a smile. "So, look, we can do this—"

"For that matter, I can take the paper," said Bette, interrupting the consul. "I will give it back to him, and tell him that I have been forced to raise some money and that the moneylender has insisted on this formality. I know my Pole; he will not even unfold the paper! He will light his pipe with it!"

"Ah! Not a bad idea, not at all bad, Miss Fischer! Well, don't worry; the thing can be wangled! But wait a moment! Shutting a man up is not everything; people only indulge in that legal luxury in order to get their money. By whom will you be paid?"

"By those who give him money."

"Ah! Yes, I was forgetting that the Minister of War had commissioned him to make the monument erected to one of our customers. Ah! The firm has supplied many a uniform for General Montcornet, and he soon blackened them in the smoke of cannons, that fellow! A brave man! And he paid on the nail!"

A Marshal of France may have served his Empire or his country, but from a tradesman "he paid on the nail" is still his highest praise.

"Then that is all right; you shall have your tassels on Saturday, Monsieur Rivet. By the way, I am leaving the Rue du Doyenné; I am going to live in the Rue Vanneau."

"A good thing, I hated to think of you in that hole, which in spite of my aversion to everything to do with the Opposition is a disgrace—yes! I venture to say, is a disgrace to the Louvre and the Place du Carrousel. I honor Louis-Philippe; he is my idol, he is the august representative of the class on which he has established his throne, and I shall never forget what he did for the trimming business by re-establishing the National Guard—"

"When I hear you talk like that," Lisbeth said, "I wonder why you are not a deputy."

"They are afraid of my attachment to the Royal House," replied Monsieur Rivet; "my political enemies are those of the King. Ah! a noble character, a noble family! In short," he went on, developing his argument, "he is our ideal: in morality, in economics, in everything! But the completion of the Louvre is one of the conditions on which we gave him the crown, and the civil list, to which no limit was set, has, in my opinion, left the heart of Paris in a deplorable state. It is because I am in favor of the happy medium[4] that I would like to see the middle of Paris in a very different state. Your neighborhood makes one shudder. You would have been murdered there one fine day.... Well, I see your Monsieur Crevel has been nominated major of his legion; I hope we shall be making his big epaulette for him."

"I am dining there today. I will send him to see you."

Lisbeth reckoned on having her Livonian in her power, by breaking off all his means of communication with the outer world. If he could no longer work, the artist would be forgotten like a man buried alive in a vault, where she alone could visit him. So she had two days of happiness, for she hoped to inflict a mortal blow on the Baroness and her daughter.

In order to get to Crevel's house in the Rue des Saussayes, she crossed the Carrousel bridge, went along the Quai Voltaire, the Quai d'Orsay, the Rue Belle Chasse, the Rue de l'Université, the Pont de la Concorde, and the Avenue de Marigny. This illogical route was traced by the logic of passion, always the worst enemy of the legs. Cousin Bette all the time she was on the quays, watched the right bank of the Seine, walking very slowly. Her calculation proved correct. She had left Wenceslas dressing, and she guessed that once she was out of the way the lover would go to visit the Baroness, taking the shortest way. And, in fact, just as she was sauntering along by the parapet of the Quai Voltaire, in imagination blotting out the river and walking on the opposite bank, she recognized the artist as he came out of the Tuileries on his way to the Pont Royal. There she overtook the faithless one, and was able to follow him unobserved, for lovers seldom turn around: she accompanied him as far as Madame Hulot's house, and saw him go in with the air of a familiar visitor.

At this final proof, confirming Madame Marneffe's confidences, Lisbeth was beside herself.

She arrived at the house of the newly elected major in that state of mental derangement in which murders are committed, and found old Crevel waiting for his children, Monsieur and Madame Hulot the younger, in his drawing room.

But Célestin Crevel is so naïvely and perfectly the type of the

Parisian parvenu that it would be wrong to enter the presence of César Birotteau's fortunate successor without ceremony. Célestin Crevel is a world to himself, and he deserves, even more than Rivet, the honors of the palette, for he plays an important part in this domestic drama.

Chapter XII

Have you ever noticed how, in childhood, or at the beginning of our social lives, we construct a model for ourselves, often quite unawares? A bank clerk, for instance, when he enters his manager's drawing room, dreams of possessing one just like it. If he makes his fortune twenty years later, it will not be the luxury then in fashion that he will introduce into his house, but the out-of-date luxury that fascinated him long ago. There is no end to the follies that issue from these retrospective envies, nor can we measure the effect of those secret rivalries that drive men to imitate the type that they have set themselves, and to waste their strength merely in order to be reflected moonshine. Crevel was a deputy mayor because his predecessor had been a deputy mayor; he was a major because he had coveted César Birotteau's epaulettes. Moreover, impressed by the marvels created by the architect Grindot at the time when fortune had raised his master to the top of her wheel, Crevel, as he said in his own words, "never thought twice" when it came to decorating his flat; he addressed himself with closed eyes and open purse to Grindot, an architect by that time quite forgotten. Who can say how long an extinct fame may last, with the help of such out-of-date admiration?

So Grindot had started work all over again, for the thousandth time, on his white-and-gold drawing room, paneled with crimson damask. The furniture in rosewood, carved, as common furniture is carved, without taste or skill, had won for Paris workmanship well-merited glory in the eyes of the provinces at the time of an exhibition of manufactured goods.

The sconces, the firedogs, the fenders, the chandelier, and the clock, all approximated the rococo style. The round table, a fixture in the middle of the drawing room, which displayed a marble top inlaid with every kind of Italian and antique marble, came from Rome, where mineralogical charts of this kind—like nothing so much as tailor's samples—are made; this table never failed to call forth the admiration of Crevel's bourgeois guests. The portraits of the late Madame Crevel, of Crevel himself, of his daughter and his son-in-law (the work of Pierre Grassou, the most popular painter in middle-class circles, to whom Crevel owed his absurd Byronic pose), that adorned the walls, were all done to match. The frames, which cost a thousand francs each, harmonized well with all this café splendor, which, to be sure, would have made any real artist shrug his shoulders.

Money has never yet lost the smallest opportunity of proving its own stupidity. We would by now have ten Venices in Paris if our retired businessmen had had that instinct for fine things that distinguishes the Italians. Even in our own times a Milanese lawyer left five thousand francs to the *Duomo* for the building of the colossal Virgin that crowns the cupola: Canova in his will requested his brother to build a church costing four millions, and the brother added something on his own account. Would a Parisian businessman (and they all, like Rivet, at least love their Paris) ever think of building the spires that are missing from the towers of Notre Dame? And yet, consider the sums that revert to the State from money left without heirs. The whole of Paris could be made beautiful for the price of the absurdities in stucco casts, gilded plaster, in imitation sculptures bought during the last fifteen years by individuals of Crevel's stamp.

At the end of this drawing room was a magnificent study, furnished with tables and cabinets, in imitation Boulle.[1] The bedroom, with its chintzes, opened out of the drawing room. Mahogany in all its glory infested the dining room, whose panels were adorned with views of Switzerland, richly framed. Old Crevel, who dreamed of one day visiting Switzerland, was determined to possess that country in painting until the time should come when he would go there in reality.

Crevel, deputy mayor, officer of the National Guard, and of the Legion of Honor, had, as we see, faithfully reproduced all the grandeurs, even to the furniture, of his unfortunate predecessor. Where, under the Restoration, the one had fallen, the other, altogether overlooked, had risen, not by any singular turn of fortune, but by force of circumstances. In revolutions, as in storms at sea, solid worth goes to the bottom, and the waves carry light trash to the surface. César Birotteau, a royalist and in favor at court, had been envied, and became the target of middle-class hostility, while Crevel was the typical representative of the triumphant middle class.

This flat, whose rent was a thousand crowns per annum, bursting with all the vulgarities that money can buy, occupied the first floor of an old mansion, between a court and a garden. Everything in it was preserved like beetles in a naturalist's cabinet, for Crevel lived there very little.

This sumptuous residence was the official domicile of the ambitious bourgeois. He kept a cook and a valet, paid additional maids to help them, and ordered his dinners from Chevet when he entertained his political friends, people he wanted to impress, or his family. The seat of Crevel's real existence, formerly in the Rue Notre Dame de Lorette, at Mademoiselle Héloise Brisetout's, had been transferred, as we have seen, to the Rue Chauchat. Every evening the retired merchant (all ex-shopkeepers called themselves retired merchants) spent two hours in the Rue des Saussayes attending to business, and devoted the rest of his time to Zaïre,[2] much to Zaïre's annoyance. Orosmanes (alias Crevel) had a private arrangement with Mademoiselle Héloise; she gave him five hundred francs' worth of happiness every week, and nothing "on account." Crevel paid, besides, for his dinner and all extras. This contract, even with bonuses—for he gave a fair number of presents—

seemed economical to the ex-lover of the famous singer. On this subject he would say to widowed merchants who were devoted to their daughters that it paid better to hire horses by the month than to have your own stable. Nevertheless, if we recall the confidences made by the porter of the Rue Chauchat to the Baron, Crevel did not escape either the groom or the coachman.

Crevel had, as is easily seen, turned his great devotion to his daughter to the advantage of his pleasures. The immorality of the situation was justified on the highest moral grounds. Besides this, the ex-perfumer acquired from this way of life (it was the done thing, emancipated, Regency, Pompadour, Marshal de Richelieu,[3] etc.) a veneer of superiority. Crevel saw himself as a broad-minded man, a gentleman of style, an openhanded man, not narrow in his ideas, and all for twelve or fifteen hundred francs a month. This was not the outcome of deliberate hypocrisy, but an effect of middle-class vanity, which comes to much the same thing, to be sure. At the Bourse, Crevel passed for a man with ideas in advance of his time, and above all, for a man who knew how to live. In this respect Crevel flattered himself on having gone several degrees better than César Birotteau.

"Well," exclaimed Crevel, flying into a rage at the sight of Cousin Bette, "and so it is you who are marrying Mademoiselle Hulot to this young Count you have been bringing up by hand for her?"

"One would think you were not pleased at the news?" Bette replied, directing a penetrating glance on Crevel. "What interests have you in preventing my cousin from marrying? For you were responsible, I am told, for her marriage with Monsieur Lebas's son[4] having fallen through?"

"You are a sensible woman, and can keep your mouth shut," said the good Crevel. "Very well, do you think I shall ever forgive *Monsieur* Hulot for the crime of having taken Josépha away from me?... Especially as he turned an honest girl, whom I would in the end have married in my old age, into a slut, showgirl, an Opera singer?... No, no, never!"

"Baron Hulot is very likable, all the same," said Cousin Bette.

"Likable, very likable, too likable!" replied Crevel. "I wish him no harm; but I want to have my revenge, and I will have it. I have set my heart on it."

"Is it because of that wish that you don't visit Baroness Hulot any more?"

"That may be."

"Ah! So you were paying court to my cousin?" said Lisbeth, smiling. "I thought as much!"

"And she has treated me like a dog—worse than that, like a lackey; I would almost say like a political prisoner! But I will succeed yet!" he said, clenching his fist and striking his brow with it.

"Poor man! It would be a terrible thing to find his wife unfaithful, after having been sent packing by his mistress!"

"Josépha!" exclaimed Crevel. "Josépha has thrown him over, sent him packing, turned him out!... Bravo, Josépha! Josépha, you have avenged me! I shall send you two pearls to wear in your ears, my ex-gazelle! This is the first I have heard of it, because since seeing you, the evening after the day when the fair Adeline showed me the door yet again, I have been staying with the Lebas, at Corbeil, and I have only just got back. Héloise did all she could to send me into the country, and I have only just discovered the reason for her little game. She wanted to have a housewarming, and without me, at Rue Chauchat, with artists and ham actors and writers. I was taken in! She is an unpublished Déjazet.[5] She is a character, that girl! Look at the note I had yesterday evening!"

Dear Old Thing,

I have pitched my tent in the Rue Chauchat. I took the precaution of letting some friends take the chill off first. All goes well. Come whenever you like. Hagar[6] awaits her Abraham.

"Héloise will tell me the news; she knows her Bohemia."[7]

"But my cousin has taken this unpleasantness very well," Lisbeth replied.

"It isn't possible," said Crevel, stopping as he walked up and down like the pendulum of a clock.

"Monsieur Hulot has reached a certain age," Lisbeth observed maliciously.

"I know that," Crevel went on. "But we are alike in one respect: Hulot cannot do without an attachment. He might go back to his wife," he thought to himself. "That would be a change for him, but goodbye to my revenge! You are smiling, Mademoiselle Fischer.... Ah! you know something?"

"I am laughing at your ideas," Lisbeth replied. "Yes, my cousin is still beautiful enough to inspire passions; I would be in love with her myself if I were a young man."

"Whoever has drunk must drink again!" exclaimed Crevel. "You're making fun of me. The Baron must have found some consolation."

Lisbeth inclined her head affirmatively.

"Well, he is very lucky if he has replaced Josépha overnight!" Crevel went on. "But I'm not surprised, for he told me one evening at supper that when he was young he always had three mistresses, so as never to be without one: the one he was giving up, the queen of the moment, and the one whom he was courting for the future. He must have had some little shopgirl in reserve in his fish pond! In his deer park![8] He is very Louis XV, that fellow! What it is to be a handsome man! All the same, he is not as young as he was—time is beginning to tell! He must have taken up with some little working-girl."

"Oh no!" replied Lisbeth.

"Ah!" said Crevel, "what would I not give to prevent him from being able to hang up his hat! It was impossible for me to get Josépha back from him; women of that sort never go back to their first love. Besides, a return is never the same, as the saying goes. But, Cousin Bette, I would give a lot—in fact, I would willingly spend fifty thousand francs to take that big handsome fellow's mistress away from him, just to show him that a fat old chap with a major's belly and the bald pate of a future mayor of Paris doesn't let his queen be taken without making his pawn a queen."

"In my position," Bette replied, "I have to hear everything and know nothing. You can speak freely to me, for I never repeat a word of anything that is confided to me. Why should I break that rule of my conduct? No one would trust me any more."

"I know," replied Crevel. "You are the pearl of all spinsters. But look here! Damn it, there are exceptions. After all, the family has never paid you any allowance."

"But I have my pride. I would not like to depend on anyone!" said Bette.

"Ah, if you would help me to get my revenge," went on the retired merchant, "I would make over to you investments worth ten thousand francs.[9] Tell me, pretty cousin, tell me who has replaced Josépha, and you shall have the wherewithal to pay your rent, and your breakfasts in the morning. The good quality coffee that you like so much—you might even get the best Mocha, eh? Oh, and very nice, too—pure Mocha!"

"I do not set so much store by ten thousand francs in investments, which would bring in nearly five hundred francs in income, as on absolute secrecy," said Lisbeth, "because, you know, my dear Monsieur Crevel, the Baron is very kind to me; he is going to pay my rent!"

"Yes, for how long! Consider that!" exclaimed Crevel. "Where is the Baron going to find the money?"

"Ah! That I don't know. Meanwhile, he is spending more than thirty thousand francs on the flat that he is preparing for a certain little lady."

"Already! What, is she a society woman? The scoundrel! Lucky devil! He has all the luck!"

"A married woman, and a real lady," the cousin repeated.

"Really?" exclaimed Crevel, opening eyes animated with envy, and also at that magic word "lady."

"Yes," Bette replied. "Talented, musical, twenty-three, a pretty, innocent face, a dazzling fair skin, teeth like a puppy's, eyes like stars, a fine brow ... and tiny feet. I *have never seen such tiny feet; they are no wider than her* stays."

"And her ears?" asked Crevel, much moved by this catalogue of charms.

"Finely set ears," she replied.

"Little hands?"

"I can tell you, in one word, she is a gem of a woman, and such good manners, so modest, so refined ... a lovely soul, an angel altogether; very distinguished, for her father was a Marshal of France."

"A Marshal of France!" exclaimed Crevel, giving a great bound of excitement. "Good Lord! Upon my soul! Gracious heavens! In the name of all the—! Ah! the scamp! You must excuse me, Cousin, I'm going crazy. I believe I would give a hundred thousand francs. I believe ..."

"Yes; my word, I can tell you she is an honest woman, a respectable wife. And the Baron has done things very well."

"And he hasn't got a penny, that I can tell you."

"There is a husband that he has pushed."

"Where to?" said Crevel with a little laugh.

"He is already appointed deputy head clerk, that same husband, who will presumably raise no difficulties ... and nominated for the Cross."

"The government ought to take care to respect those whom it has decorated by not giving Crosses to all and sundry," said Crevel, in the tone of one piqued on political grounds. "But what has he got to him, that old dog of a Baron?" he went on. "It seems to me that I'm as good as he is," he added, admiring himself in a mirror and taking his pose. "Héloise has often told me, under circumstances in which women never lie, that I was astonishing."

"Oh!" replied the cousin, "women love fat men—they are nearly all kind; and if I had to choose between you and the Baron, I would choose you. Monsieur Hulot is brilliant, a handsome man, and he has a fine presence, but you—you are solid; and besides, you know ... I believe you are even more of a bad lot than he is!"

"It is incredible how all women, even the most devout, love men who give that impression!" exclaimed Crevel, coming up and putting his arm round Bette's waist, he was so delighted.

"That is not the difficulty," Bette went on. "But you must see that a woman who is enjoying so many advantages will not be unfaithful to her protector for trifles, and *that* will cost more than a hundred and something thousand francs, because the little lady hopes to see her husband head clerk of a department two years from now.... It is poverty that is driving this poor little angel into the abyss!"

Crevel walked up and down his drawing room in a frenzy.

"He must be very much taken with this woman?" he asked, after a moment, during which his desire, inflamed by Lisbeth, rose to a sort of madness.

"What do you expect?" Lisbeth replied. "I don't think he has had *that* as yet," she said, snapping her thumbnail against one of her enormous white teeth, "and he has already forked out ten thousand francs' worth of presents."

"Oh! What a joke," exclaimed Crevel, "if I were to get in first!"

"Oh dear, I really ought not to have put these ideas into your head," said Lisbeth, with an air of sudden remorse.

"No. I shall make your family blush. Tomorrow I shall place in your name, in investments, a sum in five-per-cents, enough to buy you an income of six hundred francs, but you must tell me everything: the name and the address of this Dulcinea.[10] I don't mind telling you that I have never had a real lady and it has always been my highest ambition to have one for a mistress. Mahomet's houris[11] are nothing in comparison with what I imagine of society women. In fact, it is my ideal—I am mad about it; so much so, do you know, that the Baroness Hulot will never seem fifty to me," he said, unconsciously echoing one of the finest wits of the last century.[12] "Listen, my good Lisbeth, I have made up my mind to sacrifice a hundred, two hundred.... Quiet! Here are the young people; I see them coming across the court. You have told me absolutely nothing, I give you my word of honor, because I don't want you to lose the Baron's confidence—quite the contrary. The old boy must be jolly well in love with this woman."

"Oh! He is mad about her!" said the cousin. "He didn't know where to find forty thousand francs to establish his daughter, but he has raised them for this new flame."

"And do you think she loves him?" asked Crevel.

"At his age!" replied the spinster.

"Oh! What a fool I am!" exclaimed Crevel. "Putting up with Héloise's artist,[13] just as Henry IV allowed Bellegarde to Gabrielle.[14] Oh! old age, old age!... How are you, Célestine, how are you, my jewel? And your brat? Ah, there he is! Upon my word, he is beginning to look like me.... How are you, Hulot my boy, all right? We shall soon be having another wedding in the family."

Célestine and her husband made a sign toward Lisbeth, and the daughter replied coolly to her father, "Really, whose?"

"Hortense's," he replied; "although, of course, it is not quite settled yet. I have just come from Lebas, and they are mentioning Mademoiselle Popinot for our young friend the Councilor, who has set his heart on becoming the president of a provincial court.... Let us go in to dinner."

Chapter XIII

By seven o'clock Lisbeth was already on her way home on an omnibus, for she was impatient to see Wenceslas, whose dupe she had been for three weeks; she was bringing him her basket filled with fruit by Crevel himself, whose consideration for *his* cousin Bette had redoubled. She ran upstairs to the attic so fast that she was quite out of breath, and found the artist busy finishing the decorations of a box intended as a present for his beloved Hortense. The lid was bordered with hydrangeas, among which played *amoretti.*

The poor lover, in order to cover the expense of this box, which was to be carried out in malachite, had made two sconces, two fine pieces of work, for Florent and Chanor, and sold them the copyright.

"You have been working too hard lately, my dear boy," said Lisbeth, wiping his brow that was damp with sweat, and kissing it. "Such activity seems to me dangerous in August. Really, you may damage your health. Look, here are some peaches and plums from Monsieur Crevel.... Now, there is no need to worry, for I have borrowed two thousand francs, and all being well we can pay them back when you sell your clock!... All the same, I am a little doubtful about the moneylender; he has just sent this document."

She placed the writ under a sketch of Marshal Montcornet.

"Who are you making that lovely thing for?" she asked, taking the sprays of hydrangeas in red wax that Wenceslas had put down while he ate the fruit.

"For a jeweler."

"What jeweler?"

"I don't know; it was Stidmann who asked me to do the work for him, because he is very busy."

"But these are *hortensias,*" she said in a hollow voice. "Why have you never worked in wax for me? Would it have been so difficult to design a brooch or a little box, or some little thing, as a keepsake?" she said, darting a terrible look at the artist, whose eyes, fortunately, were lowered. "And you say you love me!"

"How can you doubt it... Mademoiselle?"

"Oh! That is a very cold *mademoiselle.* Why, you have been my only thought since I saw you dying in here.... When I saved you, you became mine; I have never spoken to you of that obligation, but I was pledged to it myself. I said to myself, 'As this boy has placed himself in my hands, I will make him rich and happy!' Well, I have succeeded in making your future!"

"How?" asked the poor artist, at the height of happiness, and too naïve to suspect a trap.

"I will tell you," said the peasant.

Lisbeth could not resist the agonizing pleasure of gazing at Wenceslas, who was looking up at her with a filial love, radiant also with his love for Hortense, which deceived the old maid. Seeing for the first time in her life the fires of passion in a man's eyes, she believed that she herself had kindled them.

"Monsieur Crevel will settle on us a hundred thousand francs to start a business if, he says, you will marry me; he has strange notions, that fat old fellow.... What do you think about it?" she asked.

The artist, who had turned pale as death, looked at his benefactress with dull eyes that spoke all his thoughts. He was left stunned and gasping.

"No one has ever told me so plainly," she went on, "that I was hideous."

"Mademoiselle," Steinbock replied, "my benefactress can never be ugly in my eyes; I have a very deep affection for you, but I am not thirty, and—"

"And I am forty-three!" said Bette. "Men still fall desperately in love with my cousin, the Baroness Hulot, who is forty-eight, but, of course, *she* is beautiful!"

"Fifteen years between us, Mademoiselle! How could we ever get on? For our own sakes, I think we would be wise to hesitate.... My gratitude will not fall short of your perfect kindness. And what is more, I will be able to return your money in a few days."

"My money!" she cried. "Oh! you treat me as though I were a heartless usurer!"

"Forgive me," went on Wenceslas, "but you have spoken to me about it so many times.... And you have made me, don't destroy me!"

"You want to get away from me, I can see," she said, shaking her head. "Who has given you the power of ingratitude, you who are as frail as papier mâché? Don't you trust me—me, your good angel? I who have sat up so many nights working for you? I who have given you my whole life's savings? I who for four years have shared my bread, the bread of a poor worker, with you—who have given you everything, even my courage!"

"Mademoiselle, don't say any more, don't!" he gasped, going on his knees and stretching out his hands to her. "Not another word! In three days I will explain to you—I will tell you everything; let me—" he said, kissing her hand—"let me be happy. I am in love, and loved."

"Very well, be happy, my child," she said, raising him. Then she kissed his brow and his hair with all the desperation that a condemned man must feel, living through his last morning.

"Ah! You are the noblest and best of women; you are equal to the woman I love!" cried the poor artist.

"I still love you enough to tremble for your future," she went on, gloomily. "Judas hanged himself! The ungrateful always come to a bad end! If you leave me, you will never do anything worth while again! Don't you think that, without marrying—because I know I am an old maid, and I don't want to stifle the flower of your youth, your poetry as you call it, in my arms that are like vine-stocks, I know—but, without marrying, could we not stay together? Listen, I have a head for business; I could make you a fortune in ten years of work, for Thrift is my name; but with a young wife, who would bring you nothing but expenses, you will waste everything—you will only work to make her happy. Happiness leaves nothing but memories. When I think of you I myself spend hours with my arms dangling.... So stay with me, Wenceslas.... Truly I understand everything; you shall have mistresses, pretty women like that little Madame Marneffe who wants to meet you, and she could give you the kind of happiness that you could not find with me. And then you can marry when I have saved you enough to bring you in an income of thirty thousand francs."

"You are an angel, Mademoiselle, and I shall never forget this moment," Wenceslas replied, drying his eyes.

"Now you are as I like to see you, my child," she said, gazing at him in rapture.

Vanity is so strong in all of us that Lisbeth thought she had won. She had made such a great concession, offering him Madame Marneffe! She experienced the strongest emotion of her life: for the first time joy flooded her heart. For another such moment she would have sold her soul to the devil.

"I am engaged," he replied, "and I love a woman against whom no other can prevail. But you are, and always will be, the mother whom I have lost."

These words descended like an avalanche of snow on that burning crater. Lisbeth sat down and looked despondently at his youth, his distinguished beauty, the artist's brow, the fine hair that stirred in her all her womanly instincts, and little quickly drying tears dimmed her eyes for a moment. She looked like one of those meager statues that sculptors in the Middle Ages carved on tombs.

"I don't bear you any grudge," she said, rising abruptly; "you are only a child. May God protect you!"

She went downstairs and shut herself up in her room.

"She is in love with me," Wenceslas said to himself, "poor soul! How burningly eloquent she was! She is mad!"

This last effort of her arid and matter-of-fact nature to keep with her that image of beauty and poetry had been so violent that it can only be compared to the savage energy of a shipwrecked man, trying for the last time to reach the shore.

Two days later, at half-past four in the morning, when Count Steinbock was sunk in the deepest sleep, he heard a knock at the door of his attic; he went to open it, and saw two shabbily dressed men, accompanied by a third, in the dress of a third-rate bailiff.

"You are Monsieur Wenceslas Count Steinbock?" said this latter.

"Yes."

"My name is Grasset, sir, successor to Louchard, sheriff's officer."

"Well?"

"You are under arrest, sir, you must come with us to the Clichy prison. So please get dressed. We have done this without any unpleasantness, as you see; I have not brought any police, and there is a cab downstairs."

"You are properly caught," said one of the bailiff's men. "It is up to you to come quickly!"

Steinbock dressed and went downstairs, with a bailiff's man holding each arm; when he was in the cab, the driver set off at once like a man who knows where to go; in half an hour, the wretched alien found himself well and truly under lock and key, without having made any protest, so great was his astonishment.

At ten o'clock he was summoned to the office of the prison, where he found Lisbeth, who, in tears, gave him some money so that he could live, and pay for a room large enough to work in.

"My child," she said, "don't mention your arrest to anyone. Do not write to a living soul; it would ruin your future. This disgrace must be kept hidden. I will soon get you out. I shall raise the money, never fear. Write down for me what you would like me to bring so that you can work. If I live, you shall soon be free."

"Oh, I shall owe you my life for the second time!" he cried. "I should lose more than my life if I were to lose my reputation."

Lisbeth left with joy in her heart; she hoped, by keeping her artist under lock and key, to be able to wreck his marriage with Hortense by saying that he was married, had been pardoned by the efforts of his wife, and had left for Russia. And in order to carry out this plan, she went to see the Baroness at about three o'clock, although it was not the day when she generally dined there; but she wanted to enjoy the tortures that her young cousin would go through at the time when Wenceslas generally arrived.

"You will stay to dinner, Bette?" the Baroness asked, concealing her disappointment.

"Yes, if I may ..."

"Good," replied Hortense. "I shall go and tell them to be punctual, because I know you don't like to be late."

Hortense made a sign to her mother not to worry, for she proposed to tell the footman to send Steinbock away if he came; but as the footman was out, Hortense had to give this instruction to the parlormaid, and the parlormaid went upstairs to fetch her needlework and sit in the hall.

"And my sweetheart?" said Cousin Bette to Hortense when she returned. "You don't ask me about him any more."

"To be sure, how is he?" said Hortense. "Because now he is famous. You must be pleased!" she added, whispering to her cousin. "Everybody is talking about Wenceslas Steinbock."

"Far too much," she replied aloud. "He is losing his head. If it was only a matter of bewitching him and involving him in the pleasures of Paris, I know my power; but they say that the Czar Nicholas is going to pardon him, so as to secure the services of an artist of such talent."

"Oh, nonsense!" said the Baroness.

"How do you know that?" Hortense asked, seized by a sudden spasm of the heart.

"But," replied the atrocious Bette, "a person to whom he is united by the most sacred bonds, his wife, wrote to him yesterday. He intends to go. Ah! he will be mad to leave France for Russia!"

Hortense looked imploringly at her mother, as her head dropped to one side; the Baroness had only just time to reach her daughter as she fainted, white as the lace of her fichu.

"Lisbeth, you have killed my daughter!" cried the Baroness. "You were born to bring us misfortune!"

"Why, what have I done, Adeline?" asked the peasant woman, getting up with a threatening air, which the Baroness in her distress did not notice.

"I was wrong," Adeline replied, supporting Hortense. "Ring the bell!"

At that moment the door opened, and the two women looking around together, saw Wenceslas Steinbock, whom the cook, in the parlormaid's absence, had admitted.

"Hortense!" cried the artist, bounding toward the group of three women. And he kissed his fiancée's brow under her mother's very eyes, but so respectfully that the Baroness could not object. This was a better restorative than smelling salts. Hortense opened her eyes, saw Wenceslas, and her color returned. In a few minutes she had entirely recovered.

"So this is what you have been hiding from me!" said Cousin Bette, smiling at Wenceslas and seeming to guess the truth from the confusion of her two cousins. "How did you manage to steal my sweetheart?" she asked Hortense, leading her into the garden.

Hortense naïvely told her cousin the romance of her love. Her mother and father, convinced that Bette would never marry, had, she said, allowed Count Steinbock's visits. Only Hortense, like a full-blown Agnes,[1] put down to chance the purchase of the group and the arrival of the artist, who, according to her story, had wished to find out the name of his first purchaser. Steinbock presently came out and joined the two cousins, and thanked the spinster effusively for her prompt deliverance. Lisbeth replied Jesuitically[2] to Wenceslas that, the creditor having made to her only vague promises, she had not expected to free him before the next day, and that their moneylender, ashamed of an unjust enforcement of the law, had no doubt anticipated her. The old maid, moreover, seemed delighted, and congratulated Wenceslas on his good fortune.

"Naughty boy!" she said, before Hortense and her mother. "If you had told me two evenings ago that you were in love with my cousin Hortense and that she loved you, you would have spared me many tears. I was afraid you were going to abandon your old friend, your governess, whereas, on the contrary, you are going to be my cousin; that will be a very slender bond, to be sure, but one that fully justifies the affection that I have for you."

And she kissed Wenceslas on the brow. Hortense flung herself into her cousin's arms and burst into tears.

"I owe you my happiness!" she said. "And I will never forget."

"Cousin Bette," the Baroness added, kissing Lisbeth in her delight at seeing everything turning out so well, "the Baron and I owe you a great deal, and we will repay it; come and talk things over in the garden," she said, leaving her seat.

So Lisbeth seemed to be playing the part of the good angel of the family; she was in the position of being adored by Crevel, Hulot, Wenceslas, and Hortense.

"We don't want you to work any more," said the Baroness. "If you earn forty sous a day, not counting Sundays, that comes to six hundred francs a year. Well, how much have you managed to save?"

"Four thousand five hundred francs."

"Poor cousin!" said the Baroness.

She raised her eyes to heaven, so much was she moved at the thought of all the painful privations represented by that sum, saved in the course of thirty years. Lisbeth, who misunderstood the meaning of that exclamation, read into it the mocking disdain of the successful woman, and her hatred acquired a new rancor at the very moment when her cousin had abandoned all her feelings of mistrust toward the tyrant of her childhood.

"We will add to that sum ten thousand five hundred francs," said Adeline. "We will make it over in trust, the interest to go to you and the capital to revert to Hortense; that means you will have an income of six hundred francs a year."

Lisbeth to all appearances was overjoyed. When she went in, her handkerchief to her eyes, wiping away tears of happiness, Hortense described to her all the favors that were being rained down on Wenceslas, the favorite of all the family.

So when the Baron came home he found his family all present, for the Baroness had officially addressed Count Steinbock by the name of son, and fixed the marriage, subject to her husband's approval, in a fortnight's time. And as soon as he had set foot in the drawing room the Councilor of State was set upon by his wife and his daughter, who ran up to him, one to speak to him privately, the other to hug him.

"You have gone too far in assuming my agreement in this way," said the Baron severely. "This marriage is not settled," he said, with a look at Steinbock, who turned pale.

"He knows of my arrest," the unfortunate artist said to himself.

"Come, children," added the father, leading his daughter and future son-in-law into the garden.

And he went and sat down with them on one of the moss-grown benches of the summerhouse.

"Monsieur le Comte, do you love my daughter as much as I loved her mother?" the Baron asked Wenceslas.

"More, sir," said the artist.

"Her mother was the daughter of a peasant, and had not a penny in the world."

"Give me Hortense just as she is, without a trousseau."

"That would be a nice thing!" said the Baron, smiling. "Hortense is the daughter of Baron Hulot d'Ervy, Councilor of State, a director of the Ministry of War, senior officer of the Legion of Honor, brother of Count Hulot, whose glory is immortal and who will shortly be a Marshal of France. And . . . she has a dowry!"

"It is true," said the artist, "that I must seem ambitious, but if my dear Hortense were the daughter of a laborer, I would marry her."

"That is what I wanted to know," continued the Baron. "Run away, Hortense, I want to talk to the Count; he really loves you, you see."

"Oh, Father, I knew that you were only joking!" replied the happy girl.

"My dear Steinbock," said the Baron, gracefully choosing his words, and putting on all his charm of manner when he was alone with the artist, "I settled on my son a dowry of two hundred thousand francs, of which the poor boy has not received a farthing; he will never get a penny of it. My daughter's dowry will be two hundred thousand francs, for which you will give me a receipt."

"Yes, Monsieur le Baron!"

"Not so fast!" said the Councilor of State. "Be so good as to let me speak. One cannot expect from a son-in-law the same devotion that one has the right to expect from a son. My son knew how much I could do, and would do, for his future: he will be a minister, he will easily find his two hundred thousand francs. But your case, young man, is a different matter. You will receive sixty thousand francs in five-per-cent government stock, in your wife's name. This sum will be diminished by the small allowance to be paid to Lisbeth, but she will not live long—she has a weak chest, I know. Do not mention this to anyone; it is a secret. Let the poor soul die in peace. My daughter will have a trousseau worth twenty thousand francs; her mother will add to it six thousand francs' worth of her diamonds."

"Sir, you overwhelm me!" said Steinbock, stupefied.

"As for the remaining hundred and twenty thousand francs—"

"Say no more, sir," said the artist. "I ask for nothing but my beloved Hortense!"

"Will you listen to me, you ardent young man! As for the remaining hundred and twenty thousand francs, I have not got them; but you will receive them. . . ."

"Sir!"

"You will receive them from the government, in the form of commissions that I shall obtain for you, I give you my word of honor. You shall see. You are going to be given a studio at the statuary depot. Exhibit a few good statues, and I will get you elected to the Institute. In high circles my brother commands good will, and indeed I hope to succeed in obtaining for you works in sculpture at Versailles that will bring in a quarter of the sum. And you will also receive commissions from the City of Paris and from the House of Peers. You will have so many in fact, my dear boy, that you will have to employ assistants. I will pay my debt to you in this way. You must consider whether a dowry so paid will suit you, whether you are equal to it; consult your talents."

"I believe in my power to make my own and my wife's future, singlehanded, if all else fails!" said the high-minded artist.

"That is what I like to hear!" exclaimed the Baron. "Splendid youth, doubting nothing! I would have scattered armies for a woman! Well," he said, taking the young sculptor's hand and shaking it, "you have my consent. Next Sunday the contract, and the following Sunday to the altar; it is my wife's birthday."

"It is all right," said the Baroness to her daughter, glued to the window. "Your father and your fiancé are shaking hands!"

On his return that evening Wenceslas discovered the explanation of the mystery of his deliverance; he found at the porter's lodge a large sealed envelope containing the account of his debt, with an official receipt attached to the bottom of the writ, and accompanied by the following letter:

My Dear Wenceslas,

I came to see you this morning at ten o'clock in order to introduce you to a Royal Highness who wishes to meet you. There I learned that the English had taken you off to one of their small islands called Clichy Castle.[3]

I went at once to see Léon de Lora,[4] whom I told, as a joke, that you could not leave the country you were in for want of four thousand francs, and that your future would be compromised if you failed to present yourself to your royal patron. Fortunately, Bridau[5] was there, a man of genius who has been poor himself and who knows your story. My boy, they have raised the sum between them, and I am going to pay on your behalf the Turk[6] who has committed the crime of contempt of genius by having you locked up. As I have to be at the Tuileries by twelve I shall not be able to see you breathing the air of liberty once more. I know you are a man of honor and I have answered for you to my two friends; but go and see them tomorrow.

Léon and Bridau don't want money from you; they each want you to do them a group, and they are right. That, at least, is the opinion of one who would like to be able to call himself your rival, but who is only, your sincere friend,

Stidmann.

P.S.—I told the Prince that you would not be back from a journey until tomorrow, and he said, "Very well, tomorrow."

Count Wenceslas went to bed in those purple sheets, soft as rose petals, laid out by Favor, without one crease; that celestial fairy godmother is even slower to bestir herself for men of genius than either Justice or Fortune, because Jupiter has decreed that she shall wear no bandage over her eyes, so that she is continually taken in by the displays of charlatans, attracted by their fancy dress and trumpets, and wastes, watching their parades, the time that she should spend in seeking out men of merit in the obscure corners where they are hidden.

We must next explain how Baron Hulot had managed to raise the money for Hortense's dowry, and at the same time to meet the enormous expenses of the charming flat into which Madame Marneffe was soon to move. His financial maneuver bore the mark of the talent that leads wasters and men at the mercy of passion into those quagmires in which so many disasters await them. It is a perfect example of the remarkable genius that vices inspire, to which we must attribute those *tours de force* that ambitious or voluptuous men, or for that matter all servants of the devil, sometimes manage to carry off.

Chapter XIV

On the previous day the old man Johann Fischer, unable to pay back the thirty thousand francs which he had raised for his nephew, had found that it would be necessary for him to file a petition for bankruptcy unless the Baron repaid him.

This worthy old man, with white hair, seventy years of age, had such a blind faith in Hulot, who for this Bonapartist was a beam of the Napoleonic sun, that he was walking calmly up and down with the banker's clerk in the back room of the little ground-floor property, rented for eight hundred francs a year, in which he directed his extensive corn and forage business.[1]

"Marguerite has gone to get the money close by," he told him.

The other man, in the gray and silver uniform, was so sure of the Alsatian's honesty that he was prepared to leave his bills for thirty thousand francs with him; but the old man made him stay, observing to him that it was not yet eight o'clock. A cab drove up, and the old man hurried out and held out his hand in sublime confidence to the Baron, who handed him thirty thousand-franc notes.

"Go three doors further down. I will explain later," said old Fischer. "Here you are, young man," said the old man, returning and counting out the notes to the bank's representative, whom he then saw to the door.

When the man from the bank was out of sight Fischer called back the cab in which sat his eminent nephew, Napoleon's right hand, and said as he led him into the house, "You don't want the Bank of France to know that you have advanced me the thirty thousand francs after endorsing the bills? It is bad enough as it is that they should bear the signature of a man like yourself!"

"Come to the end of your garden, Uncle Fischer," said the high official. "How's your heart?" he went on, seating himself beneath an arbor of vine and scrutinizing him as a slave-dealer might scrutinize a substitute.[2]

"Good enough to put your money on," the little dry, thin, bright-eyed old man replied gaily.

"Does the heat worry you?"

"On the contrary."

"What do you say to Africa?"

"A fine country! The French went there with the Little Corporal."[3]

"If we are all to be saved, it means your going to Africa."

"What about my business?"

"An official of the Ministry of War who is retiring and who has nothing to live on will buy your business from you."

"And what am I to do in Algeria?"

"Raise supplies of food for the Army, grain and forage; I have your commission already signed. You will be able to buy your provisions in the country at seventy per cent less than the price that you will enter on your accounts to us."[4]

"How shall I raise them?"

"By raids, and levies, and from the khalifats. There are quantities of grain and fodder in Algeria; very little is known about the country, although we have been there for eight years.[5] When this produce is in the hands of Arabs we take it from them on a number of pretexts; then when it is in our hands the Arabs try to get it back. There is a great deal of competition, but nobody knows exactly how much is stolen on both sides one way and another. There is not time, in the open field, to measure corn in hectoliters as they do in the Paris market, or fodder as they do in the Rue de l'Enfer. The Arab chiefs are like our own Spahis; they prefer hard cash, and therefore they sell the goods very cheap. The requirements of the Army, on the other hand, are constant, and we are willing to pay exorbitant prices, calculated on the difficulty of getting supplies and on the risks of transport. That is Algeria from the standpoint of an Army contractor. It is a chaos, tempered by the red tape of all new administrations. We shall have no clear notion of what is going on there for the next twelve years, we bureaucrats, but private individuals have eyes in their heads, so I am sending you there to make a fortune. I am putting you there as Napoleon used to put a poor marshal in charge of a kingdom where smuggling could be carried on secretly. I am ruined, my dear Fischer; I must have a hundred thousand francs within a year from now."

"I see no harm in getting it out of the Arabs," replied the Alsatian calmly. "It was done under the Empire."

"The man who is going to buy your business will be coming to see you this morning, and will give you ten thousand francs," Baron Hulot continued. "Is that enough for you to get to Africa?"

The old man nodded his assent.

"As for funds, you need not worry once you are out there," the Baron went on. "I will keep the rest of the price for your business. I need it."

"You are welcome to everything, even my blood," said the old man.

"Oh! don't worry," said the Baron, attributing to his uncle greater perspicacity than he in fact had; "as far as our dealings with the excise are concerned, your honesty will not be questioned. Everything depends on the central authority; and since I have made all the appointments out there myself, I have confidence in them. This, Uncle Fischer, is a dead secret; I can trust you and I have spoken to you frankly and without mincing matters."

"It shall be done," said the old man. "And for how long?"

"Two years! You will have made a hundred thousand francs on your own account, that you can retire on happily in the Vosges!"

"It shall be done just as you wish; my honor is yours," said the little old man calmly.

"That is what I like to see in men. And by the way, you will see your great-niece happily married before you leave; she is going to be a Countess."

But levies, raiding the raiders, and the price given by the officer for the Fischer business, could not immediately raise the sixty thousand francs of Hortense's dowry, including the trousseau, worth another five thousand francs, and the forty thousand francs already spent, or shortly to be spent, on Madame Marneffe. How, then, had the Baron raised the thirty thousand francs that he had just brought? As follows. A few days before Hulot had taken out life insurance policies for the sum of a hundred and fifty thousand francs, for three years, with two different insurance companies. Provided with these insurance policies, on which he had paid the premium, he had spoken as follows to Baron de Nucingen,[6] Peer of France,[7] as he sat with him in the cab in which they were both leaving a sitting of the Chamber, on his way, in fact, to dine with him.

"Baron, I need seventy thousand francs, and I am going to ask you to lend them to me. You must nominate a deputy to whom I will make over the right to draw my salary; this amounts to twenty-five thousand francs per annum, which comes to seventy-five thousand francs, in three years. You will say, 'But supposing you die.' "

The Baron nodded his assent.

"Here is an insurance policy for a hundred and fifty thousand francs, which I will hand over to you until eighty thousand francs have been paid to you," the Baron continued, drawing a paper from his pocket.

"And what if you are dismissed?" said the millionaire Baron in his inimitable German-Jewish accent,[8] with a smile.

The other Baron, non-millionaire, became thoughtful.

"But do not worry, I did not raise the objection except only to point out to you that I have some merit in giving you the money. You must be in great straits, then, for the bank has your signature?"

"I am marrying my daughter," said Baron Hulot, "and I have no money, like all those who have continued to serve the government in these thankless times, when five hundred bourgeois sitting on benches do not know how to reward servants of the state as the Emperor did."

"Well, you kept Josépha!" the Peer of France went on, "which explains everything! Between ourselves, the Duc d'Hérouville did you a great service in taking off that leech who was draining your purse. 'I, too, have known that sorrow, and withstood it,' "[9] he added, under the impression that he was quoting French verse. "Listen to good advice, my friend: shut up shop, or you will be ruined."

This dubious transaction was put into execution through the intermediary of a little moneylender called Vauvinet, one of those agents that large banking houses keep in the background, like the small fish that attend upon sharks. This apprentice jackal promised to Baron Hulot (so eager was he to obtain the favor of that eminent man) to raise thirty thousand francs for him in exchange-notes for ninety days, with the option of renewing them four times, and pledging himself not to put them into circulation.

Fischer's successor had to give forty thousand francs for his business, with the promise of the good will of the fodder trade in a department near Paris.

Such was the terrible maze in which this passion had involved a man whose honesty had hitherto been beyond reproach, one of the most able administrators in the Napoleonic government; peculation[10] to pay for usury, usury to pay for his passions and to marry off his daughter. And this elaborate science of prodigality, all these efforts, were expended in order to impress Madame Marneffe, to be a Jupiter to that middle-class Danaë.[11] A man would not have had to spend more energy, more intelligence, more enterprise, in order to make an honest fortune than the Baron displayed in running his head into a hornet's nest: he attended to the affairs of his department, he hurried up the upholsterers, he saw the workmen, he supervised even the minutest details of the Rue Vanneau establishment. Although his time was wholly taken up with Madame Marneffe, he attended the sittings of the Chamber; he managed to be everywhere at once, and neither his family nor anyone else observed his preoccupations.

Adeline, astonished to learn that her uncle was saved, on seeing a dowry included in the contract, in the midst of her happiness that Hortense's marriage was accomplished upon such honorable terms, felt a trace of anxiety, but on the eve of her daughter's marriage, which the Baron arranged should coincide with the day on which Madame Marneffe was to take possession of her flat in the Rue Vanneau, Hector brought his wife's astonishment to an end by the following ministerial announcement:

"Adeline, our daughter is now married, and our worries on that account are at an end. The moment has come for us to withdraw from the world, because now I am within three years of retirement, when I shall have qualified for my pension. Why should we continue with expenses that are no longer necessary? The rent of our house is six thousand francs a year, we have four maids, we spend thirty thousand francs per annum on housekeeping. If you want me to fulfill my engagements—for I have mortgaged my salary for three years in exchange for the sums necessary for establishing Hortense, and for paying your uncle—"

"Ah! You have done right, my dear!" she said, interrupting her husband and kissing his hands.

This confession put an end to Adeline's fears.

"I shall have a few little sacrifices to ask of you," he went on, withdrawing his hands and placing a kiss on his wife's forehead. "I have heard of a very good first-floor flat in the Rue Plumet, very handsome, with fine carved paneling, which would cost only fifteen hundred francs, where you would only need one maid for yourself, and I would make do, for myself, with a boy."

"Yes, my dear."

"By cutting down our housekeeping expenses, and at the same time preserving appearances, you would no longer need to spend more than six thousand francs a year, apart from my personal expenses, for which I will make myself responsible."

The generous wife flung her arms around her husband's neck, entirely happy.

"What a pleasure to be able to prove to you once more how much I love you!" she cried. "And what a resourceful man you are!"

"We will have our family to dinner once a week, and, as you know, I rarely dine at home; you can very well dine twice a week with Victorin, and twice with Hortense, and, as I hope to manage a complete reconciliation with Crevel, we will dine with him once a week, and these five dinners and our own will make up the week, if we allow for a few invitations outside the family."

"I will economize for you," said Adeline.

"Ah!" he exclaimed. "You are the pearl of women."

"My dear divine Hector! I shall bless you to my dying day," she replied, "for having married darling Hortense so well."

This was the beginning of the end of beautiful Baroness Hulot's home, and of her abandonment, solemnly promised to Madame Marneffe.

Crevel, fat and self-important, who was, as a matter of course, invited to be present at the signing of the marriage contract, behaved as if the scene with which this narrative opened had never taken place, as if he bore no grudge against Baron Hulot. Célestin Crevel was amiable; he was, as usual, a little too much the ex-perfumer, but he had begun to aspire to a majestic bearing since he had become a major. He talked of dancing at the wedding.

"Fair lady," he said graciously to Baroness Hulot, "people like ourselves know how to forget. Do not banish me from your home, and deign to adorn my house sometimes by visiting it with your children. Don't worry, I will never say a word of that which lies at the bottom of my heart. I don't know what possessed me, because I should lose too much if I were never to see you again."

"Sir, an honest woman has no ears for speeches like those you refer to, and if you keep your promise you may be sure that no one will be more glad than myself to see the end of the coolness—these things are always painful in families."

"Well, you great sulky brute," said Baron Hulot, leading Crevel into the garden by force, "you are always avoiding me, even in my own house. Why should two old admirers of the fair sex quarrel over a skirt? Really, you know, it's too vulgar altogether!"

"Sir, I am not a handsome man like you, and my few attractions make it impossible for me to make good my losses as easily as you can."

"You are being sarcastic," said the Baron.

"That is permissible on the part of the vanquished toward the victor."

The conversation begun on this note ended in a complete reconciliation; all the same, Crevel reserved his right to have his revenge.

Madame Marneffe was eager to be invited to Mademoiselle Hulot's wedding. In order to see his future mistress in his own drawing room, the Councilor of State was obliged to ask all the staff of his department, down to and including the grade of deputy head clerk, therefore a large ball became necessary. The Baroness, with an eye to economizing, calculated that an evening party would cost less than a dinner, and would make it possible to invite more people. Hortense's marriage, therefore, created quite a stir. Marshal Prince Wissembourg and the Baron de Nucingen were the witnesses on behalf of the bride, and the Counts de Rastignac and Popinot for Steinbock. Besides this, since Count Steinbock had risen to fame, members of the highest circles of the Polish colony had taken him up, and the artist felt bound to invite them. The State Council, as well as the Baron's own department, and the Army, out of compliment to Count de Forzheim, were all represented at their highest levels. It was estimated that there would be two hundred indispensable invitations. What was more natural, then, that little Madame Marneffe should be all eagerness to appear in her glory in the midst of such an assembly?

It was now a month since the Baroness had devoted the price of her diamonds to furnishing her daughter's house; she had, however, kept the best for her trousseau. This sale brought in fifteen thousand francs, five thousand of which went toward the cost of Hortense's trousseau. And what were ten thousand francs toward furnishing the young couple's flat, if we consider the requirements of modern luxury? But young Monsieur and Madame Hulot, old Crevel, and the Count de Forzheim gave handsome presents, for the old uncle had kept a sum in reserve for the purchase of silver plate. Thanks to these various contributions, the most exacting woman in Paris would have been satisfied with the way in which the young couple were set up in the flat they had chosen in the Rue Saint-Dominique, near the Invalides. Everything in it seemed in harmony with their love, so pure, so open, and so sincere on both sides.

At last the great day came, for it was to be a great day for the father as well as for Hortense and Wenceslas, for Madame Marneffe had decided to give a housewarming at her home the day after the one on which she was to become the Baron's mistress, that of the marriage of the two lovers.

Who has not, once in his life, been a guest at a wedding ball? I refer every reader to his own memories; each of us will smile, to be sure, as we evoke again all those people in their Sunday best and faces to match. If any social event proves the influence of surroundings surely it is a wedding reception. The festive mood of some reacts so powerfully on the rest that even those most accustomed to wearing dress clothes soon look as if they belonged to the number of those for whom a wedding is a great event in their lives. And think of those serious ones, old men to whom all events are so equally indifferent that they have kept to their everyday black suits; the older married men whose faces bear the marks of the bitter experiences of the life that the young are only beginning; the gay sparks like carbon-dioxide bubbles in Champagne; and the young girls full of envy, the women taken up with the thought of their clothes, and poor relations whose skimped finery contrasts with the men in full dress; think of the gourmands who are interested only in the refreshments and the gamblers with no thought except for the games ... there they all are, rich and poor, envious and envied, the cynics and the dreamers, all arranged like flowers in a basket about that rarest blossom, the bride. A wedding reception is a world in miniature.

When the excitement was at its height Crevel took the Baron's arm and whispered to him in the most natural manner possible, "By Jove, what a pretty woman, over there in pink, making eyes at you!"

"Which one?"

"The wife of that deputy head clerk you're promoting, heaven knows why! Madame Marneffe."

"How do you know that?"

"Listen, Hulot, I will try to forgive all the injuries you have done me if you will introduce me to her, and in return I will ask you to meet Héloise. Everybody is asking who that charming creature can be. Are you sure that no one in your department will tumble to the way in which her husband's nomination was signed? You lucky devil, she is worth more than a department. I would gladly work in her office.... Come on, Cinna,[12] let us be friends."

"Never better," said the Baron to the perfumer, "and I promise to behave myself. Within a month I will ask you to dine with that little angel ... for she is an angel, old boy. Take my advice and follow my example—give up the devils."

Cousin Bette, who had moved to the Rue Vanneau, to a pretty little flat on the third floor, left the ball at ten o'clock to go home and look at her bonds representing an income of twelve hundred francs; one of them was in the name of Count Steinbock, the other of the young Madame Hulot. This will explain how Monsieur Crevel came to speak of Madame Marneffe to his friend Hulot, and to know of a matter of which the rest of the world was ignorant; for in Monsieur Marneffe's absence only cousin Bette, the Baron, and Valérie were in the secret.

The Baron had made the mistake of giving Madame Marneffe a dress obviously much too expensive for the wife of a deputy head clerk; other wives were jealous, both of Valérie's dress and of her beauty; there were whisperings behind fans, because the fact that the Marneffes were hard up was common knowledge in the department; the clerk had been asking for more money at the very time when the Baron had fallen for his wife. And besides, Hector was unable to conceal his delight at the spectacle of Valérie's success, as, decorous, ladylike, and envied, she underwent that attentive scrutiny that so many women dread when they enter a new environment for the first time.

Having seen his wife, his daughter, and his son-in-law into a carriage, the Baron looked for an opportunity to slip away unnoticed, leaving his son-in-law and daughter to play the host and hostess. He got into Madame Marneffe's carriage to see her home; but he found her silent and thoughtful, almost melancholy.

"My happiness makes you very sad, Valérie," he said, drawing her toward him in the darkness of the cab.

"Why, my dear, must not a poor woman always be a little sad when she first falls from virtue, even when her husband's ill-treatment entitles her to her freedom? Do you imagine that I have no soul, no faith, no religion? Your exultation this evening was most indiscreet, and you have drawn attention to me in the most odious way. Really, a schoolboy would have had more idea of how to behave. And all those women have been picking me to pieces with the aid of looks and sarcastic remarks! What woman does not value her reputation? You have ruined me! Oh! I am yours now! and I have no longer any means of justifying my fault except by being faithful to you.... Monster!" she said, laughing, and letting him kiss her. "You knew very well what you were doing! Madame Coquet, the wife of our chief clerk, came and sat beside me to admire my lace. 'It is English,' she said. 'Was it very expensive?' 'I don't know,' I said to her. 'It was my mother's; I can't afford to buy things like that.' "

Madame Marneffe had succeeded, in fact, in so fascinating the old Empire beau that he thought that he was persuading her to be unfaithful for the first time, and that he had inspired her with a passion strong enough to make her forget her duties. She told him that the odious Marneffe had neglected her from the vilest of motives. Ever since, she had gladly lived the life of the most virtuous young girl, for marriage seemed to her so horrible. This was the reason for her present sadness.

"What if love should be like marriage?" she said tearfully.

These lying coquetries, that nearly all women in Valérie's situation can produce wholesale, filled the Baron with visions of the roses of the seventh heaven. So Valérie played up to the Baron, while the lovesick artist and Hortense waited, a little impatiently perhaps, until the Baroness had bestowed her last blessing and her last kiss on the young girl.

At seven in the morning the Baron, at the height of happiness—for he had found in his Valérie all the innocence of a young girl, combined with the most consummate deviltry—returned to relieve young Monsieur and Madame Hulot of their fatigue duty. Those merrymakers, most of them strangers to the house, who end by taking possession of the place at all weddings, were still dancing their interminable figure dances called cotillions, and the bouillotte players were still clustering round the tables, where old Crevel had won six thousand francs.

The papers distributed by the news vendors next morning contained the following short item in the Paris gossip column:

> The marriage was celebrated this morning at the Church of St. Thomas d'Aquin, of Count Steinbock and Mademoiselle Hortense Hulot, daughter of Baron Hulot d'Ervy, Councilor of State and a Director of the Ministry of War, niece of the famous Count de Forzheim. This ceremony drew a large gathering. Amongst those present were several of our artistic celebrities: Léon de Lora, Joseph Bridau, Stidmann, Bixiou; eminent officials of the Ministry of War, the Council of State, and several members of both Chambers; besides distinguished members of the Polish colony, Counts Paz, Laginski, etc.

Count Wenceslas Steinbock is a grand-nephew of the famous general who served under Charles XII, King of Sweden. The young Count, after taking part in the Polish rising, found refuge in France, where his well-merited fame as a sculptor has gained for him his papers of naturalization.

So, in spite of the desperate financial straits of Baron Hulot d'Ervy, nothing was wanting that public opinion demands, not even the publicity given by the newspapers to his daughter's marriage, whose celebration was in every particular the same as that of his son and Mademoiselle Crevel. This occasion went some way toward stifling the current rumors about the Director's financial situation, and at the same time the dowry given to his daughter explained the necessity he was in of having to borrow money.

Here, then, ends the introduction to this story. This account is, to the drama that follows it, what premises are to a proposition, and what the prologue is to a classical tragedy.

Chapter XV

In Paris, when a woman decides to make a trade and profession of her beauty, it does not necessarily follow that she will make her fortune. One meets in that city lovely creatures, full of wit, living in dreadful shabbiness, and ending in squalor lives begun in pleasure. The reason is this. It is not enough to adopt the shameful career of the courtesan, hoping to profit by its advantages, while retaining the externals of a respectable middle-class wife. Vice does not come by its triumphs so easily; it is like genius in this respect, that both require a whole concourse of favorable circumstances to bring into play the happy combination of fortune and talent.

Eliminate the strange prelude of the Revolution, and the Emperor could no longer have existed; he would have been nothing more than a second Fabert.[1] Venal beauty without amateurs,[2] without celebrity, without the cross of dishonor that is won by squandering fortunes, is a Correggio in an attic, genius dying in a garret. In Paris a Laïs,[3] then, must first of all find a rich man to fall for her charms sufficiently to pay their price. Above all, she must keep up a high standard of elegance—for this is her trade-mark—have sufficiently good manners to flatter men's self-respect, and possess that Sophie Arnould[4] wit that stimulates the apathy of rich men; and finally she must arouse the desires of libertines by seeming to be faithful to one only, whose good fortune is envied by the rest.

These conditions, which women of that class call *luck,* are quite difficult to realize in Paris, for all that it is a city of millionaires and idlers, the bored and the sophisticated. Providence, it seems, has set a strong defense about the homes of clerks and the lower-middle classes in general, for whom such difficulties are at least doubled by the society in which they move. All the same, there are enough Madame Marneffes in Paris for Valérie to represent a type in this history of manners. Among these women, some follow, at the same time, real passion and financial necessity, like Madame Colleville,[5] who was for so long attached to one of the most distinguished orators of the Left, Keller the banker; others are inspired by vanity, like Madame de la Baudraye, who remained almost respectable in spite of her elopement with Lousteau; some are drawn in by their desire for fine clothes, others by the impossibility of making ends meet in a household run on obviously too little money. The meanness of the State, or Parliament, if you like, is at the root of many misfortunes, and engenders many kinds of corruption. It is at present the fashion to express much sympathy with the lot of the working classes, who are presented as being exploited by the capitalist manufacturers; but the State is a hundred times harder than the most grasping industrialist—it carries its economy in the matter of salaries to the point of absurdity. If you work hard, industry will pay you in proportion to your effort; but what does the State do for all its obscure and conscientious workers?

To stray from the paths of virtue is, for a married woman, an inexcusable fault, but there are degrees even here. Some women, far from becoming depraved, hide their faults and remain respectable women, like the two whose stories have just been mentioned, while others add to their other faults the shame of becoming gamblers. Madame Marneffe is, as it were, the type of ambitious married courtesan who from the first accepts depravity in all its implications, and who sets out to make her fortune by amusing herself, with no scruples as to the means; nearly all of these have, like Madame Marneffe, husbands who are their confederates and accomplices. These Machiavellis in petticoats are the most dangerous; and of all the kinds of evil women in Paris they are the worst. Real courtesans like Josépha, Madame Schontz and Malaga, Jenny Cadine and the rest, by the very openness of the situation, carry a warning as unmistakable as the red lamp of prostitution, or the flares of gambling dens. A man knows, therefore, that he goes that way at his peril. But the sugary respectability, the appearances of virtue, and the hypocritical bearing of a married woman who never lets anything be seen except the vulgar necessities of housekeeping, and who appears to refuse all excesses, involve men in unspectacular ruin, all the more remarkable in that the victims can find excuses, without, however, being able to account for it. It is the ignoble bills of household accounts, not gay dissipation, that eat up fortunes. The father of a family goes ingloriously to his ruin, and without the major consolation of gratified vanity.

This little lecture will go home to the hearts of many a family. Madame Marneffes are to be found on all levels of society, even at Court; for Valérie is a sad reality, painted from the life down to the smallest detail. Unfortunately, this portrait will cure no one of the folly of falling for those sweetly smiling angels with pensive looks, innocent faces, and cash-boxes for hearts.

About three years after Hortense's marriage, in 1841, everybody said that Baron Hulot d'Ervy had settled down, "put up his horses," as the first surgeon of Louis XV[6] put it, when, in fact, Madame Marneffe was costing him twice as much as he had spent on

Josépha. But Valérie, although always very nicely dressed, affected the simplicity of the wife of a subordinate official; she confined her luxury to her dressing gowns and house frocks. In this way she sacrificed her Parisian vanity to her dear Hector. Nevertheless, when she went to the theater she always appeared in a charming hat, wearing a dress in the latest fashion; the Baron fetched her in a carriage, to an expensive box.

The flat, which occupied the whole of the second floor of a modern building in the Rue Vanneau, between a forecourt and a garden, exuded respectability. Its luxury consisted in good-quality chintz curtains and in good, solid furniture. The bedroom was the exception, and offered the rich profusion of the Jenny Cadines and the Madame Schontzes. There were lace curtains, cashmere hangings, brocade portieres, a chimney-piece whose ornaments were designed by Stidmann, and a little cabinet crammed with knicknacks. Hulot would not consent to see his Valérie in any setting inferior in magnificence to Josépha's dunghill of iniquity in gold and pearls. As to the two principal rooms, the drawing room had been furnished in red damask and the dining room in carved oak. And, wishing to have everything to match, the Baron, at the end of six months, had added solid luxury to ephemeral, by giving her such valuable household property as, for example, a set of silver plate costing over twenty-four thousand francs.

Within two years Madame Marneffe's house had acquired the reputation of being a very pleasant one. There was gambling. Valérie herself was soon known as a pleasant and amusing woman. A rumor was spread, in order to explain her changed circumstances, of an enormous legacy from her natural father, Marshal Montcornet, left in trust. With forethought, Valérie had added religion to social hypocrisy. She was punctilious in her Sunday observance, and enjoyed all the honors due to piety. She collected for the Church, belonged to a women's charitable association, contributed consecrated bread, and did a certain amount of good among the poor of the neighborhood, and all at Hector's expense. So that everything in her household had the mark of respectability, and many people affirmed that her relations with the Baron were perfectly pure, pointing out the age of the Councilor of State, and attributing to him a platonic liking for Madame Marneffe's pleasant wit, charming manners, lively conversation, rather like the late Louis XVIII's partiality for a well-phrased letter.

The Baron always left at midnight with everybody else—and returned a quarter of an hour later. The secret of this profound secret was as follows.

The porters of the house were Monsieur and Madame Olivier, who, through the Baron's influence, as a friend of the landlord, who was looking for a caretaker, had risen from their obscure and ill-paid post in the Rue du Doyenné to the lucrative and splendid one in the Rue Vanneau. Now, Madame Olivier, one-time serving-maid in the household of Charles X, who had fallen from that situation, together with the Royal House,[7] had three children. The eldest, who was already a junior lawyer's clerk, was the apple of his parents' eyes. This Benjamin,[8] under the shadow of six years' conscription for military service, saw his brilliant career in danger of interruption, when Madame Marneffe managed to get him exempted on account of one of those slight physical defects which the examining boards can always find when they are privately requested to do so by some power in the Ministry. Olivier, once a King's huntsman, and his wife would, therefore, have crucified Jesus over again for Baron Hulot and for Madame Marneffe.

What could people possibly find to say who did not even know of the earlier episode of the Brazilian, Monsieur Montès de Montejanos? Nothing. People, besides, are very tolerant toward the mistress of a house where they are well entertained. Finally, Madame Marneffe added to her other advantages the highly prized virtue of being a hidden power. For this reason Claude Vignon,[9] who had become Marshal Prince de Wissembourg's secretary, and who dreamed of becoming a Councilor of State in the post of Master of Appeals, frequented her drawing room, to which came also several deputies who were gamblers and sociably inclined. Madame Marneffe's circle was built up with deliberate care; a circle was formed consisting exclusively of men of similar tastes and outlook, all interested in maintaining and proclaiming the infinite merits of the mistress of the house. The real Holy Alliance in Paris, they say, is that of complicity in vice. Interests always fall apart in the end, but there is always an understanding among the wicked.

Within three months of moving into the Rue Vanneau flat Madame Marneffe was entertaining Monsieur Crevel, who had just been made mayor of his borough[10] and an officer of the Legion of Honor. Crevel had hesitated for a long time; it had meant giving up the well-known uniform of the National Guard, in which he strutted at the Tuileries, thinking himself as much a soldier as the Emperor himself; but ambition, urged on by Madame Marneffe, proved stronger than vanity. The Mayor had decided that his liaison with Mademoiselle Héloise Brisetout was quite incompatible with his political status. Long before his accession to the bourgeois throne of the mayor his gallantries had been wrapped in the deepest mystery. But Crevel, as the reader may have guessed, had purchased the right of taking, as often as possible, his revenge for the loss of Josépha at the price of a settlement yielding an interest of six thousand francs in the name of Valérie Fortin—for the wife of the good Marneffe owned her property independently. Valérie, inheriting perhaps from her mother the particular talent of the kept woman, had read the character of that grotesque admirer at a glance; the phrase "I have never had a lady," spoken by Crevel to Lisbeth, and repeated by Lisbeth to her dear Valérie, had counted for a great deal in the transaction to which she owed her six thousand francs of interest in five-per-cents. From that time she had never allowed her prestige to diminish in the eyes of César Birotteau's one-time traveling salesman.

Crevel had married the daughter of a miller of Brie, the only child, what is more, whose inheritance had brought him three-quarters of his fortune; for as a rule, when shopkeepers grow rich it is not so much from their business as by a combination of trade and rural economy. Any number of farmers, millers, graziers, and market gardeners round Paris covet for their daughters the glories of the counter, and regard a retailer, a jeweler, a moneylender, as a much more desirable son-in-law than a solicitor or an attorney, whose social status makes them uneasy; they are afraid of later being despised by these exalted members of the middle class. Madame Crevel, rather plain, very vulgar and stupid, had died early, having given her husband no other pleasures but those of paternity; therefore, in the early days of his business career, this libertine, restricted by the duties of his position, and held in check by poverty, had suffered the torments of Tantalus. In touch with—to use his own expression—the most elegant women in Paris he ushered them to the door with the servility of a shopkeeper, at the same time admiring their grace, their way of wearing their clothes—all the indefinable marks of what we call good breeding. To aspire to one of these fairies of the drawing room had been the dream of his youth, since hidden in the depths of his heart. To win the favors of Madame Marneffe was, therefore, not only the realization of his chimera, but also a matter of pride, vanity, and self-respect, as we have seen. His ambition increased with success; his head was completely turned, and when the mind is captivated, the heart responds, and every pleasure is increased tenfold. Besides this, Madame Marneffe offered him refinements of pleasure that he had never before experienced, for neither Josépha nor Héloise had loved him; whereas Madame Marneffe thought fit to deceive completely a man in whom she saw an inexhaustible source of money. The deceptions of feigned love are more bewitching than the reality itself. True love involves lovers' quarrels that cut to the quick, but a quarrel in fun, on the contrary, flatters the vanity. The rare opportunities accorded to Crevel kept his passion at white heat. He was forever pitting himself against Valérie's virtuous severity, her feigned remorse; she would ask what her father must be thinking of her in the Heaven of the brave. He had to overcome a kind of coldness, over which the clever leading lady, in seeming to yield before the shopkeeper's consuming passion, allowed him to think he triumphed; but she would always resume, as if ashamed, her bearing of a respectable woman, and her airs of virtue, like any Englishwoman; and always crushed her Crevel with the weight of her dignity, for Crevel had, from the very first, swallowed her claim to be virtuous. Valérie had, in fact, special lines of tenderness that made her no less indispensable to Crevel than she was to the Baron. In public she presented an enchanting combination of modest and pensive innocence, an irreproachable propriety, wit enhanced by charm, grace, and Creole indolence; but in private she outdid any courtesan; then she was daring, amusing, and fertile in her inventiveness. A contrast of this kind is a source of delight to a man of Crevel's stamp; he flatters himself that he is the unique author of this comedy, and thinking that it is played exclusively for his benefit, laughs at the exquisite hypocrisy of it while he admires the woman who acts the part.

Valérie had taken complete possession of Baron Hulot, and had induced him to grow old by one of those subtle forms of flattery that so well illustrate the diabolical talent of such women. Even with the best of constitutions, a moment comes when, like a besieged fort that for a long time has kept up a gallant defense, the true state of affairs will out. Foreseeing the approaching collapse of the old beau of the Empire, Valérie made up her mind to hasten it.

"Why do you take so much trouble, my old veteran?" she said to him six months after their clandestine and doubly adulterous marriage. "Have you still pretensions? Do you want to be unfaithful to me? I should like you so much better if you stopped using make-up. Surely you don't imagine that I love you for a halfpennyworth of polish on your boots, your rubber stays, your tight waistcoat, and your dyed hair? Besides, the older you look the less I shall be afraid that my Hulot will be carried off by a rival!"

Trusting, therefore, in the heavenly friendship no less than in the love of Madame Marneffe, with whom, moreover, he intended to end his days, the Councilor of State followed this private hint and gave up dyeing his hair and whiskers. After receiving this touching declaration from Valérie, the splendid, handsome Hector appeared one fine morning gray-haired. Madame Marneffe easily convinced her dear Hector that she had noticed the white line made by the growth of his hair a hundred times.

"White hair suits your face beautifully," she said when she saw him; "it softens it, you look so much nicer, absolutely charming."

And the Baron, having once started on this course, abandoned his leather waistcoat and his stays; he left off all his bracings; his stomach fell, and he became noticeably portly. The oak became a tower, and the heaviness of his movements was all the more alarming because the Baron had aged enormously in the role of Louis XII.[11] His eyebrows were still black, and vaguely recalled the handsome Hulot, as in some feudal wall a faint detail of sculpture remains to suggest what the château must have been in its great days. This discordant detail made his expression, still youthful and lively, all the more strange in his tanned face; for where the ruddy coloring of a Rubens had so long flourished a certain reddening and the deep tension of the wrinkles betrayed the struggles of passion in rebellion against the course of nature. Hulot was at this time one of those splendid human ruins in which virility asserts itself in tufts of hair in the ears and nose and on the hands, like that moss that grows on the all but eternal monuments of the Roman Empire.

How had Valérie managed to keep Crevel and Hulot side by side in her house, while the vindictive Mayor was all for open triumph over Hulot? Leaving this question unanswered for the moment, to be unfolded in the course of the story, we will merely observe that Lisbeth and Valérie had between them constructed an enormous piece of machinery whose operation was tending toward this result. Marneffe, seeing his wife improved by the setting in which she was now enthroned, like the sun at the center of a solar system, seemed also, in the eyes of the world, to have been kindled once more by her fires, and to be quite mad about her. But if this jealousy on the part of the good Marneffe made him something of a spoilsport, it also added enormously to the value of Valérie's favors. Marneffe nevertheless evinced a confidence in his director that degenerated into an absurd complaisance. But he would not stand Crevel at any price.

Marneffe, wrecked by debaucheries peculiar to great cities, described by the Roman poets, but for which our modern decency has no name, had become as hideous as an anatomical specimen in wax. But this walking disease, dressed in a good suit, balanced its spindle shanks in elegant trousers. That shrunken chest was perfumed in fine linen, and musk disguised the fetid odors of human corruption. This hideous example of expiring vice, shod in red-heeled shoes (for Valérie had dressed Marneffe in a style suitable to his part, his position, and his cross),[12] put the fear of God into Crevel, who could not bear to meet the white eyes of the deputy head clerk. Marneffe was the Mayor's nightmare. And this evil rascal, aware of the singular power which Lisbeth and his wife had conferred upon him, took pleasure in the situation; he played on it as on an instrument, and, as cards in the drawing room were the last resource of a mind as worn out as his body, he fleeced Crevel, who felt himself obliged to "go easy" with the respectable official whom *he* was deceiving.

Seeing Crevel such a child at the mercy of that hideous and vile mummy, whose particular brand of corruption was a closed book to the Mayor, and seeing him, above all, such an object of contempt to Valérie, who laughed at Crevel as at a buffoon, the Baron apparently thought himself so secure from any rivalry from that quarter that he constantly invited him to dinner.

Valérie, protected by these two vigilant passions keeping guard over her, and by a jealous husband, drew all eyes, excited all desires, in the circle in which she shone. Thus, while keeping up appearances, she had succeeded, in about three years, in realizing the difficult conditions of that success that courtesans desire but so seldom attain by means of the scandal, the audacity, and the dazzling glitter of publicity. Like a well-cut diamond exquisitely set by Chanor, Valérie's beauty, once hidden in the mud of the Rue du Doyenné, was now worth more than its real value; she could break hearts! Claude Vignon loved Valérie in secret.

This retrospective account, necessary when we meet people again after a three years' interval, shows Valérie's balance sheet. And now let us turn to that of her partner, Lisbeth.

Chapter XVI

Cousin Bette played, in the Marneffe household, the part of a relation who has assumed the functions of companion and housekeeper; but she suffered none of those humiliations which most women unlucky enough to be forced to accept these ambiguous situations have to put up with. Lisbeth and Valérie offered the touching spectacle of one of those friendships between women, so warm and yet so improbable, in which Parisians, who are always too clever by half, see occasion for scandal. The contrast between Bette's dry masculine nature and Valérie's easy indolence lent weight to the calumny. Madame Marneffe had, moreover, given encouragement to this scandal by the trouble she took on her friend's behalf with an eye to a certain marriage which was, as we shall see, to complete Lisbeth's vengeance. An immense change had taken place in Cousin Bette. Valérie, who had decided to take her clothes in hand, had turned this change to the best possible advantage. This strange woman had taken to corsets and tight lacing, used bandoline lotion for her smooth hair, and consented to wear her dresses as they came from the dressmaker; she wore neat little boots and gray silk stockings, which were put down on Valérie's accounts, to be settled by the one entitled to do so.

Thus smartened up, but still wearing the yellow cashmere shawl, no one would have recognized the Bette of three years ago. This other diamond, black, the rarest diamond of all, trimmed by a skilled hand and mounted in a setting that became her, was fully appreciated by certain ambitious clerks. Anyone seeing Bette for the first time might have shuddered involuntarily at the air of savage poetry that the clever Valérie, by her attention to the dress of this Bleeding Nun,[1] had succeeded in bringing out, skillfully framing her dry sallow face in thick bands of hair as black as her eyes, and making the most of her rigid figure. Bette, like a Virgin by Cranach or Van Eyck, or a Byzantine virgin stepped out of its frame, kept the stiffness, the precision, of these mysterious figures, first cousins of Isis and the sheathed goddesses of Egyptian sculpture. She was like animated granite, or basalt, or porphyry. Secure from want for the rest of her days, Bette became quite charming, and took her gaiety with her wherever she went to dine. The Baron, besides, paid the rent of her little flat, furnished, as we know, with the remnants of Valérie's former boudoir and sitting room.

"I started life," she said, "as a hungry nanny-goat, and I am ending it as a lioness." She still continued to work some of the finer and more elaborate trimmings for Monsieur Rivet, but only in order, as she said, not to waste her time. And besides, her life was, as we shall see, fully occupied, too fully occupied. But it is an ingrained habit of the country-bred never to give up their work; in this they resemble the Jews.

Every morning, very early, Bette went herself to the market with the cook. It was part of Bette's plan that the household accounts, which were ruining Baron Hulot, should enrich her dear Valérie—and they did so to good purpose.

What mistress of a house has not, since 1838,[2] experienced the disastrous results of the antisocial doctrines spread among the lower classes by inflammatory writers? In all households the servant problem is nowadays the worst of all financial problems. With a few rare exceptions, which deserve the Montyon prize[3]—cooks, male and female, are domestic robbers, paid thieves, utterly brazen, with the Government complacently playing the part of fence, in allowing the natural tendency to steal, almost proverbial among cooks, in the old joke about the "handle of the basket," to develop to such lengths. Where these women used to steal forty sous for their lottery tickets they now take fifty francs to put into their savings. And the cold Puritans who amuse themselves in France with philanthropic projects think that they have made the common people moral! Between the market and the master's table the servant class has established a clandestine customs toll, and the city of Paris is much less efficient in collecting its duties than they are in taking their percentages on everything they purchase. Besides the fifty per cent that they charge on all kinds of grocer's provisions, they demand large commissions from the tradesmen. Even the most highly reputable tradesmen tremble before this secret menace, but they all pay up without protest—coach-makers, jewelers, tailors, and all. At any attempt at interference servants retaliate with insolence, or with those stupidly deliberate accidents that are so expensive; nowadays servants make inquiries about their employers' characters, just as in the old days employers made inquiries about theirs. This evil, which has now reached a head, and which the law courts are at last trying to stem, cannot be dealt with except by a law compelling domestic servants to have passbooks of good conduct, like laborers. If this were done, the evil would cease at once, like magic. Servants being obliged to produce their books, and masters being obliged to enter the reasons for dismissal, this corruption would encounter a powerful check. Our rulers, who are so preoccupied with the high politics of the moment, have no conception of the lengths to which the demoralization of the lower classes of Paris has gone: it is equaled only by their consuming jealousy. Statistics are silent on the alarming number of workingmen of twenty who marry cooks of forty and fifty who have grown rich by thieving. It is alarming to contemplate the consequences of such unions, from the threefold standpoint of criminality, degeneracy of the race, and unhappy family life. Even the purely financial consequences of these domestic thefts have immense political repercussions. Life being twice as expensive, there is no financial margin in many households—that margin that comprises half the trade of a nation, as it does the elegance of life. Books and flowers are to many people as necessary as bread.

Lisbeth, well aware of this fearful plague of Parisian households, first had the idea of supervising Valérie's housekeeping during that terrible scene in the course of which the two had come to be like sisters. She had, therefore, brought up from the depths of the Vosges a relation on her mother's side, a pious and extremely honest old maid who had been cook to the Bishop of Nancy. Anxious, nevertheless, on account of her want of experience of Paris, and even more fearing the effect of those evil counsels that destroy so many fragile loyalties, Lisbeth accompanied Mathurine to the big market, and set about teaching her what to buy. In Paris one must have a sense of domestic economy in order to know the real prices of goods and command the respect of the salesman; in order to buy luxuries, such as fish, only when they are cheap; to keep a watch on the prices of groceries, so as to buy cheap when a rise in price is likely. As Mathurine was paid good wages, and given any number of presents, she was sufficiently loyal to the household to be glad to be economical. And for some time now she had been almost a match for Lisbeth herself, who regarded her as sufficiently trained and reliable to do the marketing alone, except on days when Valérie was entertaining, which, incidentally, were frequent. The reason for this was as follows. At first the Baron had maintained the most strict decorum; but his passion for Madame Marneffe soon became so excessive, so all-absorbing, that he wished to be away from her as little as possible. At first he dined there four days a week, and later he found that it was pleasanter to dine there every day. Six months after his daughter's marriage he gave Madame Marneffe an allowance of two thousand francs a month for his board. Madame Marneffe invited any friends that her dear Baron wished to entertain. The dinner, therefore, was always arranged for six, so that the Baron could bring three without warning. Lisbeth's economy solved the difficult problem of entertaining lavishly for the sum of a thousand francs a month, and of handing over the other thousand to Madame Marneffe. Valérie's clothes were mostly paid for by Crevel and the Baron, and the two friends made another thousand francs a month out of this. In this way that pure and innocent creature had already amassed a hundred and fifty thousand francs in savings. She had saved her allowance and her monthly bonus, which produced enormous interest, thanks to the generosity with which Crevel allowed the capital of his "little duchess" to be invested in his own financial ventures. Crevel had initiated Valérie into the jargon and procedure of the Stock Exchange, and, like all Parisian women, she had soon surpassed her master. Lisbeth, who never spent a farthing of her twelve hundred francs, whose rent and dress allowance were paid for, and who never spent a penny out of her own pocket, also possessed a small capital of five or six thousand francs which Crevel watched over for her with paternal care.

All the same, the Baron's love, and Crevel's, put a heavy strain on Valérie. On the day on which this narrative is resumed, irritated by one of those small incidents that have, in life, the effect that the ringing of a bell has on a swarm of bees, making them aggregate into a solid mass, Valérie had gone up to Lisbeth to give vent to one of those lengthy lamentations with which, rather as they smoke cigarettes, women soothe life's minor miseries.

"Lisbeth darling, two hours of Crevel this morning! Such a bore! How I wish I could send you instead."

"That, unfortunately, is impossible," said Lisbeth, smiling. "I shall die a virgin."

"Belonging to those two old men! Sometimes I am positively ashamed of myself. If my poor mother could see me!"

"You are talking to me as if I were Crevel," replied Lisbeth.

"Bette darling, you don't despise me, do you?"

"Ah, if I had been pretty, wouldn't I have had some adventures!" exclaimed Lisbeth. "That is your excuse."

"But you would have obeyed only your heart," said Madame Marneffe with a sigh.

"Bah!" replied Lisbeth. "Marneffe is a corpse that they have forgotten to bury, the Baron is to all intents and purposes your husband, and Crevel your admirer; that seems to me quite in order for any married woman."

"But that is not the point, my dear darling girl, that is not the real trouble, but you choose not to understand me."

"To be sure I understand you," exclaimed the peasant from Lorraine, "for what you refer to is part of my plan of vengeance. But what can I do? I am doing my best!"

"To love Wenceslas so that I am growing thin, and not to be able to see him!" said Valérie, stretching her arms. "Hulot asks him to dinner here, and my artist declines! He doesn't know how he is adored, the monster! What has his wife got, after all? A fine body! Yes, she is beautiful, but I—I know it instinctively—I am worse!"

"Don't worry, my dear girl, he will come," said Lisbeth in the tone in which nurses speak to impatient children. "I am determined."

"But when?"

"This week, perhaps."

"Let me kiss you."

As may be seen, these two women were as one; all Valérie's actions, even her most reckless, her pleasures, her ill-humors, were decided upon only after careful deliberation on the part of the two women.

Lisbeth, who found this courtesan existence strangely exciting, advised Valérie in everything, and pursued the course of her vengeance with pitiless logic. Besides, she adored Valérie; she had made of her a daughter, a friend, the object of her love; and in her she found the docility, the softness and voluptuousness of a Creole; she enjoyed chatting with her every morning much more than she had with Wenceslas, for they could laugh together over the mischief that they planned, over the stupidity of men, and count up together the accumulating interest of their respective hoards. Lisbeth had indeed found, in her great plan, and in her new friendship, far greater scope for her activity than in her insane love for Wenceslas. The pleasures of hate satisfied are the fiercest and strongest that the heart can know. Love is the gold, but hate the iron of that mine of emotions that lies buried within us. And besides, Valérie was, in Lisbeth's eyes, beauty in all its glory—that beauty that she adored, as we only adore what we cannot possess, beauty far more malleable than that of Wenceslas, who, to her, had always been cold and remote.

By the end of nearly three years Lisbeth was beginning to see the progress of the underground tunnel on which she was expending her life and the energies of her mind. Lisbeth thought, Madame Marneffe acted. Madame Marneffe was the ax, Lisbeth the hand that was demolishing by blow after blow the family which was daily becoming more hateful to her, because we hate more and more, just as each day, when we love, we love more and more. Love and hate are emotions that feed on themselves; but of the two hate is the more enduring. Love is limited by our limited strength—it draws its power from living and giving; but hate is like death and avarice—it is a sort of active abstraction, apart from people and things. Lisbeth, having entered upon an existence that was her natural self-expression, brought all her faculties into play; she ruled, like the Jesuits, behind the scenes; and the regeneration of her appearance was no less complete. Her face shone. And Lisbeth dreamed of becoming Madame la Maréchale Hulot.

This episode, in the course of which the two friends had bluntly expressed their most secret thoughts without the slightest reserve, had taken place just after Lisbeth's return from the market, where she had been to buy the materials for an elegant dinner. Marneffe, who coveted Monsieur Coquet's position, had invited him, with the virtuous Madame Coquet, and Valérie hoped to arrange that very evening for Hulot to dismiss the head clerk. Lisbeth was dressing to visit the Baroness, with whom she was to dine.

"You will come back in time to pour out tea for us, Bette my dear?" said Valérie.

"I hope so."

"What do you mean, you hope so? Are you going to bed with Adeline, to drink her tears while she is asleep?"

"If only I could!" replied Lisbeth with a laugh. "I would not refuse. She is expiating her happiness, and I am glad of it, for I remember my childhood. Turn and turn about. She will be in the gutter, and I will be Countess de Forzheim!"

Chapter XVII

Lisbeth set out for the Rue Plumet, where she had been in the habit of going for some time, as one goes to the theater, as an emotional luxury.

The flat that Hulot had found for his wife consisted of a large bare hall, a drawing room, and a bedroom with a dressing room. The dining room opened into the drawing room on one side. Two servants' rooms and a kitchen on the third floor completed the accommodation, which was, however, not unworthy of a Councilor of State and a Director of the Ministry of War. The house, courtyard, and stairs were imposing. The Baroness, who had to furnish her drawing room, bedroom, and dining room with the relics of her former splendor, had brought the best of the furniture from her home in the Rue de l'Université. Besides, the poor woman was attached to these silent reminders of her happiness, and for her they had an almost consoling eloquence. Her flowers of memory had not faded, like the roses on the carpets, that now were scarcely visible to eyes other than her own.

In that great hall twelve chairs, a barometer, and a huge stove, and long white calico curtains with red borders, suggested the dreariness of waiting rooms in ministries, and struck a chill to the heart; one felt the oppressive solitude in which she lived. Sorrow, like happiness, creates an atmosphere. One knows at a glance whether love or despair reigns in any home. Adeline was to be found in an immense bedroom furnished with beautiful furniture by Jacob Desmalters, in speckled mahogany decorated in the Empire style, with those ormolu ornaments that manage to look even colder than Louis XVI bronzes. It was enough to make anyone shudder to see this woman, seated on a Roman chair with the sphinxes of a worktable before her, all her color gone, affecting a false cheerfulness, preserving her imperial air as carefully as she did the blue velvet dress that she wore in the house. Her proud spirit sustained her strength and preserved her beauty. But the Baroness, by the end of the first year of her exile in this apartment, had plumbed the depths of misfortune.

"Even though he has banished me here, my Hector has made my life much better than a simple peasant woman had any right to expect," she told herself. "It is his decision, and his will be done. I am Baroness Hulot, the sister-in-law of a Marshal of France, I have done nothing with which I can reproach myself, my two children are settled, and I can wait for death shrouded in the immaculate veil of a chaste wife, in the crepe[1] of my past happiness."

A portrait of Hulot, in the uniform of a Commissary General of the Imperial Guard, painted in 1810 by Robert Lefebvre, hung above the worktable, into a drawer of which, if visitors were announced, Adeline would hastily thrust a copy of the *Imitation of Christ*,[2] which she read constantly. For this blameless Magdalene heard the voice of the Holy Spirit in her desert.

"Mariette, my dear," Lisbeth asked the cook who opened the door to her, "how is my dear Adeline?"

"Oh, she seems quite well, Mademoiselle. But between ourselves, if she goes on like this, she won't last long," said Mariette in a whisper. "Really, you must make her promise to eat more. Yesterday Madame told me to give her two sous' worth of milk and a roll for breakfast; and a herring or a little cold veal for lunch; she told me to cook a pound to last her the week, that is, for the days when she dines alone and at home. She doesn't want to spend more than ten sous a day on her food. It is not right. If I was to tell Monsieur le Maréchal about it, he would quarrel with Monsieur le Baron and disinherit him; unless you, who are so kind and clever, can manage things."

"Well, why don't you ask my cousin the Baron?" said Lisbeth.

"Oh, dear Mademoiselle, it's more than three weeks since he was here; in fact, not since you were last here! Besides, Madame has made me promise, on pain of dismissal, not to ask the master for money. But talk about troubles! Ah! Poor Madame has plenty. This is the first time that the master has neglected her for so long. Every time the bell rang she used to fly to the window; but for the last five days she has just gone on sitting in her chair. She reads! And whenever she goes to see Madame la Comtesse she says to me, 'Mariette,' she says, 'if the master should come, say I am at home, and send the porter to fetch me at once; and I will pay him well for his trouble.' "

"Poor cousin!" said Bette. "It goes to my heart to hear of it. I speak to my cousin the Baron about her every day. But what can I do? He says, 'You are quite right, Bette, I am a wretch, my wife is an angel, and I am a monster; I will go tomorrow ...' and he stays with Madame Marneffe; that woman will be his ruin, and he dotes on her, he cannot bear her out of his sight. I do all I can. If I were not there, and if I had not Mathurine with me, the Baron would have spent twice the money; and as he has very little left, he might already have blown his brains out. And you know, Mariette, her husband's death would kill Adeline, of that I am sure. At least I try to make ends meet, and to stop my cousin from throwing away too much money."

"Yes, that is just what the poor mistress says! She knows how much she owes to you," Mariette replied. "She says she misjudged you for a long time."

"Oh!" said Lisbeth. "Did she say anything else?"

"No, Mademoiselle. If you want to make her happy, talk to her about the master; she thinks you are lucky to see him every day."

"Is she alone?"

"Oh, I beg pardon, the Marshal is with her. Oh! he comes every day, and she always says that she has seen the master that morning, and that he comes in very late at night."

"And is there a good dinner today?" asked Bette.

Mariette hesitated and could not meet the peasant woman's eye; just then the drawing-room door opened, and Marshal Hulot came out in such a hurry that he greeted Bette without looking at her, and dropped a paper. Bette picked up this paper, and ran to the stairs, for it was useless to call after a deaf man; but she managed not to overtake the Marshal, and as she returned she furtively read the following note, written in pencil:

> MY DEAR BROTHER,
>
> My husband has given me my allowance for this quarter; but my daughter Hortense was in such straits that I have lent her the whole amount, which is barely enough to set her right. Could you lend me a few hundred francs? Because I don't want to ask Hector for money; I could not bear it if he were to be angry with me.

"Ah!" thought Lisbeth, "she must be in desperate straits to humble her pride to this extent!"

Lisbeth went in, and finding Adeline in tears, she put her arms around her neck.

"Adeline, my poor darling, I know everything!" said Cousin Bette. "Look, the Marshal dropped this paper; he seemed very distressed, for he was running like a greyhound.... How long is it since that dreadful Hector gave you any money?"

"He pays me regularly," answered the Baroness, "but Hortense needed it, and—"

"And you had nothing to pay for our dinner," said Bette, interrupting her cousin. "Now I understand why Mariette was so embarrassed when I said something about the soup to her. Now, no nonsense, Adeline, let me give you my savings!"

"Thank you, my kind Bette," replied Adeline, wiping away a tear, "this little difficulty is only temporary, and I have made arrangements for the future. In the future I shall not be expecting more than two thousand four hundred francs a year, including rent, and I shall have enough. But whatever happens, Bette, don't say a word to Hector! How is he?"

"As sound as the Pont Neuf and as gay as a lark; he talks of nothing but the bewitching Valérie."

Madame Hulot was looking at a great silver fir outside the window, and Lisbeth could read nothing of the expression in her cousin's eyes.

"Did you remind him that this is the day when we all dine here?"

"Yes, but Madame Marneffe is giving a big dinner, if you please; she is trying to get Monsieur Coquet dismissed! And that takes precedence over everything! Look here, Adeline, listen to me. You know how fiercely independent I am on the subject of money. Your husband, my dear, will most certainly ruin you. I had hoped to be able to be useful to you all with that woman, but there is no end to the depravity of the creature; she will extract so much from your husband that he will bring you all to disgrace."

Adeline recoiled as if she had received a sword thrust in her heart.

"Yes, my dear Adeline, I am certain of it. It is my duty to enlighten you. Well, we must think of the future! The Marshal is old, but he will last a long time yet—he has a fine constitution; his widow, after his death, would receive a pension of six thousand francs. With that amount I would give you my word to look after you all! Use your influence over the old man to persuade him to marry me. It isn't that I care about being Madame la Maréchale—I set no more store by such nonsense than by Madame Marneffe's conscience; but then you would all have enough to eat. Hortense must be in great want, since she has to borrow from you."

The Marshal appeared; the old soldier had hurried so much that he was mopping his brow with his handkerchief.

"I have given two thousand francs to Mariette," he whispered in his sister-in-law's ear.

Adeline turned crimson to the roots of her hair. Two tears trembled on her still-long eyelashes, and she pressed in silence the hand of the old man, whose face shone with the happiness of a favored lover.

"I had intended to spend the money on a present for you, Adeline," he went on; "instead of paying it back to me, I want you to choose yourself whatever you would like best."

He advanced to take the hand that Lisbeth held out to him, and so carried away was he by his happiness that he kissed it.

"That looks promising," Adeline said to Lisbeth, doing her best to smile.

The younger Hulot and his wife now arrived.

"Is my brother dining with us?" asked the Marshal sharply.

Adeline took up a pencil and wrote on a slip of paper:

> I am expecting him, he promised me this morning to dine here; but if he does not come, it will be because the Marshal has kept him; he is terribly busy.

And she handed him the paper. She had invented this mode of conversation with the Marshal, and a supply of little slips of paper and a pencil were placed ready on her table.

"I know," replied the Marshal, "that he is overwhelmed with work in connection with Algeria."

Hortense and Wenceslas came in at this moment, and, with her family about her, the Baroness looked at the Marshal with an expression the meaning of which was understood only by Lisbeth.

Happiness had greatly improved the appearance of the artist, who was adored by his wife and flattered by the world.

His face was now almost full, and his elegant figure was enhanced by those advantages that good breeding imparts to all true gentlemen. His early success, his eminence, and those deceptive praises that the world bestows on artists as lightly as we say "good afternoon," or talk about the weather, had given him that sense of self-importance that degenerates into fatuity when talent wanes. The cross of the Legion of Honor completed, in his own eyes, the picture of the great man he imagined himself to be.

After three years of marriage Hortense behaved toward her husband like a dog to its master; she followed his every movement with a look, as it were, of inquiry; she never took her eyes from him, watching him as a miser watches over his treasure; her admiring self-effacement was quite touching. One saw in her the marks of her mother's character and upbringing. Her beauty, as great as ever, was now modified, though poetically, to be sure, by the gentle shadows of a secret melancholy.

As she saw her cousin come in Lisbeth had the impression that a spirit of protest, too long repressed, would soon break the fragile bonds of discretion. For Lisbeth's opinion, from the first day of the honeymoon, had been that the young couple had too small an income to sustain so great a passion.

Hortense, as she kissed her mother, exchanged a few whispered heart-to-heart phrases, whose secret was betrayed to Bette by their shakes of the head.

"Adeline will have to earn her own living, like me," thought Cousin Bette. "I must find out what she is going to do. Those pretty fingers will know at last, like mine, what it is to have to work."

At six o'clock the family went into the dining room. Hector's place was laid.

"Leave it," said the Baroness to Mariette. "The Baron is sometimes late."

"Oh, yes, my father is certainly coming," said young Hulot to his mother. "He told me that he would be here when we left the Chamber."

Lisbeth, like a spider in the middle of her web, observed all their faces. She had known Hortense and Victorin ever since they were born, and their faces were, for her, like glass through which she could read their young minds. And, to judge by certain inadvertent glances that Victorin directed toward his mother, she saw that some misfortune was about to descend upon Adeline, and that Victorin was reluctant to break it to her. The eminent young lawyer had some secret anxiety. His profound respect for his mother was abundantly clear in the unhappiness with which he looked at her. Hortense, for her part, was evidently preoccupied with troubles of her own; and for the last fortnight Lisbeth knew that she had been experiencing for the first time those anxieties that lack of money brings to honest people, to young women on whom life has always smiled, and who hide their anxieties. Moreover, Cousin Bette had divined at a glance that the mother had given nothing to her daughter. Adeline, in her delicacy, had descended to those deceits that necessity suggests to borrowers. Hortense's preoccupation, and her brother's, the Baroness's profound melancholy, cast a cloud over the dinner party, with the added chill of the old Marshal's deafness. Three people were cheerful, Lisbeth, Célestine, and Wenceslas. Hortense's love had developed in the artist all his Polish animation, that lively boastfulness, that noisy high spirits that distinguishes these Frenchmen of the North. His state of mind and his expression left no doubt that he believed in himself, and that poor Hortense, faithful to her mother's precepts, hid from him all her domestic troubles.

"You ought to be pleased," Lisbeth said to her young cousin as they left the dining room, "as your mother has come to the rescue by giving you her money."

"Mamma?" Hortense replied, astonished. "Oh! poor Mamma! I wish I could make some for her! Do you know, Lisbeth, I strongly suspect that she works in secret."

They were just crossing the great dark unlit drawing room, following Mariette, who was carrying the lamp from the dining room into Adeline's bedroom, when Victorin touched the arms of Lisbeth and Hortense; both, understanding the meaning of this gesture, allowed Wenceslas, Célestine, the Marshal, and the Baroness to go into the bedroom, and remained standing in the bay of a window.

"What is it, Victorin?" said Lisbeth. "I dare swear that it is some disaster caused by your father."

"Yes, unfortunately," said Victorin. "A moneylender called Vauvinet has bills of my father's amounting to sixty thousand francs, and he wants to prosecute! I tried to talk to my father about this dreadful business at the Chamber, but he refused to understand me; he almost avoided me. Ought we to warn Mother?"

"No, no," said Lisbeth, "she has too many troubles; it would be a death blow to her. We must be tactful with her. You don't know what straits she is in. If it hadn't been for your uncle, you would not have got any dinner tonight."

"Good Heavens, Victorin, what monsters we are!" Hortense said to her brother. "Lisbeth has to tell us what we should have guessed. My dinner chokes me."

Hortense could say no more; she covered her mouth with her handkerchief to stifle a sob, and burst into tears.

"I have told this Vauvinet fellow to come and see me tomorrow," said Victorin. "But will he be satisfied with my guarantee on the mortgage? I doubt it. These people want ready money with which to bleed others with their usurious dealings."

"We could sell out our capital," said Lisbeth to Hortense.

"That would not amount to much! Fifteen or sixteen thousand francs," Victorin replied, "and we need sixty thousand."

"Dear Cousin!" exclaimed Hortense, kissing Lisbeth with all the enthusiasm of an innocent heart.

"No, Lisbeth, keep your little income," said Victorin, pressing the peasant woman's hand. "I will see tomorrow what this man has up his sleeve. If my wife will agree, I shall be able to prevent, or at least delay, the proceedings; because it would be a frightful thing to see my father's honor attacked. What would the Minister of War have to say? My father's salary, which was pledged for three years, will not be available until December; this Vauvinet has renewed the bills of exchange eleven times, so you may imagine the sums that my father must have been paying in interest! We must close this bottomless pit."

"If only Madame Marneffe would leave him!" said Hortense bitterly.

"Heaven forbid!" said Victorin. "My father might go elsewhere. And there, at least, the original outlay has been made already."

What a change in these children, once so respectful, whose mother had so long instilled in them an absolute veneration for their father! Now they had judged him for themselves.

"But for me," Lisbeth went on, "your father would have been even more completely ruined than he is."

"We must go in," said Hortense. "Mamma is very quick; she will suspect something, and as our kind Lisbeth says, we must let her see nothing . . . we must be careful."

"Victorin, you don't know what your father will bring you to with his passion for women!" said Lisbeth. "Try to make sure of some future resources by marrying me to the Marshal; you can say something to him this very evening. I shall go early on purpose."

Victorin went into the bedroom.

"Well, my poor dear," said Lisbeth softly to her little cousin, "and what are you going to do?"

"Come to dinner with us tomorrow, and we will talk it over," Hortense replied. "I don't know which way to turn. You know how difficult life is, and you must advise me."

While the whole family with combined forces was preaching marriage to the Marshal, and Lisbeth was on her way back to the Rue Vanneau, there happened one of those incidents that infuse new energy into the vice of women like Madame Marneffe, by compelling them to bring into play all their resources of depravity. Let us admit at least so much: Life in Paris is too busy for vicious people to go out of their way to do evil; they use vice as a defensive weapon, that is all.

Chapter XVIII

Madame Marneffe's drawing room was full of her faithful admirers, and she had just settled her guests to play whist, when the footman, an old soldier engaged by the Baron, announced, "Monsieur le Baron Montès de Montejanos."

Valérie's heart beat fast, but she hurried to the door, exclaiming, "My cousin!"

And as she met the Brazilian, she whispered to him, "You are my relation, or everything is over between us! So," she went on aloud, as she led the Brazilian to the fire, "you were not shipwrecked, then, Henri, as they told me? I have been in mourning for you these three years."

"How are you, my friend?" said Monsieur Marneffe, holding out his hand to the Brazilian, who was every inch a Brazilian millionaire.

Baron Henri Montès de Montejanos, on whom the equatorial climate had bestowed the physique and complexion that we all associate with the part of Othello, had an alarming look of gloom, but this was only a plastic effect; for his character was of that gentle and affectionate kind that is predestined to fall victim to the kind of exploitation that weak women practice on strong men. The scorn that his face expressed, the muscular strength to which his massive build bore witness, all his powers, in fact, were only brought into play against men, a form of flattery that women relish so much that whenever a man gives his arm to his mistress he assumes instinctively an absurd matador swagger. Looking superb in a blue coat with buttons of solid gold, black trousers, fine boots irreproachably polished, and fashionable gloves, the only Brazilian touch about the Baron's dress was an enormous diamond, worth about a hundred thousand francs, that shone like a star in his sumptuous silk cravat, tucked into a white waistcoat in such a way as to allow a shirt of incredibly fine texture to be seen. His brow, which was bossy like that of a satyr—a sign of stubborn tenacity in passion—was surmounted by tufted jet-black hair like a virgin forest, beneath which flashed a pair of clear eyes, so wild as to suggest that the Baron's mother had been frightened by a jaguar before he was born.

This magnificent specimen of the Portuguese in Brazil took up his stand with his back to the fireplace in a pose that revealed his Parisian habits; and, with his hat in one hand, resting his arm on the velvet overmantel, he leaned toward Madame Marneffe in order to carry on a conversation with her in a low voice, caring little for all those frightfully common people who, to his mind, were very much in the way in the drawing room.

This dramatic entry, and the Brazilian's pose and behavior, produced similar stirrings of curiosity mingled with anxiety in the minds of Crevel and the Baron. Both wore the same expression, manifested the same fear. And the maneuver inspired by these two deep passions was, by simultaneous timing, so comical that it made those who were observant enough to notice it smile to themselves. Crevel, still every inch a middle-class shopkeeper, in spite of being a mayor of Paris, unfortunately was slower in his reactions than his opposite number, and the Baron was able to read in a flash Crevel's involuntary self-revelation. This was yet another blow to the heart of the elderly lover, who determined to have the matter out with Valérie.

"This evening," Crevel likewise said to himself as he arranged his cards, "this thing must be settled!"

"*You have a heart,*" Marneffe challenged him, "and you have just revoked!"

"I beg your pardon," said Crevel, trying to take back his card. "This new Baron is one too many," he went on thinking to himself. "If Valérie lives with my Baron and me, that is my revenge, and I know how to get rid of him—but the cousin! Another Baron is too much of a good thing. I don't want to be made a fool of. I would like to know exactly how they are related!"

That evening, by one of those lucky chances that only happen to pretty women, Valérie was looking charming. Her dazzling white breast was displayed by a lace tucker whose russet shade set off the dull satin of her lovely shoulders, for Parisian women (by what means, none knows!) manage to have lovely skins, and to remain slim at the same time. She was wearing a black velvet dress that seemed every moment about to slip from her shoulders, and she wore a lace headdress trimmed with flowers and grapes. Her arms, at once slender and firm, emerged from puffed sleeves frilled with lace. She looked like one of those rare fruits, coquettishly served on a beautiful plate, that make the knife blade itch to be cutting them. "Valérie," said the Brazilian to the young woman in a low voice, "I am still faithful to you; my uncle is dead, and I am twice as rich as I was when I went away. I want to live and die in Paris, near you, for you!"

"Speak more quietly, Henri, for Heaven's sake!"

"Nonsense, I must talk to you this evening, even if I have to throw all these people out the window, especially as I have wasted two days trying to find you. I can stay till they have gone, can't I?"

Valérie smiled at her supposed cousin, and said to him, "Remember that you must be the son of a sister of my mother's, who married your father during Junot's campaign in Portugal."

"I, Montès de Montejanos, great-grandson of one of the conquerors of Brazil, tell a lie?"

"Quietly, or you will not be able to come back."

"Why not?"

"Marneffe, like all dying men who pursue some last fancy, has conceived a passion for me."

"That fellow?" said the Brazilian, who knew his Marneffe. "I'll soon settle him!"

"You are violent!"

"Dear me, where does all this luxury come from?" asked the Brazilian, who had at last noticed the splendors of the drawing room.

She began to laugh.

"What bad taste, Henri!" she said.

She had just been subjected to two glances of such burning jealousy that she was now compelled to take notice of the two souls in torment. Crevel, who was playing against the Baron and Monsieur Coquet, had Marneffe for his partner. The odds were even, because Crevel and the Baron were equally distracted, and both made one mistake after another. These two old men had both, in one moment, let out the secret that Valérie had succeeded in persuading them to keep for three years; but she herself had been unable to hide the pleasure in her eyes at seeing again the first man who had ever made her heart beat faster, her first love. For the rights of these happy mortals live as long as the woman over whom they hold sway.

In the center of these three absolute passions, one based on the insolence of money, the second on the right of possession, and the third on youth, strength, fortune, and priority, Madame Marneffe remained as calm and clear-headed as Bonaparte at Mantua, when he had to contend with two armies while continuing to besiege the city.

Hulot's face, distorted with jealousy, was as terrible as that of the late Marshal Montcornet leading a cavalry charge against a Russian army lined up for battle. As a handsome man, the Councilor of State had never known jealousy, just as Murat never experienced fear. He had always been sure of his triumph. His setback with Josépha, the first of his life, he had put down to her love of money; he told himself that he had been supplanted by millions, not by an abortion, as he called the Duc d'Hérouville. The poisons and deliriums in which that mad passion so abounds, began in that instant to pour into his heart. He turned from the whist table toward the fireplace, à la Mirabeau,[1] and when he put down his cards in order to direct a look of challenge upon the Brazilian and Valérie, the company experienced that sense of alarm, mingled with curiosity, which is aroused by the spectacle of violence whose outbreak is to be expected from one moment to the next. The so-called cousin looked at the Councilor of State as he might have looked at some large Chinese vase. This situation could not continue. It was bound to lead to some dreadful scene. Marneffe was as much afraid of Baron Hulot as Crevel was of Marneffe, because he did not intend to die a deputy head clerk. Dying men believe in life as convicts do in liberty. This man was determined to be head of an office at all costs. Alarmed, and with good reason, by the pantomime of Crevel and the Councilor of State, he got up and said a word to his wife; and to the great astonishment of all present, Valérie went into the bedroom with the Brazilian and her husband.

"Has Madame Marneffe ever mentioned this cousin to you?" Crevel asked Baron Hulot.

"Never!" replied the Baron, getting up. "That's enough for this evening," he added. "I have lost two louis;[2] here you are!"

He threw down two gold pieces on the table, and went and sat on the divan with an expression that everybody interpreted as a hint to go. Monsieur and Madame Coquet, after chatting for a moment, left the room, and Claude Vignon, in despair, followed their example. These two departures served to move the less sensitive guests, who now realized that they were in the way. The Baron and Crevel remained there alone, neither of them saying a word. Hulot presently forgot about Crevel, and went on tiptoe to listen at the bedroom door; he retreated with a great bound, because Monsieur Marneffe at that moment opened the door and appeared with a calm face, apparently astonished to find only two people left.

"What about tea?" he said.

"Where is Valérie?" said the Baron, furious.

"My wife?" said Marneffe. "She has gone up to your cousin; she is coming back."

"And why has she left us for that stupid nanny?"

"Well," said Marneffe, "Mademoiselle Lisbeth came back from Madame the Baroness your wife with an attack of indigestion, and Mathurine asked Valérie for some tea for her, and so she has gone up to see what is the matter."

"And the cousin?"

"He has gone."

"Do you really think so?" said the Baron.

"I saw him to his carriage," Marneffe replied with a hideous smile.

The noise of a carriage was heard in the Rue Vanneau. The Baron, to whom Marneffe's word counted for less than nothing, left the room and went up to Lisbeth's flat. An idea flashed through his mind of the kind that the heart puts into the head when it is influenced by jealousy. Marneffe's baseness was so well known to him that he suspected a shameful connivance between the husband and the wife.

"Where has everybody gone?" Marneffe asked, on finding himself alone with Crevel.

"When the sun goes to bed so does the poultry yard," Crevel replied. "Madame Marneffe has disappeared, and her admirers have departed. What about a game of piquet?" he added, for he was determined to stay on.

He, too, believed that the Brazilian was in the house. Monsieur Marneffe agreed. The Mayor was a match for the Baron; he could stay on indefinitely, playing with the husband, who, since the suppression of public gambling,[3] had to make do with the restricted and paltry opportunities of private play.

Baron Hulot hurried upstairs to his cousin Bette's flat; but he found the door shut, and the usual inquiries through the door gave the two alert and clever women time enough to stage a scene of indigestion, with cups of tea. Lisbeth was in such pain that Valérie was seriously alarmed; so that Valérie scarcely paid any attention to the Baron's furious entrance. Illness is one of the commonest screens that women erect to ward off the storm of a quarrel. Hulot looked about stealthily, but could see no place in Cousin Bette's bedroom where a Brazilian might be hidden.

"Your indigestion, Bette, does credit to my wife's dinner," he said, looking at the old maid, who was in the best of health and doing her utmost to imitate the convulsions of hiccups as she drank tea.

"You see what a good thing it is that dear Bette is living in my house! Without me the poor girl would have died," said Madame Marneffe.

"You look as if you don't believe me," added Lisbeth, speaking to the Baron, "and that would be a shame."

"Why!" asked the Baron. "Do you know the reason of my visit?" And he eyed the door of the dressing room, from which the key had been removed.

"Are you talking Greek?" Madame Marneffe replied, with a melting look of misunderstood tenderness and fidelity.

"But it is on your account, my dear Cousin; yes, it is your fault that I am in such a state," said Lisbeth with emphasis.

This outburst diverted the Baron's attention, and he looked at the old maid in profound surprise.

"You know that I am devoted to you," Lisbeth continued. "I am here, which is proof enough. I use every ounce of my strength to watch over your interests by looking after dear Valérie's. Her household expenses would be ten times as much in any other house run on the same scale. But for me, Cousin, instead of two thousand francs a month, you would have to pay out three or four thousand."

"I know all that," replied the Baron impatiently. "You look after us in all kinds of ways," he added, going over to Madame Marneffe and putting his arm around her neck. "Does she not, my little beauty?"

"Upon my word," Valérie exclaimed, "I think you are mad!"

"Well, you have no occasion to doubt my attachment," said Lisbeth, "but I also love my cousin Adeline, and I found her in tears. She has not seen you for a month! No, that is not good enough! You leave poor Adeline without any money. Hortense nearly broke down when she discovered that it was only thanks to your brother that we had any dinner! There was not even any bread in your house today. Adeline has taken the heroic decision to keep everything to herself. She said to me, 'I shall be like you.' That went to my heart; and after dinner I thought of what my cousin was in eighteen eleven and compared it with what she is in eighteen forty-one, thirty years later. I had a violent attack of indigestion. I tried to get over it, but when I got home I thought I should die."

"You see, Valérie," said the Baron, "what my adoration of you has brought me to! To domestic crimes!"

"Oh, I did well to remain an old maid," exclaimed Lisbeth, with savage joy. "You are the best of men, Adeline is an angel, and look at the reward of her blind devotion!"

"But an old angel!" said Madame Marneffe softly, as she looked half tenderly, half amusedly, at her Hector, who was looking at her as an examining judge looks at the accused.

"Poor woman!" said the Baron. "It is more than nine months since I gave her any money, and I have always found it for you, Valérie, at any price! No one will ever love you as I do, and what troubles you bring me in return."

"Troubles?" she said. "What do you call happiness, then?"

"I still do not know on what terms you have been with this so-called cousin whom you have never mentioned before," the Baron continued, without paying any attention to Valérie's interruption. "But when he came in it was like a knife wound to my heart. Hoodwinked I may be, but blind I am not. I could read his eyes, and yours. Well, that ape's eyes shone into yours, and your look—oh, you have never looked at me like that, never! As for that mystery, Valérie, it must be cleared up. You are the only woman who has ever made me know what jealousy means, so you need not be surprised at what I am saying. But another mystery has come to light, one that seems to me infamous."

"Go on," said Valérie.

"That is, that Crevel, that cube of grossness and stupidity, loves you and that you have encouraged him at least enough to give him the right to display his passion in public."

"That makes three! Can't you find any others?" asked Madame Marneffe.

"There may be others!" said the Baron.

"If Monsieur Crevel is in love with me, he is perfectly within his rights as a man; if I encouraged his passion, that would be the act of a coquette, of a woman who would certainly leave much to be desired. Well, take me as I am, or leave me. If you give me back my freedom, neither you nor Monsieur Crevel shall ever come here again; I shall take my cousin as a lover, so as not to lose all the charming habits that you accuse me of having. Goodbye, Monsieur le Baron Hulot."

She got up, but the Councilor of State seized her by the arm and forced her to sit down. The old man could never again replace Valérie; she had, for him, become more indispensable than the necessaries of life, and he chose rather to remain uncertain than to have even the smallest proof of Valérie's infidelity.

"My dear Valérie," he said. "Don't you see how I am suffering? I only ask you to explain . . . give me some explanation."

"Very well, wait for me downstairs, because I am sure you do not want to look on while I attend to your cousin."

Hulot drew back slowly.

"You old libertine!" exclaimed Cousin Bette. "You have not even asked how your children are! What are you going to do about Adeline? For a start, I am going to take her my savings tomorrow."

"At least a man owes his wife common bread," said Madame Marneffe, smiling.

The Baron, without taking offense at the way in which Lisbeth had rated him, as roundly as Josépha, left the room, glad to avoid such a difficult question.

When the door had been bolted the Brazilian came out of the dressing room, where he had been waiting, his eyes full of tears, in a pitiable state. It was plain that Montès had heard everything.

Chapter XIX

"You don't love me any more, Henri—I can see it," said Madame Marneffe, hiding her face in her handkerchief and bursting into tears.

It was the cry of real love. The outcry of a woman's despair is so persuasive that it draws forth the forgiveness that is latent in every lover's heart when the woman in question is young, beautiful, and wearing a dress so low cut that she could slip out at the top in the garb of Eve.

"But if you love me, why do you not leave everything for me?" asked the Brazilian.

This son of America, logical, as are all children of nature, immediately resumed the conversation at the point at which he had left it, putting his arm around Valérie's waist again.

"Why?" she said, raising her head and gazing at Henri, dominating him with a look eloquent with love. "Because, my sweet, I am married; because we are in Paris and not in the savannahs, or in the pampas, in the wide open spaces of America! My darling Henri, my first and only love, do listen to me. This husband of mine, who is only an under clerk in the War Ministry, has set his heart on being a head clerk and an officer of the Legion of Honor. Can I help his being ambitious? And for the same reason that made him leave us entirely free—it was nearly four years ago, do you remember, you bad boy!—he's now forcing Monsieur Hulot upon me. I cannot get rid of that dreadful bureaucrat who puffs like a grampus and has fins of hair in his nostrils, and is sixty-three, and who has aged ten years in the last three in the attempt to keep young; I hate him so much that on the day that Marneffe is a head clerk and an officer of the Legion of Honor—"

"How much more will your husband be getting then?"

"A thousand crowns."

"I will pay him that as an annuity," Baron Montès persisted. "We will leave Paris and go—"

"Go where?" asked Valérie, with one of those pretty grimaces with which women make fun of men they are sure of. "Paris is the only city where we could be happy. Your love means too much to me to risk seeing it fade away when we find ourselves alone in a desert. Listen, Henri, you are the only man in the whole universe that I love; get that into your tiger's head."

A woman always persuades a man that he is a lion, with a will of iron, when she is making a sheep of him.

"Now listen to me! Marneffe has not five years to live; he is rotten to the marrow. He spends seven months out of twelve drinking medicine and tonics, and he lives in flannel, and as the doctor says, death may cut him off at any moment; an illness that would be slight for a man in good health would be fatal to him; his blood is infected, his life is undermined at the roots. I have not let him kiss me once in five years—the man is a disease! Some day, and that day is not far off, I shall be a widow. Well—and I have already had a proposal from a man with sixty thousand francs a year, who is as completely in my hands as if he were a lump of sugar—I swear to you that if you were as poor as Hulot and as diseased as Marneffe, and if you beat me, you are still the man that I want to marry, only you, for I love you, and I want to bear your name. And I am ready to give you any pledge of my love that you may ask—"

"Tonight, then—"

"But, you son of Rio, my lovely jaguar from the virgin forests of Brazil," she said, taking his hand and kissing it and caressing it, "show some consideration for the woman you intend to marry . . . shall I be your wife, Henri?"

"Yes," said the Brazilian, overcome by the intoxicating language of passion.

And he went down on his knees.

"Listen, Henri," said Valérie, taking both his hands and looking deep into his eyes. "Will you swear to me here, in the presence of Lisbeth, my best and only friend, my sister, to take me for your wife at the end of my year of widowhood?"

"I swear."

"That's not enough! Swear by your mother's ashes and her eternal salvation, swear it by the Virgin, and by your hopes as a Catholic!"

Valérie knew that the Brazilian would keep his word, into whatever social depths she should have fallen. The Brazilian took his solemn oath, his nose almost touching Valérie's white bosom, and his eyes fascinated; he was intoxicated, as men are when they see again the woman they love, after a voyage of a hundred and forty days.

"Very well, now don't worry. And treat Madame Marneffe with the respect due to the future Baroness de Montejanos. Do not spend a farthing on my account. I forbid it. Wait here, in the front room—you can lie on the sofa. I will come myself and tell you when you can leave. Tomorrow we will breakfast together, and you can leave about one o'clock, as if you had come to visit me at twelve. Do not be anxious, the porters are as devoted to me as if they were my father and mother. And now I must go down to serve tea."

She signed to Lisbeth, who came with her as far as the landing. There Valérie whispered in the old maid's ear.

"This blackamoor has come back a little too soon! Because I shall die if I cannot give you your revenge on Hortense!"

"Don't worry, my dearest little demon," said the old maid, kissing her on the brow. "Love and revenge, hunting in couple, will never lose the game. Hortense is expecting me tomorrow. She is in distress about money. Wenceslas would give you a thousand kisses for a thousand francs."

After leaving Valérie, Hulot had gone down to the lodge, and taken Madame Olivier by surprise.

"Madame Olivier?"

On hearing this imperious interrogation, and observing the gesture which accompanied it, Madame Olivier came out of her lodge and into the court, to the place where the Baron beckoned her.

"You know that if there is anyone who can one day help your son to a practice, it is myself; it is thanks to me that he is at this moment third clerk in a solicitor's office, and reading for the law."

"Yes, Monsieur le Baron; and Monsieur le Baron can count on our gratitude. Not a day passes but I pray to God for Monsieur le Baron's happiness."

"Not so much talk, my good woman," said Hulot, "but action!"

"What do you want me to do?" asked Madame Olivier.

"A man came tonight in a carriage. Do you know him?"

Madame Olivier had, of course, recognized Montès; how should she have forgotten him? Montès always used to slip five sous[1] into her hand in the Rue du Doyenné whenever he left the house rather too early in the morning. If the Baron had approached Olivier, perhaps he would have learned everything. But Olivier was asleep. Among the lower orders the woman is not only superior to the man, she also has, almost always, the upper hand. Madame Olivier had long since decided which side she would take in case of a collision between her two benefactors; she regarded Madame Marneffe as the stronger power.

"Do I know him?" she replied. "No, indeed; no, I have never seen him before."

"What! Did Madame Marneffe's cousin never go to see her when she lived in the Rue du Doyenné?"

"Oh! Was it her cousin?" exclaimed Madame Olivier. "Perhaps he did come, but I did not recognize him. Next time, sir, I will take notice."

"He will be coming down," said Hulot, interrupting Madame Olivier sharply.

"But he has gone," replied Madame Olivier, who had taken in the situation. "The carriage has left."

"Did you see him go?"

"As plainly as I see you. He told his man to drive to the Embassy."

Her tone of conviction and this assurance drew a sigh of relief from the Baron, who took Madame Olivier's hand and pressed it.

"Thank you, my dear Madame Olivier; but there is something else. What about Monsieur Crevel?"

"Monsieur Crevel? What do you mean? I don't understand," said Madame Olivier.

"Listen to me! He is in love with Madame Marneffe."

"I can't believe it, Monsieur le Baron; I can't believe it."

"He is in love with Madame Marneffe!" the Baron repeated emphatically. "What they are up to I do not know; but I mean to know, and you must find out. If you can put me on the track of that intrigue, your son shall be a solicitor."

"Don't you take on like this, Monsieur le Baron!" said Madame Olivier. "Madame loves you, and nobody else; her maid knows that for sure, and we are often saying that you are the luckiest man alive, because you know what Madame is—she is simply perfect! She gets up at ten every day; and then she has breakfast; well, and then she takes an hour to dress, and all that takes up two hours; well, then, she goes and walks in the Tuileries, where anybody can see her, and she is always back by four, in time to be ready for you. Oh, she's as regular as the clock. She has no secrets from her maid, and Reine doesn't keep anything from me, you may be sure! She couldn't if she wanted to, on account of my son—she's sweet on him. So you see, Monsieur, if Madame was to have any goings-on with Monsieur Crevel, we should be sure to know it."

The Baron went up again to Madame Marneffe's flat, with a beaming face, convinced that he was the only man who enjoyed the love of that shameless courtesan, as treacherous, but as lovely and as charming, as any siren.

Crevel and Marneffe were beginning a second game of piquet. Crevel was losing, like a man whose mind was not on the game. Marneffe, who knew the reason for the Mayor's absentmindedness, was taking unscrupulous advantage of it. He was looking at the cards on the table and discarding accordingly. Knowing, by this means, what his opponent had in his hand, he was playing with confidence. The stakes were twenty sous a point, and he had already cheated the Mayor out of thirty francs when the Baron returned.

"Dear me," said the Councilor of State, surprised to find no one else there, "are you alone? Where has everyone gone?"

"Your pleasant temper frightened them away," replied Crevel.

"No, it was my wife's cousin arriving," said Marneffe. "These ladies and gentlemen thought that Valérie and Henri must have a great deal to say to each other after three years' absence, and so they discreetly retired. If I had been there, I would have made them stay; but as it happens, it is just as well, because Lisbeth is not very well, and her not being able to make the tea as usual at half-past ten has upset everything."

"Then is Lisbeth really ill?" asked Crevel, furious.

"So they say," replied Marneffe, with the amoral indifference of a man for whom women have ceased to exist.

The Mayor looked at the clock, and, by his calculation, it seemed that the Baron must have spent forty minutes with Lisbeth. Hulot's jubilant expression seriously compromised Valérie, Lisbeth, and Hector himself.

"I have just been seeing her. She is in great pain, poor dear," said the Baron.

"The sufferings of others seem to cause you great pleasure, my friend," retorted Crevel with acrimony, "because you have come back positively beaming with jubilation! Is Lisbeth in serious danger? Your daughter is her heir, I believe. You are like a different man. You went off with a face like the Moor of Venice, and you come back looking like Saint-Preux![2] I would very much like to see Madame Marneffe's face!"

"Exactly what do you mean by that?" said Marneffe to Crevel, gathering up his cards and laying them down in front of him.

The dull eyes of this decrepit man of forty-seven kindled, and a faint color flushed his cold and flabby cheeks; he opened his toothless mouth, and his blackened lips caked with a sort of white chalky foam. That impotent rage of a man whose life hung on a thread, and who in a duel would have had nothing to risk, whereas Crevel would have had everything to lose, scared the Mayor.

"I said," Crevel replied, "that I should like to see Madame Marneffe's face, and I have all the more reason because your own is not very pleasant at this moment. Upon my word, you are as ugly as sin, my dear Marneffe."

"Do you realize that you are very uncivil?"

"A man who has won thirty francs off me in forty-five minutes never looks particularly handsome to me."

"Ah!" replied the under clerk. "If only you had seen me when I was seventeen!"

"Were you very attractive?"

"That has been my ruin. Now, if I had been like you, I might have been a mayor and a peer of France."

"Yes," replied Crevel with a smile, "you have been in the wars too much. And of the two metals that can be gained by cultivating the god of commerce, you have come in for the worse—the dross!"

Crevel roared with laughter. And if Marneffe took offense when his honor was in peril, he always took these vulgar and coarse pleasantries in good part; they were the small change of conversation between Crevel and himself.

"Eve has cost me dear, to be sure; but, by Jove, short and sweet, that's my motto."

"Happy ever after is more in my line," replied Crevel.

Madame Marneffe, coming in, saw only her husband playing cards with Crevel, and the Baron, in the drawing room. She guessed from the expression of the municipal dignitary all that had been agitating his mind, and she took her cue.

"Marneffe, my dear," she said, going over and leaning on her husband's shoulder, and running her pretty fingers through his dingy gray hair, but without succeeding in covering his bald head with it, as she gathered it together, "it is very late for you; you ought to go to bed. You know that tomorrow you have to dose yourself, the doctor has ordered Reine to give you your herb broth at seven. If you value your life, you must finish your game now."

"Shall we stop after five more points?" Marneffe asked.

"Very good. I have made two already," said Crevel.

"How long will it take?" asked Valérie.

"Ten minutes," replied Marneffe.

"It is eleven already," said Valérie, "and really, Monsieur Crevel, anyone would think you wanted to kill my husband. In any case, don't be long."

This double-edged remark made Crevel, Hulot, and even Marneffe himself smile. Valérie went over to talk to her Hector.

"Go now, my dear," Valérie whispered to Hector. "Walk up and down in the Rue Vanneau, and come back when you see Crevel leave."

"I would rather leave the flat and come back to your room by the dressing-room door. You could ask Reine to open it for me."

"Reine is upstairs with Lisbeth."

"Very well, shall I go back to Lisbeth's flat?"

Valérie saw danger on all sides; foreseeing a scene with Crevel, she did not want Hulot in her room, where he would hear everything.... And the Brazilian was waiting in Lisbeth's flat.

"Really, you men," said Valérie to Hulot, "when you get an idea into your heads, you would set fire to the house to get to it. Lisbeth is in no fit state to receive you. Are you afraid of catching cold in the street? Wait there—or good night!"

"Good night, gentlemen," said the Baron aloud.

His old man's vanity was piqued; Hulot was determined to prove that he could play the young man by waiting for the hour of surrender in the street, and he left.

Marneffe said good night to his wife, and took her hands with a demonstration of seeming devotion. Valérie pressed her husband's hand in a way which meant: "Get rid of Crevel for me."

"Good night, Crevel," said Marneffe. "I hope you won't stay long with Valérie. You see, I am jealous. A little late in the day, but it has got me! I shall come back to see whether you have gone."

"I want to talk to Valérie, but I won't stay long," said Crevel.

"Talk quietly," said Valérie in a low voice. "Now, what is it?" she said aloud, giving Crevel a look of mingled pride and contempt.

Before this haughty look Crevel, who had rendered great services to Valérie, and who had intended to point out this fact, became at once humble and submissive.

"This Brazilian ..." Crevel, quailing before Valérie's fixed expression of contempt, broke off.

"Well?" she said.

"This cousin."

"He is not my cousin," she replied. "He is my cousin to the world, and to Monsieur Marneffe. And if he were my lover, that would be no affair of yours. A shopkeeper who buys a woman in order to have his revenge is, in my opinion, lower than one who buys her for love. You were not in love with me; to you I was only Monsieur Hulot's mistress, and you paid for me as one might buy a pistol to shoot an enemy. I needed money, so I consented."

"You have not kept your side of the bargain," said Crevel, lapsing into the shopkeeper.

"Ah! You want Baron Hulot to know that you have robbed him of his mistress in revenge for his having taken Josépha? Nothing could prove your baseness more clearly. You say you love a woman, you treat her like a duchess, and then you want to dishonor her! But after all, my dear, you are quite right; I am not to be compared with Josépha. That young lady has the courage of her shame, while I am only a hypocrite, who deserves to be whipped in public. Oh dear!

Josépha is protected by her talent and her wealth. I have only my reputation to protect me; I am still a respectable and virtuous middle-class wife. But if you make a scandal, what shall I be? If I were rich, it would not matter! But you know very well that at most I have fifteen thousand francs a year."

"Much more," said Crevel. "I have doubled your savings during the last two months in Orléans shares."[3]

"Well, one has no status in Paris on less than fifty thousand; just give me the equivalent in money for the reputation I shall lose! All I ask is to see Marneffe made a head clerk; then he will draw a salary of six thousand francs. He has twenty-seven years of service, and in three years I shall be entitled to a pension of fifteen hundred francs if he dies! And you, whom I have loaded with kindness, whom I have made entirely happy, you cannot wait! And you call that love!" she exclaimed.

"I may have begun with an ulterior motive," said Crevel, "but now I am at your beck and call. You trample on my affections, you crush me, you humiliate me, and I love you as I have never loved before. Valérie, I love you as much as I love Célestine! I would do anything for you. Listen, instead of coming twice a week to the Rue du Dauphin, come three times!"

"Is that all? You are growing quite young again, my dear!"

"Let me send Hulot packing, humiliate him, get rid of him for you," said Crevel, disregarding this insult. "Don't see that Brazilian again, be mine entirely! You will have no reason to regret it. To begin with, I will give you a bond for eight thousand francs a year; it will be an annuity to begin with—I will only give you the capital after five years of fidelity."

"More bargains! Shopkeepers can never learn to give! You want to invest in love by installments, all through your life, by means of security bonds! Tradesman! Hair-oil seller! You put a price on everything! Hector told me that the Duc d'Hérouville gave Josépha bonds for thirty thousand a year in a packet of sugar almonds! And I am worth six Joséphas! Ah! To be loved!" she said, setting her curls, and going over to the mirror. "Henri loves me. I have only to lift my finger and he would kill you like a fly. Hulot loves me; his wife is sleeping on straw! Go and be a good family man, my dear. You have three hundred thousand francs pocket money, over and above your fortune—in fact, a gold mine—and all you think about is increasing it."

"For you, Valérie, for I offer you half of it!" he said, going down on his knees.

"Are you still here?" exclaimed the hideous Marneffe, coming in in his dressing gown. "What are you doing?"

"He is apologizing to me, my dear, for an insulting proposal that he has just made to me. As I did not agree to it, he proposed to buy me!"

Crevel would have liked a trapdoor to open and let him down into the cellar, as in a theater.

"Get up, my dear Crevel," said Marneffe, smiling. "You look quite ridiculous. I see from Valérie's expression that I am in no danger."

"Go to bed and sleep well," said Madame Marneffe.

"How clever she is!" thought Crevel. "She is adorable! She has saved me!"

When Marneffe had gone back to his room the Mayor took Valérie's hands and kissed them, leaving on them the traces of a few tears.

"All in your name!" he said.

"That is the way to love," she murmured in his ear. "Very well, love for love. Hulot is down below, in the street. The poor old thing is waiting to come up, when I stand a candle in one of my bedroom windows. I give you my permission to tell him that I love only you; he will not believe you, so take him to the Rue du Dauphin, give him proofs, shatter him. You have my permission; I order you to do it. I am bored with that old seal, bored to death with him. Keep your man in the Rue du Dauphin all night, kill him by inches. Have your revenge for the loss of Josépha. It may kill Hulot; but we shall be saving his wife and children from utter ruin. Madame Hulot is working for her living!"

"Oh! Poor woman! Upon my word, it is abominable!" exclaimed Crevel, his native good nature reviving.

"If you love me, Célestin," she whispered in Crevel's ear, brushing it with her lips as she did so, "keep him away, or I am undone. Marneffe is suspicious, and Hector has a key to the outer gate, and is expecting to come back!"

Crevel pressed Madame Marneffe in his arms, and left in a state of supreme happiness; Valérie accompanied him affectionately as far as the landing, and then, like a woman bewitched, followed him down to the first floor, and to the bottom of the stairs.

"My own Valérie! Go back; do not compromise yourself before the porters! Go, my life and my happiness, everything is yours. Go back, my duchess!"

"Madame Olivier!" Valérie called softly, as soon as the door was closed.

"Why, Madame, you here?" exclaimed Madame Olivier, bewildered.

"Bolt the main door top and bottom, and don't open it again."

"Very good, Madame!"

When she had bolted the door Madame Olivier gave an account of the attempted bribery on the part of the high official.

"That was angelic of you, dear Olivier; but we will talk about that tomorrow."

Valérie went up to the third floor like an arrow, knocked three times on Lisbeth's door, and returned to her own flat, where she gave instructions to Mademoiselle Reine; for a woman must make the best of her opportunities when a Montès comes back from Brazil.

Chapter XX

"No, by Jove, only women of the world know how to love like that!" Crevel said to himself. "How she came down the stairs, lighting it up with her look, and she was following me! Josépha! She is no catch at all," continued the ex–commercial traveler. "What was that I said? 'No catch . . .' Oh Lord! I might come out with that one day at the Tuileries. . . . No, unless Valérie sees to my education I shall never be up to much—and I am set on passing for a gentleman. . . . Ah! What a woman! She upsets me like an attack of colic when she looks at me coldly. . . . What grace! What wit! Josépha never gave me such emotions. And what unsuspected perfections! . . . Ah, now, there's my man."

In the darkness of the Rue de Babylone he perceived Hulot, his tall figure a little bowed, stealing along beside the scaffolding of a house that was being built, and he went straight up to him.

"Good morning, Baron, for it is past midnight, my friend. What the devil are you doing here? You are taking a walk in a fine drizzle. At our age that is not wise. Would you like me to give you a piece of advice? Let us both go home. For between you and me you will not see the light in the window."

On hearing that last phrase, the Baron became suddenly aware that he was sixty-three, and that his cloak was wet.

"Who on earth told you?" he asked.

"Valérie, naturally, our Valérie, who is henceforth going to be only *my* Valérie. We are even now, Baron; we will play the final round whenever you like. You cannot complain. You know that I always retained the right to take my revenge. It took you three months to take Josépha from me; and I took Valérie in . . . but we won't go into that," he went on. "Now I mean to have her all to myself. But we can still be good friends all the same."

"Crevel, do not joke," the Baron replied in a voice choked with rage. "This is a matter of life and death."

"Is that how you take it? Come, Baron, don't you remember what you said to me on the day of Hortense's marriage? Are two old beaus like ourselves going to quarrel over a skirt? It is common, it is ill-bred! We are Regency, we agreed, blue waistcoats, Pompadour, eighteenth century, positively, Maréchal de Richelieu, rococo, and, I might even say, *Liaisons dangereuses*!"[1]

Crevel might have continued to pile up his literary allusions indefinitely; the Baron heard them but indistinctly, like a man who is beginning to go deaf. But seeing, by the light of the gas lamp, that the face of his enemy had turned pale, the victor stopped short. This was a shattering blow for the Baron, after Madame Olivier's assurances, after Valérie's parting glance.

"Good heavens! There are plenty of other women in Paris!" he exclaimed at last.

"That's what I said to you when you took Josépha," said Crevel.

"But really, Crevel, it is impossible. Give me proofs! Have you a key, as I have, to let yourself in?"

And the Baron, who had now reached the house, put a key into the lock; but the door was immovable, and he tried in vain to open it.

"Don't make a disturbance at night," said Crevel calmly. "Take my word for it, Baron, I have better keys than yours."

"Prove it! Prove it!" the Baron repeated, exasperated by misery to the point of madness.

"Come with me, and I will give you proofs," replied Crevel.

And following Valérie's instructions, he led the Baron toward the quay, by the Rue Hillerin-Bertin. The unfortunate Councilor of State went, like a tradesman on the day before he declares himself bankrupt. He was absorbed in conjectures on the reasons for the secret depravity hidden in Valérie's heart, and thought that he must be suffering from some kind of delusion. Going over the Pont

Royal, he felt his existence to be so blank, so utterly at an end, so entangled financially, that he all but yielded to an evil impulse to fling Crevel into the river, and to jump in after him.

When they reached the Rue du Dauphin, which at that time had not yet been widened, Crevel stopped before a door in the wall. This door opened into a long corridor paved with black and white tiles that served as an entrance hall, and at the end of which was a staircase and a porter's lodge lighted from a small inner courtyard, of a type not uncommon in Paris. This courtyard, which was shared with the neighboring house, was a singular instance of unequal division. Crevel's little house[2]—for he was the owner—had an annex with a glass roof, built on the adjoining plot, and under the restricting condition that no higher story should be built on this structure, which was entirely concealed by the lodge and by the corbeling of the staircase.

This property had for a long time been used as a storeroom, back premises, and kitchen of one of two shops facing on to the road. Crevel had separated off these three ground-floor rooms from the rest of the building, and Grindot had transformed them into a small economically planned house. There were two entrances: one from the front, through the shop of a furniture dealer to whom Crevel let the premises at a low rent, and by the month, so that he could get rid of him if he talked; the other by a door so well concealed in the wall of the corridor as to be almost invisible. This little residence, consisting of a dining room, a drawing room, and a bedroom, lit from above, built partly on Crevel's ground and partly on his neighbor's, was therefore very hard to find. With the exception of the secondhand furniture dealer, the tenants were unaware of the existence of this little paradise. The porter's wife, who was in Crevel's pay, was an excellent cook; the Mayor could therefore enter his compact little house or leave it at any hour of the night without any fear of being spied upon. During the day a woman dressed as women dress in Paris to do their shopping, provided with a key, ran no risk in going into Crevel's rooms. She could stop to look at a piece of secondhand furniture, ask its price, go into the shop or leave it, without arousing the slightest suspicion if anyone should chance to meet her.

When Crevel had lit the candles in the drawing room the Baron was astonished to see the clever and expensive smartness of the place. The ex-perfumer had given Grindot a free hand, and the old architect had distinguished himself by producing an interior in the Pompadour style which had, incidentally, cost sixty thousand francs.

"I should like a duchess to be impressed if she was brought here," Crevel had said to Grindot.

He wanted a perfect Parisian Eden in which to enjoy his Eve, his woman of the world, his Valérie, his duchess.

"There are two beds," said Crevel to Hulot, indicating a divan with a bed that pulled out like a drawer from a chest of drawers. "Here is one; the other is in the bedroom. So we can both spend the night here."

"What about the proofs?" said the Baron.

Crevel took a candlestick and led his friend into the bedroom, where, on a sofa, he saw an expensive dressing gown belonging to Valérie that she had brought from Rue Vanneau, where she had the pleasure of showing it off before bringing it to Crevel's little house. The Mayor opened the secret drawer of one of those pretty little inlaid writing tables called *bonheur-du-jours,* rummaged in it, and drew out a letter which he handed to the Baron.

"Read this."

The Councilor of State read the following note, written in pencil:

> I waited for you in vain, you old villain. Women like me never wait for retired perfumers. Dinner had not been ordered, and there were no cigarettes. I will pay you out for this.

"Is it her writing?"

"My God!" Hulot exclaimed, sitting down, completely crushed.

"I recognize all her things—her caps, her slippers. Good Lord! How long have you—"

Crevel indicated that he understood, and took out a handful of bills from the little inlaid desk.

"Look at these, old boy. I paid the builders in December—eighteen thirty-eight. This delightful little house was first used two months before."

The Councilor of State bowed his head.

"But how on earth did you manage it? Because I know how she spends every hour of her time."

"What about the walk in the Tuileries?" said Crevel, rubbing his hands triumphantly.

"Well?" said Hulot, still mystified.

"Your supposed mistress goes to the Tuileries, where she is supposed to be walking from one to four; but, hey presto! she is here in a trice. You know your Molière? Well, Baron, there is nothing imaginary in *your* title."[3]

Hulot, no longer in doubt, remained ominously silent. Disasters impel strong and intelligent minds toward philosophy. But the Baron was, morally, like a man lost in a forest at night. This gloomy silence and the change that had come over the Baron's shrunken features alarmed Crevel, who did not wish to cause the death of his collaborator.

"As I was saying, old chap, we are even now, so let us play for the rubber. Won't you play for the rubber? Come! The deciding round!"

"Why is it," said Hulot, addressing himself, "that out of ten pretty women at least seven are false?"

The Baron was too much shaken to find any answer to the question. Beauty is the strongest of all human powers. All power that is entirely unchecked, without autocratic restraint, leads to abuse, to excess. Despotism is power gone mad. Among women, despotism is a matter of whims.

"You have no cause to complain, my good friend; you have a beautiful wife, and she is virtuous."

"I deserve it all," said Hulot. "I have not appreciated my wife; I have made her suffer—and she is an angel! Oh, my poor Adeline, you are avenged! She suffers in silence, alone, and she deserves to be adored; she is worthy of my love! I ought to . . . because she is still beautiful, innocent, almost virginal again. . . . But was there ever a more worthless, contemptible, vicious woman than this Valérie?"

"She is a good-for-nothing hussy who deserves to be whipped in the Place du Châtelet," said Crevel. "But, my dear Canillac,[4] even though we are such gallants, so very much Maréchal de Richelieu, rakes, Pompadour, du Barry, old profligates, and as eighteenth century as you please, we have no longer a lieutenant of police."

"How does one succeed in being loved?" Hulot asked himself, without paying any attention to Crevel.

"It is mere folly for the likes of you and me," said Crevel, "to expect to be loved; at most we can hope to be tolerated, for Madame Marneffe is a hundred times more corrupt than Josépha."

"And more avaricious! She has cost me a hundred and ninety-two thousand francs!" exclaimed Hulot.

"And how many centimes?" asked Crevel, with a tradesman's insolence, thinking that the sum was a small one.

"It is obvious that you do not love her," said the Baron sadly.

"I have had enough of her," said Crevel. "She has had more than three hundred thousand francs from me."

"What does she do with it? Where does all that money go to?" said the Baron, holding his head in his hands.

"If we had had an arrangement between us, like the poor young devils who go shares in keeping a twopenny tart, she would have cost us less."

"That is an idea!" the Baron replied; "but she would still deceive us, because, my portly friend, what do you make of that Brazilian?"

"Yes, you old fox, you are right, we are cheated like—like shareholders!" said Crevel. "All women of her sort are liabilities."

"Was it really she who told you about the light in the window?" asked the Baron.

"My dear old boy," said Crevel, striking his attitude, "she has fooled us both. Valérie is a— She told me to keep you here.... Now I understand. She has her Brazilian with her. Ah! I am finished with her. If you hold her hands, she manages to cheat you with her feet! Really, she is vicious, utterly immoral."

"She is worse than a prostitute," said the Baron. "Josépha and Jenny Cadine had a perfect right to deceive us; after all, they make a trade of their charms."

"But she plays the saint, the prude!" said Crevel. "Look here, Hulot, you should go back to your wife. Your finances are not too good; people are beginning to talk about certain bills of exchange in the possession of a shady moneylender called Vauvinet, whose special line is lending money to prostitutes. As for me, I have had enough of the ladies. Besides, at our age, what do we want with these chits, who, frankly, are bound to deceive us. You have white hair and false teeth, Baron. And I look like Silenus. I am going to save money. Money never lets you down. Even if the Treasury is open to everybody every six months, at least it pays your interest, and that woman spends it. . . . With you, friend Gubetta,[5] my old comrade, I might have accepted an unseemly, or perhaps I ought to say a philosophical, situation; but a Brazilian who may have brought some dubious colonial currency from his country—"

"Women," said Hulot, "are inexplicable creatures."

"I can explain them," said Crevel. "We are old, and the Brazilian is young and handsome."

"Yes, that is true," said Hulot. "I must admit that we are not as young as we were. But, my friend, how is one to live without seeing these lovely creatures undressing, rolling up their curls, smiling at us meaningly through their fingers as they twist up their curling-papers, and going through all their repertoire, telling their lies, saying that we do not love them when we are preoccupied with our work, and taking our minds off our troubles?"

"Yes, upon my word it is the only pleasure in life!" exclaimed Crevel. "When a saucy puss smiles at you and says 'Darling, you don't know how nice you are! I suppose I am different from other women, who fall in love with youths with goats' beards, fellows who smoke, with manners like lackeys, because being young they think they can dispense with common courtesy! And besides, they come and go as they please, and then they say goodbye, and go their ways. . . . You think I am a flirt, but I prefer men of fifty to these whippersnappers; one can keep them longer. They are devoted, they know that women are not so easily come by, they appreciate us. That is why I love you, you old rascal!' And they throw in all kinds of petting and caresses— Oh, there is no more truth in it than in the posters on the Town Hall!"

"Lies are often preferable to the truth," said Hulot, thinking of several charming occasions, evoked by Crevel's mimicry of Valérie. "They have to act up to their lies and sew spangles on their stage costumes."

"And we have them, after all, the bitches," said Crevel brutally.

"Valérie is a witch," said the Baron; "she can turn an old man into a young one."

"Yes, that's true enough," said Crevel; "she is an eel that wriggles out of your hands; but the prettiest of eels, white, and sweet as sugar . . . as amusing as Arnal,[6] and what a sense of humor!"

"Oh, yes, she is very witty!" said the Baron, forgetting all about his wife.

The two comrades went to bed the best of friends, recalling to one another Valérie's perfections, the intonations of her voice, her little ways, her gestures, the amusing things she did, her sallies of wit and demonstrations of affection. For she was expert in the art of love, and had remarkable moments, just as a tenor may sing an air better at one performance than at another. And they both fell asleep, lulled in these tender and diabolical reminiscences, lit up by the fires of hell.

Next day, at nine, Hulot set out for the Ministry; Crevel had business in the country. They left together, and Crevel offered the Baron his hand, as he said, "No ill feeling, is there? Because we are both done with Madame Marneffe."

"Oh, this is the end!" replied Hulot, with an expression almost of horror.

At half-past ten Crevel was going up Madame Marneffe's stairs four steps at a time. He found that infamous creature, that adorable enchantress, in the most attractive dressing gown, eating an exquisite breakfast in the company of Baron Henri Montès de Montejanos and Lisbeth. In spite of his shock at the sight of the Brazilian, Crevel asked Madame Marneffe to give him two minutes in private. Valérie went with Crevel into the drawing room.

"Valérie, my angel," said the amorous Crevel, "Monsieur Marneffe will not last long; if you will be faithful to me, when he dies we can be married. Think it over. I have got rid of Hulot for you. So just consider whether that Brazilian is worth a Mayor of Paris, a man who would attain the highest dignities for your sake, and who, as it is, has an income of eighty-odd thousand a year."

"I will think it over," she said. "I will be at the Rue du Dauphin at two, and we can talk about it. But see that you behave yourself! And do not forget the shares you promised to make over to me yesterday!"

She returned to the dining room, followed by Crevel, who was congratulating himself on having hit upon a plan for having Valérie to himself; but he now saw Baron Hulot, who had come in during this short conference, with a similar motive. The Councilor of State asked, as Crevel had done, for a few moments alone with Valérie. Madame Marneffe rose to go back to the drawing room, smiling at the Brazilian as she did so, as much as to say: "They are mad! Can they not see you here?"

"Valérie my child," said the Councilor of State, "that cousin is an American cousin."[7]

"Don't say any more!" she cried, interrupting the Baron. "Marneffe has never been, and never will be, my husband. The first and the only man that I have ever loved has just returned when I least expected him. It is not my fault! But look at Henri, and look at yourself! And ask yourself whether any woman, especially when she is in love, could hesitate. My dear, I am not a kept woman. From today I am not going to continue to play Susannah[8] between the two elders. If I mean anything to you, you can be our friends, you and Crevel; but everything else is over, because I am twenty-six, and from now on I intend to be an absolute saint—a good and worthy woman—like your wife."

"Really?" said Hulot. "Is this how you receive me, when I come like a pope offering you indulgences with both hands? Very well, then, your husband shall never be a senior clerk, or an officer of the Legion of Honor!"

"That remains to be seen!" said Madame Marneffe, with a significant look at Hulot.

"Don't let us quarrel," said Hulot in despair. "I will come this evening, and then we can discuss everything."

"In Lisbeth's flat, then."

"Very well, at Lisbeth's," said the amorous old man.

Hulot and Crevel went downstairs together to the street without saying a word. But on the pavement they looked at one another and laughed bitterly.

"We are two old fools," said Crevel.

"I have got rid of them," said Madame Marneffe to Lisbeth as she returned to the table. "I have never loved and I never shall love any man but my jaguar," she added, smiling at Henri Montès. "Lisbeth, my dear, do you know? Henri has forgiven me all the infamies to which I was driven by poverty."

"It is my fault," said the Brazilian. "I ought to have sent you a hundred thousand francs."

"Poor darling!" said Valérie. "I ought to have worked for my living, but my fingers are not made for that—ask Lisbeth."

The Brazilian went away the happiest man in Paris.

At noon Valérie and Lisbeth were talking in the splendid bedroom where this dangerous Parisian was adding to her toilet those finishing touches that no maid can give. Behind locked doors and drawn curtains, Valérie gave an account of everything that had happened the previous evening, night, and morning, down to the last detail.

"Are you pleased, duckie?" she asked Lisbeth finally. "Which shall I be, Madame Crevel or Madame Montès? What do you advise?"

"Crevel will not last more than ten years, libertine that he is," said Lisbeth, "and Montès is young. Crevel would leave you an income of about thirty thousand francs a year. Let Montès wait; he will be quite pleased to be the Benjamin.[9] And at about thirty-three, my dear girl, if you take care of your looks, you will be able to marry your Brazilian and live in style with sixty thousand a year of your own—and with a Marshal's wife to protect you!"

"Yes, but Montès is a Brazilian; he will never get anywhere," observed Valérie.

"We live in the age of railways," said Lisbeth, "and foreigners nowadays rise to high positions in France."

"We shall see," said Valérie. "When Marneffe is dead. He has not very much longer to suffer."

"These attacks of his," said Lisbeth, "are a sort of remorse of the body. Now I must go and see Hortense."

"Yes, go, there's an angel!" said Valérie. "And bring me my artist! In three years I have not gained so much as an inch of ground! That is a disgrace to both of us! Wenceslas and Henri are my only two passions. One is love, and the other is a fancy!"

"How beautiful you are this morning!" said Lisbeth, putting her arm around Valérie's waist and kissing her brow. "I enjoy all your pleasures, your good fortune, your dresses.... I never knew what it was to live until the day when we became sisters."

"Wait a moment, my dear tigress!" said Valérie, smiling. "Your shawl is crooked. You still don't know how to wear a shawl, after three years, after all my lessons; you will never be Madame la Maréchale Hulot!"

Chapter XXI

Lisbeth, wearing prunella boots, gray silk stockings, and fortified with a dress made of beautiful Levantine cloth, her braided hair surmounted by a very pretty black velvet bonnet lined with yellow satin, made her way to Rue Saint-Dominique by way of the Boulevard des Invalides, wondering as she went whether discouragement would at last break down Hortense's courageous spirit, and whether Slavonic instability, taken at a weak moment, would make Wenceslas's fidelity waver.

Hortense and Wenceslas lived in the ground-floor flat of a house at the corner of the Rue Saint-Dominique and the Esplanade des Invalides. This flat, which was originally in harmony with the honeymoon, now had that half-new, half-faded look that one might describe as the autumn of furnishing. Young couples are extravagant and wasteful without realizing it, or meaning to be so, with all their belongings and with their love as well. They are entirely self-centered, and take little thought for the future that, later on, preoccupies the mother of a family.

Lisbeth found her cousin Hortense just as she had finished dressing a tiny Wenceslas, who had been carried out into the garden.

"Good afternoon, Bette," said Hortense, who opened the door to her cousin herself.

The cook had gone out shopping; the housemaid, who was also the nurse, was doing the washing.

"Good afternoon, dear child," said Bette, kissing Hortense. "Is Wenceslas at his studio?" she added in a whisper.

"No, he is talking to Stidmann and Chanor in the drawing room."

"Is there anywhere that we can talk privately?"

"Come into my bedroom."

The chintz hangings of this bedroom, with a pattern of pink flowers and green leaves on a white ground, had faded in the sun, and so had the carpet. The curtains had not been washed for some time. The smell of cigar smoke hung about the room, for Wenceslas, now that he had become a famous artist, and having been born a gentleman, dropped his ash on the arms of the chairs, and on the prettiest pieces of furniture, as a man does for whom love puts up with everything, a rich man, who is above bourgeois carefulness.

"Now let us talk about your affairs," said Lisbeth, seeing her lovely cousin sitting silent in the armchair into which she had thrown herself. "But what is the matter? You look a trifle pale, my dear."

"There have been two more articles tearing my poor Wenceslas to shreds; I have read them, but I have hidden them from him, because they would discourage him altogether. The statue of Marshal Montcornet is condemned outright. And they only allow the bas-reliefs to pass and praise his talent for ornament out of treachery, to give more weight to their statement that serious art is beyond his reach! I begged Stidmann to tell me the truth, and he has completely shattered me by confessing that his own private opinion is in agreement with that of all the other artists, the critics, and the public. He said to me here in the garden, just after breakfast, that if Wenceslas does not exhibit something first-rate this autumn he might as well give up serious sculpture and confine himself to trifles and figurines, pieces of jewelry and high-class goldsmith's work. This setback is terrible, because Wenceslas would never accept it; he feels that he has so many wonderful ideas."

"Ideas don't pay the tradesmen," said Lisbeth. "I used to tell him so until I was tired. Bills are paid with money. Money is only given for work completed, and work that ordinary people like well enough to buy. When it comes to making a living, an artist had much better have a model for a candlestick or a fender or a table on his counter, than a group or a statue; because everybody needs these things; but he might wait for months for a buyer of his group—and for his money."

"You are right, dear Lisbeth! I wish you would tell him so, because I simply have not the courage. Besides, as he said to Stidmann, if he went back to decorative art and miniature sculpture, he would have to give up the Institute, and large works, and then we should not get the three hundred thousand francs commission for work at Versailles, and the City of Paris, that the Ministry has promised us. We shall lose all that because of those dreadful articles inspired by rivals who want to step into our shoes."

"And you never dreamed of that possibility, poor little lamb!" said Bette, kissing Hortense on the brow. "You wanted a gentleman and a leading artist, the most distinguished sculptor alive! But that is all imagination, you know. That dream needs an income of fifty thousand francs a year, and you only have two thousand four hundred so long as I am alive; and three thousand after my death."

Tears rose in Hortense's eyes, and Bette drank them up with a look, as a cat drinks milk.

The story of that honeymoon is briefly as follows—the account will perhaps not be lost on artists.

Mental work, labor in the higher regions of the mind, is one of the most strenuous kinds of human effort. The quality that above all deserves the greatest glory in art—and by that word we must include all creations of the mind—is courage; courage of a kind of which common minds have no conception, and which perhaps is here described for the first time. Under the terrible stress of poverty, and kept by Bette rather like a horse in blinkers, unable to look to the right or to the left, spurred on by that hard old maid, Necessity personified, a sort of deputy Fate, Wenceslas, a born poet and dreamer, had proceeded from conception to execution, leaping over the abyss that divides these two hemispheres of art without even noticing it. To plan, dream, and imagine fine works is a pleasant occupation to be sure. It is like smoking magic cigars, like leading the life of a courtesan who pleases only herself. The work is then envisaged in all the grace of infancy, in the wild delight of its conception, in fragrant flowerlike beauty, with the ripe juices of the fruit savored in anticipation. Such are the pleasures of invention in the imagination. The man who can explain his design in words passes for an extraordinary man. All artists and writers possess this faculty. But to produce, to bring to birth, to bring up the infant work with labor, to put it to bed full-fed with milk, to take it up again every morning with inexhaustible maternal love, to lick it clean, to dress it a hundred times in lovely garments that it tears up again and again; never to be discouraged by the convulsions of this mad life, and to make of it a living masterpiece that speaks to all eyes in sculpture, or to all minds in literature, to all memories in painting, to all hearts in music—that is the task of execution. The hand must be ready at every instant to obey the mind. And the creative moments of the mind do not come to order. These, like the moments of love, are discontinuous.

This creative habit, the indefatigable maternal love that makes a mother (that natural masterpiece that Raphael so well understood)—in short, this intellectual maternal faculty that is so difficult to acquire, may easily be lost. Inspiration gives genius its opportunity. She runs, not on a razor's edge, but in the air itself, and flits away with all the suspicious wildness of a crow; she wears no scarf by which the poet may catch hold of her, her hair is a flame, she is as elusive as those lovely rose and white flamingos that are the despair of sportsmen. And work is a weary struggle at once dreaded and loved by those fine and powerful natures who are often broken under the strain of it. A great contemporary poet has said, speaking of this appalling labor, "I begin it with despair, but I leave it with regret." Let the ignorant take note! If the artist does not throw himself into his work like Curtius[1] into the gulf, like a soldier into the breach, unreflectingly; and if, in that crater, he does not dig like a miner buried under a fall of rock; if, in fact, he thinks about the difficulties instead of overcoming them one by one, like those mortals favored by the fairies, who, in order to win their princesses, fight a whole series of combats against successive enchantments, the work will never be completed; it will perish in the studio, where production becomes impossible, and the artist looks on at the suicide of his own talent. Rossini, whose talent was of an order comparable with that of Raphael, provides a striking example of this, with his youthful days of poverty, contrasting with the wealth and success of his riper years. And it is for that reason that the same reward, the same triumph, the same laurels, are accorded to great poets as to great generals.

Wenceslas, by nature a dreamer, had devoted so much energy to production, study, and work under Lisbeth's despotic rule, that love and happiness had produced a reaction. His true character reasserted itself. The idleness, the carelessness, and the weakness of the Slav returned, to occupy once more in his nature those comfortable corners from which the rod of the schoolmistress had driven them. During the first months the artist was in love with his wife. Hortense and Wenceslas abandoned themselves to the adorable childishness of a legitimate, happy, and unbounded passion. Hortense, during this time, was the first to excuse Wenceslas from his work, proud of being thus able to triumph over her rival, his sculpture. And a woman's caresses drive away the muse, and weaken the fierce, resolute determination of the worker. Six or seven months went by, and the sculptor's fingers were forgetting the use of their tools. When work became urgently necessary, when the Prince de Wissembourg, president of the committee of subscribers, asked to see the statue, Wenceslas produced the phrase so characteristic of all idlers, "I am just beginning work on it." And he lulled his beloved Hortense with deceptive words, with the magnificent schemes of an artist's daydreams. Hortense loved her poet more than ever; she imagined a sublime statue of Marshal Montcornet. Montcornet was to be the idealization of bravery, the very type of the cavalry officer, courage in the style of Murat.[2] Why, one would only have to look at that statue to picture all the Emperor's victories! And what execution! The pencil was very accommodating, and bore out the artist's words.

But the only statue that was produced was an exquisite little Wenceslas.

When Wenceslas was on the point of going to the studio at the Gros-Caillou, to work the clay and finish the maquette, the prince's clock required his presence at the studio of Florent and Chanor, where the figures were being filed; or the day was dull and dark; on one day business had to be attended to, on another there was a family dinner, not to mention indispositions of talent or of health, besides those spent in dalliance with his adored wife. The Marshal Prince de Wissembourg was obliged to get positively angry before he could succeed in seeing the model, and to say that he would go back on his choice. It was only after endless complaints and by dint of strong words that the committee of subscribers succeeded in seeing the plaster model. After a day at work, Steinbock would return home visibly tired, complaining of having to work like a common mason, and of his physical weakness. During this first year the household was comfortably off. Countess Steinbock, madly in love with her husband, in the exultation of her required affection, bitterly reproached the War Minister. She went to see him, and told him that great works were not manufactured like cannon, and that the State ought to take its orders from genius—as under Louis XIV, Francis I, and Pope Leo X. Poor Hortense, who imagined that she held a Phidias[3] in her arms, had, in respect to her Wenceslas, all the maternal cowardice of a woman who carries love to the point of idolatry.

"Do not hurry," she would say to her husband. "Our whole future depends upon this statue; take your time, produce a masterpiece."

She would go to the studio. And Steinbock, in love, would waste five hours out of seven with his wife, describing the statue instead of working on it. In this way he spent eighteen months in completing this work that was of such supreme importance for him. When the plaster had been cast, and the model actually existed, poor Hortense, who had been a witness of her husband's tremendous efforts, who had seen his health suffer from that physical exhaustion to which the body, the arms, and the hands of a sculptor are subject—Hortense thought the result altogether admirable. Her father, who knew nothing about sculpture, and the Baroness, who was equally ignorant, praised it as a masterpiece; then they brought the Minister of War, and he, carried away by their persuasion, and seeing this model, by itself, well lighted, and carefully displayed against a green baize background, gave his approval. But alas! At the exhibition of 1841 unanimous condemnation soon degenerated, in the mouths of those inclined to be hostile toward an idol who had risen so quickly to fame, into howls of mockery. Stidmann, who tried to advise his friend, was accused of jealousy. The articles in the newspapers Hortense read simply as the utterances of envy. Stidmann, like a true friend, had articles written challenging the critics, and pointing out that sculptors alter their works very considerably in transposing them from the plaster to the marble, and that it is the marble that matters. "Between the plaster model and the marble," wrote Claude Vignon, "a masterpiece may be ruined, or a great work made from a poor model. The plaster is the manuscript, the marble is the book."

In two and a half years Steinbock had produced a statue and a son; the son was exquisitely beautiful; the statue was deplorable.

The clock for the Prince and the statue paid off the young couple's debts. Steinbock had acquired the habits of social life; he went to plays, and to the opera; he talked brilliantly about art, and he maintained his reputation as a great artist, so far as the world of fashion was concerned, by his conversation, by his critical disquisitions. There are men of talent in Paris who spend their lives in talk, and who are satisfied with a sort of drawing-room celebrity. Steinbock, in imitation of these attractive eunuchs, contracted an ever-growing disinclination for work. From the outset he would see all the difficulties involved in any undertaking, and the consequent discouragement undermined his will to work. Inspiration, that mania of intellectual generation, took flight from such a half-hearted lover.

Sculpture, like drama, is at once the easiest and the most difficult of all the arts. You have simply to copy a model, and the work is done; but to endow it with life, and while representing a man or a woman, to create a type, is a Promethean task. Those who, in the annals of sculpture, have succeeded in doing this are as few in number as the poets of mankind. Michelangelo, Michel Columb, Jean Goujon, Phidias, Praxiteles, Polycleitus, Puget, Canova, and Albert Dürer, are the companions of Milton, Virgil, Dante, Shakespeare, Tasso, Homer, and Molière. Work like theirs is on so grand a scale that a single statue is enough to make a man immortal, just as *Figaro, Lovelace,* and *Manon Lescaut* suffice to immortalize Beaumarchais, Richardson, and the Abbé Prévost.[4] Superficial minds (and there are all too many of these among artists) have said that sculpture depends entirely upon the nude, that it died with Greece and that modern dress makes it impossible. But, in the first place, there are sublime statues, fully draped, among the works of antiquity—the *Polyhymnia* and the *Julia,* for example—and we have not seen a tenth part of their work; and furthermore, true lovers of art have only to go and see Michelangelo's *Thinker* in Florence, or in the Cathedral of Mainz the *Virgin* of Albert Dürer, who has made, in ebony, a living woman clad in triple robes, whose hair falls in waves more soft than any that a lady's maid ever combed. The ignorant have but to look at these works to be convinced that genius can inspire drapery, armor, and dress with a soul, and clothe a body in it just as a man imparts to his clothes the stamp of his character and habits. Sculpture is the continual realization of the quality that, in painting, has but one name, once and for all: Raphael! The solution of this tremendous problem can only be reached by dint of constant, sustained work, for the material difficulties must be so completely mastered, the hand be under such perfect control, so ready to obey the mind, that the sculptor is able to struggle in naked conflict with that indefinable moral element that it is his task to embody and transfigure. If Paganini, who could utter his soul in the sounds of his violin, went for three days without practicing, he lost, besides his expression, the register of his instrument—as he called that intimate harmony existing between the wood, the bow, the strings, and himself; and, this union dissolved, he would have been no more than any ordinary violinist.

Constant labor is the law of art, as it is of ordinary life; for art is the creative activity of the mind. And neither great artists nor true poets wait for commissions or purchasers; they create today, tomorrow, every day. And this produces a habit of work, that perpetual struggle with the difficulties of their art that keeps them in constant relations with the muse, with their creative powers. Canova lived in his studio, Voltaire in his study; so must Homer and Phidias[5] also have lived.

Wenceslas Steinbock had kept to the hard road trodden by these great men, the road that leads to the height of glory, so long as Lisbeth had kept him shut up in his garret. Happiness, in the person of Hortense, had reduced the poet to indolence. A normal state of all artists, for to them idleness is in itself an occupation. In it they enjoy the pleasures of the pasha in his seraglio; they toy with ideas, they get drunk at the springs of the intellect. Some great artists who, like Steinbock, have wasted themselves in reverie have been truly described as dreamers. These opium-eaters all sink into poverty, whereas, had they been upheld by the discipline of life, they might have been great men. These semi-artists are charming, to be sure, and the world is fond of them, and turns their heads with applause. They seem to be superior to real artists, who are objected to on the grounds of their alleged egoism, bad manners, and rebellion against the rules of society. This is because great men belong to their work. Their entire detachment, their devotion to their work, brands them as egoists in the eyes of stupid people, who would like to see them dressed like men about town, performing those worldly evolutions called social duties. Such people would like to see the lions of Atlas combed and perfumed like a lady's lapdog. Such men, who rarely encounter their equals, for of these there are few, fall into solitary exclusiveness. They become incomprehensible to the majority, which, as we know, is composed of the fools, the envious, the ignorant, and the superficial. Imagine, then, the part that a woman must play in the life of one of these exceptional beings! A wife would have to be all that Lisbeth was for five years, and give love besides—humble and discreet love, always ready, and always smiling.

Hortense, made wise by her sufferings as a mother and impelled by dire necessity, had realized too late the mistakes that, in her excessive love, she had unwittingly committed; but as a true daughter of her mother, the very thought of being hard on Wenceslas broke her heart; she loved her poet too much to endure the idea of being his taskmaster, and she foresaw the day when poverty would overtake herself, her son, and her husband.

"There, there, my dear," said Bette, seeing tears fall from her cousin's lovely eyes, "there is no need to despair. A whole bucketful of tears will not buy a plate of soup! How much do you need?"

"Five or six thousand francs."

"I have not more than three thousand. What is Wenceslas doing now?"

"He has been asked to work with Stidmann on a dessert service for the Duc d'Hérouville, for six thousand francs. And if he does Monsieur Chanor has promised to advance four thousand francs that we owe to Monsieur Léon de Lora and Monsieur Bridau—a debt of honor."

"Do you mean to say that you have been paid for the statue and the bas-reliefs for the monument to Marshal Montcornet, and you have not settled these debts yet?"

"But," said Hortense, "we have been spending twelve thousand francs a year for the last three years, and I have an income of only a hundred louis. The Marshal's monument, after all the expenses had been paid, only brought us sixteen thousand francs. In fact, if Wenceslas does not work, I do not know what is going to become of us. Ah! If only I could learn to make statues, how I would mold the clay!" she exclaimed, stretching her beautiful arms.

The promises of girlhood were plainly realized in the mature woman. Hortense's eyes shone. Impetuous blood, strong and red, flowed in her veins. She chafed against the necessity of wasting her energy in looking after her baby.

"Ah! my dear little goose, a sensible girl should marry an artist when he has made his fortune, and not before."

At this moment they heard the voices of Stidmann and Wenceslas, who were seeing Chanor to the door. Presently Wenceslas came in with Stidmann. Stidmann, an artist much in favor in journalistic circles, and with actresses and courtesans of the better class, was a distinguished-looking young man whom Valérie was anxious to take up, and whom Claude Vignon had already introduced to her. Stidmann had just broken with the notorious Madame Schontz,[6] who had married some months ago, and gone to live in the country. Valérie and Lisbeth, who had heard of this break from Claude Vignon, thought it advisable to draw Wenceslas's friend into the Rue Vanneau circle.

Stidmann, from motives of tact, did not visit the Steinbocks often, and Lisbeth had not been present when he was brought by Claude Vignon. She now saw him, therefore, for the first time. As she watched this well-known artist, she noticed the way in which he looked at Hortense from time to time, and this gave her the idea that he might be offered to the Countess Steinbock by way of consolation if Wenceslas were to be unfaithful. Stidmann had, as a matter of fact, dallied with the idea that, if Wenceslas were not his friend, Hortense, the marvelously beautiful young Countess, would make an adorable mistress. But this thought, held in check by a sense of honor, was in itself a reason for keeping away from the house. Lisbeth observed the revealing embarrassment that overcomes a man in the company of a woman with whom he will not allow himself to flirt.

"He is very attractive, that young man," she whispered to Hortense.

"Do you think so?" she replied. "I have never noticed him."

"Stidmann, my dear fellow," Wenceslas said in an aside to his friend, "you know we don't stand upon ceremony with one another—well, we have to talk business with this old girl."[7]

Stidmann took his leave of the two cousins, and departed.

"It is settled," said Wenceslas when he came back after seeing

Stidmann off; "but the work will take six months and meanwhile we must live."

"There are my diamonds!" exclaimed the young Countess Steinbock, with the superb impulsiveness of a woman in love.

A tear came into Wenceslas's eye.

"Oh, but I shall work," he replied, going over and sitting down beside his wife, and drawing her on to his knee. "I shall do odds and ends, a wedding chest, bronze groups—"

"But, my dear children," said Lisbeth, "you know, you are my heirs, and believe me, I shall leave you a nice little pie, especially if you help me to marry the Marshal—if we manage it quickly, I will take you all in as boarders, you and Adeline. Oh, we could live together very happily. But for the moment listen to the voice of my long experience. Don't rush off to a moneylender; that spells ruin. I have seen it happen again and again; the borrowers never have the money when the interest falls due, and lose everything. I can get you the money at five per cent on your note of hand alone."

"Oh, then we should be saved!" said Hortense.

"Well, my child, Wenceslas had better come with me to see the person who will lend it if I ask her. It is Madame Marneffe. If she is flattered—for she has all the vanity of a parvenue—she will make no difficulty about getting you out of your trouble. Come and see her yourself, my dear Hortense."

Hortense looked at Wenceslas with the expression of the condemned on their way to the scaffold.

"Claude Vignon took Stidmann there," said Wenceslas. "It is a very pleasant house."

Hortense bowed her head. What she felt can be described only by one word; it was not pain, it was illness.

"But, my dear Hortense, you must learn what life is like!" Lisbeth exclaimed, understanding Hortense's eloquent gesture, "otherwise you will be like your mother, abandoned in a deserted room where you will weep like Calypso[8] after the departure of Ulysses, and at an age when there will be no hope of a Telemachus!" she added, repeating a witticism of Madame Marneffe's. "You must regard people in the world as fools that can be made use of, taken up or put down according to their usefulness. Make use of Madame Marneffe, my children, and drop her afterwards. Are you afraid that Wenceslas, who adores you, will fall for a woman four or five years older than you are, faded as a sheaf of fodder, and—"

"I would rather pawn my diamonds," said Hortense. "Oh, never go there, Wenceslas! It is hell!"

"Hortense is right!" said Wenceslas, kissing his wife.

"Darling, thank you!" said the young wife, delighted. "You see what an angel my husband is, Lisbeth. He doesn't gamble, and we go everywhere together, and if he could only settle down to work … no, I should be too happy. Why should we be shown off to my father's mistress, a woman who is ruining him, and is the cause of all the troubles that are killing our heroic Mamma?"

"My dear child, that is not what is ruining your father! It was that singer who ruined him, and then your marriage!" replied Cousin Bette. "Good Heavens! Madame Marneffe is very useful to him … however, I must not talk."

"You have a good word for everyone, Bette dear." Hortense was just then summoned to the garden by her baby's cries, and Lisbeth remained alone with Wenceslas.

"Your wife is an angel, Wenceslas!" said Cousin Bette; "love her well, and never give her any cause for unhappiness."

"Yes, I love her so much that I have not told her our situation," Wenceslas replied, "but I can speak freely to you, Lisbeth.… Well, if we were to pawn my wife's diamonds, that still would not help."

"Well then, borrow from Madame Marneffe," said Lisbeth. "Persuade Hortense to let you go, Wenceslas, or, good gracious me, go there without telling her!"

"That is just what I was thinking," said Wenceslas, "when I refused to go, for fear of hurting Hortense."

"Listen, Wenceslas, I am much too fond of both of you not to warn you of the danger. If you go there, hold on to your heart with both hands, because that woman is a demon! Everyone who sees her adores her; she is so wicked, and so tempting! She fascinates men, like a work of art. Borrow her money, but don't leave your soul as a pledge! I should never forgive myself if you were to be unfaithful to my cousin. Here she comes!" exclaimed Lisbeth. "Say no more; I will arrange things for you."

"Give Lisbeth a kiss, my darling," said Wenceslas to his wife. "She is going to help us out of our difficulties by lending us her savings." And he gave Lisbeth a look which she understood.

"Then I hope that now you are really going to work, my angel!" said Hortense.

"Yes," replied the artist. "I shall start tomorrow."

"Tomorrow is our ruin!" said Hortense, smiling at him.

"Well, darling child, you know very well that there has not been a single day when something has not happened to prevent it, interruptions, or things to be seen to."

"Yes, you are right, my love."

"Here," went on Steinbock, tapping his brow, "I have ideas! Oh, I am going to astonish my enemies! I am going to make a dinner service in the eighteenth-century German style—the fantastic style! Foliage twined with insects, with sleeping children among the leaves, and absolute chimeras, straight from our nightmares! I see it all; it will be confused, light and yet cluttered, all at once. Chanor was tremendously impressed . . . and I needed some encouragement, because the last article on the statue of Montcornet really depressed me."

When Wenceslas and Lisbeth were alone for a moment, later in the day, the artist arranged with the spinster to visit Madame Marneffe the following day, for by then either his wife would have agreed, or he would go without telling her.

Chapter XXII

Valérie, who was told of this triumph that same evening, insisted that Baron Hulot should go and invite Stidmann, Claude Vignon, and Steinbock to dinner; for she was beginning to tyrannize over him as such women know well how to tyrannize over old men, who trot around town and run all the errands required by the vanity or interests of these exacting mistresses.

Next day Valérie prepared her weapons, by making one of those toilets that Parisian women know how to invent when they want to make the most of themselves. She studied herself, for this purpose, as a man about to go into battle practices feints and lunges. Not a speck, not a wrinkle were to be seen. Valérie had never been more white, and soft, and delicate. And her beauty spots attracted the eye unawares. We imagine that eighteenth-century patches are out of date, or at least unfashionable; this is a mistake. Women today are cleverer than they used to be, and deceive the eye by daring devices. One is the first to invent a knot of ribbons, with a diamond in the center, and draws all eyes for a whole evening; another revives the hairnet, or sticks a pin in her hair in a way that makes you think of her garters; another ties black velvet around her wrists and yet another appears in feather plumes. These sublime efforts, these Austerlitzes[1] of vanity, or love, later become fashionable in lower spheres, by which time their happy innovators are thinking up new ones. For this particular evening Valérie, who was bent on success, arranged three beauty spots. She had dyed her hair with a lotion to change its color, for a few days, from fair to a dimmer shade. Madame Steinbock was a red-blonde, and she wished to be altogether unlike her. This new color lent Valérie a piquancy and strangeness that puzzled her faithful admirers so much that Montès asked her, "What have you done to yourself this evening?" Next she put on a black velvet neckband, wide enough to emphasize the whiteness of her bosom. The third beauty spot can be compared to the *assassine* of our grandmothers' days.[2] Valérie placed the loveliest little rosebud in the middle of her bodice, just at the top of her stays, in the daintiest of little hollows. It was enough to make any man under thirty lower his eyes.

"I am delicious!" she said to herself, posing before her mirror, for all the world like a dancer practicing her attitudes.

Lisbeth had gone to the market, and the dinner was to be one of those special dinners that Mathurine used to cook for her Bishop when he entertained the prelate of the neighboring diocese.

Stidmann, Claude Vignon, and Count Steinbock arrived almost together, just before six. An ordinary, or, if you like, a natural woman, would have hurried down on hearing the name she had so ardently desired; but Valérie, who had been waiting in her room since five, left her three guests alone together, certain that she would be the subject of their conversation, or of their secret thoughts. She herself had supervised the arrangement of her drawing room, and had placed in evidence those delicious pieces of nonsense produced only in Paris—and which only Paris can produce—that reveal the woman and, as it were, announce her presence; scrapbooks bound in enamel and encrusted with pearls; dishes full of pretty rings; pieces of Sèvres and Dresden, exquisitely mounted by Florent and Chanor, beside statuettes and albums—all those trifles that cost fantastic sums and are commissioned from the makers either in the first ardor of passion or in its last reconciliation. Besides, Valérie was drunk with success. She had promised to marry Crevel if Marneffe were to die; and the amorous Crevel had transferred to the account of Valérie Fortin bonds bringing in an income of ten thousand francs a year, the whole amount of his profits in railway speculations during the past three years, the fruits of the capital of a hundred thousand crowns that he had offered to Baroness Hulot. So that Valérie's income now amounted to thirty-two thousand francs. Crevel had just made another promise even more considerable than the gift of his profits. In the paroxysm of passion into which his "duchess" (for this was the title he gave to Madame *de* Marneffe,[3] in order to complete his illusion) had plunged him between the hours of two and four—for Valérie had surpassed herself that day in the Rue du Dauphin—he felt compelled to encourage the promised fidelity by mentioning a beautiful little house that a rash speculator had built in Rue Barbette and now wanted to sell. Valérie already saw herself in this charming house, with its own court and garden, keeping her own carriage.

"What respectable life could ever produce so much in so short a time, and with so little trouble?" she had said to Lisbeth as she dressed.

Lisbeth was dining that evening with Valérie, in order to be able to say to Steinbock things that no woman can say about herself. Madame Marneffe, her face radiant with pleasure, entered the drawing room with graceful modesty, followed by Bette, who, in black and yellow, served, as they say in the studios, as a foil.

"Good evening, Claude," she said as she gave her hand to the distinguished old critic.

Claude Vignon, like many another, had gone into politics—a phrase invented to describe an ambitious man in the first stages of his career. The man in politics of 1840 is more or less the equivalent of the abbé of the eighteenth century. No drawing room is complete without its politician.

"My dear, this is my cousin, Count Steinbock," said Lisbeth, as she introduced Wenceslas, whom Valérie appeared not to have noticed.

"Yes, indeed; I recognized Monsieur le Comte," said Valérie, with a gracious inclination to the artist. "I often used to see you in the Rue du Doyenné. I had the pleasure of being present at your wedding. My dear," she said to Lisbeth, "it would be difficult to forget your ex-son, even after seeing him only once. Monsieur Stidmann, how good of you," she continued, greeting the sculptor, "to have accepted my invitation at such short notice; but necessity is above the law! I knew that you were the friend of these two gentlemen. And there is nothing more chilling and dreary than a dinner when the guests do not know each other, and so I dragged you in for their sakes; but you will come another time just for mine, won't you? Do say yes!"

And she moved off for a few moments with Stidmann, seeming to be entirely taken up with him. First Crevel, then Baron Hulot, and lastly a deputy named Beauvisage, were announced. This personage, a provincial Crevel, one of those born to make up the undistinguished crowd, voted under the banner of Giraud, the Councilor of State, and of Victorin Hulot. These two politicians were trying to form a nucleus of progressives in the broad ranks of the Conservative party. Giraud sometimes came in the evenings to visit Madame Marneffe, who flattered herself that she would also capture Victorin Hulot; but the puritanical barrister had so far found excuses for refusing both his father and his father-in-law. To visit the house of the woman who caused his mother so many tears seemed to him a crime. Victorin Hulot was, among the puritans of politics, what a pious woman is among the devout. Beauvisage, a one-time hosier of Arcis, was anxious to "pick up the Paris style." This man, one of the outer circle of the Chamber, was under the tutelage of the charming, ravishing Madame Marneffe, having been lured there by Crevel, whom he had accepted, on Valérie's advice, as model and master. He consulted him on all points, asked for the address of his tailor, imitated him, and tried to strike an attitude like Crevel; in short, Crevel was a great man to him. Valérie, surrounded by these great personages, and by the three artists, well seconded by Lisbeth, impressed Wenceslas as a woman of distinction, all the more so as Claude Vignon spoke of her in the tones of a man in love.

"She is Madame de Maintenon[4] in Ninon's skirts!" said the old critic. "You may please her in a single evening, if you are in a witty mood; but to make her love you—that would be a triumph to satisfy a man's ambition, and fill his life!"

Valérie, by seeming cold and indifferent to her old neighbor, wounded his vanity, though quite unconsciously, for she knew nothing of the Polish character. All Slavs have a childish side, like all primitive races, that have not so much become really civilized as irrupted among the civilized nations. This race has spread like a wave, and covered an immense area. It inhabits deserts in whose vast spaces it has room to expand; there is no crowding, as in Europe, and civilization is impossible where there is not a continual jostling of minds and interests. The Ukraine, Russia, the plains of the Danube, in other words, the Slav race, provides a link between Europe and Asia, between civilization and barbarism. And so it is that the Poles, the richest of the Slav nations, have in their character the childish and inconsistent strain of the beardless races. They possess courage, spirit, and energy; but undermined by inconstancy, this courage, and that energy, that spirit, has neither method nor direction, for a Pole is as unstable as the wind that blows on those immense plains, broken with swamps; and although he has the impetuosity of those snowstorms that carry off houses, he is, like those aerial avalanches, lost in the first pool and dissolved into water. Man always assimilates from the environment in which he lives. Forever at war with the Turks, the Poles have become infected with the taste for Oriental magnificence—they often forgo necessities for the sake of display; the men are as vain as women, and yet the climate has given them constitutions as hard as those of Arabs.

The Poles, sublime in suffering, have wearied the armies of their oppressors by dint of their endurance in defeat, and in the nineteenth century have re-enacted the spectacle of the early Christians. Add ten per cent of English caution to the Polish character, so frank and open, and the generous white eagle would reign today in all those regions into which the two-headed eagle[5] has insinuated itself. A little Machiavellianism would have prevented Poland from going to the rescue of Austria, who has partitioned her; from borrowing from Prussia, the usurer who has undermined her; and from breaking up at the time of the first Partition. At the christening of Poland a wicked fairy, forgotten by the genial spirits who doted on that enchanting nation, with all its brilliant qualities, must certainly have come and said: "Keep all the gifts that my sisters have bestowed upon you, but you shall never know what you want!" If, in her heroic duels with Russia, Poland had been victorious, the Poles would have been at war among themselves today, as they formerly fought in their Diets to hinder one another from becoming king. The day when that nation, entirely made up of reckless courage, has the good sense to seek out a Louis XI[6] among her progeny, to accept a tyranny and a dynasty, she will be saved.

What Poland is in politics, most Poles are in their private lives, especially under the stress of disaster. And so Wenceslas Steinbock, who had adored his wife for three years, and who knew that in her eyes he was a god, was so piqued at being hardly noticed by Madame Marneffe that it became a point of honor with him to attract her attention. Comparing her with his wife, he gave Valérie the advantage. Hortense was a beautiful body, as Valérie had said to Lisbeth; but Madame Marneffe was spirited to her finger tips, and had all the attraction of vice. Hortense's devotion was such as a husband takes as his due. The sense of the immense worth of an absolute love is soon lost, just as a debtor, in the course of time, begins to look upon the loan as his. Such high loyalty becomes, as it were, the soul's daily bread, whereas infidelity has the seductiveness of a delicacy. A disdainful woman, and above all a dangerous woman, stimulates curiosity, as spices season good food. Besides, disdain—so well feigned by Valérie—was a new experience for Wenceslas, after three years of pleasures easily enjoyed. Hortense was a wife, but Valérie was a mistress.

Many men wish to possess these two editions of the same work; however, it is a sign of great inferiority in a man to be unable to make his wife his mistress. Vanity, in this respect, is a mark of weakness. Constancy will always be the genius of love, evidence of immense power, the power that makes a poet! A man should be able to find all women in his wife, as the disreputable poets of the seventeenth century did in their Manons as Irises and Chloes.[7]

"Well," said Lisbeth to Wenceslas, when she observed that he was fascinated, "what do you think of Valérie?"

"All too charming," said Wenceslas.

"You would not listen to me," went on Cousin Bette. "Ah, my dear boy, if you and I had remained together you might have been that siren's lover; you could have married her when she became a widow, and had her forty thousand francs a year!"

"Really?"

"Certainly," said Lisbeth. "But now you must be careful. I warned you of the danger; don't go too near the candle flame! Give me your arm—dinner is served."

No words could have been more demoralizing, for you have only to point out a precipice to a Pole and he will immediately throw himself over it. This race has the mentality of a cavalry regiment; they fancy that they can ride down all obstacles and come through victorious. This spur to his vanity, applied by Lisbeth, was driven home by the sight of the dining room, shining with silver plate; here Steinbock saw all the refinement and taste of Parisian luxury.

"I should have done better to marry Célimène,"[8] he thought to himself.

All through dinner Hulot was charming; he was glad to see his son-in-law present, and still more happy because he was certain of a reconciliation with Valérie, whose fidelity he flattered himself that he would be able to assure by the promise of Coquet's post. Stidmann responded to the Baron's amiability by the best sallies of Parisian wit, and his artist's verve. Steinbock would not allow himself to be eclipsed by his friend, and he too exerted his wit, made brilliant sallies, made an impression, and was highly pleased with himself; Madame Marneffe smiled at him several times in order to show him that she entirely understood him. The good food and the heady wines completed the work; Wenceslas was plunged into what one might call the slough of pleasure. After dinner, excited by a shade too much wine, he stretched himself on a divan, and gave himself up to physical and mental well-being, which Madame Marneffe raised to the seventh heaven by coming and sitting beside him, light, scented, and pretty enough to damn the angels. She leaned toward Wenceslas—she almost brushed his ear as she whispered to him.

"We cannot talk business this evening unless you stay till the others have gone. Then you and Lisbeth and I can arrange matters for you."

"You are an angel!" Wenceslas replied in the same low tones. "I was a great fool not to listen to Lisbeth."

"What did she say?"

"She told me, in the Rue du Doyenné, that you were in love with me!"

Madame Marneffe looked at Wenceslas, seemed to be much confused, and got up quickly. A young and beautiful woman cannot with impunity arouse in a man the idea of an immediate success. This gesture of a virtuous woman suppressing a secret passion was a thousand times more eloquent than the most eloquent declaration. Wenceslas's desire was now so thoroughly aroused that he redoubled his attentions to Valérie. A woman in the public eye is a woman coveted! Hence the terrible power of actresses. Madame Marneffe, knowing that she was being looked at, behaved like a popular actress. She was charming, and her triumph was complete.

"My father-in-law's follies no longer surprise me," said Wenceslas to Lisbeth.

"If you talk like that, Wenceslas," said the cousin, "I shall repent to my dying day ever having got you the loan of those ten thousand francs. Are you going to be like the rest of them," she asked, indicating the guests, "madly in love with that creature? Just think, you would be your father-in-law's rival. And besides, think of all the unhappiness you would bring on Hortense."

"That is true," said Wenceslas. "Hortense is an angel. I would be a monster."

"One in the family is quite enough," Lisbeth replied.

"Artists should never marry," Steinbock exclaimed.

"Ah! That is exactly what I said to you in the Rue du Doyenné. Your group and statues, your works, are your children."

"What are you talking about over there?" Valérie asked, coming and joining Lisbeth. "Pour out the tea, Cousin."

Steinbock, out of Polish boastfulness, was eager to appear on terms of familiarity with this drawing-room fairy. Having defied Stidmann, Claude Vignon, and Crevel with a look, he took Valérie's hand, and forced her to sit down beside him on the divan.

"You are much too lordly, Count Steinbock!" she exclaimed, resisting a little.

And she began to laugh as she dropped down beside him, arranging the little rosebud displayed on her bodice as she did so.

"Alas! If I were, I should not come here to borrow money!" he said.

"Poor boy! I remember how you used to work half the night at the Rue du Doyenné. You have been rather a goose! You went and married like a starving man grabbing a loaf. You didn't know Paris! Look where you have landed yourself! But you turned a deaf ear to Bette's devotion, to say nothing of the love of a woman who knows her Paris by heart."

"Don't say any more!" cried Steinbock. "I give in!"

"You shall have your ten thousand francs, my dear Wenceslas; but on one condition," she said, playing with his fine wavy hair.

"What is that?"

"Well, I do not want any interest—"

"Madame!"

"Oh, don't be angry; you shall repay me with a bronze group. You began the story of Samson—finish it. Do Delilah cutting off the hair of her Jewish Hercules! But you, who would be a great artist if you listened to me, I hope that you understand the subject! What you must express is the power of woman. Samson doesn't count. He is the dead body of strength. Delilah is passion, that destroys everything. How much finer," she concluded, seeing Claude Vignon and Stidmann coming over to them, hearing them talking about sculpture, "is that *replica*—is that the right word?—of the story of Hercules at the feet of Omphale[9] than the Greek myth! Did the Greeks copy the Jews, or was it the Jews who took the story from Greece?"

"There, Madame, you raise an important question, that of the period when the different books of the Bible were written. The great and immortal Spinoza, so wrongly ranked among the atheists, who proved the existence of God by mathematics, claimed that Genesis and the political portions, so to speak, of the Bible date from the time of Moses, and he demonstrated the interpolations by means of philological proofs. And for that he was stabbed three times as he went into the synagogue."

"I had no idea I was so learned," said Valérie, annoyed at the interruption of her tête-à-tête.

"Women know everything, by instinct," replied Claude Vignon.

"Well, do you promise?" she said to Steinbock, taking his hand as shyly as a young girl in love.

"You are very lucky, my dear fellow," said Stidmann, "if Madame Marneffe has asked you a favor!"

"What is it?" asked Claude Vignon.

"A little group in bronze," said Steinbock. *"Delilah cutting Samson's hair."*

"Difficult," said Claude Vignon, "because of the bed—"

"On the contrary, nothing could be easier," replied Valérie, with a smile.

"Ah! Let us all become sculptors!" said Stidmann.

"Madame should be your subject!" Vignon replied, with a keen glance at Valérie.

"Well," she went on, "this is how I imagine the composition. Samson has awakened with no hair, like many another dandy with a false wig. The hero is sitting on the bed, so you have only to show the foot of it, hidden by hangings and draperies. He sits there like Marius on the ruins of Carthage, his arms crossed, his head shaved—Napoleon on Saint Helena, don't you know! Delilah is kneeling, more or less like Canova's *Magdalene.* When a woman has ruined her man she adores him. As I see it, the Jewess was afraid of Samson, terrible and strong, but she must have loved Samson the little child again. So Delilah is bewailing her crime; she would gladly give her lover back his hair; she hardly dares to look at him, but she does look at him, with a smile, because in his weakness she reads her forgiveness. This group, and another, of ferocious Judith,[10] is the whole truth about women. Virtue cuts off your head, but vice only cuts off your hair. So look out for your wigs, gentlemen!"

And she left the two artists, quite overcome, to sing her praises, along with the critic.

"She couldn't be more delightful!" exclaimed Stidmann.

"Oh," said Claude Vignon, "she is the most witty and attractive woman I have ever met! The combination of beauty and intelligence is rare indeed!"

"If you, who had the honor of knowing Camille Maupin,[11] can talk like that, what are we to think?" Stidmann went on.

"If you are going to make your Delilah a portrait of Valérie, my dear Count," said Crevel, who had left the card table for a moment, and had overheard the conversation, "I would give a thousand crowns for the group. Yes, by Jove! I will stump up a thousand crowns!"

"Stump up? What does that mean?" Beauvisage asked Claude Vignon.

"If Madame Marneffe will do me the honor of sitting," said Steinbock, to Crevel. "Ask her."

At this moment Valérie herself brought Steinbock a cup of tea. This was more than a mark of attention; it was a favor. There is a whole language in the way in which a woman performs this small action, and women are well aware of this; it is fascinating to study their movements, their expression, their looks, their tone, their accent, when they accomplish this seemingly simple act of politeness. From the question, "Do you take tea?" "Will you have some tea?" "A cup of tea?" coldly asked, and the order given to the nymph presiding over the urn to bring it, to the endless poem of the odalisque[12] coming from the tea table, cup in hand, toward the pasha of her heart, presenting it to him with submissive air, offering it with caressing voice, with a look eloquent with voluptuous promise, a physiologist might observe all the feminine emotions, from aversion, through indifference, to the declaration of Phaedra to Hippolytus.[13] Women can at will make this act contemptuous to the point of insult, or humble to the point of Oriental servility. Valérie was more than a woman. She was the serpent in female form, and she achieved her diabolical work by going up to Steinbock with a cup of tea in her hand.

"I will take," the artist whispered in Valérie's ear, rising and touching her fingers lightly with his own, "as many cups of tea as you care to offer me, to have them brought to me like this!"

"What were you saying about posing?" she asked, without showing that this utterance, so frantically desired, had gone straight to her heart.

"Old Crevel has offered me a thousand crowns for a copy of your group."

"He! A thousand crowns for a bronze?"

"Yes, if you will pose as Delilah," said Steinbock.

"I hope he will not be there!" she said. "For then the group would be worth more than his whole fortune, because Delilah is very scantily clad."

Just as Crevel liked to strike his attitude, so all women have a victorious gesture, a studied pose, in which they know that they are irresistible. There are some who, in a drawing room, spend the whole time looking down at the lace of their tuckers, or adjusting the shoulders of their dresses; others who make play with the brilliance of their eyes by looking up at the cornices. But Madame Marneffe did not triumph front-face like other women. She turned away abruptly, to return to Lisbeth at the tea table. That dancer's gesture, with the movement of her skirts, that had captivated Hulot, bewitched Steinbock.

"Your vengeance is complete," Valérie whispered to Lisbeth.

"Hortense will weep bitter tears, and curse the day when she took Wenceslas from you."

"Nothing is complete until I am Madame la Maréchale," replied the peasant; "but *they* are all beginning to want it. This morning I saw Victorin. I forgot to tell you. The young Hulots have bought back the Baron's notes of hand from Vauvinet, and tomorrow they are going to put their names to a guarantee for seventy-two thousand francs at five per cent, payable in three years, with a mortgage on their house. So the young Hulots are in straits for the next three years, and they won't be able to raise any more money on that property. Victorin is terribly upset; he has discovered the truth about his father. And Crevel is quite capable of refusing to see them again; he will be so annoyed about this act of self-sacrifice."

"Has the Baron nothing left?" Valérie whispered to Lisbeth, smiling at Hulot as she did so.

"Nothing that I know of. But he will draw his salary again from next September."

"And he has his insurance policy; he has renewed it. Dear me, it is time he made Marneffe a head clerk—I will fix him this evening."

"My dear Wenceslas," Lisbeth said, going over to the artist, "you really must go home; you are making a fool of yourself, looking at Valérie in that compromising way, and her husband is madly jealous. Don't follow the example of your father-in-law. Go home. I am sure Hortense will be waiting up for you."

"Madame Marneffe asked me to wait until the others had gone, to arrange our little business together," Wenceslas replied.

"No," said Lisbeth, "I will send you the ten thousand francs. Her husband has his eye on you; it would be unwise to stay. Bring the bill of exchange at eleven tomorrow; that yellow-faced[14] Marneffe is in his office at that time and Valérie will be free. Have you really asked her to pose for a group? Come up to me first. Ah! I always knew," said Lisbeth, catching a look that Steinbock flashed at Valérie, "that you were a budding libertine. Valérie is very beautiful, but try not to bring trouble on Hortense."

Nothing is so irritating to a married man as to have his wife, at every turn, interposed between himself and his desire, however transient.

Chapter XXIII

Wenceslas returned home at about one in the morning. Hortense had been expecting him since half-past nine. From half-past nine to ten she had listened to the sound of carriages, thinking to herself that Wenceslas had never come home so late from dining with Chanor and Florent. She sat and sewed beside her son's cradle, for she had begun to economize on the wages of a sewing-woman by doing some of the mending herself. From ten to half-past a suspicion crossed her mind, and she wondered.

"Has he really gone to dine with Chanor and Florent, as he told me? He chose his best cravat and best tie-pin when he dressed. He took as long over his toilet as a woman who wants to look her best.... Ridiculous! He loves me.... And here he is."

Instead of stopping, the carriage that the young wife had heard went past. From eleven until midnight Hortense was tormented by every kind of fear, for the quarter where they lived was deserted.

"If he set out on foot," she thought to herself, "some accident may have happened to him! Men have been known to kill themselves by tripping over a curb, or by not noticing holes in the road. Artists are so careless. What if he has been stopped by thieves? This is the first time he has left me here alone for six hours and a half. But what am I worrying about? He is not in love with anyone except me."

Men ought to be faithful to wives who love them, if only because of the perpetual miracles wrought by real love in that sublime region that we call the world of the spirit. A woman in love is, in relation to the man she loves, in the position of a somnambulist to whom the hypnotist has given the unfortunate faculty of knowing, as a woman (when she has ceased to be the mirror of the world), what she observed as a somnambulist. Passion induces in a woman's nervous system that ecstatic condition in which presentiment is as acute as the vision of a clairvoyant. A woman knows when she is betrayed, but she will not let herself know it; she doubts her own knowledge, because she loves. She refuses to listen to the voice of the Pythian oracle within her. This extremity of love should command an all-but-religious veneration. In noble minds respect for this holy phenomenon will always be a barrier against infidelity. How should a man not love a beautiful and intelligent being whose soul attains to such heights? . . . By one in the morning Hortense had reached such a degree of anxiety that she rushed to the door when she recognized Wenceslas's ring. She flung her arms around him and clasped him like a mother.

"Here you are at last!" she said, recovering her powers of speech. "Darling, after this wherever you go I shall go with you, because I could not endure the torture of waiting like this for you again. I imagined you tripping over a curbstone and fracturing your skull! Killed by thieves! No, if it happened again I should go mad. So you enjoyed yourself? Without me? How could you!"

"What can I say, darling angel? Bixiou was there, and he brought us some new commissions; Léon de Lora, whose wit never dries up; Claude Vignon, to whom I am indebted for the only favorable notice I have had on the monument of Marshal Montcornet. There was—"

"There were no women?"

"The worthy Madame Florent—"

"You told me it was at the Rocher de Cancale.[1] Was it at their house, then?"

"Yes, it was. I made a mistake."

"Did you not take a cab home?"

"No."

"You walked all the way from Rue des Tournelles?"

"Stidmann and Bixiou walked back with me along the boulevards as far as the Madeleine, talking all the way."

"It must have been dry, then, on the boulevards, and the Place de la Concorde and the Rue du Bourgogne, because your shoes are not muddy," said Hortense, looking at her husband's patent-leather boots.

It had been raining; but Wenceslas had not got his feet wet between the Rue Vanneau and the Rue Saint-Dominique.

"Look, here are five thousand francs that Chanor has very kindly lent me," said Wenceslas, in order to cut short this cross-questioning.

He had divided his ten thousand-franc notes into two packets, one for Hortense, another for himself; for he had some five thousand francs' worth of debts that Hortense did not know about. He owed money to his figure-carver and his workmen.

"Now you need not worry, my darling," he said, kissing his wife. "I am going to work from tomorrow on. Tomorrow I shall be off to the studio at half-past eight. I shall go to bed at once, so as to get up in good time, if you will forgive me, my sweet."

The suspicion that had formed in Hortense's mind vanished; she was a thousand miles away from the truth. Madame Marneffe! The idea never entered her head. What she feared for her Wenceslas was the company of courtesans. The names of Bixiou and Léon de Lora, two artists notorious for their wild life, had alarmed her.

Next day she saw Wenceslas off at nine o'clock, entirely reassured.

"Now he has started work," she thought to herself, as she dressed her baby. "I see he is in the mood. Well, if we cannot have the glory of Michelangelo, we shall at least have that of Benvenuto Cellini."

Lulling herself in her own hopes, Hortense dreamed of a happy future; and she was talking to her son, aged twenty months, in that nonsense language that makes babies laugh when, at about eleven, the cook, who had not seen Wenceslas go out, announced Stidmann.

"Do forgive me," said the artist. "Has Wenceslas gone out already?"

"He is at his studio."

"I came to talk over our work with him."

"I will send someone to fetch him," said Hortense, offering Stidmann a chair.

The young wife, thanking Heaven inwardly for this lucky chance, was anxious to keep Stidmann in order to hear more about the previous evening. Stidmann bowed to the Countess in acknowledgment of this favor. Madame Steinbock rang, the cook appeared, and she sent her off to the studio in search of the master.

"Did you have an amusing evening last night?" said Hortense. "Wenceslas did not get back until one."

"Amusing? I would not exactly say that," said the artist, who had been trying to "make"[2] Madame Marneffe the night before. "Society is not very amusing unless one is hoping to get something out of it. That little Madame Marneffe is certainly very amusing, but she is a flirt."

"And what did Wenceslas think of her?" poor Hortense asked, trying to keep calm. "He didn't tell me."

"I will only tell you one thing," said Stidmann, "and that is, that I think she is a very dangerous woman."

Hortense turned as pale as a woman in childbirth.

"So then it was . . . at Madame Marneffe's . . . and not at the Chanors' that you dined . . ." she stammered, ". . . last night . . . with Wenceslas, and he . . ."

Stidmann, without realizing the nature of his blunder, realized that he had made one. The Countess did not finish her sentence, but fainted completely.

The artist rang, and the maid came in. When Louise tried to help the Countess Steinbock to her room she fell into a fit of alarming hysterics. Stidmann, like all those who have destroyed the carefully erected fabrication of a man's lie to his family, could not imagine why his words had had such an effect; he supposed that the Countess must be in a delicate state, in which the slightest contradiction was dangerous. The cook returned and said—in a loud voice, unfortunately—that the master was not at his studio. In the midst of her attack the Countess heard this answer, and the hysterics began again.

"Go and fetch Madame's mother!" said Louise to the cook. "Run!"

"If I knew where to find Wenceslas, I would go and tell him," said Stidmann, in despair.

"He is with that woman!" cried poor Hortense. "He dressed very differently from when he goes to his studio."

Stidmann rushed to Madame Marneffe's, realizing the likelihood of this guess, the product of passion's second sight. At this moment Valérie was posing as Delilah. Stidmann was too clever to ask for Madame Marneffe, but went straight past the porter's lodge, and quickly ran up to the second floor, thinking to himself: "If I ask for Madame Marneffe she will certainly be out; if I ask bluntly for Steinbock they will laugh in my face. I will take them by storm." Reine came in answer to his ring.

"Please tell Count Steinbock to come at once; his wife is dying."

Reine, who was a match for Stidmann, looked at him with an expression of convincing stupidity. "But, sir, I don't understand . . . what did you . . ."

"I tell you my friend Steinbock is here; his wife is dying, and the matter is serious enough for you to disturb your mistress."

And Stidmann went away.

"He is there, all right," he thought to himself. And sure enough, Stidmann, who waited for a few minutes in the Rue Vanneau, saw Wenceslas come out, and signed him to hurry. Having told him of the tragedy that was in progress at Rue Saint-Dominique, Stidmann scolded Steinbock for not having warned him to keep quiet about the dinner of the previous evening.

"I am done for," said Wenceslas, "but I forgive you. I forgot all about our appointment for this morning, and I ought to have told you that—we were supposed to be dining with Florent. Well, there it is. That Valérie has made me mad; but, my dear fellow, she is worth the price of glory, and of misfortune ... Ah, she is ... Good Lord, what a dreadful situation I am in! Give me some advice! What shall I say? What excuse shall I make?"

"Give you advice? I have none to give," said Stidmann. "But your wife loves you, doesn't she? Well, she will believe anything. Tell her, anyhow, that you had gone to find me, while I was looking for you. That will at least explain this morning's session. Goodbye!"

Bette, warned by Reine, hurried after Steinbock and overtook him at the corner of Rue Hillerin-Bertin. She was afraid on account of his Polish naïveté. Not wishing to be compromised, she said a few words to Wenceslas, who, in his joy, kissed her in the public street. She had, no doubt, given the artist a plank on which to cross this pitfall of married life.

On seeing her mother, who had hurried to her side, Hortense had burst into floods of tears. The nervous crisis took a favorable turn.

"He has deceived me, Mamma dear!" she said to her. "Wenceslas, after giving me his word of honor not to visit Madame Marneffe, dined there yesterday, and did not come home until a quarter past one! If you only knew! Last night we had not exactly a quarrel, but an explanation, and I begged and pleaded with him! I said I was jealous, and that I should die if he were to be unfaithful; that I knew I was suspicious, but that he ought to have some consideration for my failings, when they come from my love for him; that I had my father's blood in my veins, as well as yours. That if I were to discover an infidelity I was capable of anything, of taking my revenge, of dishonoring us all—himself, his son, and myself! And that I was even capable of killing him, and myself afterwards! And more besides. And he went there, and he is there now! That woman is determined to ruin us all! Yesterday Victorin and Célestine pledged themselves to pay back seventy-two thousand francs, borrowed in the name of that wretched man! Yes, Mamma, they were going to sue my father, and send him to prison! That abominable woman—is she not content with my father, and with your tears? Need she take Wenceslas from me? I shall go there and stab her!"

Madame Hulot, stricken to the heart by the dreadful secret that Hortense in her fury had betrayed without realizing that she had done so, controlled her grief by one of those heroic efforts of which really great mothers are capable, and drew her daughter's head on to her bosom and covered it with kisses.

"Wait until Wenceslas comes, my child, and he will be able to explain everything. It may not be so bad as you think! I have been deceived too, darling Hortense. You think I am beautiful, and I have been faithful, but in spite of that I have been deserted for twenty-three years now, for women like Jenny Cadine, and Josépha, and this Marneffe! Did you know?"

"You, Mamma, you! You have endured that for twenty—" She stopped short, appalled by her own thoughts.

"Do as I have done, my child," the mother continued. "Be gentle, and kind, and your conscience will be at peace. If a man can say on his deathbed, 'My wife has never caused me the smallest pain!' God, who hears these last words, counts it in our favor. If I had abandoned myself to rages like yours, what would the result have been? Your father would have become embittered; perhaps he would have left me, and he would not have been held in check by the fear of hurting me; our ruin, that is complete today, to be sure, might have come about ten years ago, and the world would have seen the spectacle of a husband and wife living apart—the worst kind of scandal, heartbreaking, because it means the death of the family. Neither you nor your brother would have been given a start in life. I have sacrificed myself and put such a brave face on it that until this last intrigue of your father's the world has always imagined that I was happy. My opportune, not to say courageous, dissembling has protected Hector so far; he is still respected; only this old man's passion is carrying him too far, I can see. His folly, I am afraid, will break through the screen that I have kept between us and the world. But I have kept it up for twenty-three years, this curtain behind which I have wept, without a mother, or a friend, or any other support than that of religion; I have saved the honor of the family for twenty-three years."

Hortense listened to her mother with a fixed gaze. Her calm voice, and the resignation of that supreme suffering, soothed the smart of the young wife's first wound. Her tears came, and fell in torrents. In an excess of filial love, overcome by her mother's nobility, she knelt at her feet, and kissed the hem of her dress as pious Catholics kiss the holy relics of a martyr.

"Get up, my Hortense," said the Baroness. "Such understanding from my daughter wipes out many sad memories. Come into my arms. Your own trouble is all you need be distressed about. The desperation of my own poor little girl, whose happiness was my only joy, has broken the seal of absolute silence that nothing else would have made me break. Yes, I hoped to take my sorrow to the grave, like one more shroud. I only spoke in order to quiet your frenzy, God forgive me! Oh, if you were to have my life, I do not know what I should do! Men, the world, fate, nature, and even God, I believe, make us pay for love with the worst of torments. I shall have paid for ten years of happiness with twenty-four years of despair, ceaseless sorrow, and bitterness."

"You had ten years, dearest Mamma, and I have had only three!" she exclaimed, in the egoism of her own love.

"Nothing is lost, my child. Wait until Wenceslas comes."

"Mother," she cried, "he lied to me! He deceived me! He said that he would not go, and he went! And that beside his child's cradle!"

"My angel, men will commit the most cowardly, shameful acts for the sake of their pleasures—crimes even; that is their nature, it seems. We wives are marked out for sacrifice. I thought my troubles were over, but they are only just beginning, for I never expected to suffer all over again for my daughter. Courage, and silence! My Hortense, promise not to speak of your troubles to anyone except me, not to let any third person suspect them.... Come, be as proud as your mother!"

Hortense started at this moment, for she heard her husband's step.

"I hear that Stidmann came to look for me here, while I was looking for him in his rooms."

"Indeed!" exclaimed poor Hortense, with the savage irony of an injured woman, who uses words as weapons.

"Yes, we have only just met," replied Wenceslas, feigning astonishment.

"And yesterday?" Hortense continued.

"Well, yes, I did deceive you, darling love, and your mother shall judge."

This frankness was a relief to Hortense's heart. All really noble women prefer truth to lies. They cannot bear to see their idol degraded; they like to be proud of the man whom they allow to dominate them. The Russians have something of the same feeling in relation to their Czar.

"Listen, Mother dear," said Wenceslas. "I love my good sweet Hortense so much that I concealed our financial straits from her. What else could I have done? She was still a nursing mother, and worries would have been very bad for her. You know how much a woman risks at that time. Her beauty, her health, and her youth are all in danger. Was that wrong? She thought that we owed only five thousand francs, but I owed another five thousand. . . . The day before yesterday we were in despair! Nobody in the world will lend money to an artist. They no more believe in our talents than in our imaginations. I have knocked at all the doors in vain. Lisbeth offered us her savings."

"Poor soul!" said Hortense.

"Poor soul," said the Baroness.

"But what use were Lisbeth's two thousand francs? They are her all, and they would have been no help to us. And then our cousin spoke, as you know, Hortense, of Madame Marneffe, who, from a sense of honor, as she owes everything to the Baron, would not take even the smallest interest. Hortense wanted to pawn her diamonds. They would have brought us a few thousand francs, but we needed ten thousand. And those ten thousand were available, for a year, and without interest! I said to myself, 'Hortense need not know. I shall take them.' This woman invited me to dinner yesterday, through my father-in-law, giving me to understand that Lisbeth had spoken to her, and that I could have the money. Between despair for Hortense, and accepting that invitation, I did not hesitate. That is all. How could Hortense, at twenty-four, pure and faithful, who is all my happiness and my pride, whom I have never left since we were married, imagine that I could prefer—what? A hard-mouthed, hard-baked, hard-boiled creature," he said, using vulgar slang in order to drive home his contempt by one of those exaggerations that women like.

"Ah! if your father had ever been so open with me!" exclaimed the Baroness.

Hortense threw her arms affectionately around her husband's neck.

"Yes, I would have done the same," said Adeline. "Wenceslas, my dear, your wife might have died," she went on, in a serious tone. "You see how much she loves you, and, alas, she is yours." And she sighed deeply.

"He could either make her a martyr or a happy woman," she thought to herself, thinking those thoughts that all mothers think when their daughters are married. "It seems to me," she added aloud, "that I am unhappy enough to be allowed to see my children happy."

"Do not worry, Mother dear," said Wenceslas, delighted beyond measure to see this crisis happily ended. "Within two months I shall have paid the money back to that dreadful woman. What else could I have done?" he went on, repeating his typically Polish phrase with Polish grace. "There are times when one would borrow from the Devil himself. After all, the money belongs to the family, and since she invited me, should I have been able to get this money, that has cost us so dear, if I had responded rudely to her politeness?"

"Oh, Mamma, what trouble Papa is bringing on us!" cried Hortense.

The Baroness laid her finger to her lips, and Hortense wished she had not spoken. These were the first words of blame that she had ever spoken of the father so heroically protected by her mother's sublime silence.

"Goodbye, my children," said Madame Hulot. "The sun is shining again; but don't quarrel any more."

When Wenceslas and his wife had returned to their room, after seeing the Baroness to the door, Hortense said to her husband, "Tell me about your evening!"

And she scrutinized Wenceslas's face as he told his story, interrupting him with all those questions that rise to the lips of a wife in such circumstances. This account made Hortense thoughtful, because she divined the diabolical amusement that artists must find in such vicious company.

"Be honest, Wenceslas! Stidmann was there, and Claude Vignon, and Vernisset, and who else? In fact, it was amusing?"

"For my part, I was thinking only of our ten thousand francs, and I thought to myself, 'My Hortense will be worrying.' "

The Livonian found this cross-questioning very exhausting, and he took advantage of a moment of gaiety to say to Hortense, "And what would you have done, my angel, if your artist had been guilty?"

"I?" she said, with an air of decision. "I would have taken Stidmann for a lover, but without being in love with him, of course."

"Hortense!" exclaimed Steinbock, getting up abruptly, with a theatrical gesture. "You would not have had time. I would have killed you!"

Hortense flung herself into her husband's arms and clung to him, covered him with kisses, and exclaimed, "So you love me, Wenceslas! Come, you have nothing to fear! But no more Marneffe! Never plunge into a sink of vice like that again!"

"I swear to you, my darling Hortense, that I will never go back there, except to redeem my bill of exchange!"

She sulked, but only as women in love sulk, in order to make her point. Wenceslas, exhausted by such a morning, let his wife sulk; and went off to his studio, where he made a *maquette* for the group of *Samson and Delilah,* the sketch for which was in his pocket.

Hortense, repentant because she had sulked, and thinking that Wenceslas was annoyed, arrived at the studio just as her husband had finished molding the clay with the rage that inspires artists when the creative mood is on them. At the sight of his wife Wenceslas hastily threw a damp cloth over the rough design for the group, and took Hortense in his arms, saying, "We are not angry, are we, my puss?"

Hortense had seen the group, and the cloth thrown over it, and said nothing. But before she left the studio she turned back, took off the rag, and looked at the *maquette.*

"What is this?"

"A group that I thought of doing."

"Why did you hide it from me?"

"I didn't want you to see it until it was finished."

"The woman is very pretty!" said Hortense. And a thousand suspicions sprang up in her soul, like the dense rank tropical vegetation that in India springs up overnight.

Chapter XXIV

By the end of about three weeks Madame Marneffe was becoming profoundly irritated by Hortense. Such women have their pride; they want men to kiss the Devil's hoof, and they never forgive virtue that does not fear their power or that stands its ground against them. Now, Wenceslas had not paid a single visit to the Rue Vanneau, not even the courtesy visit that he owed to a woman who had posed as Delilah. Whenever Lisbeth had gone to visit the Steinbocks she had found them out. They were living in the studio. Lisbeth, tracking the two turtledoves to their nest at Gros-Caillou, found Wenceslas hard at work, and was told by the cook that

Madame never left him. Wenceslas had submitted to the despotism of love. Valérie, therefore, took sides with Lisbeth for reasons of her own in her hatred of Hortense. Women refuse to let go of a lover for whom another woman is competing, just as men do of women who are desired by more fools than one. And any reflections here made on the subject of Madame Marneffe apply equally well to male adventurers, who are the equivalent of courtesans. Valérie's whim became an obsession; she was determined to have her group at all costs, and she was promising herself to go, one morning, to see Wenceslas at his studio, when a serious event occurred, of a kind that for a woman like herself can only be called one of the fortunes of war.

Valérie announced the news of this very personal event as follows. She was breakfasting with Lisbeth and Monsieur Marneffe.

"Tell me, Marneffe, what would you say to being a father for the second time?"

"Are you pregnant, really? May I kiss you?" He rose, went to the other side of the table, and his wife offered him her brow in such a way as to receive his kiss on her hair.

"Then I am a head clerk and officer of the Legion of Honor at one go! All the same, my dear, I don't want to see Stanislaus suffer for it! Poor little fellow!"

"Poor little fellow?" said Lisbeth. "You haven't set eyes on him for seven months; they think at the school that I am his mother, because I am the only person in this house who ever does anything about him!"

"A child that costs us a hundred crowns every three months!" said Valérie. "And besides, he at least is your child, Marneffe! You ought to pay for his schooling out of your salary. The new one, instead of reminding us of shopkeepers' bills, will save us from want."

"Valérie," said Marneffe, imitating Crevel's pose, "I hope that Monsieur le Baron Hulot will look after his son, and that he will not lay the burden on a poor civil servant. I propose to take a firm line with him. So get your evidence, Madame! Try to get letters from him in which he speaks of his happiness, because he isn't being very forthcoming over my nomination."

And Marneffe set out for the Ministry, at which, thanks to the valuable friendship of his director, he did not need to arrive before eleven; he did, moreover, very little work when he got there, for his inefficiency was as notorious as his aversion to work.

When they were alone Lisbeth and Valérie looked at each other for a moment like two Augurs, and broke simultaneously into a great fit of laughter.

"Look here, Valérie, is it true?" said Lisbeth. "Or just a farce?"

"It is a physical fact!" said Valérie. "I am sick of Hortense. And last night it occurred to me that I might throw this infant like a bombshell into Wenceslas's household."

Valérie went into her room, followed by Lisbeth, and showed her the following letter, already written:

> WENCESLAS MY DEAR,
>
> I still believe in your love, although I have not seen you for nearly three weeks. Do you despise me? Delilah can hardly believe it. Is it not, rather, the result of the tyranny of a woman whom you told me you would never be able to love again? Wenceslas, you are too great an artist to allow yourself to be dominated like that. The home is the tomb of glory. Is there nothing left of the old Wenceslas of the Rue du Doyenné? You failed with my father's statue; but in you the lover is greater than the artist, and you had better luck with his daughter; and you are a father, my adored Wenceslas. If you don't come and see me in my present condition, your friends will have a very poor opinion of you, but I love you so madly that I feel I should never have the strength to blame you. May I still sign myself,
>
> YOUR VALÉRIE?

"What do you say to my sending this letter to the studio to arrive when our dear Hortense is alone there?" said Valérie to Lisbeth.

"Last night I found out from Stidmann that Wenceslas is going to fetch him at eleven to go and see Chanor about some commission; so that great lump Hortense will be alone."

"After such a trick," Lisbeth replied, "I would not be able to remain your friend openly. I would have to break with you, to be thought not to visit you any more, or even to speak to you."

"Obviously," said Valérie, "but—"

"Oh, don't worry," Lisbeth broke in. "We shall meet again when I am Madame la Maréchale; *they* are all for it now; the Baron is the only one who does not know of the scheme, but you can bring him around."

"But," said Valérie, "it is quite possible that I shall soon be on cool terms with the Baron."

"Madame Olivier is the only person who can make sure of Hortense getting the letter," said Lisbeth; "we must send her first to Rue Saint-Dominique, before she goes on to the studio."

"Oh! Our little beauty will be at home," replied Madame Marneffe, ringing for Reine, to send in search of Madame Olivier.

Ten minutes after the dispatch of that fatal letter Baron Hulot arrived. Madame Marneffe, with the grace of a kitten, flung her arms around the old man's neck.

"Hector! You are a father!" she whispered in his ear. "That is what comes of quarreling and making it up again!"

Noticing a look of astonishment that the Baron did not conceal quickly enough, Valérie put on a cold manner, which reduced the Councilor of State to despair. She made him draw from her one by one the most convincing proofs. When conviction, led on by vanity, had taken possession of the old man's mind, she told him of Monsieur Marneffe's wrath.

"My dear old veteran," she said, "you can scarcely refuse to get your acting editor,[1] or our managing director if you like, nominated as a head clerk and officer of the Legion of Honor, because, poor man, you have ruined him; he adores Stanislaus, that little monstrosity who is so like him, and whom I cannot endure. Unless you would prefer to settle an annuity of twelve hundred francs on

Stanislaus—the capital to be his, I mean, and the interest in my name?"

"But if I make any settlement, I should prefer it to be in the name of my son, and not on the monstrosity!" said the Baron.

This rash utterance, in which the phrase "my son" came out as roundly as a river in flood, was transformed by the end of an hour's discussion into a formal promise to settle an annuity of twelve hundred francs on the future child. And this promise was, on Valérie's tongue and in her face, what a drum is to a child; she played on it incessantly for three weeks.

Just as Baron Hulot was leaving the Rue Vanneau, as happy as a husband after a year of marriage who wants an heir, Madame Olivier had allowed Hortense to extract from her the letter that she had been asked to deliver only into the Count's own hands. The young wife paid a twenty-franc piece for this letter. The suicide pays for his opium, or his pistol, or his charcoal. Hortense read and reread the letter; she could see only a white paper crossed by black lines—there was nothing in the whole universe but this letter. She was in utter darkness. The light of the conflagration that was devouring the edifice of her happiness lit up this paper in the blackness of night that surrounded her. The voice of her little Wenceslas, playing near, reached her ears as if he had been at the bottom of a valley, and herself on the summit. To be thus outraged, at twenty-four, in the full splendor of her beauty, enhanced by a pure and devoted love, was more than a wound: it was death itself. The first attack had been purely nervous—her body had given way under the stress of jealousy; but now that certainty attacked her soul she was unconscious of her body. Hortense remained thus stunned for about ten minutes. Her mother's image rose to her mind, and wrought a revolution in her; she became calm and cold, and recovered the use of her reason. She rang.

"My dear, ask Louise to help you," she said to the cook. "You must pack, as quickly as possible, everything here that belongs to me, or to my son. I give you an hour. When everything is ready go to the square and fetch a cab, and tell me. Don't ask any questions!

I am leaving the house, and I shall take Louise with me. You must stay with the master; take good care of him. . . ."

And she went into her room, sat down at her table, and wrote the following letter:

MONSIEUR LE COMTE,

The enclosed letter will explain to you the resolution that I have taken.

When you read these lines I shall have left your house, and returned to my mother's, with our child. Do not imagine that I shall ever go back on this decision. If you attribute this act to the impetuosity of youth, or impulse, or the rashness of young love, outraged, you will be utterly mistaken.

I have thought a great deal, during the last fortnight, about life, and love, and our marriage, and our mutual responsibilities. I know all about my mother's devotion, for she has told me of her sufferings. She has been heroic, daily, for the past twenty-three years; but I do not feel that I have the strength to imitate her, not because I love you less than she loves my father, but by reason of my character. Our home would become a hell, and I might lose my head to the point of disgracing you, myself, and our child. I do not wish to be a Madame Marneffe; and, in that career, a woman of my temperament would probably stop at nothing. I am, unluckily for myself, a Hulot and not a Fischer.

Alone, and away from the spectacle of your dissipations, I can keep control of myself, especially with our child to look after, and with my strong and noble mother, whose example will restrain the wild impulses of my emotions. There I can be a good mother, bring up our son well, and live. With you, the wife would destroy the mother, and incessant quarrels would embitter my character.

I can accept a death blow, but I could not endure to suffer for twenty-five years, like my mother. If you have, after three years, betrayed an absolute, constant love, for your father-in-law's mistress, what sort of rivals would you give me later? Alas, you have begun your career as a libertine much earlier than my father, with the looseness that is a disgrace to the father of a family, that loses the respect of his children, and that leads at last to shame and despair.

I am not unforgiving. Implacable resentment is not becoming in any frail creature, living under the eye of God. If you achieve success and fame by continuous work, if you give up courtesans, and ignoble and unworthy courses, you will still find in me a wife worthy of you.

I believe you to be too much of a gentleman to go to law. You will respect my wish, Monsieur le Comte, in leaving me with my mother; and above all, do not ever come there. I am leaving you all the money that you borrowed from that vile woman. Good-bye.

HORTENSE HULOT.

This letter was written with difficulty. Hortense repeatedly broke down in tears, and the cries of murdered passion. She laid down her pen, and took it up again, to express simply what love commonly proclaims in such testamentary letters. She poured out her heart in exclamations, cries, and tears; but her letter was dictated by reason.

The young wife, on being told by Louise that all was ready, went slowly round the little garden, the bedroom, and the drawing room, looking at everything for the last time. Then she gave the cook the most urgent instructions to look after the master well, promising to reward her if she would be honest. At last she got into the cab to go to her mother's, her heart broken, weeping so much that her maid was quite distressed, kissing little Wenceslas in a way that betrayed her still great love for his father.

The Baroness had already heard from Lisbeth that the father-in-law was largely to blame for the son-in-law's fault, and she was not surprised to see her daughter arrive, approved of her action, and agreed to keep her with her. Adeline, seeing that sweetness and devotion had never checked Hector, for whom her respect was beginning to grow less, thought that her daughter had done right in taking another course. Within three weeks the poor mother had received two wounds that caused her greater suffering than all the tortures that she had endured hitherto. The Baron had placed Victorin and his wife in difficulties; and now he was the cause, according to Lisbeth, of Wenceslas's lapse, and had corrupted his son-in-law. The dignity of the father of the family, so long upheld at the price of so many absurd sacrifices, had been degraded. Although they did not grudge their money, the younger Hulots felt both mistrust and anxiety with regard to the Baron. This ill-concealed sentiment was a cause of deep distress to Adeline, who foresaw the breakup of the family. The Baroness gave her daughter the dining room, which was quickly transformed into a bedroom, with the help of the Marshal's money; and the hall was made, as in many households, into the dining room.

When Wenceslas returned home, and had read both the letters, he felt a kind of joy, mingled with sadness. Kept so constantly under observation, so to speak, by his wife, he had inwardly rebelled against this new servitude, after the style of Lisbeth. Sated with love for three years, he, too, had been thinking during the past fortnight; and he found the family burdensome. He had just been congratulated by Stidmann on the passion he had inspired in Valérie; for Stidmann, with an ulterior motive not difficult to guess, thought fit to flatter the vanity of Hortense's husband in the hope of consoling the victim. So Wenceslas was glad to be able to return to Madame Marneffe. And yet he remembered the perfect and pure happiness that he had enjoyed with Hortense, all her perfections, her wisdom, her innocent and unfeigned love, and he missed her desperately. He would gladly have gone at once to his mother-in-law to beg for forgiveness, but, like Hulot and Crevel, he went instead to see Madame Marneffe, to whom he took his wife's letter to show her what a disaster she had caused, and to diminish this misfortune, so to speak, by demanding in return the pleasures his mistress could bestow. He found Crevel with Valérie. The Mayor, puffed up with pride, was walking up and down in the drawing room in the manner of a man laboring under a violent emotion. He took up his position, as if he were about to speak, but dared not. His face was radiant, and he went to the window, tapping the panes with his fingers. He looked at Valérie with a soft and tender expression. Fortunately for Crevel, Lisbeth came in.

"Cousin," he whispered to her, "do you know the news? I am a father! I do not seem to love my poor Célestine so much. Oh! What it is to have a child by a woman that one adores! To combine paternity of the heart with that of the blood! Look here, tell Valérie! I shall work for that child; I will make him rich! She tells me that she thinks, from certain indications, that it will be a boy! If it's a boy, I want him to have the name Crevel: I shall see my lawyer."

"I know how much she loves you," said Lisbeth; "but for the sake of your future and hers control yourself, and don't rub your hands every two minutes."

During this aside between Lisbeth and Crevel, Valérie had asked Wenceslas to return her letter, and whispered in his ear proposals that banished all his grief.

"Now you are free, my dear," she said. "Ought great artists ever to marry? Freedom and impulse is life to you. Come, I shall love you so much, my dearest poet, that you will not miss your wife. All the same, if, like a great many men, you wish to preserve appearances, I promise you that I can arrange for Hortense to return to you in no time."

"Oh! If only that were possible!"

"I am sure of it," said Valérie, annoyed. "Your poor father-in-law is finished, in every way, and out of vanity he wants to have it thought that he is loved, wants people to think that he has a mistress; and he is so vain in this matter that I can persuade him to do anything. The Baroness is still so much in love with her old Hector—I always feel as if I were talking about the *Iliad*—that the two old people will manage to persuade Hortense to patch things up with you. Only, if you want to avoid trouble at home, don't stay away from your mistress for three weeks . . . I was dying. My dear, a gentleman owes some consideration to a woman he has compromised as you have compromised me, especially when the woman has to be so careful about her reputation ... stay to dinner, my angel ... and remember that I shall have to be all the more cold with you, as you are the author of this all-too-obvious mistake."

Baron Montès was announced. Valérie rose, ran to meet him, and whispered to him for a few moments, impressing on him the same conditions of reserve in behavior as she had just done with Wenceslas; for the Brazilian wore a diplomatic expression appropriate to the great news that filled him with joy, for he, at least, was certain of his paternity!

Thanks to this strategy, based on the vanity of men in the capacity of lovers, Valérie sat at her table surrounded by four men, all happy, animated, and under her spell, believing themselves adored, whom Marneffe called, jokingly, to Lisbeth, including himself, the five Fathers of the Church.

Only Baron Hulot at first looked worried. For on leaving his office he had been to see the head of the Personnel Department, a general, his comrade for thirty years, and he had raised the question of appointing Marneffe to Coquet's place, the latter having agreed to resign.

"My dear fellow," he said, "I would not ask this favor of the Marshal without talking it over with you, and having your agreement."

"My dear fellow," replied the Director of Personnel, "allow me to observe that for your own sake you would do well not to press for this appointment. I have already given you my views. It would create a scandal in the department, where there is already a great deal too much talk about yourself and Madame Marneffe. This is absolutely between ourselves. I do not want to touch you on a sensitive spot, or to disoblige you in any way, and I will prove it. If you absolutely insist, if you are determined to ask for Coquet's place—and he will be a real loss to the War Ministry, for he has been here since 1809—I shall go into the country for a fortnight, and leave you a clear field with the Marshal, who loves you like a son. In that way I shall be neither for nor against, and I shall have a clear conscience as an administrator."

"Thank you," said the Baron. "I shall think over what you have said."

"If I have spoken in this way, my dear fellow, it is much more in your own interest than because it concerns me or my vanity. In the first place, the Marshal has the last word. And besides, my dear fellow, we are all blamed for so many things—what is one more or less? We are not new to it, when it comes to being criticized. Under the Restoration men were nominated just in order to give them appointments, regardless of their fitness for the job. You and I are old comrades."

"Yes," the Baron broke in, "and it is just because I do not want to compromise an old and valued friendship that I—"

"Well, well," said the Director of Personnel, seeing embarrassment written on Hulot's face, "I will go off, my dear fellow.... But be careful! You have enemies—that is to say, men who would like to have your high appointment—and you are only held by one anchor. Ah! if you were only a deputy, like me, you would have nothing to worry about. So go carefully."

This speech, delivered in all friendship, made a deep impression on the Councilor of State.

"But after all, Roger, what is all the fuss about? Don't keep things back from me!"

The individual addressed as Roger looked at Hulot, took his hand, and pressed it.

"We have been friends too long for me not to warn you. If you want to keep your place, you will have to look after your own interests. In fact, in your position, instead of asking the Marshal to give Coquet's place to Marneffe, I would ask him to use his influence to reserve a place for me on the General Council of State, where I could die in peace; and like the beaver, I should abandon my Director-Generalship to the hunters."

"What! The Marshal would surely never forget—"

"My dear fellow, the Marshal spoke so warmly on your behalf at a general meeting of Ministers that there is no longer any question of sacking you. But it was discussed! So do not give them any pretexts. I will say no more. At the moment you can make your own terms, be a Councilor of State and a Peer of France. If you leave it too long, if you give them any weapons against you, I cannot answer for the consequences.... Do you still want me to go?"

"Wait a bit. I will see the Marshal," said Hulot, "and I will ask my brother to sound him first."

It is easy to imagine the frame of mind in which the Baron returned to Madame Marneffe's; he had almost forgotten that he was a father, for Roger had played the part of a true and kind friend in telling him the real state of affairs. Nevertheless, Valérie's influence was so great that halfway through dinner the Baron was in tune again, and was all the more gay because he had worries to forget; but the unfortunate man did not know that, this very evening, he would have to choose between his happiness and the danger of which the Director of Personnel had warned him—in short, to choose between Madame Marneffe and his position.

Chapter XXV

At about eleven, when the party was at its height—for the drawing room was full of guests—Valérie drew Hector on to a corner of her sofa.

"My dear old thing," she whispered to him, "your daughter is so annoyed because Wenceslas comes here that she has walked out on him. Hortense seems to be very headstrong. Ask Wenceslas to let you see the letter that the little fool wrote him. This separation of two lovers, for which I am supposed to be to blame, might do me incalculable harm, because this is how virtuous women attack one another. It is monstrous to play the victim in order to throw the blame on to a woman whose only fault is that her house is a pleasant one. If you love me, you will clear me by reconciling the two turtledoves. I do not particularly want to receive your son-in-law; it was you who brought him here; take him away again! If you have any authority with your family, it seems to me that you could insist on your wife's making the reconciliation. Tell the worthy old lady from me that if I am unjustly blamed for having broken up their marriage, and dividing the family, and annexing both the father and the son-in-law, then I shall live up to my reputation, and cause them trouble, after my own fashion! Now Lisbeth is talking of leaving me! She prefers her family, and I don't blame her. She will not stay, she says, unless the young people are reconciled. We shall be in a fine fix; the housekeeping here would cost three times as much."

"Oh, leave that to me!" said the Baron, on hearing of his daughter's scandal. "I will soon settle that!"

"Now," said Valérie, "there is something else. What about Coquet's place?"

"That," said Hector, looking down, "is more difficult, not to say impossible!"

"Impossible, my dear Hector?" Madame Marneffe said in a low voice. "But you don't know to what extremes Marneffe is capable of going. I am in his power; he is immoral, in his own interests, like most men, but he is also extremely vindictive, like all petty minds. In the situation in which you have placed me, I am at his mercy. I shall have to live with him for a few days, and he is quite capable of refusing to leave my room again."

Hulot gave a great start.

"He will leave me free only on condition he is made a head clerk. It is infamous—but logical."

"Valérie, do you love me?"

"In my present condition, my dear, that question is the lowest kind of insult!"

"Very well. If I were to attempt—only to attempt—to ask the Marshal for Marneffe's promotion, I should be finished, and Marneffe would be out of a job."

"I thought that you and the Prince were old and intimate friends."

"That is true, and he has amply proved it. But, my child, there is an authority higher than the Marshal—there is the Council of Ministers, for example. Given a little time, and maneuvering, we shall manage it. In order to succeed, I must wait for an opportunity—when I have been asked to do some service. Then I could say, 'One good turn deserves another.' "

"If I say that to Marneffe, my poor dear Hector, he will do us some bad turn or other. Listen—tell him yourself that he will have to wait. I really cannot be responsible. Oh! I know what my position would be; he knows how to punish me—he would never leave my bedroom!... Don't forget the twelve hundred francs annuity for the little one!"

Hulot, seeing his pleasure threatened, took Marneffe aside; and for the first time he dropped the lofty tone that he had hitherto maintained, so appalled was he by the thought of that moribund creature in his pretty wife's bedroom.

"Marneffe, my dear fellow," he began, "I was talking about you today! But you cannot be promoted to a head clerkship just yet.... We must wait."

"Oh, can't I, Monsieur le Baron?" said Marneffe curtly.

"But my dear fellow—"

"Oh, can't I, Monsieur le Baron?" Marneffe repeated coldly, looking from the Baron to Valérie and back again. "You have put my wife in a situation in which she will have to be reconciled with me, and I shall keep her; because, *my dear fellow,* she is charming!" he added with horrible irony. "I am master here—which is more than you are at the Ministry."

The Baron experienced one of those pangs that produce in the heart the same effect as violent toothache, and he could not conceal the tears in his eyes. During this brief scene Valérie had confided this supposed determination of Marneffe to Henri Montès, so getting rid of him for a time.

Of her four faithful ones, only Crevel, as the possessor of the economical little house, was exempted from this measure; therefore his face wore an expression of truly insolent beatitude, in spite of the silent reproofs that Valérie administered to him, by frowns and meaning looks; but his radiant paternity shone in every feature. At a word of whispered reproach from Valérie, he clasped her hand and replied, "Tomorrow, my duchess, you shall have your little house! I shall be signing the lease tomorrow."

"And the furniture?" she replied, smiling.

"I have a thousand shares in the Versailles *Rive Gauche* railway,[1] bought at twenty-five francs, and they will soon be at three hundred, as a result of the amalgamation of the two lines, a secret I was let into. You shall have furniture fit for a queen! But you will be only mine from then on, won't you?"

"Yes, Big Mayor!" said that middle-class Madame de Merteuil.[2] "But behave yourself! Respect the future Madame Crevel!"

"My dear cousin," Lisbeth was saying to the Baron, "I went to see Adeline early yesterday, because, you know, I cannot in common decency stay on here. I am going to keep house for your brother the Marshal."

"I am going home tonight," said the Baron.

"Very well, I will come to breakfast tomorrow," said Lisbeth with a smile.

She knew how necessary her presence would be at the family scene that would take place the next day. Therefore, first thing in the morning, she went to see Victorin, whom she told of the separation of Hortense and Wenceslas.

When the Baron returned to his home, at half-past ten, Mariette and Louise, who had had a hard day, were closing up the flat so that Hulot did not need to ring. The husband, very much put out by his compulsory virtue, went straight to his wife's bedroom; and through the half-open door he saw her kneeling before her crucifix, lost in prayer, and in one of those poses that are the glory of painters or sculptors who have the good luck to invent and reproduce them. Adeline, carried away in her exaltation, was praying aloud.

"O God, have mercy on us and enlighten him!"

The Baroness was praying for her Hector. At this sight, so different from the one he had just left, and on hearing this phrase, inspired by the events of that day, the Baron was touched, and a sigh escaped him. Adeline turned her face wet with tears. She believed so completely that her prayer had been answered that she jumped up and clasped Hector in her arms with all the strength of happiness. Adeline had stripped herself of all a woman's instincts, and sorrow had obliterated even the memory of them. There were no feelings left in her except those of maternity, of family honor, and the pure attachment of a Christian wife for an erring husband, that saintly tenderness that survives all else in a woman's heart. All this was easy to divine.

"Hector," she said at last, "are you coming back to us? Has God taken pity on our family?"

"Dear Adeline!" replied the Baron, coming in and drawing his wife down beside him on a sofa. "You are the saintliest creature that I have ever known, and I have long ceased to be worthy of you."

"It would need very little, my dear," she said, holding Hulot's hand and trembling so much that she seemed to have no control of her nerves. "Very little indeed to set things right again."

She dared not continue; she felt that every word would be a reproach, and she was unwilling to mar the happiness with which this meeting was flooding her soul.

"I have come here because of Hortense," Hulot began. "That girl may do us far more harm by her precipitate action than my absurd passion for Valérie has done. But, we will talk of all that tomorrow. Hortense is asleep, Mariette tells me; we will not disturb her."

"Yes," said Madame Hulot, suddenly overcome by deep sadness.

She divined that the reason for the Baron's return was not so much the wish to see his family as some ulterior motive.

"Do not worry her tomorrow, either, the poor child is in a dreadful state; she has not stopped crying all day," said the Baroness.

Next morning at nine the Baron, while he waited for his daughter, whom he had sent for, walked up and down the great deserted drawing room, trying to think of arguments with which to overcome the most difficult of all forms of obstinacy—that of a young wife, injured and powerless, as blameless youth ever is, knowing nothing of the shady compromises of the world, because she is ignorant of the world's passions and interests.

"Here I am, Papa!" said Hortense in a tremulous voice, and looking pale from unhappiness.

Hulot, sitting down on a chair, put his arm around his daughter's waist, and made her sit on his knee.

"Well, my child," he said, kissing her brow, "so there is trouble at home, and you have been headstrong? That is not good form. My Hortense should not take so decisive a step on her own initiative—to leave her house, and desert her husband—without consulting her parents. My darling Hortense, if you had only come to see your kind and admirable mother, you would not have been the cause of the great distress that you make me suffer. You do not know the world. It is very wicked. People might say that your husband has sent you back to your parents. Girls brought up, as you were, under your mother's wing, remain children longer than the others—they know nothing of life! Naïve, innocent love, like yours for Wenceslas, unfortunately never calculates; it acts only on its first impulses. The little heart takes the lead, and the head follows. You would burn down Paris to have your revenge, without giving a thought to the police court! When your old father tells you that you have not shown due regard to the proprieties, you must believe him. And I have said nothing of the deep pain that I feel; it is very bitter, because you throw the blame on a woman whose heart you do not know, whose enmity might become terrible. Alas! you are so open, so innocent and pure, that you suspect nothing; you may be calumniated, slandered. And besides, my dearest little angel, you have made too much of a mere joke, and I can personally assure you that your husband is innocent. Madame Marneffe—"

So far the Baron, artist in diplomacy that he was, had formulated his remonstrances with admirable tact. He had, as we see, skillfully led up to the introduction of that name. Nevertheless, on hearing it, Hortense started as if wounded to the quick.

"Listen to me—I have great experience, and I have seen the whole thing," her father continued, preventing his daughter from speaking. "That lady treats your husband very coldly. Yes, you have been the victim of a practical joke. I can prove it to you. Wenceslas was there at dinner yesterday—"

"He went to dinner?" exclaimed the young wife, starting up, and looking at her father with horror painted on her face. "Yesterday! After reading my letter? Oh, my God! Why did I not bury myself in a convent, instead of getting married? My life is no longer my own. I have a child!" she added, sobbing.

These tears went to Madame Hulot's heart. She came out of her bedroom, ran to her daughter, and took her in her arms, asking her those pointless questions of grief, the first that came into her mind.

"Now we have tears," thought the Baron. "Just when everything was going so well! What is to be done now, with crying women?"

"My child," said the Baroness to Hortense, "listen to your father. He loves us. There there."

"Come now, Hortense, my dear little girl, don't cry; it will spoil your looks," said the Baron. "Come now, be sensible. Go quietly home and I promise you that Wenceslas shall never set foot in that house. I ask you to make that sacrifice, if it is a sacrifice to forgive such a small fault in a husband you love! I ask you to do it for the sake of my gray hairs, and for the sake of the love you owe your mother. Surely you do not want to darken my old age with bitterness and grief?"

Hortense flung herself in a frenzy at her father's feet, with a gesture of such violent desperation that her hair, loosely pinned up, came down and she held up her hands to him with an expression in which was written her despair.

"Father, you are asking me to sacrifice my life! Take it, if you must, but at least take it pure and stainless. I will lay it down for you gladly. But do not ask me to die in dishonor, a criminal! I am not like my mother! I cannot swallow outrages! If I return to my husband's house, I might smother Wenceslas in a fit of jealousy, or do something even worse. Do not demand of me things that are beyond my power! Do not have to mourn for me while I am still alive! Because the least thing that can happen is that I should go mad! I feel on the verge of madness already! Last night! Last night! He dined with that woman after reading my letter! Are other men like that? I will give you my life, provided that my death is not dishonorable! His fault! Light! To have a child by that woman!"

"A child?" exclaimed Hulot, starting back. "Come! This must be some joke."

At this moment Victorin and Cousin Bette came in, and stood speechless at this spectacle. The daughter was lying prostrate at her father's feet. The Baroness, silent, and torn between her maternal instincts and her duty as a wife, presented an anxious and tear-stained face.

"Lisbeth," said the Baron, seizing the spinster's hand, and indicating Hortense, "you must help me. Poor Hortense is beside herself. She thinks that Madame Marneffe is Wenceslas's mistress, and all she wanted was a group by him."

"Delilah!" cried the young woman. "The only thing he has done without endless delays since our marriage! The man would not work for me, or for his son, and yet he worked for that worthless creature with such energy— Oh! kill me outright, Father, because every word you speak is a sword thrust!"

Turning to the Baroness and Victorin, Lisbeth indicated the Baron, who could not see her, with a pitying shrug of the shoulders.

"Listen, Cousin," said Lisbeth. "When you asked me to go and live above her, and keep house for her, I did not know what Madame Marneffe was. But one can learn a lot in three years. That woman is a whore! And a whore whose depravity can only be compared with that of her vile and hideous husband. You are the dupe, the Lord Provider for these people, and they will lead you farther than you think! I must speak frankly to you, for you are at the bottom of a pit!"

Hearing Lisbeth speak in these terms, the Baroness and her daughter looked at her with an expression with which the devout might thank the Madonna for having saved their lives.

"She has made up her mind, that dreadful woman, to wreck your son-in-law's marriage. I do not know more than that, for my intelligence is too weak to see clearly into such dark, ignoble, perverse intrigues. Your Madame Marneffe is not in love with your son-in-law, but she has vowed to have him at her feet, out of revenge. I have just been talking to this wretched woman as she deserves. She is a shameless courtesan. I told her that I was leaving her house, that I could no longer smirch my honor in that sink of vice. I belong to my family, before everything. I heard that my little cousin had left Wenceslas, so I came. Your Valérie, whom you think is a perfect saint, is the cause of this cruel separation. How can I stay with such a woman? Our poor darling Hortense," she said, touching the Baron's arm significantly, "is perhaps the victim of a whim, for which women of her sort will sacrifice a whole family in order to possess some trifle. I do not think Wenceslas is guilty, but I do think him weak, and I should not like to say that he would not succumb to her refinements of temptation. I have made up my mind. That woman is fatal to you; she will have you all out in the street. I do not want to seem to be involved in the ruin of my family, after staying three years there simply in order to prevent it. You are being deceived, Cousin! Say firmly that you will have nothing to do with the appointment of that contemptible Marneffe, and just see what will happen! There is fine trouble in store for you if that happens!"

Lisbeth raised her young cousin, and kissed her warmly.

"My dear Hortense, don't give way," she whispered.

The Baroness embraced Lisbeth with the eagerness of a woman who sees herself avenged. The whole family stood in silence around the father, who was intelligent enough to know the meaning of that silence. An expression of fearful anger passed over his brow and his face; its signs were unmistakable. All his veins swelled, and his eyes became bloodshot, and his face showed blotches. Adeline flung herself on her knees before him, and took his hands.

"My dear, my dear, have mercy!"

"I am hateful to you!" said the Baron, putting into words the cry of his conscience.

We are all in the secret of our own misdoings. We nearly always imagine in our victims the sentiments of hate that vengeance might well inspire in them; and in spite of the efforts of hypocrisy, our words or our expression give us away under the stress of some unforeseen ordeal, just as in the past the criminal used to confess under the hands of the torturer.

"In the end," he went on, in order to retract his avowal, "our children turn against us."

"Father!" Victorin exclaimed.

"You are interrupting your father!" the Baron continued in a voice of thunder, looking at his son.

"Listen, Father," said Victorin in a clear, firm tone, the tone of a puritanical deputy. "I am too fully aware of the respect I owe you ever to fail in it, and you will certainly always find in me the most obedient and submissive of sons."

Those who are in the habit of attending the sittings of the two Chambers will recognize the technique of parliamentary debate in these attenuated phrases, calculated to calm irritation and gain time.

"We are so far from being your enemies," Victorin continued, "that I have quarreled with my father-in-law, Monsieur Crevel, because I have redeemed Vauvinet's notes of hand for sixty thousand francs, and there is not a shade of doubt that that money is in the hands of Madame Marneffe. Oh, I am not criticizing you in the least, Father," he added, in reply to a gesture of the Baron's, "but I wish merely to join my protest to Cousin Lisbeth's, and to point out to you that although my devotion to you is blind, and indeed unlimited, Father, my dear Father, unfortunately our financial resources are not!"

"Money!" exclaimed the excited old man, dropping into a chair, quite crushed by this argument. "And this is my son! Your money shall be repaid, sir!" he said, rising.

He went toward the door.

"Hector!"

At this cry the Baron turned, and suddenly revealed to his wife a face bathed in tears. She flung her arms around him with the strength of despair.

"Don't go away like this... do not leave us in anger. I at least have not said a word!"

At this heart-rending cry the children went on their knees before their father.

"We all love you!" exclaimed Hortense.

Lisbeth, immobile as a statue, watched this tableau with a scornful smile on her lips. At this moment Marshal Hulot's voice was heard in the hall. The family realized the importance of concealment, and the scene abruptly changed. The two young people rose, and everyone endeavored to conceal all traces of emotion.

Meanwhile an altercation was taking place at the door between Mariette and a soldier, that presently became so pressing that the cook came into the drawing room.

"Sir, a regimental quartermaster just back from Algiers insists on seeing you."

"Tell him to wait."

"He told me, sir, to tell you privately that it has something to do with your uncle."

The Baron started, for he thought that at last the funds had arrived which for the last two months he had been secretly asking for, in order to pay his bills. He left his family and hurried into the hall. He saw there a typically Alsatian figure.

"Are you *Mennesir the Paron Hilotte*?"[3]

"Yes."

"Himself?"

"Himself."

The quartermaster had been fumbling in the lining of his cap during this dialogue, and drew out a letter which the Baron hurriedly tore open, and read as follows:

> DEAR NEPHEW,
>
> Far from being able to send you the hundred thousand francs that you ask me for, my position has become untenable unless you can take drastic steps to save me. We have the Public Prosecutor on our tracks, talking moral nonsense, and going on about the administration. It is impossible to make this wretched civilian keep his mouth shut. If the Ministry of War lets these black-coated individuals feed out of its hand, I am done for. I can trust the bearer. Try to get him promoted, because he has done good service for us. Do not leave me to the crows!

This letter was a thunderbolt. The Baron saw in it the early signs of the internal disputes between the civil and military authorities that are vexing the Algerian administration to this day, and realized that he must invent some palliative for the trouble that stared him in the face. He told the soldier to return the next day; and having dismissed him with fine promises of promotion, he returned to the drawing room.

"Hail and farewell, brother," he said to the Marshal. "Goodbye, children. Goodbye, Adeline, my dear. And what are you going to do, Lisbeth?" he asked.

"I am going to keep house for the Marshal, because I must end my days doing what I can for one or other of you."

"Don't leave Valérie until I have seen you," Hulot whispered to his cousin. "Goodbye, Hortense, my little rebel; try to be sensible. I have important matters to attend to, and we will talk about your reconciliation some other time. Think it over, there's a good little puss!" he said, kissing her.

He left his wife and children so obviously worried that they continued to feel the gravest apprehensions.

"Lisbeth," said the Baroness, "we must find out what is worrying

Hector. I have never seen him in such a state. Stay a few days longer with that woman; he tells her everything, and so we may find out what has upset him so suddenly. Don't worry. We will arrange your marriage with the Marshal, for it really is necessary."

"I shall never forget your courage this morning," said Hortense, kissing Lisbeth.

"You have avenged our poor mother," said Victorin.

The Marshal looked on with a puzzled air at these marks of affection lavished on Lisbeth, who went home to describe this scene to Valérie.

This sketch will enable innocent readers to divine the various ravages that the Madame Marneffes bring about in a family, and the means by which they can attack poor virtuous wives, apparently beyond their reach. But if we transpose, in imagination, these troubles into the highest social sphere, about the throne, and consider what kings' mistresses must have cost them, we can form some idea of the indebtedness a nation owes to those sovereigns who set an example of well-conducted domestic life.

Chapter XXVI

In Paris every Ministry is a little town, from which women are excluded. But just as much scandal and detraction goes on there as if the feminine population were admitted. After three years, Monsieur Marneffe's position had been, so to speak, clarified, brought to light, and in the offices everybody was asking, "Will Monsieur Marneffe be Monsieur Coquet's successor or will he not?" just as in the Chamber they asked, "Will the Budget be passed or not?" Every sign from the Personnel Department was carefully watched, as was everything that went on in the Baron's department. The astute

Councilor of State had won over to his side the victim of Marneffe's promotion, a capable worker, telling him that if he could arrange Marneffe's promotion he should certainly be his successor, pointing out that Marneffe was a dying man. This clerk was canvassing for Marneffe.

As Hulot went through his outer office, full of visitors, he noticed Marneffe's colorless face in a corner, and sent first for him.

"What do you want to see me about, my dear fellow?" said the Baron, concealing his anxiety.

"Monsieur le Directeur, I am the laughingstock of the department, because it is known that the head of the Personnel Department has left this morning on sick leave, and will be away for about a month. Waiting a month—I know what that means. You have put me in the position of being laughed at by my enemies, and it is bad enough to be drummed on one side; both sides at once, Monsieur le Directeur, is enough to burst the drum."

"My dear Marneffe, it takes a lot of patience to get what one wants. You cannot be made a head clerk—if you ever are—in less than two months from now. A time when I am obliged to consolidate my own position is not the moment to ask for a promotion that would cause a scandal."

"If you are sacked I shall never get the job," said Monsieur Marneffe coldly. "And if you get me appointed it will make no difference in the end."

"Am I to sacrifice myself for you, then?"

"If you do not, I shall be very much mistaken in you."

"You are too Marneffe altogether, Monsieur Marneffe!" said the Baron, rising and showing the deputy clerk the door.

"I wish you good morning, Monsieur le Baron," said Marneffe in humble tones.

"The infamous scoundrel," thought the Baron to himself. "This looks very much like a summons to pay up within twenty-four hours on pain of distraint."

Two hours later, just as the Baron was briefing Claude Vignon, whom he was sending to the Ministry of Justice to get the information about the judicial authorities under whose jurisdiction Johann Fischer was working, Reine opened the door of the Director's office, and handed him a little note, saying she would wait for the answer.

"Why has she sent Reine?" thought the Baron. "Valérie is mad; she will compromise us all, and she is certainly compromising the abominable Marneffe's appointment!"

He dismissed the Minister's private secretary, and read as follows:

> Oh, my dear, what a scene I have had to endure! If you have given me three years of happiness, I have certainly had to pay for it! He came in from his office in a rage that made me really frightened. He is ugly at the best of times, but he looked like a monster. His four real teeth were chattering, and he threatened me with his hateful attentions if I continued to receive you. My poor dear, alas! our door is henceforth closed against you. You can see my tears—they are dripping on the paper and making it quite wet. Can you read this at all, Hector dear? Oh! Not to see you again, give you up, when I have within me a part of your life, as I hope I have your heart also, is enough to kill me! Think of our child. Do not forsake me! But do not compromise yourself for Marneffe; don't give in to his threats! Oh, I love you more than I have ever loved you! I remember all the sacrifices you have made for your Valérie, and I shall never cease to be grateful; you are, and you will always be, my only husband. Do not give another thought to the twelve hundred francs annuity that I asked you to settle on that dear little Hector who will be born not many months from now. . . . I will not be a financial burden to you. Indeed, my money will always be yours.
>
> Ah! if only you loved me as I love you, my Hector, you would retire; we would both say goodbye to our families, our troubles and our present lives, entangled with so much hate, and go right away, taking Lisbeth, and live in some pretty place—in Brittany, or anywhere you like. There we should see no one, and we

should be happy, far away from all these people. Your pension, and the little I have saved in my own name would be quite enough for us. If you are jealous—well, then you would see your Valérie giving all her thought to her Hector, and you would never have to scold me, as you did the other day. I should have only one child—ours—of that you may be sure, my darling old veteran. No, you cannot imagine the state I am in, because you don't know how he behaved to me, and the insults that he spat out at your Valérie! The very words would soil the paper; but a woman like me, Montcornet's daughter, ought never in all her life to have heard such words! Oh, I wish you had been there, so that I could have punished him by showing him how utterly I love you! My father would have killed the wretch! As for me, I am only a weak woman; I love you desperately! Indeed, my love, in my present state of distress I simply cannot give up seeing you. Yes, I am determined to see you in secret every day! We women are like that; I share your resentment. For pity's sake, if you love me, do not promote him—let him die a deputy clerk! At this moment I simply can't think; I can still hear him abusing me. Bette, who was going to leave me, has taken pity on me, and is staying on for a few days.

My dearest darling, I don't know yet what to do. I can only think of flight. I have always adored the country, Brittany, Languedoc, anywhere you like, so long as there I should be free to love you. Poor darling, I am sorry for you. Here you are compelled to go back to your old Adeline, to that tear filled urn, because that brute meant what he said: he will watch me day and night. He even spoke of the police! Do not come! I know that he is capable of anything, for he is using me for the purposes of the most ignoble kind of speculation. So I would like to be able to give you back everything I owe to your generosity. Oh, my darling Hector, I may have flirted, and seemed light to you, but you don't know your Valérie! She loves to tease you, but she loves you more than anyone else in the world. Nobody can stop you from going to see your cousin, so I will plan with her some means of our seeing each other. My dear old thing, I do beg you to write me just one line to reassure me, in the absence of your dear presence! (Oh! I would give my right hand to have you by my side on our divan!) A letter would be like a charm to me; write me something full of your noble heart. I shall return your letter, for we must be careful. I don't know where I could hide it; he rummages everywhere. But do please reassure your Valérie, your wife, the mother of your child. To have to write to you, after seeing you every day! As I said to Lisbeth, I never realized how happy I was! A thousand loving kisses, dear old thing. And always love

YOUR VALÉRIE.

"And tears!" thought Hulot, as he finished reading this letter. "Tears that have quite blotted out her name." "How is she?" he said to Reine.

"Madame is in bed; she has had dreadful hysterics," replied Reine. "Madame had an attack that twisted her like a bent twig after she had finished writing. That comes of crying. She heard the master's voice on the stairs."

The Baron in his distress wrote the following letter on a sheet of headed official notepaper:

Don't worry, my angel; he shall die a deputy clerk! Your idea is excellent; we will go and live right away from Paris, and we shall be happy with our little Hector. I shall retire, and shall certainly be able to find a good place in some railway company. Ah, my darling love, your letter makes me feel young again! I shall start life over again, you shall see, and make a fortune for our dear little one. As I read your letter, a thousand times more ardent than those of the *Nouvelle Héloise*,[1] it worked a miracle in me! I never imagined that I could love you more. You shall see me this evening at Lisbeth's.

YOUR
HECTOR (FOR LIFE!).

Reine went off with this reply, the first letter that the Baron had ever written to his *very dear friend*!

Emotions such as these to some extent counterbalanced the disasters whose distant thunder was growling on the horizon; but at this moment the Baron, believing that he could certainly avert the blow aimed at his uncle Johann Fischer, was concerned only with the deficit.

One of the peculiarities of the Bonapartist character is faith in the power of the sword, and the conviction of the superiority of the military over the civil authorities. Hulot felt nothing but scorn for the Public Prosecutor in Algiers, where the Ministry of War was supreme. Men remain what they have once been. How should officers of the Imperial Guard forget having seen the mayors of the largest towns of the Empire, the Emperor's prefects, Emperors themselves on a small scale, coming out to receive the Imperial Guard to do it honor on the frontiers of the departments through which it passed—in fact, to accord it the honors accorded to sovereigns?

At a quarter past four the Baron went straight to Madame Marneffe's; his heart beat fast as that of a young man as he went upstairs, for he was asking himself this question: "Shall I see her? Or shall I not see her?" How could he possibly remember the scene of the morning, in which his children had knelt weeping at his feet? Did not Valérie's letter, placed forever in a slim note-case lying against his heart, prove that he was adored more than the most adorable of young men? After ringing, the unfortunate Baron heard the shuffling of slippers, and the invalid Marneffe's hateful cough. Marneffe opened the door, but only in order to strike an attitude and indicate the stairs to Hulot with a gesture exactly like the one with which Hulot had shown him the door in his office.

"You are altogether too Hulot, Monsieur Hulot!" he said.

The Baron tried to push past him, but Marneffe drew a pistol from his pocket and cocked it.

"Monsieur Councilor of State, when a man is as vile as I am—for you think me very vile, don't you?—he would be the worst of galley slaves if he did not extract all the benefits due to the honor he has sold. You have asked for war; it will be lively, and no quarter. Don't come here again, and don't attempt to get past me; I have told the police of my situation with regard to you."

And while Hulot was still dumfounded with amazement, he pushed him out and shut the door.

"The low scoundrel!" Hulot thought to himself, as he went upstairs to Lisbeth's flat. "Now I understand her letter! Valérie and I will leave Paris. Valérie is mine for the rest of my life; she will close my eyes!"

Lisbeth was not at home. Madame Olivier told Hulot that she had gone to see the Baroness, expecting to find him there.

"Poor girl! I could never have believed she could be so subtle as she was this morning," thought the Baron, recalling Lisbeth's conduct, as he made his way from Rue Vanneau to Rue Plumet.

At the corner of Rue Vanneau and Rue de Babylone he looked up at the Eden from which Hymen[2] had banished him with the sword of the law. Valérie, at her window, was watching Hulot. When he looked up she waved her handkerchief, but the infamous Marneffe struck a blow at his wife's cap and dragged her violently away from the window. Tears came into the eyes of the Councilor of State.

"To be loved like this! To see a woman maltreated, and to be nearly seventy!" he thought.

Lisbeth had gone to give the family the good news. Adeline and Hortense already knew that the Baron, unwilling to dishonor himself in the eyes of the entire Ministry by appointing Marneffe to a head clerkship, had been turned out by the husband, who had turned violently against him. In her happiness Adeline had planned a dinner that should be better than her Hector would find at Valérie's, and the devoted Lisbeth had helped Mariette to achieve this difficult result. Cousin Bette was the idol of the hour: mother and daughter had kissed her hands, and had told her with touching delight that the Marshal had consented to take her as his housekeeper.

"And from that, my dear, to becoming his wife is but a step," said Adeline.

"And he did not say no when Victorin suggested it to him," added Countess Steinbock.

The Baron was welcomed by his family with such charming, touching expressions of affection, so overflowing with love, that he was forced to conceal his worry. The Marshal came to dinner. After dinner, Hulot did not leave. Victorin and his wife came in, and they made up a party for whist.

"It is a long time, Hector," said the Marshal gravely, "since you have given *us* such a pleasant evening."

This speech from the old soldier, so indulgent to his brother, and who in these words implicitly rebuked him, made a deep impression. It showed how wide and deep were the wounds in a heart in which all the sorrows at which he guessed found their echo.

At eight the Baron insisted on seeing Lisbeth home himself, promising to return.

"You know, Lisbeth, he ill-treats her!" he said to her, on the way. "Ah! I have never loved her so much!"

"Ah! I never realized how much Valérie loved you!" Lisbeth replied. "She is light, she is a flirt, she likes to be flattered, to see the comedy of love played for her benefit, as she says; but you are her only real attachment."

"What message did she give you for me?"

"This," said Lisbeth. "She has, as you know, encouraged Crevel. You must not hold it against her, for that is why she is now secure from utter poverty for the rest of her days; but she detests him, and it is practically over. Well, she has kept the key of some rooms—"

"Rue du Dauphin!" exclaimed the delighted Baron. "Just for that I will forgive her for Crevel! I have been there; I know—"

"Here is the key," said Lisbeth. "Get another like it made tomorrow—two if you can."

"And then?" said Hulot eagerly.

"Well, I will come to dinner with you again tomorrow, and you can give me back Valérie's key—because old Crevel might ask her to give it back to him—and you can go and meet her the day after. You can arrange matters then. You will be quite safe, because there are two entrances. If Crevel should by any chance come in by the back way—for he has Regency habits, as he always says—you can leave by the shop, and vice versa. Well, you old wretch, you owe all this to me. What are you going to do for me?"

"Anything you like!"

"Well then, you would not oppose my marrying your brother!"

"You the Maréchale Hulot, Countess of Forzheim?" exclaimed Hulot, taken by surprise.

"Well, Adeline is a Baroness!" Bette replied in a sharp and threatening tone. "Listen, you old libertine, you know the state of affairs you are in! Your family may find itself starving and in the gutter—"

"That is what I dread!" said Hulot, startled.

"If your brother were to die, who would look after your wife and daughter? The widow of a Marshal of France would be given a pension of at least six thousand francs, would she not? Well, I only want to marry in order to make sure that your daughter and your wife will have bread to eat, you old imbecile!"

"I never thought of it in that light," said the Baron. "I will talk to my brother, for we can depend upon you. Tell my angel that my life is *hers.*"

And the Baron, having seen Lisbeth go into the house in Rue Vanneau, returned to play whist and remained at home. The Baroness was at the height of happiness, for it seemed that her husband had returned. For nearly a fortnight he went to the Ministry at nine, returned for dinner at six, and spent the evening with his family. He took Adeline and Hortense twice to the theater. Mother and daughter had three Thanksgiving Masses said, and prayed to God to keep with them the husband and father that He had restored.

CHAPTER XXVII

One evening Victorin Hulot, as he saw his father going off to bed, said to his mother, "Well, we have every reason to be happy. My father has come home; and my wife and I will never grudge the sacrifice of our capital if this lasts."

"Your father is nearly seventy," said the Baroness. "He is still thinking about Madame Marneffe, I can see; but presently he will forget; a passion for women is not like gambling, or speculation, or avarice—there is an end to it."

But the beautiful Adeline—for she was still beautiful in spite of her fifty years and her sorrows—was mistaken in this. Libertines, those men on whom nature has bestowed the rare faculty of loving beyond the limits that she sets for love, are rarely as old as their age. During this relapse into virtue the Baron had gone three times to the Rue du Dauphin, where he had certainly not behaved like a man of seventy. His rekindled passion rejuvenated him, and he would have thrown away his honor, his family, everything, for Valérie, without a regret. But Valérie, completely changed, now never spoke to him about money, or the twelve hundred francs a year to be settled on their son; on the contrary, she offered him money, and loved Hulot as a woman of thirty-six might love a handsome law student, poor, poetic, and in love. And poor Adeline thought that she had recaptured her beloved Hector! The lovers' fourth meeting had been arranged at the last moment of the third, exactly as in the old days the play for the next night was announced at the Italian theaters. The hour agreed upon was nine in the morning. On the day on which the happiness was due, in anticipation of which the infatuated old man had resigned himself to family life, at about eight o'clock Reine came and asked for the Baron. Hulot, fearing some catastrophe, went to speak to Reine, who would not come into the flat. The faithful maid gave the following note to the Baron:

DEAR OLD THING,

Do not go to Rue du Dauphin. Our bad dream is ill, and I must look after him; but be there tonight at nine. Crevel is at Corbeil, with Monsieur Lebas, and I am quite sure he will bring no princesses to his little villa. I can arrange to spend the night there, as I need not be back before Marneffe wakes. Please confirm this; for perhaps your great elegy of a wife does not leave you free as formerly. They say she is still beautiful, and you might be unfaithful to me—you are such a libertine! Burn this note. I am suspicious of everyone.

Hulot wrote the following brief reply:

MY LOVE,

My wife has never, for the last twenty-five years, interfered with my pleasures, as I have told you. I would sacrifice a hundred Adelines for you! I will be there this evening at nine, in Crevel's temple, waiting for my divinity. Oh, that your deputy clerk might soon die! Then we need never be parted again. That is the dearest wish of

YOUR
HECTOR.

In the evening the Baron told his wife that he had some work to attend to with the Minister at Saint-Cloud, and that he would be back at four or five in the morning, and set out for the Rue du Dauphin. It was toward the end of the month of June.

Few men in their lives have really experienced the terrible sensation of going to their death, for those who return from the scaffold can be easily counted; but a few have vividly experienced that agony in dreams, lived through it all, even to feeling the knife at their neck at the moment when awakening and day come to deliver them. Well, the sensation to which the Councilor of State was prey at five in the morning, in Crevel's elegant and stylish bed, far surpassed in horror that of feeling himself tied to the fatal block, while ten thousand spectators looked on through twenty thousand fiery eyes. Valérie was asleep in a graceful attitude. She was as lovely as beautiful women are, women beautiful enough to be so even in sleep. It is art invading nature—literally a living picture.

In his horizontal position the Baron's eyes were three feet above the floor; his gaze, straying at random, like those of a man who has just awakened, and who is collecting his thoughts, fell on the door, covered with flowers painted by Jan,[1] an artist who could afford to despise fame. The Baron did not see, like the man condemned to death, twenty thousand living eyes, but only one, whose look was, however, more truly piercing than that of the ten thousand in the public square. This sensation was of an intensity, coming as it did in the midst of enjoyment, greater than that of a man condemned to death; and any number of melancholic Englishmen[2] would have paid a high price for it. The Baron lay there, still horizontal, literally bathed in a cold sweat. He tried to doubt his senses; but that deadly eye babbled. There was a murmur of whispering voices behind the door.

"If only it is nothing worse than Crevel playing a trick on me!" the Baron thought, no longer in doubt that some person was present in the temple.

The door opened. The majesty of the French law, which, on all the public notices, comes after that of the king, made its appearance in the shape of a little police officer accompanied by a tall justice of the peace, both ushered in by friend Marneffe. The police officer, who began with a pair of shoes whose flaps were tied with ribbons with bedraggled bows, ended with a yellow cranium almost bare of hair; he seemed to be a sly fellow, with a broad sense of humor, who no longer cherished any illusions on the subject of Paris life. His eyes, from behind his spectacles, glittered through the glass with a knowing and mocking expression. The justice of the peace, a retired solicitor, and an old admirer of the fair sex, envied the delinquent.

"We have to do our duty, you know, Monsieur le Baron!" said the officer. "We are acting for the plaintiff. The justice of the peace is here to authorize entering a private residence. I know who you are, and who the lady is."

Valérie opened her eyes, astonished, and gave a piercing scream of the kind that actresses use when they are impersonating madness in the theater, and twisted in convulsions on the bed like a medieval witch in her yellow vest, on a bed of fagots.

"Death! My dearest Hector, but a police court? Oh, never!"

She leaped from the bed, and passed like a white cloud between the three spectators, and crouched under the writing table, hiding her face in her hands.

"I am lost! Let me die!" she cried.

"Sir," said Marneffe to Hulot, "if Madame Marneffe goes mad, you will be worse than a libertine; you will be a murderer!"

What can a man do, or say, when he is found in a bed that does not belong to him, even as a tenant, with a woman who does not belong to him either? This.

"Mr. Justice of the Peace, and you, Officer," said the Baron with dignity, "be so good as to attend to this unfortunate lady, whose reason appears to me to be in danger... and proceed with your report afterward. The doors are no doubt locked, and you need not fear that either she or I will escape, in our present condition."

The two officials followed the injunction of the Councilor of State.

"Come here to me, you miserable flunky," said Hulot aside to Marneffe, taking his arm and drawing him toward him. "It is not I who will be a murderer, but you! You want to be a head clerk, and an officer of the Legion of Honor?"

"Before everything, Monsieur le Baron," said Marneffe with a bow.

"You shall be both; reassure your wife, and send these fellows away."

"Oh, no!" said Marneffe cunningly. "These gentlemen must draw up their action as witnesses to the fact, because without that document, the basis of my claim, where should I be? High officialdom is choked with swindlers. You have taken my wife, and have not made me a head clerk, Monsieur le Baron! I give you just two days to do so! Here are some letters!"

"Letters!" exclaimed the Baron, interrupting Marneffe.

"Yes, letters proving that the child my wife is carrying at this moment is yours. Do you understand? You ought to settle on my son an income equal to what he will lose through this bastard. But I will be moderate; it is no business of mine; I am not enamored of paternity! I will be satisfied with a hundred louis a year. Tomorrow I succeed Coquet, and go on the July honors list for the Legion of Honor or . . . the documentary evidence will be laid before the Bench, along with my charge. I am letting you off lightly, am I not?"

"My word! That's a pretty woman!" said the J.P. to the police officer. "A loss to the world if she goes mad!"

"She's not mad," replied the officer sententiously. The police are always skepticism incarnate.

"Baron Hulot has walked into a trap," he added, loud enough for Valérie to hear him.

Valérie gave the officer a look that would have killed him, if looks could put into force the rage that they express. The policeman smiled, for he, too, had set his trap, and the woman had fallen into it. Marneffe asked his wife to go into the dressing room and dress, for he had settled with the Baron.

"Gentlemen," he said to the two functionaries, "I need not ask you to keep this matter secret."

The two officials bowed. The police officer rapped twice on the floor, his secretary entered, sat down at the desk, and proceeded to write, as the officer dictated in a low voice. Valérie continued to weep hot tears. When she had finished her toilet Hulot went in and dressed. Meanwhile the report was finished. Marneffe then waited to take his wife home; but Hulot, believing that he was seeing her for the last time, implored the husband, with a look, to allow him to speak to her.

"Sir, your wife has cost me too dear for you not to allow me to bid her goodbye ... in the presence of you all, of course."

Valérie went over to him, and Hulot whispered to her, "The only thing left for us is to fly; but how can we communicate? We have been betrayed ..."

"By Reine!" she replied. "But, my dear, after this scene, we cannot see each other again. I am dishonored. And people will tell you dreadful things about me—and you will believe them!"

The Baron made a gesture of denial.

"You will believe them, and thank Heaven you will, because then perhaps you won't regret me."

"He shall not die a deputy clerk," Marneffe muttered in the ear of the Councilor of State, as he returned to take away his wife, to whom he said, brutally, "That's enough! I am weak with you, but I will not be made a fool of by anyone else!"

Valérie left Crevel's little house with a last look at the Baron, so piquant that he thought that she adored him. The J.P. gallantly offered his hand to Madame Marneffe as he saw her into the cab. The Baron, who had to sign the report, remained completely shattered, alone with the police officer. When the Councilor of State had signed, the officer looked at him keenly, over his glasses.

"You are very fond of that little lady, sir?"

"Yes, to my cost, as you see."

"And what if she did not care for you?" the officer went on. "If she was deceiving you?"

"I know that already, Officer—here, in this very house . . . We talked it over, Monsieur Crevel and I."

"Oh! then you knew that you were in the Mayor's little villa?"

"Perfectly."

The officer touched his cap respectfully.

"You must be very much in love. I will say no more," he said. "I respect incurable passions, as doctors respect incurable invalids. . . .

I remember Monsieur de Nucingen, the banker, when he was attacked by an infatuation like that."

"He is a friend of mine," said the Baron. "I often dined with the beautiful Esther. She was worth the two million she cost him."

"More than that," said the officer. "That whim of the old banker cost four people their lives. Oh! Infatuations like that are like the cholera."[3]

"What were you going to say to me?" asked the Councilor of State, who did not like indirect warnings.

"Why should I destroy your illusions?" replied the police officer. "It is rare enough to have any at your age!"

"Rid me of them!" cried the Councilor of State.

"You will curse the doctor later," replied the policeman with a smile.

"I ask you as a favor, Officer."

"Well, then, that woman was in collusion with her husband."

"Oh!"

"That is so, sir, in two cases out of every ten. Oh, we know all about it!"

"What proof have you of this complicity?"

"To begin with, the husband," said the knowing police officer, with all the calm of a surgeon accustomed to searching wounds. "Speculation is stamped on every line of his ugly face. But you must have set great store by a certain letter written by that woman, in which there is mention made of the child?"

"That letter means so much to me that I always carry it with me," Baron Hulot replied to the police officer, rummaging in his side pocket to find the little note-case that he carried with him everywhere.

"You can leave the note-case where it is," said the officer, thundering out his indictment. "Here is the letter. Now I know all I wanted to know. Madame Marneffe must have known what was in that note-case."

"No one else in the world."

"That is what I thought. Now, here is the proof that you asked me for, of the complicity of that little lady."

"What do you mean?" said the Baron, still incredulous.

"When we came in, Monsieur le Baron," the officer proceeded, "that miserable Marneffe came in first, and he took that letter, which his wife had no doubt put on that table," indicating the dressing table. "Evidently the husband and wife had agreed upon the place, if she managed to steal the letter from you while you were asleep; because the letter that the lady wrote you, along with those you wrote to her, would be decisive evidence in a police court."

The policeman showed Hulot the letter that Reine had brought to him in his office at the Ministry.

"It is one of the documents in the case," said he. "You must return it to me, sir."

"Well, Officer," said Hulot, whose face changed, "that woman serves out profligacy in fixed rations. I am sure now that she has three lovers!"

"That is obvious," said the police officer. "Oh! they are not all walking the streets! When a woman follows that trade, sir, with a carriage, in drawing rooms, or in her own house, it is not a matter of francs and centimes. Mademoiselle Esther, whom you just mentioned, and who poisoned herself, ran through millions.... Take my advice, Monsieur le Baron; settle down to a quiet life. This little party will cost you a tidy sum; that crook of a husband has the law on his side . . . and what is more, but for me the little lady would have caught you again."

"Thank you, Officer," said the Councilor of State, struggling to keep his dignity.

"Well, sir, we must lock up, the farce is over, and you can return the key to the Mayor."

Hulot[4] returned home in a state of depression that reduced him almost to the breaking point, and plunged him in thoughts of the deepest gloom. He woke his noble, saintly, and virtuous wife, and poured out to her the story of those three years, sobbing like a child whose toy has been taken away from him. This confession from an old man, still young at heart, this frightful and heart-rending saga, while it moved Adeline to pity, also secretly caused her the liveliest joy, and she thanked heaven for this final blow, because she now saw her husband as settled for good in the bosom of his family.

"Lisbeth was right!" said Madame Hulot quietly, and without any useless recriminations. "She warned us in advance."

"Yes! Oh, if I had only listened, instead of getting angry, the day I tried to persuade poor Hortense to return home, so as not to compromise the reputation of that— Oh, my dear Adeline, we must save Wenceslas! He is in that mire up to the neck!"

"My poor darling, so the middle-class wife turned out to be no better than the actresses!" said Adeline, smiling.

The Baroness was alarmed at the change in Hector; when she saw him unhappy, suffering, bowed under the weight of his troubles, her heart went out to him in pity and love; she would have laid down her life to make Hulot happy.

"Stay with us, Hector my dear. Tell me how these women manage to attract you so much. I will try.... Why have you not taught me to be what you want? Is it because I am not clever enough? There are still men who think me beautiful enough to pay court to."

Many married women, faithful to their duties and to their husbands, may well ask at this point why strong and affectionate men, so tenderhearted to the Madame Marneffes of this world, do not make their wives the objects of their fancies and their passions, especially when these wives are like Adeline Hulot. This is one of the profound mysteries of human nature. Love cuts clean across reason; the virile and austere delight of great minds, and pleasure—the vulgar commodity sold in the marketplace—are two aspects of the same reality. The women who can satisfy these two great appetites of the two sides of human nature are as rare, in sexual life, as great generals, great writers, great artists, and great inventors, in the life of a nation. Men of superior qualities, as well as fools—the

Hulots no less than the Crevels—feel the double need for the ideal and for pleasure; all alike go in search of that mysterious androgyne, that rare work of nature, which in most cases proves to be in two volumes. This search is a depravity produced by society. To be sure, marriage must be accepted as a duty; it is life, imposing its tasks and stern sacrifices equally on both sides. Libertines, those treasure-hunters, are as guilty as other malefactors punished more severely than they. This reflection is not merely a moral platitude; it reveals the cause of many unexplained misfortunes. This Scene of Paris life[5] has, however, its moral—morals, rather, more than one, and of various kinds.

The Baron went without delay to see the Marshal Prince de Wissembourg, whose high protection was his last resource. The old soldier's protégé, for thirty-five years, he had access to him at all times, and could call at his rooms first thing in the morning.

"Ah, good morning, my dear Hector," said that great and worthy leader. "What is the matter? You look worried. But the session is ended—one more over! I speak of these things now as I used to of our campaigns. And upon my word, I believe the newspapers refer to the sessions as 'parliamentary campaigns.' "

"Yes, we have been in difficulties, Marshal. But the times are hard," said Hulot. "It can't be helped; that is what the world is like. Every period has its drawbacks. In 1841 the worst trouble is that neither the King nor his Ministers are free to act, as the Emperor was."

The Marshal gave Hulot one of those eagle looks whose pride, clearness, and perspicacity revealed that, in spite of his years, that great mind was still strong and vigorous.

"You want me to do something for you?" he said in a jovial tone.

"I find myself in the position of having to ask you, as a personal favor, for the promotion of one of my deputy clerks to the grade of head clerk of a department, and for his nomination as an officer of the Legion of Honor."

"What is his name?" said the Marshal, piercing the Baron with a lightning glance.

"Marneffe."

"He has a pretty wife; I saw her at your daughter's marriage. If Roger . . . but Roger is away. Hector, my boy, this is a matter of your pleasure. What! You are still at it? Well, you do credit to the Imperial Guard! That is what comes of having been in the Commissariat; you have reserves! Drop this business, my dear boy; it is too much a matter of gallantry to be brought up in administrative quarters."

"No, Marshal, it is a bad business, for the police are involved. You don't want to see me in a police court?"

"The deuce!" exclaimed the Marshal, becoming serious. "Go on."

"I am in the position of a fox caught in a trap. You have always shown me so much kindness that I hope you will consent to get me out of the shameful position in which I am placed."

And Hulot described his misadventures as wittily and lightly as he could.

"And, my dear Prince," he concluded, "you will surely not allow my brother, who is your friend, to die of grief, and allow one of your directors, a Councilor of State, to be dragged in the mud? This Marneffe is a miserable specimen. He can be made to retire in a year or two."

"How you talk of two or three years, my dear fellow!"

"But, Prince, the Imperial Guard is immortal."

"I am the last of the first batch of Marshals," said the Minister. "Listen, Hector. I am more fond of you than you know; I will prove it! The day I quit the Ministry we will both go. You are not a deputy, my friend! Any number of men would like your place; and but for me, you would have been out by this time. Yes, I have broken several lances in your defense. Very well, I will grant your two requests, because it would never do to see you in the dock at your age and in your position. But you have stretched your credit almost to breaking point. If this appointment gives rise to any talk, we shall be held responsible. For myself, I do not mind, but it is another thorn in your path. At the next session you will be sacked. Your place is held out as a bait to five or six influential men, and you have only been saved so far by the force of my arguments. I said that on the day you retired and your place was filled there would be five malcontents to one happy man; whereas by letting them stew in their own juice for two or three years we should have six votes. They laughed, in the Council meeting, and declared that the Veteran of the Old Guard, as they said, was becoming very strong on parliamentary tactics. I tell you this frankly. And besides, you are getting on in years. You are fortunate to be able still to get into difficulties of that kind. It is a long time since Sub-Lieutenant Cottin[6] had mistresses!"

The Marshal rang.

"That police report must be torn up," he added.

"You are acting like a father, sir. I did not venture to mention my anxiety on that account."

"I wish Roger were here!" the Marshal exclaimed, as Mitouflet, his batman, came in. "I was going to send for him. No, you can go, Mitouflet. And you go, too, my friend. I will have this nomination drawn up, and sign it. But that low schemer shall not enjoy the fruit of his crimes for long. He shall be watched, and drummed out of the regiment on the first pretext. Meanwhile, you are saved, Hector my dear fellow; but be careful. Do not strain friendship too far. You shall have the nomination this morning, and your man shall be an officer of the Legion of Honor. How old are you now?"

"I shall be seventy in three months' time."

"What a fellow you are!" said the Marshal, smiling. "It is you who ought to be promoted; but, by Jove, we are not under Louis XV!"

Such is the strength of the comradeship that unites the glorious survivors of the Napoleonic phalanx; they feel always as if they were still in camp together, and bound to stand by one another against any attack.

"One more favor like that," Hulot thought as he crossed the court, "and I am finished."

The unfortunate official went to see the Baron de Nucingen, to whom he now owed only a mere trifle; he succeeded in borrowing forty thousand francs by pledging his salary for another two years; but the Baron stipulated that, in the case of Hulot's retirement, the whole of his pension should be devoted to the repayment of the debt, until both interest and capital were repaid. This new arrangement, like the first, was made through Vauvinet, to whom the Baron signed bills of exchange for twelve thousand francs. Next day the fatal police report, the husband's charge, letters and all, were destroyed. The scandalous promotions of Monsieur Marneffe passed over almost unnoticed during the July celebrations[7] and did not give rise to a single comment in the newspapers.

Chapter XXVIII

Lisbeth, who had to all appearances broken with Madame Marneffe, had moved in to Marshal Hulot's household. Ten days after these events the first banns of marriage were published between the old maid and the illustrious old soldier, to whom, in order to obtain his consent, Adeline had given an account of Hector's financial catastrophe, begging him never to mention it to the Baron, who, she said, was despondent, deeply depressed, and quite crushed.

"I am afraid he is feeling his age!" she added.

So Lisbeth had triumphed! She was about to attain the goal of her ambition, see her schemes accomplished, her hatred gratified. She was rejoicing in advance at the prospect of the pleasure of ruling the family which had so long looked down upon her. She vowed to patronize her patrons, to play the lady bountiful keeping the ruined family alive; she greeted herself in the mirror as *Madame la Comtesse* or *Madame la Maréchale*! Adeline and Hortense should end their days in misery, struggling with penury, while she, cousin

Bette, was received at the Tuileries, and paraded in the world of fashion.

But a terrible event occurred which threw the old maid down from the social heights where she sat so proudly enthroned.

On the very day that these first banns were published the Baron received another message from Africa. A second Alsatian arrived, and handed him a letter, having first made sure that he was giving it to Baron Hulot in person; he gave him the address of his lodgings, and left the high official utterly overwhelmed by the first few lines that he read:

Dear Nephew,

You will receive this letter, by my calculations, on August 7th. Supposing it takes you three days to send us the help we need, and that it takes a fortnight to get here, that brings us to September 1st.

If you can act within that time, you will have saved the honor of your humble servant Johann Fischer.

This is what the clerk that you have given me as an accomplice tells me to ask; for I am, it seems, liable to be brought before either the Court of Assizes or a court-martial. You will understand that Johann Fischer will never appear before any tribunal; he will go, by his own act, before the tribunal of God.

Your clerk seems to me a bad lot, quite capable of compromising you; but he is as astute as a thief. He says that your best line is to protest louder than anyone else, and send out an inspector with a special commission to find out who is guilty, to discover abuses, in fact to make a fuss; but I don't know who will stand between us and the law if any trouble starts.

If your commissioner arrives here by September 1st and you give him the word, if you can send by him two hundred thousand francs to make good the quantities of stores that we say we have bought in remote districts, we shall be regarded as solvent and blameless.

You can trust the soldier who is the bearer of this letter with a check made out to me payable through an Algerian bank. He is a sound man, a relation of mine, and would never think of trying to find out what he is carrying. If you cannot do anything, I will die willingly for the man to whom we owe our Adeline's happiness.

The anguish and pleasures of passion, the catastrophe that had just brought his career of gallantry to an end, had prevented Baron Hulot from giving a thought to poor Johann Fischer, although his first letter had given clear enough warning of the danger that had now become so pressing. The Baron left the dining room in such a state of agitation that he literally dropped into a chair in the drawing room. He was stunned, and overcome by the dizziness caused by his heavy fall. He stared at a rose in the carpet, without noticing that he was still holding Johann's fatal letter in his hand. Adeline was in her bedroom, when she heard her husband drop into the chair like a dead weight. The sound was so unusual that she thought he must have had a stroke. She looked up in breathtaking, paralysing fear, at her mirror, in which the room was reflected through the open door, and saw her Hector in a state of collapse like a broken man. The Baroness entered on tiptoe, and as Hector did not hear her, she was able to approach, see the letter, take it, and read it, trembling in every limb. She experienced one of those violent nervous shocks that leave their mark forever on the body. Several days later she became affected with a continual nervous tremor; for after the first moment the need to act caused her to summon up such strength as can only be drawn from the very sources of life itself.

"Hector, come into my bedroom," she said in a voice that was scarcely above a whisper. "Don't let your daughter see you like this. Come, my dear, come."

"Where can I find two hundred thousand francs? I could manage to have Claude Vignon sent out on a special commission. He is a clever, intelligent fellow . . . that could be managed in a couple of days. But two hundred thousand francs! My son hasn't got the money; his house is already mortgaged for three hundred thousand. My brother's savings at most amount to thirty thousand. Nucingen would laugh at me! Vauvinet? He was reluctant enough to lend me ten thousand to settle on the son of that scoundrel Marneffe. No, it is all up with me; I shall have to throw myself on the Marshal's mercy, confess how matters stand, hear him call me a rotter, listen to his broadside, and then sink decently to the bottom."

"But, Hector, this is not merely financial ruin; it is disgrace!" said Adeline. "My poor uncle will kill himself. Kill only us—you have the right—but you cannot be a murderer! Take courage! There must be some way."

"None!" said the Baron. "No one in the government could lay hands on two hundred thousand francs, even to save a Ministry! Oh, Napoleon, where are you now?"

"My uncle! Poor man! Hector, he cannot be allowed to kill himself, in disgrace!"

"There is just a chance," he said, "but a very slim one. Yes, Crevel is at daggers drawn with his daughter. Ah, he's got the money; he is the only one who could . . ."

"Come, Hector, better that your wife should suffer than that your uncle, your brother, and the honor of the family should be destroyed!" said the Baroness, suddenly struck by an idea. "Yes, I can save you all. Good God! what a dreadful thought! How could I think of it?"

She clasped her hands, went down on her knees, and said a prayer. As she rose she saw an expression of such wild joy on her husband's face that the diabolical thought returned, and Adeline sank into a kind of insane stupor.

"Go, my dear; hurry to the Ministry," she exclaimed, rousing herself from this torpor; "try to send out a commission. You must! Get around the Marshal! And when you come back at five perhaps you will find—yes, you will find two hundred thousand francs. Your family, your honor as a gentleman, a Councilor of State, a government official—your honesty, your son, shall all be saved. But your

Adeline will be lost; you will never see her again. Hector my dear," she said, going on her knees before him, pressing his hand and kissing it, "give me your blessing, and say goodbye to me."

It was so heart-rending that, taking his wife in his arms, raising her, and kissing her, Hulot said to her, "I don't understand."

"If you did," she said, "I should die of shame, or not have sufficient strength to carry out this last sacrifice."

Mariette came to say that breakfast was served.

Hortense came in to wish her father and mother good morning. They would have to go to breakfast, and put on an assumed cheerfulness.

"Go and begin without me; I will join you!" said the Baroness.

And she sat down at her desk and wrote the following note:

> MY DEAR MONSIEUR CREVEL,
>
> I have a favor to ask of you, and I shall expect you this morning, for I count on your gallantry, which is known to me, not to keep me waiting too long.
>
> YOUR DEVOTED SERVANT,
> ADELINE HULOT.

"Louise," she said to her daughter's maid, who waited on her as well, "give this letter to the concierge, and tell him to take it at once to this address, and to wait for an answer."

The Baron, who was reading the papers, handed a Republican paper to his wife, pointing to an article, and saying, "Will there be time?"

This was the item, one of those paragraphs of scandal with which the newspapers spice their political bread and butter:

> A correspondent writes to us from Algiers that such grave abuses have come to light in the commissariat department of the province of Oran that official inquiries are being made. It is a clear case of peculation, and the guilty parties are known. Unless severe measures are taken, we will continue to lose more men by

the embezzlement that keeps down their rations than by Arab steel and the fiery heat of the climate. We await further information before saying any more on this deplorable subject. We are no longer surprised at the alarm caused by the establishment of the press in Algeria, envisaged in the 1830 Charter.

"I will dress and go to the Minister," said the Baron, as he left the breakfast table; "time is precious, a man's life depends on every moment."

"Oh, Mamma, I have lost all hope!" exclaimed Hortense.

And, unable to hold back her tears, she passed over to her mother a copy of the *Revue des Beaux-Arts.* Madame Hulot saw a reproduction of a group entitled *Delilah* by Count Steinbock, beneath which was printed: "In the possession of Madame Marneffe." From the first line the article, signed V, bore the mark of Claude Vignon's style and friendliness.

"Poor child," said the Baroness.

Startled by the indifference of her mother's tone, Hortense looked at her, and recognized in her expression a sorrow before which her own paled; she came over and kissed her mother, saying, "What is the matter, Mamma? What has happened? Can we possibly be more wretched than we are?"

"My child, in comparison with what I am suffering today, it seems to me that the worst that I ever endured in the past was as nothing. When shall I ever cease to suffer?"

"In heaven, darling Mother," said Hortense gravely.

"Come, my angel, you must help me to dress.... No, I would rather you did not, on this occasion. Send me Louise."

Adeline, returning to her bedroom, went and examined herself in the mirror. She looked at herself, sadly and curiously, asking herself, "Am I still beautiful? Could anyone still desire me? Am I wrinkled?"

She lifted up her beautiful golden hair, and uncovered her temples. They were as fresh as a young girl's.

Adeline went further; she uncovered her shoulders, and was

satisfied, and experienced a little thrill of pride. The beauty of beautiful shoulders is the last thing a woman loses, above all when her life has been pure. Adeline selected her items of dress carefully; but a pious and chaste woman will always be chastely dressed, in spite of all the little adornments of coquetry. What use are new gray silk stockings, and high-heeled satin shoes, when she is utterly ignorant of the art of displaying, at the critical moment, a pretty foot, a few inches beyond a half-lifted skirt, in such a way as to open up horizons of desire! She did indeed put on her prettiest dress of flowered muslin, with a low neck and short sleeves, but, alarmed at this bareness, she covered her lovely arms with sleeves of transparent gauze, and veiled her bosom and shoulders with an embroidered fichu.

Her curls, *à l'Anglaise,* seemed to her too suggestive, and she extinguished their vitality under a very pretty cap; but, with or without the bonnet, would she ever have known how to make play with their golden ringlets, to show them off, to display her tapering fingers for admiration?

As for rouge, the conviction of guilt, the preparations for a deliberate sin, threw this saintly woman into such a fever that she had, for a while, all the color of her youth. Her eyes shone, and her cheeks glowed. But instead of putting on a seductive air, she saw herself as shameless, and was horrified. At Adeline's request Lisbeth had described to her the circumstances of Wenceslas's infidelity, and the Baroness had learned to her great astonishment that in one evening, in a moment, Madame Marneffe had made herself the mistress of the bewitched artist.

"How do these women do it?" the Baroness had asked Lisbeth.

Nothing exceeds the curiosity of virtuous women on this subject; they would like to possess the seductions of vice, while remaining pure.

"Why, they are seductive; that is their business," Bette had replied. "That evening, you see, Valérie was enough to damn an angel."

"Well, tell me how she did it."

"There is no theory; it is only a matter of practice, in that trade," Lisbeth had said mockingly.

The Baroness, remembering this conversation, would have liked to consult Cousin Bette; but there was no time. Poor Adeline, incapable of inventing a beauty spot or pinning a rosebud in the lovely middle of her bosom, of devising those stratagems of the toilet calculated to awake in men their slumbering desires, was merely carefully dressed. One cannot become a courtesan at will! "Woman is man's meat," as Molière wittily observed, by the mouth of the judicious Gros-René.[1] Such a comparison supposes a sort of culinary science in the art of love. Then the noble and virtuous wife would be the Homeric repast, flesh laid on burning coals. The courtesan, on the other hand, would be a dish by Carême,[2] with all its accompaniments, flavorings, and skill in preparation. The Baroness could not, did not know how to, serve up her white bosom in a magnificent dish of lace, after the manner of Madame Marneffe. The secret of certain attitudes, the effect of certain looks, were unknown to her. In fact, she did not possess any box of magic. The noble wife might have turned about a hundred times, and yet not known how to offer anything to the expert eye of a libertine.

To be an honest woman and a prude in the eyes of the world, and a courtesan for her husband, is the prerogative of the woman of genius, and these are few. Therein lies the secret of long attachments, inexplicable for women who do not possess these two magnificent faculties. Imagine Madame Marneffe virtuous, and you have the Marchesa de Pescara! But such great and illustrious women, beautiful, like Diane de Poitiers,[3] and virtuous, are few in number.

The scene with which this serious and terrible study of Paris manners opened was now to be repeated, with this one difference—that the miseries foretold by the captain of the municipal militia had reversed the roles. Madame Hulot awaited Crevel with the same intentions that had brought him, smiling at the Paris crowds from his milord, three years before. And, strangest of all, the Baroness, faithful to herself and to her love, was contemplating the worst kind of infidelity—that which is not even justified (in the eyes of certain judges at least) by the violence of passion.

"What can I do to become a Madame Marneffe?" she wondered, as she heard the doorbell.

She restrained her tears, and fever gave animation to her features, as she resolved to be a complete courtesan, poor noble creature!

"What the deuce can the worthy Baroness Hulot want with me?" thought Crevel, as he went up the wide staircase. "She is probably going to talk to me about my quarrel with Célestine and Victorin, confound it! But I shall not give way."

As he entered the drawing room, into which he was shown by Louise, he thought, as he surveyed the bareness of the *premises* (Crevel's word): "Poor woman! Here she is, like a fine picture put away in an attic by a man who knows nothing about painting."

Crevel, seeing that Count Popinot,[4] Minister of Commerce, bought pictures and statues, wanted to become famous as one of those Maecenases[5] of Paris, whose love of art consists in trying to buy for twenty sous works worth twenty francs. Adeline smiled graciously at Crevel, and motioned him to a chair facing her.

"Here am I, fair lady, at your service," said Crevel.

The Mayor, now a political figure, had taken to wearing black. His face emerged above this garb like the full moon rising above a mass of dark clouds. His shirt, adorned by three enormous pearls, worth five hundred francs apiece, gave a high idea of his capacity—his thoracic capacity—and he was fond of saying, "In me you see the future athlete of the Tribune!" His large plebian hands were encased in yellow gloves, even in the morning. His patent-leather boots suggested the little brown coupé with one horse which had brought him. In three years ambition had modified Crevel's famous pose. Like great painters, he had entered his second period. In high society, when he went to see the Prince de Wissembourg, to the Prefecture, to Count Popinot's, and the like, he held his hat in his hand in a free and easy style that Valérie had taught him, and inserted the thumb of the other hand into the armhole of his waistcoat with a waggish air, simpering and smirking at the same time. This new stance was the product of Valérie's sense of humor, who, on the pretext of rejuvenating her Mayor, had bestowed upon him yet one more ridiculous trait.

"I asked you to come, my dear kind Monsieur Crevel," the Baroness began in a stifled voice, "on a matter of the greatest importance."

"So I guessed, Madame," said Crevel with a knowing air, "but what you ask is out of the question. Oh, I am not a brutal father, a man, as Napoleon says, stiff through and through with avarice. Listen to me, fair lady. If my children were ruining themselves for their own benefit, I would come to the rescue. But to back your husband, Madame? That would be to pour water into the vessels of the Danaids![6] Their house is mortgaged for three hundred thousand francs, for an incorrigible father! They have nothing left, poor wretches! And they don't get any fun out of it. All they have got to live on now is Victorin's salary at the law courts. He will have to jabber to some purpose, that son of yours! And he was going to be a minister, that little lawyer, the hope of us all! A fine pilot, who has run aground badly; now if he had borrowed in order to get on, and got into debt entertaining deputies and canvassing votes and gaining influence, I should have said to him: 'Here is my purse; help yourself, my friend!' But to pay for his father's follies, follies that I foretold to you! Why, his father has ruined every chance he ever had of getting on—I am the one who will be a minister!"

"I'm afraid, *dear Crevel,* it was not about our children, poor dears! If you have hardened your heart against Victorin and Célestine I shall love them so much the more, and that may lessen the bitterness that your anger has caused in their kind hearts. You are punishing your children for a good action!"

"Yes, a good action ill done! That is halfway to being a crime!" said Crevel, much pleased with this epigram.

"Doing good, my dear Crevel," the Baroness continued, "does not consist in sparing money from an overflowing purse! It is to go short ourselves in order to be generous, make a sacrifice! It is being prepared for ingratitude! Heaven ignores the charity that costs us nothing."

"Saints, Madame, can go to the workhouse if they please; they know that for them it is the gate of heaven. As for me, I am a man of the world; I fear God, but I fear the hell of poverty more. To be penniless is the last degree of misfortune in society as it is today. I am a man of my time. I respect money!"

"From a worldly point of view," said Adeline, "you are right."

She found herself a hundred miles away from the point, and she felt like St. Lawrence on the gridiron as she thought of her uncle, for she could see him, in her mind's eye, blowing his brains out. She looked down and then raised her eyes, full of angelic sweetness—how unlike that provoking wantonness in which Valérie excelled—to look at Crevel. Three years earlier she would have enchanted Crevel with that adorable look.

"I have known you," she said, "to be more generous; then you used to speak of three hundred thousand francs in the most lordly way."

Crevel looked at Madame Hulot, and saw her like a lily about to fade, and a vague suspicion crossed his mind. But he felt so much respect for this saintly woman that he drove back such ideas into the unworthier regions of his heart.

"Madame, I have not changed, but there is—and ought to be—method in the lordliness of a retired businessman. He is systematic and economical in all things. He opens an account for his little amusements, and devotes certain profits to that heading; but as to touching his capital! That would be folly. My children shall have all I have to leave—their mother's fortune and my own; but surely they don't want to see their father becoming a dull dog—turning into a monk and a mummy! I enjoy life! I go gaily down the river—I fulfill all the duties that law, affection, and family life impose on me, just as I have always paid my bills promptly as they fall due. If my children manage their domestic life as well as I have, I shall be satisfied; and as for the present, so long as my follies—for I admit I am guilty of them—cost nothing to anyone except suckers—

pardon me, I don't suppose you know that piece of city slang—they will have nothing to reproach me with, and they will still come in for a tidy sum on my death. Your children cannot say as much for their father, whose goings-on are ruining his son and my daughter."

The Baroness was getting farther and farther away from her objective.

"You are very hard on my husband, my dear Crevel, and yet if you had found his wife frail you would have been his best friend."

She gave Crevel a burning glance. But then, like Dubois who gave the Regent three kicks,[7] she overdid it, and the Regency perfumer's profligate ideas returned; he thought to himself: "Does she want her revenge on Hulot? Does she like me better as a mayor than in the uniform of the National Guard? Women are unaccountable!"

And he took up his second-period position, looking at the Baroness with a Regency expression.

"One might suppose," she continued, "that you are taking your revenge on him for a virtue that resisted you—for a woman that you loved enough—to—buy her," she concluded almost inaudibly.

"For a divine woman," replied Crevel, with a meaning smile at the Baroness, who looked down to hide the tears in her eyes, "for you have swallowed some bitter pills ... in the last three years ... eh, my dear?"

"Don't let us talk about my troubles, dear Crevel; they are more than any human being can endure. But if only you still loved me you would save me from the abyss into which I have fallen. Yes, I am in hell! The regicides[8] that were tortured with red-hot tongs, and torn in quarters by four horses, were on a bed of roses in comparison with me, because only their bodies suffered, but my very heart is torn in pieces."

Crevel's hand moved from his armhole; he rested his hat on the worktable, broke his pose, and smiled! This smile was so silly that the Baroness misunderstood it, and took it for an expression of kindness.

"You see a woman not in despair, but in the death throes of her honor, prepared to do anything, *my dear,* to prevent a crime."

Fearing that Hortense might come in, she bolted the door; then, with the same impulsive gesture, she flung herself at Crevel's feet, seized his hand, and kissed it.

"Be my deliverer!" she cried.

She believed there was a generous strain in his shopkeeper's heart, and conceived the sudden hope that she might obtain the two hundred thousand francs without losing her honor.

"Buy affection—for you were ready to buy virtue," she went on, looking up at him wildly. "Put your trust in my honor as a woman, in my honor, whose integrity you know! Be my friend! Save an entire family from ruin, shame, and despair, and keep it from sinking into the mud, where there are quicksands and blood! Don't ask me to explain!" she said, as Crevel made a move, and was about to speak. "Above all, don't say to me 'I told you so!' like those friends who are glad at misfortune. Come! Put yourself in the hands of a woman you used to love, and whose humiliation at your feet is perhaps her noblest moment! Do not make terms with her, but be sure that her gratitude will withhold nothing from you! No, give me nothing, but lend me, lend to me, whom you used to call Adeline!"

At this point her tears flowed so fast, and Adeline was sobbing so uncontrollably, that Crevel's gloves were soaked through. The words "I need two hundred thousand francs" were scarcely audible in that flood of weeping, just as stones, however large, cannot be seen in Alpine torrents swollen by the melting snows.

Such is the inexperience of virtue! Vice asks for nothing, as we have seen in the case of Madame Marneffe; it succeeds in having everything offered to it. Such women only make their demands when they have made themselves indispensable, or when a man has to be "worked," as one works a quarry in which the lime has become scarce, "worked out," as the quarrymen say. On hearing these words Crevel understood everything. He raised the Baroness with a gallant air, with the insolent phrase, "Come now, bear up, Mother," which Adeline in her distraction did not even hear. The scene was changing its character, and Crevel was becoming, as he himself would have said, "master of the situation."

Chapter XXIX

The magnitude of the sum startled Crevel so much that the emotion aroused in him by seeing this beautiful woman in tears at his feet was suddenly dissipated. Besides, however angelic and saintly a woman may be, her beauty disappears when she is weeping floods of tears. The Madame Marneffes, as we have seen, cry a little on occasion, allowing a stray tear to trickle down their cheeks; but to burst into tears, in such a way as to make their eyes and noses red! Never would they make such a mistake as that!

"Come, come, my child, calm yourself," said Crevel, taking the beautiful Madame Hulot's hands in his own, and patting them. "Good Lord! Why are you asking me for two hundred thousand francs? What are you going to do with them? Who are they for?"

"Don't ask me to give an explanation, but give them to me! You will have saved the lives of three people, and our children's honor!"

"And do you suppose, little woman, that you would find a man in the whole of Paris who could go, at a word from a woman practically off her head, and produce, there and then, out of a drawer, somewhere or other, two hundred thousand francs that have been quietly simmering there, waiting until she deigns to skim them? Is that all you know of life, and business, my dear? Your people are in a bad way, send them the Sacraments; for no one in Paris, with the exception of Her Holiness the Bank,[1] the great Nucingen, or some insane miser who has fallen in love with gold, as we common men do with women, could work a miracle of that kind! Even the Civil List, however civil it may be, would ask you to call back tomorrow. Everyone has his money invested, and uses it to the best advantage. You are deceiving yourself, my dear angel, if you imagine that Louis-Philippe rules the country—he himself does not make that mistake. He knows very well, like the rest of us, that above the law is the holy, venerable, solid, adored, gracious, beautiful, noble, young, and all-powerful franc! Now, my angel, money demands interest, and it is always busy watching for its opportunities. 'God of the Jews, thou art supreme!' says Racine.[2] In short, the old story of the Golden Calf. There was financial speculation in the desert in the days of Moses, and we have returned to the biblical traditions. The Golden Calf was the first ledger," he went on. "You have lived too long in the Rue Plumet, Adeline. The Egyptians must have lent enormous sums to the Hebrews, and what they ran after was not God's Chosen People, but their capital!"

He looked at the Baroness with a look that invited her to admire his cleverness.

"You don't know how devoted citizens are to their sacred pile," he continued, after this pause. "Now if you'll have the goodness to listen to me! Get this idea into your head. You want two hundred thousand francs? No one can give them to you without selling out some of his capital. Now work it out! To raise two hundred thousand francs in ready money would mean selling out above seven hundred thousand francs in three-per-cents.[3] Well, you could not raise your money in less than two days. That would be the very least time it would take. If you want to persuade a man to hand over a fortune—and a lot of people would consider two hundred thousand francs a fortune—well, the least you can do is to say where all that money is going to, and what you want it for."

"It is going, my dear, kind Crevel, to save the lives of two men, one of whom would die of grief and the other kill himself! And for my sake, too, for I should certainly go mad. I am a little mad already, am I not?"

"Not so very mad!" he said, putting his arm around Madame Hulot's knees. "Old Crevel has his price, since you thought of applying to him, my angel."

"It seems that one has to let a man put his arms around one's knees!" thought this saintly and noble woman, hiding her face in her hands. "You offered me a fortune once," she said aloud, blushing.

"Ah! little woman, that was three years ago," said Crevel. "Oh! you are more beautiful now than I ever saw you!" he exclaimed, taking the Baroness's arm and pressing it to his heart. "By Jove, you have a good memory, my child! Well, now you see what a mistake you made in being so prudish! Because those three hundred thousand francs that you so nobly refused are in another woman's pocket. I loved you, and I still love you; but to go back to three years ago, when I said to you 'You shall be mine!' What was my motive? I wanted to have my revenge on that cad Hulot. Well, my dear, your husband took a gem of a woman as his mistress, a pearl, a knowing little hussy who must then have been twenty-three, for she is now twenty-six. I thought it would be more amusing, more complete, more Louis XV, more Marshal de Richelieu, would have more kick to it, to carry off that charming creature, who, in any case, never loved Hulot, and who for three years has been crazy about your humble servant."

As he spoke Crevel, from whose hands the Baroness had withdrawn her own, had resumed his attitude. He put his thumbs in his armholes and beat his chest with both his hands, for all the world like a flapping pair of wings, thinking that he was thus making himself desirable and charming. It was as much as to say, "This is the man to whom you showed the door!"

"So you see, my dear, I have had my revenge, and your husband knows it! I proved to him categorically that he had been duped, what you call tit for tat. Madame Marneffe is *my* mistress, and if friend Marneffe kicks the bucket she will be my wife."

Madame Hulot looked at Crevel with a fixed, distrait look.

"Hector knew that!" she said.

"And went back to her!" Crevel replied. "And I put up with it, because Valérie wanted her husband made a chief clerk; but she gave me her word to arrange things so that our Baron should be completely done for so that he won't show up any more. And my little duchess—for she was born to be a duchess, that woman, upon my word!—kept her promise. She has returned your Hector to you, Madame, as she so wittily put it, 'virtuous in perpetuity.' It has taught him a lesson, and no mistake! The Baron has had some hard knocks; he won't keep any more dancers, or pretty ladies either. He is radically cured, for he has been rinsed out like a beer glass. If you had listened to old Crevel, instead of humiliating him, and showing him the door, you should have had four hundred thousand francs, because my revenge has cost me more than that. But I hope to get my money back when Marneffe dies . . . I have invested it in my future wife. That is the secret of my extravagances. I have solved the problem of how to act the *grand seigneur* inexpensively."

"Would you give your daughter such a stepmother!" exclaimed Madame Hulot.

"You don't know Valérie, Madame," Crevel replied sententiously, taking up the attitude of his first period. "She is well born, and a lady, and extremely well connected. Why, only yesterday the vicar of her parish dined with her. We have given a superb monstrance[4] to the church—for she is very devout. She is clever, you see, and witty, charming, and well informed—she has everything. And for myself, my dear Adeline, I owe everything to that charming woman. She has broadened my outlook, and polished my speech, as you can see; she keeps me in hand, gives me ideas, and helps me to express them. I never make mistakes in grammar now. I have changed a lot—you must have noticed it. And what is more, she has inspired my ambition. I shall be a deputy, and I won't make any blunders, because I shall consult my Egeria[5] even on the smallest points. All great politicians, from Numa to our present Prime Minister,[6] have had their sybil of the fountain. Valérie entertains a score of deputies; she is becoming very influential, and now that she is going to move into a charming house, and have a carriage, she will be one of the hidden arbiters of Paris. Such a woman is a real power! Oh, yes, I have often thanked my lucky stars that you were virtuous!"

"It is enough to make anyone doubt the goodness of God!" exclaimed Adeline, whose indignation had dried her tears. "But it is impossible—divine justice must be hanging over her head!"

"You don't know the world, fair lady!" said Crevel, the great politician, deeply offended. "The world, my dear Adeline, loves success. After all, has it ever come in search of your sublime virtues, whose price is two hundred thousand francs?"

Madame Hulot shuddered at this speech, and her nervous trembling came on again. She realized that the ex-perfumer was taking a mean revenge on her, just as he had had his revenge on Hulot. Her gorge rose with disgust, in a spasm that contracted her throat so violently that she could not speak.

"Money!" she managed to say at last. "Always money!"

"You touched me deeply," said Crevel, brought back by this exclamation to the humiliation of this woman, "when I saw you there, weeping at my feet. Well, perhaps you don't believe me, but if I had my note-case with me I would have given it to you. Come, now, do you really need such a large sum?"

On hearing that question, pregnant with two hundred thousand francs, Adeline forgot the insults of this cheap imitation of a fine gentleman at the bait of success so cunningly dangled by Crevel, whose only motive was to learn Adeline's secrets so as to laugh over them with Valérie.

"Oh, I will do anything!" exclaimed the wretched woman. "Sir, I am prepared to sell myself—to become a Valérie, if need be."

"You would find that difficult," said Crevel. "Valérie is a masterpiece in her own way, you know, Mother. Twenty-five years of virtue puts men off, like a neglected disease. And your virtue has grown moldy, my child. But you shall see how fond of you I am. I shall manage to get you your two hundred thousand francs."

Adeline seized Crevel's hand, and pressed it to her heart, unable to utter a word, and tears of joy came into her eyes.

"Oh! Not so fast! it will have to be angled for! Now, I am a good sort, with no prejudices—like a good time—and I am going to speak to you plainly. You want to do as Valérie does. Very good, but that is not the whole story. You need to get hold of some sucker, a stockholder, a Hulot. Now, I know a retired tradesman, a hosier, as a matter of fact. He is dull, and stupid, hasn't an idea in his head. I am licking him into shape, but I don't know when he will do me any credit. My man is a deputy. He is vain, and a bore. Some virago of a wife buried in the provinces has preserved him in a state of complete innocence from the luxury and pleasures of Parisian life; but Beauvisage—he is called Beauvisage—is a millionaire, and he would give, as I would have given three years ago, my dear, a hundred thousand crowns to have a real lady for his mistress. Yes," he said, thinking that he had understood correctly a gesture from Adeline, "he is jealous of me, you see. Yes, he is jealous of my happiness with Madame Marneffe, and the fellow is quite capable of selling an estate to purchase a—"

"Stop, Monsieur Crevel!" said Madame Hulot, no longer concealing her disgust, her face revealing all her shame. "You have punished me enough, more than I deserved. My conscience, so sternly suppressed by the iron hand of necessity, cries out to me, at this last insult, that some sacrifices are impossible! I have no pride left—I shall not flare up, as I did in the old days, and order you to go, after receiving this mortal thrust. I have lost the right to do so. I offered myself to you like a prostitute. Yes," she went on, in reply to a movement of protest, "I have defiled my life, pure until now, with an odious intention; and . . . I have no excuse. I know that! I deserve all the insults that you can heap on me! God's will be done! If he desires the death of two beings worthy to go to him—if they die, I shall mourn them, and pray for their souls! If he wills the humiliation of our family, we must bow under the avenging sword, and kiss it, like Christians. I shall know how to expiate this shameful incident that will be the torment of all my last days. It is no longer Madame Hulot, sir, who is speaking to you, but a poor humble sinner, a Christian whose heart henceforth will know only one sentiment, that of repentance, and who will give herself up entirely to prayer and charity. With such a sin on my conscience I am the last of women and the first of penitents. You have been the means of bringing me to my senses; the voice of God is speaking in me now, and it is you whom I must thank."

She was shaking again with that nervous trembling that never left her from that hour. Her sweet voice contrasted strangely with the feverish speech of the woman who had resolved to dishonor herself to save her family. The blood left her cheeks; she was pale, and her eyes were dry.

"In any case, I played my part very badly, did I not?" she went on, looking at Crevel with the sweetness with which a martyr might have looked at a proconsul. "True love, the holy and devoted love of a woman offers quite other pleasures than those to be bought in the market of prostitution! But why say more?" she said, recollecting herself, and advancing another step up the path to perfection. "My words sound like irony, but indeed they are not! Forgive me. Besides, sir, I had no intention of hurting anyone but myself."

The majesty of virtue, its holy radiance, had driven out the transient impurity of this woman, who, resplendent in the beauty natural to her, seemed in Crevel's eyes to have grown taller. Adeline at this moment had the sublimity of one of those emblems of religion, upheld by a cross, painted by the early Venetian school; but she expressed, in her misfortune, all her greatness, and that of the Catholic Church to which she flew for refuge like a wounded dove. Crevel was dazzled and dumfounded.

"Madame, I am at your service, unconditionally!" he exclaimed, in an impulse of generosity. "We will look into this matter and . . . whatever you want . . . even the impossible . . . I will do. I will deposit securities at the bank, and within two hours you shall have the money."

"Oh, God, this is a miracle!" said poor Adeline, falling on her knees.

She repeated a prayer with a fervor that touched Crevel so profoundly that Madame Hulot saw tears in his eyes when, her prayer ended, she rose to her feet.

"Be a friend to me," she said. "Your heart is better than your conduct and your words. God gave you your heart, but you have learned your ideas from the world, and from your passions! Oh, I will really love you," she exclaimed with an angelic ardor whose expression contrasted strangely with her foolish attempts at coquetry.

"Do not tremble like that," said Crevel.

"Am I trembling?" asked the Baroness, who had not noticed this infirmity that had so suddenly come upon her.

"Yes. Why, look," said Crevel, taking Adeline's arm and showing her that she was shaking with nervousness. "Come, Madame," he added, with respect, "calm yourself. I am going to the bank."

"Come back quickly! Remember," she said, giving away her secrets, "it is a matter of preventing the suicide of my poor uncle Fischer, whom my husband has compromised, because now I can trust you, and tell you everything! Ah! if we do not succeed in time, I know the Marshal—he is so sensitive, and he would not survive the shock many days!"

"I will go, then," said Crevel, kissing the Baroness's hand. "But what has poor old Hulot been up to?"

"He has robbed the State!"

"Good Heaven! I'll be off at once. I understand, and I admire you!"

Crevel bent on one knee, kissed Madame Hulot's skirt, and vanished, saying, "I will be back presently."

Unfortunately, on his way from Rue Plumet to fetch his securities from his own house Crevel had to pass Rue Vanneau, and he could not resist the pleasure of going to see his little duchess. When he arrived his face still showed signs of emotion. He went into Valérie's bedroom, where he found her doing her hair. She examined Crevel in the mirror, and was, like all women of her sort, annoyed to see—although she still knew nothing of the occasion—that he was under the stress of an emotion of which she was not the cause.

"What is the matter, my poodle?" she said to Crevel. "Is this how you come to see your little duchess? I won't be your duchess any more, sir, and I won't be your sweetie-pie either, you old monster!"

Crevel replied with a sad smile, and a glance toward Reine.

"Reine, my child, that will do for today; I can finish my hair myself. Give me my Chinese dressing gown, because *my gentleman* seems to me in a fine Chinese puzzle."

Reine, whose face was pitted like a colander, and who seemed to have been made specially for Valérie, exchanged a smile with her mistress, and brought the dressing gown. Valérie took off her wrap—she was in her vest—and took refuge in her dressing gown like a grass-snake disappearing under a tuft of grass.

"Madame is not at home?"

"What a question!" said Valérie. "Now, tell me, my big puss, has the *Rive Gauche* gone down?"

"No."

"They have raised the price of the house?"

"No."

"You are afraid you are not the father of your little Crevel?"

"What an idea!" replied this man, so sure that he was loved.

"Well, really, I can't guess!" said Madame Marneffe. "When I have to draw out your troubles like a cork out of a wine bottle, I give it up! Go away—you bore me."

"It is nothing," said Crevel. "I must find two hundred thousand francs within two hours."

"Well, you will find them! For that matter, I have not spent the fifty thousand francs we got for the police report on Hulot, and I can ask Henri for fifty thousand."

"Henri! It is always Henri!" Crevel exclaimed.

"And do you imagine, you green old Machiavelli, that I am going to send Henri away? Is France going to disarm her fleet? Henri—he is a dagger in its sheath, hanging on a nail. That boy," she said, "serves to show me whether you love me … and this morning you don't love me."

"Not love you, Valérie?" said Crevel. "I love you a million!"

"That is not enough!" she went on, jumping on to Crevel's knees, and putting both her arms around his neck as if she were hanging herself on a hat-peg. "I want to be loved ten million, as much as all the gold in the world—and more. Henri can't be with me five minutes without telling me everything he has on his mind! Come, what is it, my big poodle? Out with it! Tell Mamma all about it!"

And she brushed Crevel's face with her hair, and pulled his nose.

"How can you have a nose like that," she went on, "and still have secrets from your Vava——lélé——ririe!"

At *Vava* she bent his nose to the right, at *lélé* to the left, and at *ririe* tweaked it straight again.

"Well, I have just seen—"

Crevel stopped, and looked at Madame Marneffe. "Valérie, my jewel, do you promise on your honor—you know, on ours—not to repeat a word of what I tell you?"

"That is understood, Mayor! Raise your right hand, thus! And your foot!"

She posed in such a way as to strip Crevel (as Rabelais puts it)[7] from his brain to his heels; she was so amusing and irresistible, her naked form visible through a mist of fine lawn.

"I have just seen virtue in despair."

"Is there any virtue in despair?" she said, shaking her head and crossing her arms like Napoleon.

"It was poor Madame Hulot. She needs two hundred thousand francs! If she does not get them, the Marshal, and old Fischer, will blow their brains out; and as you are partly responsible for all that, my little duchess, I am going to do what I can. Oh, she is a saintly woman. I know her well; she will pay me the whole lot back."

At the word Hulot, and at the mention of two hundred thousand francs, Valérie darted a look from between her long eyelashes, like the flash of a cannon in its smoke.

"How did the old girl manage to get around you? She let you see—what? Her religion?"

"Do not make fun of her, my precious; she is a truly saintly, truly noble and devout woman, who deserves respect!"

"And what about me? Do I not deserve respect?" said Valérie, with a menacing look at Crevel.

"I didn't say that," Crevel replied, realizing that praise of virtue might hurt Madame Marneffe's feelings.

"I am religious too," said Valérie, moving away from him, and sitting in an armchair. "But I don't make a parade of my religion; I go to church in secret."

She sat in silence, and took no further notice of Crevel. Dreadfully distressed, he went and stood in front of the chair where Valérie had buried herself, and found her lost in those thoughts that he had so foolishly suggested.

"Valérie, my little angel!"

Profound silence. A highly problematical tear was furtively wiped away.

"One word, my sweetie-pie!"

"Well?"

"What are you thinking, my sweetheart?"

"Ah, Monsieur Crevel, I was thinking of the day of my First Communion. How pretty I was then! How pure I was then! How good I was then! Immaculate! Ah! if anyone had said to my mother, 'Your daughter will be a kept woman; she will be unfaithful to her husband. Some day a police officer will find her in a certain little villa, and she will sell herself to a Crevel to deceive a Hulot—two horrible old men. . . .' Pah! Why, she would have died before the end of the sentence, she loved me so much, poor woman."

"Don't take on like this!"

"You do not know how much a woman must love a man in order to silence the remorse that gnaws at the heart of an adulterous wife. I am sorry that Reine has gone; she would have told you that only this morning she found me in tears, praying. I, Monsieur Crevel, for my part, do not scoff at religion. Have you ever heard me say a wrong word on that subject?"

Crevel shook his head.

"I never allow religion to be discussed in my presence. I make fun of everything under the sun: royalty, politics, money, all that is held sacred in the eyes of the world—judges, marriage, love, young girls, old men! But the Church! And God! . . . Ah, there I draw the line. I know very well that I am wicked—that I am sacrificing my future happiness for you . . . and you don't know how much love that means!"

Crevel clasped his hands.

"Ah, you would have to see into my heart, and there measure the extent of my convictions, before you could know how much I have sacrificed for you! I feel that I have the making of a Magdalene in me. And you know how much respect I show to priests! Think of the presents I have given to the Church! My mother brought me up in the Catholic faith, and I know about God. It is to sinners like us that He speaks most terribly!"

Valérie wiped away two tears that rolled down her cheeks. Crevel was appalled; in her exaltation Madame Marneffe got up.

"Calm yourself, my precious duck! You alarm me!"

Madame Marneffe went down on her knees.

"Oh, God! I am not utterly wicked!" she said, joining her hands. "Deign to rescue Thy lost lamb, strike her, wound her, to snatch her from the hands that have caused her shame, and made her an adulteress, and with what joy she will nestle upon Thy shoulder! With what joy will she return to the fold!"

She rose, looked at Crevel, and Crevel was alarmed at her lackluster eyes.

"Yes, Crevel, and do you know, I am frightened sometimes. The justice of God is exercised in this world as well as in the next. What good can we hope from God? His vengeance falls on the guilty in all kinds of ways; it assumes every form of misfortune. All kinds of misfortunes that foolish people cannot understand are punishments. That is what my mother told me on her deathbed, speaking of her old age. And if I were to lose you—" she added, seizing Crevel in an embrace of savage energy. "Ah! I should die!"

Madame Marneffe released Crevel, knelt down again in front of her armchair, clasped her hands (and in what a ravishing attitude), and recited with infinite fervor the following prayer:

"And thou, Saint Valérie, my dear patron, why dost thou not visit more often the pillow of her who was confided to thy care? Oh, come this night, as thou camest this morning; inspire me with good thoughts, and I will leave my evil ways; I will renounce, like the Magdalene, these deceptive joys, the false glamour of the world, even the man I love!"

"My own sweetie-pie!" exclaimed Crevel.

"No more sweetie-pie, sir."

She turned away proudly, like a virtuous wife, her eyes full of tears, but dignified, cold, and indifferent.

"Leave me," she said, repulsing Crevel. "What is my duty? To belong to my husband. He is a dying man, and what do I do? Deceive him at the very gates of the tomb! He believes that your son is his. I shall tell him the truth, and begin by begging his pardon, before asking God to pardon me! We must part! Goodbye, Monsieur Crevel," she added, rising, and offering him a cold hand. "Goodbye, my dear; we shall not meet again until we meet in a better world. You owe me some happiness—criminal, to be sure; but now I want . . . yes, I shall earn your respect!"

Crevel was weeping hot tears.

"You great ninny!" she exclaimed, bursting into an infernal peal of laughter. "That is how pious women set about pulling up a carrot of two hundred thousand francs! And you talk of Marshal de Richelieu, the original of Lovelace, and yet you can be taken in by that old gambit, as Steinbock would say. I could drag two hundred thousand francs out of you myself, whenever I wanted to, you big simpleton! Keep your money! If you have too much, you ought to give it to me! If you give two sous to that good woman, who has taken up religion because she is fifty-seven, you shall not see me again, and you will lose your mistress; you would come back to me the next day, all bruised with her angular caresses, and wet through with her tears, and sick of her little cotton bonnets and her whimperings, turning her favors into rainstorms."

"The fact is," said Crevel, "that two hundred thousand francs is a lot of money."

"They certainly expect a great deal, these pious women! Well, I must say they sell their sermons at a better price than we sell the most precious and most certain thing on earth—pleasure! And what long stories they can tell! No, I know them; I have seen them at my mother's. They think anything is permitted for the sake of the Church, for . . . Really, my sweetie-pie, you ought to be ashamed of yourself—you, who are not given to generosity. Why, you have not given me two hundred thousand francs altogether!"

"Oh, I have," said Crevel. "The house alone will cost that."

"Then you must have four hundred thousand francs?" she said thoughtfully.

"No."

"Well, then, you meant to lend that old horror the two hundred thousand francs for my house? That is high treason against your sweetie-pie!"

"But please listen!"

"If you were giving that money to some stupid philanthropic scheme, you would pass as a man of the future," she said, becoming animated, "and I would be the first to advise you to do it; because you are too simple to write big political books that would make you famous—you haven't enough style to dish up a pamphlet. But you might make a gesture—other men have done it in your position—written their names in gold letters by putting them to some social, moral, national, or whatnot scheme. Benevolence is quite out, quite vulgar nowadays. Little comforts for old prisoners, who have a better time than many poor honest souls, is quite played out. I would like to see you think up something more difficult to do with your two hundred thousand francs—something really useful. Then you would be talked of as a benefactor to mankind, a Montyon,[8] and I should be proud of you! But to throw two hundred thousand francs into a holy-water stoup, lend them to a pious woman deserted by her husband for some reason or other—come! There is always a reason. Would you leave me?—is a stupidity which nowadays could only germinate in the brain of an ex-perfumer! It reeks of the counter. Two days later you would not dare to look yourself in the face in your glass! Go and put your money in the bank—run, for I shall not let you come back without a receipt! Go, and go quickly—at once!"

She pushed Crevel out of her bedroom by the shoulders, seeing avarice blossoming on his face once again. When the outer door of the flat had closed, she exclaimed, "Now, Lisbeth, you are more than revenged! What a pity she is at her old Marshal's! Wouldn't we have laughed! So the old woman wants to take the bread out of my mouth, does she? I'll show her!"

Chapter XXX

Being obliged to live in a style consistent with the highest military rank, Marshal Hulot had taken a fine house in the Rue du Montparnasse, in which there are two or three princely residences. Although he rented the whole of the house, he occupied only the ground floor. When Lisbeth went to keep house she at once wanted to let the first floor, which, she said, would pay the whole rent, so that the Count would be able to live almost rent-free; but the old soldier would not agree to this. For months past the Marshal had been troubled by many sad thoughts. He had noticed his sister-in-law's poverty, and saw that she was in distress, without being able to guess the cause. The old man, so cheerful in his deafness, had become taciturn; he had it in mind that his house might one day provide a refuge for Baroness Hulot and her daughter, and it was for them that he was keeping the first floor. The modest fortune of the Count de Forzheim was so well known that the Minister of War, the Prince de Wissembourg, had insisted on his old comrade's accepting a grant for the purpose of furnishing his house. Hulot had used this grant to furnish the ground floor, in which everything was in good order; for he did not, as he said, intend to accept the Marshal's baton just to carry it about the streets. Under the Empire the house had belonged to a senator, and the ground-floor rooms had therefore been magnificently fitted with carved paneling in gold and white, which was in a good state of preservation. The Marshal had put in some good old furniture in the same style. In the coach-house he kept a carriage with two crossed batons painted on the panels, and he hired horses when he had to go anywhere in style, to the Minister's or to the Palace, to attend a ceremony or a reception.

Since he had for his batman an old soldier of sixty, who had been with him for the last thirty years, and whose sister was his cook, he was able to save about twelve thousand francs, which he was adding to a little sum that was destined for Hortense. Every day the old man walked from the Rue du Montparnasse to the Rue Plumet along the boulevard; the pensioners of the Invalides,[1] as they saw him coming, never failed to stand at attention and salute him, and the Marshal rewarded every old soldier with a smile.

"Who is that man you always stand at attention to salute?" a young workman one day asked an old captain and pensioner.

"I will tell you, my lad," the officer replied, and the "lad" prepared to resign himself to listening to a long story.

"In 1809,"[2] said the pensioner, "we were defending the flank of the *Grande Armée,* marching on Vienna, under the command of the Emperor. We came to a bridge defended by three batteries of cannon, on a kind of cliff, in three redoubts one above the other, all trained on the bridge. We were under the command of Marshal Masséna.[3] That man you see there was at that time Colonel of the Grenadier Guards, and I was one of them. Our columns held one bank of the river, and the redoubts were on the other. Three times they attacked the bridge, and three times they were driven back. 'Go and fetch Hulot,' the Marshal said. 'Nobody except him and his men can swallow that morsel.' So we arrived. The General who was just withdrawing from the attack stopped Hulot under fire to tell him how to take the position, and he took up all the road. 'I don't want any advice, but room to pass,' said our Colonel coolly, and set out to cross the bridge at the head of his men. And then—bang! Thirty guns let loose on us—"

"Ah! By gosh," exclaimed the workman, "that must have accounted for some of these crutches!"

"If you had heard the quiet way he said that, my lad, you would bow down to the ground before that man! It is not so famous as the bridge of Arcoli,[4] but it was perhaps even finer. So we followed Hulot at the double, up to those batteries. All honor to those who fell there!" said the officer, raising his cap. "The *kaiserlicks* were amazed at the style of the thing. And so the Emperor made that old man you see there a count; and he honored us all in honoring our leader, and this King had good reason to make him a Marshal."

"Long live the Marshal!" said the workman.

"Oh, you can shout all you like! The Marshal is deaf—with the cannon-fire."

This anecdote perhaps gives some idea of the respect in which the pensioners held Marshal Hulot, whose Republican views, moreover, won for him the affection of the common people of the neighborhood.

Suffering taking hold of this calm, innocent, and honorable mind was a heartbreaking spectacle. All the Baroness could do was to lie, and to hide, with all a woman's tact, the terrible truth from her brother-in-law. During this disastrous morning the Marshal, who slept very little, like all old men, had extracted from Lisbeth full particulars of his brother's situation, and promised to marry her as the price of her indiscretion. Anyone will understand the pleasure with which the old maid allowed these confidences, which she had been longing to tell her future husband ever since she had come to the house, to be dragged out of her; for in this way her marriage was made more certain.

"Your brother is incorrigible!" Lisbeth shouted into the Marshal's good ear. Her strong clear peasant's voice enabled her to talk to the old man. She wore out her lungs, so eager was she to demonstrate to her future husband that he would never be deaf with her.

"He has had three mistresses," said the old man, "and his wife was an Adeline.... Poor Adeline!"

"If you will take my advice," Lisbeth shouted, "you will use your influence with the Prince de Wissembourg to find my cousin some suitable employment. She will need it, for the Baron's salary is pledged for three years."

"I will go to the Ministry," he replied, "and talk to the Marshal, and see what he has to say about my brother, and ask him to do something to help my sister. To find some place that is worthy of her."

"The Paris Women's Charitable Organization has formed several benevolent associations under the patronage of the Archbishop; they employ inspectors, who are quite well paid, whose task it is to look into cases of real need. Work of that kind would just suit dear Adeline; it would be after her own heart."

"Send for the horses," said the Marshal. "I will go and dress. I will drive to Neuilly if need be."

"How fond he is of her! I shall always find her in the way, at every turn!" said the peasant to herself.

Lisbeth was already bossing everyone in the house, but only out of the Marshal's sight. She had put the fear of God into the three servants. She had engaged a personal maid, and used all her old maid's energy in poking her nose into everything, taking stock of everything, and in every way looking after the well-being of her Marshal. No less Republican than her future husband, Lisbeth pleased him by her democratic views, and she flattered him, besides, with amazing skill; and for the last fortnight the Marshal, whose house was better kept, and who found himself being looked after like a child by its mother, had begun to regard Lisbeth as a partner after his dreams....

"My dear Marshal," she shouted, as she saw him to the steps, "put up the windows, and don't sit in a draft—to please me!"

The Marshal, an old bachelor who had never been pampered in his life, went off smiling at Lisbeth, although his heart was sore.

At this very moment Baron Hulot was leaving the War Office and was on his way to see the Marshal Prince de Wissembourg, who had sent for him. Although there was nothing unusual in the Minister's sending for one of his directors, Hulot's conscience was so uneasy that he fancied that there was something cold and forbidding in Mitouflet's expression.

"And how is the Prince, Mitouflet?" he asked as he shut the door of his office and joined the messenger, who had gone on ahead.

"He must have a bone to pick with you, Monsieur le Baron," replied the messenger, "for his voice, his temper, and his face are set stormy."

Hulot turned pale, and said nothing; he passed through the hall, the reception rooms, and arrived, his heart beating violently, at the door of his office. The Marshal, then aged seventy, with the pure white hair and tanned complexion of old men of that age, was striking on account of a brow of such breadth that it suggested to the imagination a field of battle. Beneath that hoary dome, crowned with snow, there shone, under the hollow of his strongly projecting brows, eyes as blue as Napoleon's, whose ordinary expression was one of the sadness of bitter thoughts, and regrets. For this rival of Bernadotte[5] had hoped for a throne. But those eyes could flash formidable lightning when they expressed strong feeling. His voice, deep at all times, rang at such moments with strident tones. In anger, the Prince was a soldier once more; he spoke the language of Sub-Lieutenant Cottin, and no longer minced his words. Hulot d'Ervy found this old lion, his hair disheveled like a mane, standing in front of the fireplace, his eyebrows knit in a frown, his back against the mantelpiece, and his eyes, to all appearances, fixed on vacancy.

"Here I am at your orders, Prince!" said Hulot in his most charming manner, affecting to be quite at his ease.

The Marshal looked hard at the Director without saying a word during the time it took the Baron to walk over from the door to within a few steps of him. This leaden stare was like the eye of God; Hulot could not sustain it, and lowered his eyes in confusion.

"He knows everything," he said to himself.

"Does your conscience tell you nothing?" asked the Marshal in his deep, ringing tones.

"It tells me, Prince, that I probably did wrong in ordering *razzias* in Algeria without referring the matter to you. At my age, and with my tastes, after forty-five years of service, I have no fortune. You know the methods of the four hundred elected representatives of France. All those gentlemen envy any man in a high position, and they have pared down the salaries of Ministers, and there it is. Just try asking them for money for an old servant of the State! What can you expect of men who pay legal officials as badly as they do? Who pay thirty sous a day to the workers at the port of Toulon, when it is a physical impossibility for a family to live on less than forty sous? Who never give a thought to the atrocity of paying clerks salaries of from six hundred francs to ten or twelve hundred in Paris, and who covet our places when they carry a salary of forty thousand francs? And who now refuse to restore to the crown a piece of crown property[6] confiscated in eighteen thirty, and acquired, what is more, from Louis XV's privy purse, when they were asked for it for an impoverished Prince! If you had not your fortune, Prince, you would be left stranded, like my brother, with nothing but your salary. As for your having saved the *Grande Armée,* and myself along with it, in the swampy plains of Poland, they would never give it a thought!"

"You have robbed the State! You have made yourself liable to be brought up for trial," said the Marshal, "like that clerk in the Treasury![7] And you treat that, sir, with such levity?"

"But there was a great difference, sir!" exclaimed Baron Hulot. "Have I dipped hands into a cash-box entrusted to my care?"

"A man in your position," said the Marshal, "when he commits such an infamous crime, is doubly guilty if he does it clumsily. You have shamefully compromised our high administration, which has hitherto been the purest in Europe. And that, sir, in order to get two hundred thousand francs for a whore!" said the Marshal in a terrible voice. "You are a Councilor of State, and a simple soldier is punished by death for selling the property of his regiment! Here is a story that Colonel Poutin, of the Second Lancers, once told me. At Saverne, one of his men fell in love with a little Alsatian girl who wanted a shawl; the hussy carried on so that the poor devil, who was about to be promoted to quartermaster, after twenty years of service, the pride of the regiment, sold, in order to get that shawl, some property belonging to his company. Do you know what that lancer did, Baron d'Ervy? He ate the glass of a window, after having stolen that property, and died eleven hours later at the hospital! You had better try to die of a stroke, so that we can save your honor."

The Baron looked with haggard eyes at the old warrior; and the Marshal, seeing his expression, which betrayed the coward, flushed crimson, and his eyes blazed.

"Are you going to let me down?" Hulot stammered.

At this moment Marshal Hulot, having been told that his brother was alone with the Minister, ventured to come in, and went straight up to the Prince, in the manner of deaf people.

"Oh!" exclaimed the hero of the Polish campaign, "I know what you have come for, my old friend! But it is quite useless."

"Useless?" repeated Marshal Hulot, who had heard only that one word.

"Yes, you have come to plead for your brother; but do you know what your brother is?"

"My brother?" asked the deaf man.

"Yes," shouted the Marshal. "He is an infernal blackguard,[8] unworthy of you!"

And in his wrath the Marshal's eyes darted those flaming looks that, like those of Napoleon, broke men's wills and nerve.

"You lie, Cottin!" replied Marshal Hulot, who had turned pale. "Throw down your baton, and I will throw mine! I am at your service!"[9]

The Prince went up to his old comrade, looked him full in the face, and shouted in his ear, as he pressed his hand, "Are you a man?"

"You shall see."

"Very well, pull yourself together! This is going to be the greatest blow that could befall you."

The Prince turned around, took a folder from his table, and put it into the hands of Marshal Hulot, shouting to him, "Read this!"

The Count de Forzheim read the following letter, which lay at the top of the folder:

To His Excellency the President of the Council. Secret and Confidential.
Algiers.

MY DEAR PRINCE,

We have a very unpleasant business on our hands, as you will see from the accompanying documents.

The matter, briefly, is this. Baron Hulot d'Ervy has sent an uncle of his into the province of Oran as a buyer of grain and forage, with a storekeeper as an accomplice. This storekeeper, to gain favor, made a confession, but has since escaped. The Public Prosecutor handled the affair firmly, thinking that only two minor officials were involved; but Johann Fischer, the uncle of your Director-General, finding himself about to be brought up for trial, stabbed himself in prison with a nail.

The matter would have ended there if this worthy and honest man, who was, it would seem, deceived by his accomplice and by his nephew, had not decided to write to Baron Hulot. This letter, seized by the police, so astonished the Public Prosecutor that he came to see me. It would be such a terrible thing to arrest and try a Councilor of State, a Director-General who has such a record of good and loyal service—for he saved us all after Beresina[10] by reorganizing the administration—that I had all the documents sent to me.

Must this affair take its course? Or would it be better, now that the principal apparent culprit is dead, to bury the matter, and condemn the storekeeper in default?

The Public Prosecutor has consented to my forwarding the documents to you; and, as Baron d'Ervy is domiciled in Paris, the proceedings would lie with your superior court. We have taken this rather shabby way of getting out of the difficulty for the moment.

Only, my dear Marshal, act quickly. There is already a great deal too much talk about this deplorable business, which will do us more harm than it has already done if the complicity of the principal culprit, which is at present known only to the Public Prosecutor, the examining judge, and myself, should leak out.

At this point the letter fell from Marshal Hulot's hands; he looked at his brother, and saw that there was no need to examine the documents; but he looked for Johann Fischer's letter, and handed it to his brother, after reading it at a glance.

From the Prison at Oran.

DEAR NEPHEW,

When you read this letter I shall no longer be alive.

Be quite easy; they will not be able to find any evidence against you. With myself dead, and your Jesuit Chardin escaped, the matter will end. The thought of Adeline's face made happy by you makes death easy to me. You need not trouble to send the two hundred thousand francs now. Goodbye.

This letter will be delivered to you by a prisoner whom I think I can trust.

JOHANN FISCHER.

"I ask your pardon," said Marshal Hulot to the Prince de Wissembourg, with pathetic pride.

"Come, never be formal with me, Hulot!" the Minister replied, shaking his old friend by the hand. "The poor lancer killed no one but himself," he said, with a thunderous look at Hulot d'Ervy.

"How much did you take?" said the Count de Forzheim sternly to his brother.

"Two hundred thousand francs."

"My dear friend," said the Count, addressing the Minister, "you shall have the two hundred thousand francs within forty-eight hours. It shall never be said that a man bearing the name of Hulot has defrauded the State of a single sou."

"What nonsense!" said the Marshal. "I know where the two hundred thousand francs are, and I will get them back. Hand in your resignation and ask for your pension," he went on, tossing a double sheet of foolscap in the direction of the Councilor of State, who had sat down at the table, for his legs were trembling. "Your trial would disgrace us all; so I obtained from the Council of Ministers permission to take this course. Since you are willing to accept life without honor, without my esteem, a degraded existence, you shall have the pension to which you are entitled. Only get yourself forgotten."

The Marshal rang.

"Is the clerk Marneffe there?"

"Yes, Your Excellency."

"Send him in."

"You," exclaimed the Minister, on seeing Marneffe, "and your wife have deliberately ruined the Baron d'Ervy, whom you see here."

"I beg your pardon, Monsieur le Ministre, we are very poor; I have only my salary to live on, I have two children, of which the second will have been brought into my family by Monsieur le Baron."

"The very picture of a scoundrel!" said the Prince, pointing Marneffe out to Marshal Hulot. "That's enough of your Sganarelle[11] speeches!" he went on. "Either you hand back two hundred thousand francs, or you will go to Algeria."

"But, Monsieur le Ministre, you don't know my wife—she has spent it all! Monsieur le Baron invited six people to dinner every day. Fifty thousand francs a year were spent at my house."

"Leave the room," thundered the Minister in the terrible voice that had given the order to charge into battle. "You will receive notice of your transfer within two hours. Go!"

"I would rather hand in my resignation," said Marneffe insolently. "To be what I am and beaten into the bargain would be too much of a good thing altogether. That wouldn't suit me at all!"

And he left the room.

"What an impudent scoundrel!" said the Prince.

Marshal Hulot, who throughout this scene had remained standing, motionless, pale as death, looking askance at his brother, went over and took the Prince's hand, saying again, "Within forty-eight hours the material damage shall be repaired. But the dishonor! Goodbye, Marshal; it is the last blow that kills. Yes, this will kill me," he added in a low voice.

"What the deuce brought you here this morning?" said the Prince, deeply moved.

"I came on behalf of his wife," replied the Count, pointing to Hector; "she is without bread . . . and especially now."

"He has his pension!"

"It is pledged!"

"He must be possessed by the devil!" said the Prince with a shrug. "What philter do these women make you drink, to take away your wits?" he said to Hulot d'Ervy. "How could you, knowing as you do the minute exactness with which the French administration puts everything on record, gives an account of every detail, consumes reams of paper to certify the receipt or the outlay of a few centimes—you whom I have heard to complain that a hundred signatures are required for trifles, to release a soldier, to buy a curry-comb—how could you possibly hope to hide your theft for any length of time? To say nothing of the newspapers and the envious, and the people who would like to steal! Do these women rob you of your common sense? They must put blinkers over your eyes! Or are you made differently from the rest of us? The day you ceased to be a man and became only a temperament you should have retired from administration. If in addition to your crime you are capable of such folly, you will end—I would rather not say where."

"Promise me to do what you can for her, Cottin?" said the Count de Forzheim, who had heard nothing, and who was thinking only of his sister-in-law.

"I will do all I can!" said the Minister.

"Thank you, then, and goodbye. Come, sir,"[12] he said to his brother.

The Prince looked with apparent calm at the two brothers, so different in their conduct, build, and character—the brave and the cowardly, the puritan and the lecher, the honest man and the peculator—and he thought, "That coward will not have the courage to die! And my poor Hulot, with all his integrity, has death in his knapsack!"

He sat down in his armchair and went on reading the dispatches from Africa, with a gesture that revealed at once the coolness of the soldier and the profound pity that is aroused by the spectacle of the battlefield; for really no men are more humane than soldiers, so stern in appearance, and to whom war has imparted that icy inflexibility so necessary on the field of battle.

The following day several newspapers contained under various headings the following items:

> The Baron Hulot d'Ervy has asked to be granted his retirement. The disorders in the Algerian administration brought to light by the death and flight respectively of two officials have influenced the decision of this high administrator. On hearing of the crimes of these employees, in whom he had been so unfortunate as to place his confidence, Baron Hulot had a stroke in the War Minister's office.
>
> Monsieur Hulot d'Ervy, brother of the Marshal, has been forty-five years in the service. His decision, which has been heavily opposed, has been learned with regret by all who know Baron Hulot, whose private qualities are no less conspicuous than his administrative talents. No one can have forgotten the devotion of the Commissary-General of the Imperial Guard at Warsaw, or the remarkable energy with which he organized supplies for the army raised by Napoleon in 1815.
>
> One more of the great names of the Empire is disappearing from the scene. Since 1830 Baron Hulot has always been one of the indispensable lights of the Council of State, and of the Ministry of War.

> *Algiers.*—The affair known as the forage case, which in several newspapers has been magnified to absurd proportions, has been brought to a close by the death of the chief culprit. Mr. Johann Wisch took his own life in prison; his accomplice has absconded, but will be sentenced in default.
>
> Wisch, formerly an army contractor, was an honest man and highly respected, who could not endure the realization that he had been the dupe of Chardin, the storekeeper who has absconded.

And in the Paris news the following items appeared:

> The Minister of War, in order to prevent all irregularities in the future, has decided to create a commissariat department in Africa. It is rumored that Monsieur Marneffe, a senior clerk, will be put in charge of this organization.
>
> Baron Hulot's succession excites many ambitions. We learn from a reliable source that this directorship has been offered to Count Martial de la Roche-Hugon, Deputy, and brother-in-law to Count de Rastignac. Monsieur Massol, Master of Appeals, is to be appointed Councilor of State, and Monsieur Claude Vignon becomes Master of Appeals.

Of all kinds of rumors the most dangerous for the opposition newspapers is the official rumor. However clever journalists may be, they are sometimes the dupes, willy-nilly, of the cleverness of those amongst them who, like Claude Vignon, have risen from the press to higher spheres. It takes a journalist to circumvent a newspaper. So it may be said, to misquote Voltaire, that

Le fait-Paris n'est pas ce qu'un vain peuple pense.[13]

Chapter XXXI

Marshal Hulot drove home with his brother, who took the front seat, respectfully leaving his elder brother alone inside the carriage. Neither of the brothers spoke a single word. Hector was shattered. The Marshal remained lost in thought, like a man who is collecting his forces and rallying his strength in order to sustain a crushing weight. When they reached his house he motioned his brother, still without speaking, but with a commanding gesture, into his study. The Count had been given, by the Emperor Napoleon, a splendid brace of pistols of Versailles make; he took the box, on which was engraved the inscription: "Presented by the Emperor Napoleon to General Hulot," from his desk, on which he laid it, and pointing to it, said to his brother, "There is your medicine."

Lisbeth, who had peeped through the half-open door, ran to the carriage, and ordered the coachman to drive as fast as he could to Rue Plumet. Within about twenty minutes she returned with the Baroness, whom she had told of the Marshal's threat to his brother.

The Count, without looking at his brother, rang for his factotum, the old soldier who had served him for thirty years.

"Beau-Pied," he said, "fetch my lawyer, and Count Steinbock, my niece Hortense, and the stockbroker of the Treasury. It is half-past ten, and I want them all here at twelve. Take a cab—and go faster than *that*!" he said, reverting to a Republican expression that he had often used in the old days.

And he put on the frown that had brought his soldiers to heel when he was combing the broom of Brittany in 1799 (see *Les Chouans*).[1]

"You shall be obeyed, Marshal," said Beau-Pied, saluting.

Without paying any attention to his brother, the old man returned to his study, took a key from his desk, and opened a malachite box mounted in steel, the gift of the Emperor Alexander. By the Emperor Napoleon's[2] orders he had gone to return to the Russian Emperor his personal property captured in the Battle of Dresden, in return for which Napoleon hoped to get Vandamme. The Czar had rewarded General Hulot handsomely, presenting him with this casket, saying that he hoped one day to be able to show the same courtesy to the Emperor of France; but he had kept Vandamme. The imperial arms of Russia were inlaid in gold on the cover of this box, richly ornamented in gold. The Marshal counted out the bank notes and gold pieces that it contained. There were a hundred and fifty-two thousand francs. He seemed satisfied. At this moment Madame Hulot came in, in a condition to melt the heart of the most politic judge. She flew into Hector's arms, looking from the box of pistols to the Marshal and back again with a wild expression.

"What have you against your brother! What has my husband done to you?" she cried with a voice so penetrating that the Marshal heard her.

"He has disgraced us all!" said the old soldier of the Republic, with an effort that reopened one of his old wounds. "He has robbed the State! He has dishonored my name, he has made me wish only for death—he has killed me. I have barely enough strength left to accomplish the restitution! I have been humiliated in the presence of the Condé of the Republic,[3] in the presence of the man I most respect, and to whom I myself unjustly gave the lie—the Prince de Wissembourg! Is that a small thing? That is how his account stands with his country!"

He wiped away a tear.

"And now, as to his family!" he continued. "He is robbing you of the bread I had saved for you, the fruit of thirty years' savings, of the privations of an old soldier. This was meant for you!" he said, pointing to the bank notes. "He has killed your uncle Fischer, a good and worthy son of Alsace, who could not, as he can, endure the thought of a stain on his peasant name. And worst of all, God, in His great goodness, allowed him to choose an angel among women! He had the unspeakable happiness to marry an Adeline! He has betrayed her, plunged her into the depths of sorrow, left her for common whores, street prostitutes, chorus girls and actresses—Cadine, Josépha, Marneffe! And this is the man that I treated as a son, my pride! Go, wretched man, if you can accept the degraded life you have made for yourself! Leave my house! I have not the heart to curse a brother I have loved so much. I am as weak with him as you are, Adeline; but never let him come into my presence again. I forbid him to attend my funeral, to follow my coffin. Let him, at least, bear the shame of his crime, if he feels no remorse!"

The Marshal, who had turned pale, dropped on to the settee of his study, exhausted by this solemn speech. And perhaps for the first time in his life two tears gathered in his eyes and trickled down his cheeks.

"Poor Uncle Fischer!" Lisbeth exclaimed, putting a handkerchief to her eyes.

"Brother," said Adeline, kneeling down in front of the Marshal, "live for my sake! Help me in the task that I must undertake of reconciling Hector to life, and making him redeem his faults!"

"He!" said the Marshal. "If he lives, he is not at the end of his crimes! A man who has failed to appreciate an Adeline, who has smothered in his soul the feelings of a true Republican, the love of his country, his family, and of the poor, that I tried to inculcate into him—that man is a monster, a swine! Take him away if you still love him, because something in me is crying out to charge my pistols and blow his brains out! By killing him I should save you all, and save him from himself!"

The old Marshal rose with a gesture so threatening that poor Adeline cried, "Come, Hector!"

She seized her husband, led him away, and left the house dragging the Baron after her; he was so broken down that she had to get him into a cab to take him to Rue Plumet, where he went to bed. The man, a complete wreck, stayed in bed for several days, refusing all food and not speaking a single word. It was by dint of tears that Adeline persuaded him to swallow a little broth; she watched over him, sitting by his bed, and of all the feelings that once had filled her heart there remained only a profound pity for him.

At half-past twelve Lisbeth showed into her dear Marshal's study—where she had stayed with him, so alarmed was she by the change that was taking place in him—the lawyer and Count Steinbock.

"Monsieur le Comte," said the Marshal, "I would ask you to sign the authorization which will enable my niece, your wife, to sell for certain funds a bond of which she at present possesses only titular ownership. Mademoiselle Fischer, you will consent to this sale, and agree to relinquish the interest on it that you at present draw?"

"Yes, my dear Count," said Lisbeth, without hesitation.

"Good, my dear," said the old soldier. "I hope I shall live long enough to recompense you. I did not doubt that you would agree. You are a real Republican, a woman of the people."

He took the old maid's hand and kissed it.

"Monsieur Hannequin," he said to the lawyer, "draw up the necessary document in the form of power of attorney, and let me have it here by two, so that the stock can be sold at the Bourse today. My niece, the Countess, holds the title; she will be here presently, to sign the power of attorney when you bring it, and so will Mademoiselle Fischer. Monsieur le Comte will go back with you and sign at your office."

The artist, at a sign from Lisbeth, bowed respectfully to the Marshal, and left the room.

At ten the following day the Count de Forzheim sent in his name to the Prince de Wissembourg, and was shown in immediately.

"Well, my dear Hulot," said Marshal Cottin, holding out the newspapers to his old friend, "we have saved appearances, you see. Read this."

Marshal Hulot put down the newspapers on his old friend's table, and handed him two hundred thousand francs.

"This is the sum of which my brother robbed the State," he said.

"This is quite absurd," exclaimed the Minister. "We cannot possibly," he added, speaking into the ear-trumpet that the Marshal offered him, "manage this restitution. We should have to admit your brother's complicity, and we have done everything possible to conceal it."

"Do what you like with it. But I do not wish the Hulot family to keep one sou of what was stolen from State funds," said the Count.

"I will lay the matter before the King. We will say no more about it," said the Minister, realizing that it would be impossible to overcome the old man's sublime obstinacy.

"Goodbye, Cottin," said the old soldier, taking the hand of the Prince de Wissembourg. "My very soul is frozen."

Then, after taking a step toward the door, he turned around and looked at the Prince; and seeing how deeply he was moved, he opened his arms to him, and the two old soldiers embraced each other.

"I feel as if I were saying goodbye to all the *Grande Armée*, in your person ..."

"Goodbye, then, my good old comrade," said the Minister.

"Yes, it is goodbye; for I am going the way of all those good soldiers of ours that we have mourned."

At this moment Claude Vignon was shown in. These two old relics of the days of Napoleon saluted gravely, concealing all traces of emotion.

"I hope you were satisfied with the notices in the papers," said the Master of Appeals–elect. "I managed to make the Opposition papers believe that they were publishing official secrets."

"Unfortunately it is all useless," the Minister replied, as he watched the Marshal going out through the outer room. "I have just said a last goodbye that fills me with grief. Marshal Hulot has not three days to live; I saw that clearly yesterday. That man, the soul of integrity, a soldier that the very bullets respected, in spite of his valor—there, look you, in that armchair, he received his deathblow, and at my hands, from a piece of paper! Ring for my carriage. I am going to Neuilly," he said, squeezing the two hundred thousand francs into his ministerial portfolio.

Three days later, in spite of Lisbeth's care, Marshal Hulot was dead. Such men are the honor of the parties that they support. To Republicans the Marshal was the very archetype of patriotism; so that they were all present at his funeral, which was followed by an immense crowd. The Army, the Government, the Court, and the common people, all came to pay homage to that lofty virtue, that high integrity, that unsullied glory. Such a demonstration from the whole nation is not to be had for the asking. This funeral was marked by one of those manifestations, full of delicacy, of good taste, and true feeling, that from time to time remind us of the qualities and glory of the French nobility. For behind the Marshal's coffin walked the old Marquis de Montauran, whose brother had been Hulot's opponent—his defeated opponent—in the rising of the Chouans in 1799. The Marquis, as he lay dying from the bullets of the "Blues," had entrusted the interests of his younger brother to the Republican soldier (see *Les Chouans*). Hulot had so well carried out the dying noble's verbal will that he had managed to save the property of the young man, who was at that time an *émigré*. Hence the homage of the old French nobility accorded to the soldier who, nine years before, had conquered *Madame*.[4]

This death, which took place just four days before the last reading of the banns of her marriage, was for Lisbeth a thunderbolt that burned up the harvest already garnered in the barn. The peasant had, as often happens, succeeded too well. The Marshal had died as a result of the blows struck at the family by herself and Madame Marneffe. The old maid's spite, that had seemed mollified by success, was increased by the disappointment of all her hopes. Lisbeth went to Madame Marneffe's, where she wept with rage; for she no longer had a home, as the Marshal's tenancy was so arranged that his lease terminated with his life. Crevel, in order to console the friend of his Valérie, took charge of her savings, and considerably increased them, placing her capital in five-per-cents in the name of Célestine, to yield her life-interest. Thanks to this negotiation, Lisbeth possessed an income of two thousand francs. When the Marshal's property was examined a note was found addressed to his sister-in-law, his niece Hortense, and his nephew Victorin, requesting them to pay, between them, an income of twelve hundred francs to Mademoiselle Lisbeth Fischer, whom he had intended to marry.

Adeline, seeing the Baron between life and death, managed for several days to hide from him the fact of the Marshal's death; but Lisbeth appeared in mourning, and the fatal truth was told him eleven days after the funeral. This terrible blow put new energy into the sick man, who got up, and found his family assembled in the drawing room, all wearing mourning. They became silent when he appeared. After a fortnight Hulot, who had become as thin as a ghost, seemed to his family to have become a mere shadow of his former self.

"We must decide what to do," he said in a toneless voice, sitting down in an armchair, and looking around at the group, from which Crevel and Steinbock were absent.

"We cannot stay here," Hortense was saying as her father came in; "the rent is too high."

"As to rooms," said Victorin, breaking this painful silence, "I can offer my mother—"

On hearing these words, which seemed to exclude himself, the Baron, who, with bowed head, had been studying the pattern on the carpet, though without seeing it, raised his head, and looked at the young lawyer wretchedly. A father's rights are still so sacred, even when he is disgraced, and stripped of all honor, that Victorin paused.

"To your mother," the Baron repeated. "You are quite right, my son!"

"The rooms above ours, in our wing," said Célestine, finishing her husband's sentence for him.

"Am I disturbing you, my dears?" said the Baron, with the gentleness of a man who has condemned himself. "You need not worry about the future. You will have no further cause to complain of your father, for you will not see him again until such time as you need no longer blush for him."

He took Hortense, and kissed her brow. He opened his arms to his son, who jumped up to embrace him when he guessed his father's purpose. The Baron beckoned to Lisbeth, who went toward him, and he kissed her brow. Then he went back into his bedroom, whither Adeline, in acute distress, followed him.

"My brother was right, Adeline," he said, taking her hand. "I am unworthy to live, unworthy of my family. I dared not bless my poor children, who have behaved so splendidly, otherwise than in my heart; tell them that I could not do more than embrace them. For from a man without honor, a father who has become the assassin and the scourge of his family, instead of being the defender of its honor, a blessing could bring only evil. But I shall bless them in my thoughts, every day. As for you, God alone, for He is all-powerful, can ever reward you according to your merits. I ask your forgiveness," he said, kneeling at his wife's feet, taking her hands, and wetting them with his tears.

"Hector, Hector, your sins are great, but the Divine mercy is infinite, and you can repair it all by staying with me. Raise yourself up in a Christian frame of mind, my dear. I am your wife and not your judge. I am yours; do what you like with me, take me with you wherever you go; I feel in myself the strength to console you, and make your life supportable, by my love, and care, and my respect! Our children are settled; they don't need me any more. Let me try to be your amusement and distraction. Let me share the hardship of your exile and poverty, and make it less hard. I shall always be of some use to you, even if it is only to save you the expense of a servant."

"Do you forgive me, my dear, beloved Adeline?"

"Yes; but, my dear, please get up!"

"Well, with that pardon I can live!" he said, rising. "I came back into our bedroom so that our children should not see the abasement of their father! Think of their having to see every day a father guilty as I am! That would be something dreadful, that would undermine paternal authority and disintegrate the family. Therefore I cannot remain among you; I must leave you in order to spare you the odious spectacle of a father without dignity. Do not try to prevent me from going, Adeline. That would only be to load with your own hand the pistol with which I should blow my brains out. And do not come with me into hiding; you would drive out the only strength that remains in me, that of remorse."

Hector's determination silenced his heartbroken wife. This woman, so great in the midst of such ruin, drew her strength from her close union with her husband; for she dreamed of having him to herself—she saw it as her heaven-sent mission to comfort him, to bring him back to family life, to reconcile him with himself.

"Hector, you aren't going to leave me to die of despair, worry, and anxiety!" she said, seeing the source of her strength being removed from her.

"I will come back, my angel, descended from the sky, I think, expressly for me; I will come back, if not rich, at least with enough to live on. Listen, my darling Adeline, I cannot stay here for many reasons. To begin with, my pension, which will be six thousand francs, is engaged for four years, and consequently I have nothing. I shall be in danger of arrest, in a few days, on account of notes-of-hand in the possession of Vauvinet. So I must keep away, until my son, with whom I shall leave precise instructions, has redeemed them. My disappearance will facilitate that. When my pension is freed, when Vauvinet has been paid, I will come back to you. You would betray the secret of my exile. Do not worry, do not weep, Adeline.... It will only be for a month."

"Where will you go? What will you do? What will become of you? Who will look after you, and you no longer young? Let me go into hiding with you. We will go abroad," she said.

"Well, we shall see," he replied.

The Baron rang, and ordered Mariette to collect all his things, and pack them, at once, and secretly. Then, after embracing his wife with a demonstration of tenderness to which she was unaccustomed, he begged her but to leave him alone for a few moments so that he could write out the instructions that Victorin would need, promising not to leave the house before the evening, or without her. As soon as the Baroness had gone back into the drawing room the cunning old man slipped through the dressing room, reached the hall, and handed Mariette a slip of paper on which he had written: "Send on my baggage by rail to Corbeil." The Baron got into a cab, and was already driving across Paris before Mariette went in and showed the Baroness this note, telling her that Monsieur had just gone out. Adeline flew into the bedroom, trembling more violently than ever; her children, alarmed, followed her on hearing a piercing cry. They found that she had fainted. She had to be put to bed, for she was attacked by a nervous fever, and for a month lay between life and death.

"Where is he?" were the only words she would say.

Victorin's search was fruitless. And this is why. The Baron drove to the Place du Palais-Royal. There, this man, who had summoned up all his ingenuity in order to work out a scheme that he had been planning during the days that he had lain in bed, crushed with pain and grief, crossed the Palais-Royal and hired a splendid carriage in the Rue Joquelet. Obeying the Baron's orders, the coachman drove to the Rue de la Ville-Evêque, and into the courtyard of Josépha's house, whose gates were opened, at a shout from the coachman, for this stylish carriage. Josépha came down, prompted by curiosity, for her footman had told her that a helpless old gentleman, unable to get down from his carriage, had asked her to speak to him for a moment.

"Josépha . . . it is I!"

The celebrated singer recognized Hulot only by his voice.

"What? Is it you, my poor old thing? I declare you look like a twenty-franc piece that the German Jews have pared down and the money-changers refuse!"

"Yes, worse luck!" said Hulot. "I have been at death's door! But you are as beautiful as ever! Will you do me a kindness?"

"That depends—everything is relative!" she said.

"Listen," said Hulot, "could you put me up for a few days in a servant's room, under the roof? I haven't a sou, and I am without hope, without bread, or pension, or wife, or children, or refuge, or honor, or courage, or a single friend—and what is worse, liable to be arrested because of some notes-of-hand!"

"You poor old thing! You are certainly *sans* a lot of things. Are you also *sans culotte*?"[5]

"If you laugh at me, I am lost!" exclaimed the Baron. "And I counted on you, as Gourville counted on Ninon!"[6]

"They say it was a real lady who reduced you to this state? These girls know more than we do about how to fleece a man! And here you are like a carcass that the crows have picked clean … one can almost see daylight through you!"

"Time is short, Josépha!"

"Come in, old dear! I am alone, and my servants do not know you. Send your cab away. Have you paid for it?"

"Yes," said the Baron, getting down, with the help of Josépha's arm.

"If you like, you can say you are my father," said the singer, moved to pity.

She made Hulot sit down in the splendid drawing room where he had last seen her.

"Is it true, old dear, that you have killed your brother and your uncle, ruined your family, mortgaged your children's house, and robbed the till of the African government, all for your princess?"

The Baron bowed his head sadly.

"Well, I admire that!" exclaimed Josépha, jumping up in her enthusiasm. "That is a real flare-up! A real Sardanapalus![7] It is in the grand style, complete! I may be a common hussy, but I have a heart! Well, I would rather have an out-and-out spendthrift like you, crazy about women, than these calculating bankers without any soul, who ruin thousands of families with their railways, that are gold for them, but iron for their victims! You have only ruined your own family; you have sold no one but yourself! And besides, you have excuses, physical and moral."

And striking a tragic pose, she recited: " '*C'est Vénus tout entière à sa proie attachée.*'[8] So there you are!" she concluded, with a pirouette.

Hulot found that vice absolved him; vice smiled at him in the midst of her lavish luxury. The magnitude of his crimes was here, as before a jury, an extenuating circumstance.

"Is she pretty, your real lady, at least?" asked the singer, trying as a first act of kindness to distract Hulot, whose unhappiness grieved her.

"Upon my word, almost as pretty as you are!" replied the Baron artfully.

"And … very amusing, they tell me? What does she do, then? Is she more witty than I am?"

"Don't let us talk about her," said Hulot.

"They say she has ensnared my Crevel, and little Steinbock, and a superb Brazilian."

"Very likely."

"And that she has moved into a house as pretty as this one, that Crevel has given her. That girl is my steward; she finishes off the bottles I have broached. That is why I am so anxious to know what she is like, old boy. I once just caught a glimpse of her driving in the *Bois*,[9] but only in the distance. Carabine tells me that she is an accomplished gold-digger. She is trying to eat up Crevel! But she will only manage to nibble him. Crevel is hard-boiled! A good-natured old egg, who always says yes, but who goes his own way all the same. He is vain, and lecherous, but his cash is cold. All one gets out of that sort is a thousand or three thousand a month, but they jib at any serious expense, like a donkey at a river. They are not like you, old dear; you are a man of passion—one could make you sell your country! So, you see, I am ready to do anything I can to help you. You are my father; you started me in my career! It is a sacred duty. What do you need? Shall I give you a hundred thousand francs? I would wear out my temperament to get it for you! As for giving you bed and board, that is nothing. A place will be laid for you here every day. You can have a very nice room on the second floor, and a hundred crowns a month for pocket money."

The Baron, touched by this reception, had a last access of honor.

"No, my dear, no; I did not come here to be kept," he said.

"It would be a triumph, at your age!" she said.

"This is what I want, my child. Your Duc d'Hérouville has large estates in Normandy, and I would like to be his agent, under the name of Thoul. I could perfectly well do it, and I am honest, because one may rob the Government, but one does not pilfer from the cash-box."

"Ah! Ah!" said Josépha. "He who has drunk must drink again."

"In fact, all I want is to live incognito for three years."

"Well, I could easily manage that for you," said Josépha. "All I need do is ask him tonight, after dinner. The Duke would marry me, if I wanted him to. But I have his money, and I want something else—his respect! He's a Duke of the old school! He is as noble and distinguished and great as Louis XIV and Napoleon rolled into one, although he's a dwarf. And besides, I have followed the examples of Schontz and Rochefide:[10] my advice has earned him two millions. But listen to me, my old son of a gun. I know you of old; you can't keep your eyes off women, and you would always be running after the girls of Normandy, who are very good-looking; you would get your bones broken by their lovers or their fathers, and the Duke would have to come to the rescue. Do you think I don't see from the way you look at me that the *young man* is not by any means dead in you, as Fénelon[11] says? That plan isn't in your line. You can't break so easily with Paris and us girls, old thing! You would die of boredom at Hérouville."

"What will become of me?" exclaimed the Baron. "For I only want to stay with you until I can find something to do."

"Well, would you like to know how I propose to fix you up? Listen, you old brigand; you can't do without women. That makes up for everything. Now listen. At the end of La Courtille, Rue Saint-Maur-du-Temple, I know of a poor family who possess a treasure: a little girl, prettier than I was at sixteen! Ah! there is a light in your eye already! She works sixteen hours a day embroidering fine materials for the silk-merchants, and for that she is paid sixteen sous a day, one sou an hour—a pittance! Well, they live like the Irish, on potatoes, fried in rat's dripping, at that, with bread five days a week, and they drink canal water out of the town taps, because Seine water costs too much; and she cannot set up on her own account without six or seven thousand francs. Your wife and family bore you, don't they? Besides, one could not be a nobody where one has been a little god. All you can do with a father with no money, and without honor, is to stuff him and put him in a glass case!"

The Baron could not help smiling at these outrageous sallies.

"Well, little Bijou is coming tomorrow, bringing me an embroidered dressing gown—an absolute *honey*! They have been working on it for six months. No one else will have anything like it! Bijou is fond of me, because I give her candy, and my old dresses. Besides, I send presents of bread and firewood and meat to the family, who would break the shins of the first-comer if I asked them to. I try to do some good in the world! Oh, I know what I suffered when I was hungry! Bijou has confided all her little secrets to me. That child has the makings of a character actress at the Ambigu-Comique.[12] Bijou's dream is to wear lovely dresses like mine, and, above all, to go in a coach! I shall say to her, 'My dear, what do you say to an old gentleman friend of—' How old are you?" she asked, breaking off. "Seventy-two?"

"I have lost count."

" 'What do you say to an old gentleman of seventy-two,' I shall say, 'very neat in his ways, who does not smoke, sound as a bell, as good as a young man? He will marry you—on the wrong side of the blanket[13]—and be very kind to you; he will give you seven thousand francs to set up in business, and furnish a flat for you, all in mahogany; and if you are a good girl, he will sometimes take you to a show. He will give you a hundred francs a month pocket money, and fifty for housekeeping!' I know Bijou! I was just like her at fourteen! I jumped for joy when that awful Crevel made me those very same horrible propositions! Well, old boy, you will be fixed up there for three or four years, not more."

Hulot did not hesitate; he was determined to refuse! But so as to seem grateful to the kindhearted singer, who was trying to help him according to her lights, he appeared to hesitate between vice and virtue.

"Good gracious! You are as cold as a paving stone in December!" she exclaimed, in surprise. "Why, you would be making a whole family happy—a grandfather who toddles about, a mother worn out with work, two sisters, one of them very plain, who earn thirty-two sous a week between them by ruining their eyesight. That will make up for the trouble you have caused at home, and you can redeem your sins and have as much fun as a tart at Mabille[14] at the same time."

Hulot, in order to put an end to the temptation, made a gesture of counting out money.

"Oh, don't worry about ways and means," Josépha replied. "My Duke will lend you ten thousand francs: seven thousand to set up an embroidery establishment in Bijou's name, three thousand for furnishing, and every three months you will find a check there for six hundred and fifty francs. When you get your pension again you can pay the Duke back the whole seventeen thousand francs. Meanwhile you will be as happy as a bull in clover, and hidden in a hole where the police will never find you. If you wear a big beaver overcoat, you will look just like a comfortable householder of the quarter. Call yourself Thoul if you fancy that name. I will introduce you to Bijou as an uncle of mine, who went bankrupt in Germany. You will be looked after like a god. There you are, Papa! Who knows, you may have no regrets. And in case by any chance you are bored, you had better keep a decent suit, and you can invite yourself to dinner here now and then, to pass the evening."

"And I meant to reform, and begin a new life! Listen, lend me twenty thousand francs, and I will go abroad to seek my fortune in America, like my friend d'Aiglemont[15] when Nucingen had ruined him."

"You!" exclaimed Josépha. "Leave morals to shopkeepers, to the rank and file, to worthy French citizens who have nothing to trade on but their good character! As for you, you were never intended for a ninny. You as a man are what I am as a woman—a cad of genius!"

"I will sleep on it, and we can talk about it tomorrow."

"You must come and dine with the Duke. My d'Hérouville will receive you politely, just as if you had saved the State, and you can decide. Now, cheer up, old thing! Life is like a dress—when it gets dirty we have to brush it; when it wears into holes we patch it up. But we wear it as long as we can!"

This philosophy of vice, and her gaiety, dissipated Hulot's bitter griefs.

Next day at noon, after an excellent breakfast, Hulot saw the entry of one of those living masterpieces that Paris, alone in the world, can produce; only in Paris exists that continual concubinage of luxury and poverty, vice and virtue, repressed desire and renewed temptation, that places that city in the tradition of Nineveh, of Babylon, and of Imperial Rome. Mademoiselle Olympe Bijou,[16] a young girl of sixteen, had the exquisite face that Raphael copied for his Virgins, innocent eyes, saddened by hard work, black, dreamy eyes with long lashes, whose sparkle was dimmed by laborious nights, eyes heavy with fatigue; a complexion of alabaster, almost unhealthy in its pallor; and a mouth like a half-opened pomegranate, a heaving bosom, with full breasts, lovely hands, teeth of dazzling whiteness, and an abundance of black hair. All this beauty was set off in a dress of cotton at seventy-five centimes a yard, trimmed with an embroidered collar; stitched leather shoes, and the cheapest of gloves. The child, quite unconscious of her worth, had dressed up in her best to go and see the fine lady. The Baron, in the grip of lechery once more, felt his whole life concentrated in his eyes. He forgot everything at the sight of this exquisite creature. He was like a hunter who sees game, who cannot resist taking aim, even in the presence of an emperor!

"And she is guaranteed innocent, a pure girl!" said Josépha. "And nothing to eat! That is Paris. I was like her once!"

"It's a bargain!" said the old man, getting up and rubbing his hands.

When Olympe Bijou had gone Josépha looked mischievously at the Baron.

"If you don't want any trouble, Papa," she said, "be as strict as a judge on the bench. Keep a tight hand on her, be a Bartholo![17] Look out for the Augustes and Hippolytes and Nestors and Victors[18]—all the *ors*,[19] including gold! Heavens! Once that child is dressed and properly fed, once she gets the upper hand, she will rule you like a Tartar. I will see about setting you up. The Duke does things well; he will lend you—which means giving you—ten thousand francs, and he will deposit eight thousand with his lawyer with instructions to pay you six hundred francs every quarter, because I cannot trust you. Don't you think I am nice?"

"Adorable!"

Ten days after deserting his family, when they were all gathered around Adeline's bed, in tears—for she seemed to be dying—and while she was asking, in a feeble whisper, "Where is he?" Hector, under the name of Thoul, Rue Saint-Maur, was established, with Olympe, as proprietor of an embroidery establishment under the name of Thoul and Bijou.

Chapter XXXII

Victorin Hulot, under the stress of the disaster loosed upon his family, received those final touches that make or mar a man. He was perfected. In life's great storms we act like a captain who lightens his ship of its heaviest cargo. The lawyer lost his self-consciousness, his air of complacency, his arrogance as an orator, and his political pretensions. In fact, he became, as a man, what his mother was as a woman. He made up his mind to make the best of Célestine—who certainly did not realize his dreams—and he saw life sanely, realizing that its universal law obliges us to put up with imperfections in everything. He vowed to do his duty in all things, so appalled was he by his father's conduct. These feelings were confirmed as he watched by his mother's bed on the day that she was pronounced out of danger. Nor did this happiness come singly. Claude Vignon, who had called to inquire every day on behalf of the Prince de Wissembourg after Madame Hulot's health, asked the re-elected deputy to go with him to see the Minister.

"His Excellency wants to talk over your family affairs with you," he said.

The Minister had known Victorin Hulot for a long time, and received him with characteristic friendliness that augured well.

"My boy," said the old soldier, "I promised your uncle the Marshal, in this very room, to look after your mother. That saintly woman, I am told, is now on the way to recovery, and the time has come to pour balm on your wounds. I have here two hundred thousand francs for you, which I shall now give you."

The barrister's gesture was worthy of his uncle the Marshal.

"Be quite easy," said the Prince, smiling. "It is money entrusted to me. My days are numbered—I shall not be here forever—so take it now, and be my deputy in the bosom of your family. You may use the money to pay off the mortgage on your house. These two hundred thousand francs belong to your mother and your sister. But if I were to give this money to Madame Hulot I fear that in her devotion to her husband she would be tempted to waste it; and the intention of those who return it to you is that it should be used for the support of Madame Hulot and her daughter, Countess Steinbock. You are a sensible man; you take after your noble mother, and your uncle, my friend the Marshal. You are appreciated here, my boy, and elsewhere. So you must be your family's guardian angel, and accept this legacy from your uncle and myself."

"Your Excellency," said Hulot, taking the Minister's hand and pressing it, "a man like yourself knows that thanks in words mean nothing, and that gratitude must be proved."

"Prove yours to me," said the old soldier.

"In what way?"

"By accepting my propositions," said the Minister. "We would like to offer you the appointment of legal adviser to the War Ministry, which, on the military engineering side, is up to its ears in litigation arising out of the plan for the fortification of Paris; and also as consulting lawyer to the Prefecture of Police, and a member of the Board of the Civil List. These three appointments would bring you in a salary of eighteen thousand francs, and would leave you completely free. You would still be able to vote in the Chamber in accordance with your political views and your conscience. You must regard yourself as absolutely free on that score. After all, we should be very badly off if we had no national opposition! And one other thing. Your uncle, the Marshal, a few hours before he died, wrote me a letter suggesting what I could do for your mother, of whom he was very fond. Mesdames Popinot, de Rastignac, de Navarreins, d'Espard, de Grandlieu, de Carigliano, de Lenoncourt, and de la Bâtie[1] have made a place for your good mother, as Lady Superintendent of their charities. These ladies, as presidents of various branches of good works, cannot do everything themselves, and they need a lady of character who can supervise them actively, go and visit unfortunate cases, see that charity is not being misused, making sure that the funds reach those who have applied for them, seeking out deserving cases who are too proud to ask for help, and so forth. Your mother will fulfill the function of a good angel, and will only come into contact with the priests and these charitable ladies; she will be paid six thousand francs a year, and her traveling expenses. You see, young man, how an honorable and upright man can still protect his family from beyond the grave. Names like that of your uncle are, and must always be, a shield against misfortune in any decent society. Follow in his footsteps; you have made a good start I know—persist in it."

"Such consideration does not surprise me in a friend of my uncle's," said Victorin. "I will try to live up to your expectations."

"Go and comfort your family, then. And by the way," the Prince added, shaking hands with Victorin, "I hear your father has disappeared!"

"Yes, unfortunately."

"A very good thing! That unfortunate man has shown great intelligence—a quality which, to be sure, he never lacked."

"He was afraid of his creditors."

"I see. Well, you shall have six months' salary in advance, on your three appointments. This prepayment will no doubt help you to redeem the notes-of-hand from the usurer. I shall be seeing Nucingen, and I might be able to free your father's pension without its costing a sou to you or my Ministry. But the peer has not killed the banker in Nucingen; he will want some concession or other."

So when he returned to Rue Plumet, Victorin was in a position to carry out his plan of taking his mother and sister into his house.

The distinguished young barrister possessed, as his sole fortune, one of the most beautiful properties in Paris, a house bought in 1834, in anticipation of his marriage, and situated on the boulevard between the Rue de la Paix and the Rue Louis-le-Grand. A speculator had built two houses between the boulevard and the street, and between these, between the two gardens and courts, there stood a magnificent wing, all that now remained of the splendors of the great mansion of the Verneuils. The younger Hulot, relying on Mademoiselle Crevel's dowry, had bought this superb property for a million francs, when it was put up to auction, and he had paid five hundred thousand francs down. He lived on the ground floor of the old wing, and proposed to pay off the rest of the price by letting the remainder; but although speculations in house property in Paris are safe enough, they are sometimes capricious, or slow, owing to unforeseen circumstances. As strollers in Paris must have observed, the Boulevard between the Rue Louis-le-Grand and the Rue de la Paix developed very slowly; it took so long to be tidied up and beautified that trade did not make its appearance there, with its splendid shop fronts, the gold of money-changers, the fairy creations of fashions, and all the extravagant splendor of shop windows, until 1840.

In spite of the two hundred thousand francs given by Crevel to his daughter at the time when his vanity was still flattered by this marriage, and before the Baron had robbed him of Josépha; and in spite of a further two hundred thousand francs paid off by Victorin in the course of seven years, there was still a debt of five hundred thousand francs to be paid off on the property by reason of the son's devotion to his father. Fortunately the steady rise in rents, and the beauty of the location, had by now greatly increased the value of the two houses. The speculation was bearing its fruit, after eight years, during which the lawyer had struggled desperately to pay the interest, and an insignificant sum on the capital. Tradespeople were offering good rents for the shops of their own accord, on condition of being given eighteen-year leases. The flats went up in value by reason of the shifting of the center of Paris business life, which was by then situated between the Bourse and the Madeleine, the district thenceforth to be the seat of financial and political power.

The money returned by the Minister, together with the salary paid in advance, and the premiums paid by his tenants, would now reduce Victorin's debt to two hundred thousand francs. The two houses, now entirely let, would bring in a hundred thousand francs a year. In another two years, during which Hulot could live on his salaries, doubled by the Marshal's appointments, he would be in a splendid position. This was indeed manna from heaven. Victorin could give his mother the first floor of his wing, and his sister the second, on which Lisbeth was also to have two rooms. And with Cousin Bette in charge, this triple household could meet its expenses, and present an honorable face to the world, worthy of a barrister of note. The stars of the Law Courts were rapidly disappearing, and Hulot, gifted with eloquence, caution, and strict probity, was listened to by the Bench and the Councilors; he studied his cases, and made no statements that he could not prove. He would not plead causes in which he did not believe, and was, in fact, a credit to the Bar.

Her home in the Rue Plumet had become so hateful to the Baroness that she agreed to her son's moving her to the Rue Louis-le-Grand. Adeline now occupied a beautiful suite, and she was spared all the material details of domestic life, for of these Lisbeth took charge, and started all over again the *tour de force* of economy that she had achieved at Madame Marneffe's, seeing in this an opportunity of bringing the weight of her vengeance to bear on these three upright lives, the object of a hatred that was now aggravated by the overthrow of all her hopes. Once a month she went to see Valérie, sent there by Hortense, who was anxious to have news of Wenceslas, and by Célestine, who was very worried on account of the open liaison between her father and the woman to whom her mother and sister-in-law owed their ruin and their unhappiness. Lisbeth, needless to say, took advantage of this curiosity in order to see Valérie as often as she liked.

About twenty months passed by, during which the Baroness recovered her health, except that her nervous trembling remained. She learned her duties, which provided her with a noble distraction from her grief and an outlet for her heavenly goodness of heart. In her work she saw, moreover, a possible means of discovering the whereabouts of her husband, in the course of the various chances that took her to all parts of Paris. Meanwhile the debts to Vauvinet were paid, and the pension of six thousand francs payable to Baron Hulot was almost redeemed. Victorin paid all his mother's expenses, as well as his sister's, out of the ten thousand francs interest on the capital left in trust for them by Marshal Hulot. Adeline's salary amounted to six thousand francs a year, and this sum, together with the Baron's pension, when it was freed, would in due course produce a clear income of twelve thousand francs a year for the mother and daughter. The poor woman would have been almost happy but for her constant anxiety as to the fate of the Baron, for she would have liked him to enjoy the good fortune that was beginning to smile on the family; and but for the spectacle of her abandoned daughter, and but for the terrible blows that Lisbeth, whose diabolical character had free play, administered from time to time, apparently in all innocence.

A scene which took place early in March 1843 will illustrate the effects produced by Lisbeth's persistent hatred, still seconded by Madame Marneffe. Two important events had taken place in Madame Marneffe's life. First, she had given birth to a stillborn infant, whose coffin had been worth two thousand francs a year to her. And as to Marneffe himself, eleven months later Lisbeth was able to give her family the following news on her return from a visit of discovery to the Marneffe establishment.

"This morning," she said, "that dreadful Valérie called in Dr. Bianchon[2] to know whether the doctors who condemned her husband yesterday had made any mistake. Dr. Bianchon has said that that frightful man will be in the hell that awaits him this very night. Old Crevel and Madame Marneffe saw the doctor out, and your father, Célestine dear, gave the doctor five gold pieces for that piece of good news. When he got back to the drawing room Crevel cut capers like a dancer, and kissed that woman, and said, 'So you will be Madame Crevel at last!' And he said to me, when she left us alone to return to her husband's bedside—for his death-rattle had begun—your respected father said to me, 'With Valérie for my wife, I shall become a peer of France! I shall buy an estate I have my eye on,[3] Presles, that Madame de Sérizy wants to sell. I shall be Crevel of Presles, and a member of the Council of Seine-et-Oise, and a deputy. I shall have a son! I shall be all I ever wanted to be!' 'And what about your daughter, then?' I said to him. 'Pooh!' he said, 'she is only a daughter. Besides she has become too much of a Hulot altogether, and Valérie can't bear any of that lot. My son-in-law has always refused to come here. Who is he to set up as the family mentor, a Spartan, a puritan, a philanthropist? So I am through with my daughter. She has had half her mother's fortune, and two hundred thousand francs into the bargain! Besides, haven't I the right to do as I like? I shall judge my daughter and son-in-law by the way they take my marriage; as they behave, so shall I. If they behave properly toward their stepmother, we shall see! After all, I am a man'—and more such nonsense! And he posed like Napoleon on a monument!"

The ten months' official widowhood insisted upon by the *Code Napoléon* had now elapsed some days since. The estate of Presles had been purchased. Victorin and Célestine had sent Lisbeth that very morning to find out the latest news of the marriage of that charming widow to the Mayor of Paris, now a member of the Council of Seine-et-Oise.

Célestine and Hortense, who had become increasingly fond of one another since they had lived under the same roof, were now almost inseparable. The Baroness, carried away by her conscientiousness, that made her do far more than was necessary in her work, devoted her whole energies to the charitable works of which she was an agent; she was out nearly every day from eleven to five. The two sisters-in-law, thrown together by the care of their children, whom they looked after together, both stayed at home and shared their work. They had come to speak all their thoughts aloud and presented a touching picture of two sisters; one happy, the other sad. Beautiful, full of life, gay and witty, the sad sister seemed to belie her true situation by her exterior; while the melancholy, gentle, calm Célestine, equable as reason itself, habitually pensive and thoughtful, might have been thought to have some secret sorrow. Perhaps this contrast contributed to their warm friendship. Each of these two women supplied the other with what she lacked. Sitting in a little summerhouse in the garden that the trowel of the speculative builder had spared through a happy fancy (for he had intended to keep this hundred square feet of earth for himself), they were enjoying the first green shoots of the lilacs, the spring festival that can only be appreciated in full in Paris, whose inhabitants, for six months of the year, have lived in forgetfulness of vegetation, between cliffs of stone and the tossing tides of their human ocean.

"Célestine," said Hortense, in reply to a remark from her sister-in-law, who was saying what a pity it was that her husband had to be at the Chamber in this fine weather, "I do not think you appreciate your happiness. Victorin is a perfect angel, and you sometimes torment him."

"My dear, men like to be tormented! Some ways of teasing are a proof of affection. If your poor mother had been—not exacting, perhaps, but always ready to be exacting, you would certainly not have had all these misfortunes to lament."

"Lisbeth has not come back. I shall have to sing the song of *Malbrouck*!" said Hortense. "I do long for some news of Wenceslas! What does he live on? He has done no work for two years."

"Victorin told me that he saw him the other day with that dreadful woman, and he suspects that she keeps him in idleness. You know, if you wanted to, Hortense dear, you could still have your husband back."

Hortense shook her head.

"Believe me, the situation will become intolerable before long," Célestine continued. "At first, anger and despair and indignation gave you strength. And the awful misfortunes that have since descended on our family—two deaths, financial disaster, and Baron Hulot's ruin—have occupied your heart and your thoughts. But now that you are living in peace and quiet you will not be able to bear the emptiness in your life so easily. And as you never could—and do not want to—leave the paths of virtue, you will have to be reconciled with Wenceslas. You know how fond Victorin is of you, and that is what he thinks. There is one thing stronger than our personal feelings, and that is nature."

"But he is so worthless!" exclaimed the proud Hortense. "He is that woman's lover, because she keeps him! Has she paid his debts, do you imagine? Good Heavens, I think of his situation night and day! He is the father of my child, and he is degrading himself!"

"Think of your mother, dear child," said Célestine.

Célestine was one of those women who, when you have given them enough reasons to convince a Breton peasant, go back for a hundredth time to their original argument. Her face, rather flat, cold and common, her brown hair, braided in straight plaits, her very complexion, all marked her as a sensible woman, with no charm, but also with no weakness.

"The Baroness would gladly be with her husband in his disgrace, to comfort him, and hide him in her heart from all eyes," Célestine continued. "She has a room ready for him upstairs, just as if she expected to find him one day and bring him back."

"Oh, my mother is sublime!" Hortense replied. "She has been wonderful all the time, every day, for twenty-six years. But I have not her character! It can't be helped! I am angry with myself sometimes. But you don't know what it is, Célestine, to have to compromise with infamy!"

"What about my father?" replied Célestine calmly. "He is certainly going the way in which yours perished! My father is ten years younger than the Baron, and he was a shopkeeper, it is true. But where will it end? That Madame Marneffe has made my father obey her like a dog; she disposes of his fortune, and gives him his ideas, and nothing can open his eyes. And now that the banns of marriage are published I tremble! My husband means to try once more; he regards it as his duty to avenge society and the family and bring that woman to book for all her crimes. You know, my dear Hortense, noble minds like Victorin's, and hearts like ours, find out too late about the world and its ways! This is a secret, my dear, and I tell you in confidence because it concerns you; but don't say a word, don't give a sign, and don't tell even Lisbeth, or your mother, or anybody, because—"

"Here is Lisbeth," said Hortense. "Well, Cousin, how goes the inferno in the Rue Barbet?"

"Badly for you, my dears. Your husband, my dear Hortense, is more infatuated than ever with that woman, who, I must say, is madly in love with him. As for your father, Célestine my dear, he is gloriously blind. But that is nothing new; it is what I see once a fortnight, and really I am thankful that I have never had anything to do with men. They are beasts. Five days from now Victorin and you, dear child, will have lost your father's fortune!"

"Have the banns been published?" asked Célestine.

"Yes," Lisbeth replied, "I have just been pleading your cause. I said to that monster, who is following in the footsteps of the other one, that if he would help you out of the difficulties you are in, and pay off your house for you, that you would be grateful, and receive your stepmother—"

Hortense started in alarm.

"Victorin will decide," Célestine replied coldly.

"But do you know what the Mayor replied?" said Lisbeth. " 'Let them struggle. Horses are only broken by starving, by lack of sleep, and by going without sugar!' Monsieur Crevel is worse than Baron Hulot! So, my poor dears, start your mourning for your father's money! And what a fortune! Your father has paid three million for the Presles estate, and he still has an income of thirty thousand! Oh, he has no secrets from me! He is talking of buying the Navarreins mansion in the Rue du Bac. Madame Marneffe has forty thousand francs a year on her own account. Ah! here is our guardian angel—here comes your mother!" she exclaimed, hearing the wheels of a carriage.

And presently the Baroness came down the steps and joined the family party. At fifty-five, ravaged by so many sorrows, and constantly trembling as though shivering with ague, Adeline, who was now pale and wrinkled, still had her fine figure, her superb lines, and her natural dignity. Seeing her, anyone would have said: "She must have been beautiful!" Worn by the grief of not knowing what had become of her husband, of not being able to share with him this Parisian oasis, the peace and seclusion, the comfort that the family was beginning to enjoy, she presented the graceful majesty of a ruin. At every gleam of hope disappointed, at every useless search, Adeline sank into a deep depression that separated her from her children. The Baroness, who had left that morning with fresh hopes, was eagerly awaited. An official, under an obligation to Hulot, to whom he owed his high position, had said that he had seen the Baron in a box at the Ambigu-Comique Theater, with a woman of astonishing beauty. Adeline had gone to call on Baron Vernier. This high official, while affirming that he had indeed seen his old protector, and saying that his behavior toward the woman during the performance suggested a clandestine relationship, had told Madame Hulot that her husband, in order to avoid meeting him, had left long before the end of the performance.

"He seemed on very familiar terms with the girl, and his dress betrayed straitened circumstances," he added in conclusion.

"Well?" said the three women to the Baroness.

"Well, Monsieur Hulot is in Paris. And that is in itself, for me, a ray of hope—to think that he is not far away," Adeline replied.

"He does not appear to have reformed!" said Lisbeth, when Adeline had concluded her account of her interview with Baron Vernier. "He seems to have taken up with some little working-girl. But where can he be getting money from? I'll be bound that he gets it from his old mistresses, Mademoiselle Jenny Cadine, or Josépha!"

The Baroness's trembling grew more violent than ever; she

wiped away the tears that rose to her eyes, and looked up sadly toward heaven.

"I cannot believe that a Grand Officer of the Legion of Honor would sink so low," she said.

"For his pleasure," said Lisbeth, "there is nothing he would not do! He robbed the State; he would rob individuals; he might even commit murder!"

"Oh! Lisbeth!" cried the Baroness, "keep such thoughts to yourself!"

At this moment Louise came toward the family group, which had been joined by the two little Hulots and little Wenceslas, who came to see whether their grandmother's pockets contained any sweets.

"What is it, Louise?" they asked.

"There is a man asking for Mademoiselle Fischer."

"What kind of man?" said Lisbeth.

"He is all in tatters, Miss, and covered with fluff like a mattress-maker; he has a red nose, and smells of brandy. He is the sort who does odd jobs."

This unattractive description had the effect of making Lisbeth hurry to the court of the house in the Rue Louis-le-Grand, where she found a man smoking a pipe whose seasoning proved him a past master in the art of smoking.

"What have you come here for, Père Chardin?" she asked him. "We agreed that you would always go, on the first Saturday of the month, to the door of Madame Marneffe's house in the Rue Barbet-de-Jouy; I have just come back after staying there for five hours, and you did not come!"

"I did go there, respectable and charitable lady," said the mattress-maker. "But there was a game of snooker going on at the Café des Savants, Rue du Coeur Volant, and we all have our little weaknesses. Mine is billiards. If it hadn't been for billiards I might have been eating off silver plate. You must get this straight," he said, searching for a paper in the gusset of his torn trousers, "billiards lead on to a drop, and plum-brandy. It is ruinous, like all good things, by the little extras that come with it. I know the arrangement, but the old man is in such a fix that I came where you told me not to. If hair was all hair, we might sleep on it! But it is a mixture! God doesn't look after everybody, as they say—He has His preferences; after all, it's His right. Here is the letter from your estimable relative and my very good friend. It will tell you his political views."

Père Chardin tried to trace some zigzag lines in the air with the forefinger of his right hand.

Lisbeth, paying no attention to him, read these few lines:

DEAR COUSIN,

Be my Providence! Let me have three hundred francs today!

HECTOR.

"What does he want the money for?"

"The landlord!" said Père Chardin, who was still trying to trace figures in the air. "And then my son has come back from Algeria, through Spain, and Bayonne, and . . . he hasn't made any takings, which is not like him, because, begging your pardon, he is a sharp chap, my son! Well, there it is, he's got to live; but he will pay back all we lend him, because he wants to get up a what's-its-name. He has ideas that will take him a long way."

"To the police court!" said Lisbeth. "He killed my uncle, and I haven't forgotten it!"

"Him! He wouldn't kill a chicken, respectable lady."

"Here, take the three hundred francs," said Lisbeth, taking fifteen gold pieces from her purse. "Now—be off with you, and never come here again."

She saw the father of the Oran storekeeper to the gate, where she pointed out the old drunk to the porter.

"If that man comes here—if he ever does come here again—do not on any account let him in, and tell him that I am not at home. If he tries to find out whether Monsieur Hulot, or Baroness Hulot, lives here, say you don't know anyone of that name."

"Very good, Miss."

"It might cost you your place if you made a mistake, even unintentionally," the old maid whispered to the porter.

"Cousin," she said, turning to the barrister, who was just coming in, "you are threatened by a great misfortune."

"What is that?"

"In a few days your wife will have Madame Marneffe for a stepmother."

"That remains to be seen!" said Victorin.

For the last six months Lisbeth had been paying, regularly, a small allowance to her protector, Baron Hulot, whose protectress she had become; she knew the secret of his whereabouts, and she relished Adeline's tears, saying to her, as we have seen, when she saw her gay and hopeful: "Wait till you find my poor cousin's name in the papers, in the police-court news." And in this, as on a previous occasion, she had gone too far in her vengeance. She had aroused Victorin's suspicions. Victorin had made up his mind to put an end to this Sword of Damocles that Lisbeth was constantly pointing out, and to the she-devil to whom his mother and the whole family owed so many misfortunes. The Prince de Wissembourg, who knew all about Madame Marneffe, was secretly supporting the young barrister's enterprise; he had promised him, as President of the Council,[4] the secret help of the police in order to enlighten Crevel and save a fortune from the clutches of the diabolical courtesan, whom he had not forgiven for Marshal Hulot's death and the ruin of a Councilor of State.

Chapter XXXIII

The words "he gets it from his old mistresses," spoken by Lisbeth, kept the Baroness awake all night. Like invalids condemned by the doctors, who consult quacks, like those who have fallen into Dante's lowest circle, that of despair, or like drowning men who clutch at straws, taking them for masts, she came at last to believe in the baseness the very thought of which had shocked her; and it occurred to her that she might apply for help to one of these odious women. Next morning, without consulting her children or saying a word to anyone, she went to call on Mademoiselle Josépha Mirah, *prima donna* of the Royal Academy of Music, there to find or lose the hope that had gleamed before her like a will-o'-the-wisp. At noon the great singer's maid brought her the Baroness Hulot's card, informing her that the lady herself was waiting at the door having asked whether Mademoiselle could receive her.

"Are the rooms done?"

"Yes, Miss."

"And the flowers fresh?"

"Yes, Miss."

"Tell Jean just to look around and see that everything is all right before showing the lady in, and see that she is treated with the greatest respect. Go, and then come back and dress me, because I must look my smartest."

And she went to examine herself in her cheval glass.

"Now, brace up!" she said to herself. "Vice must arm herself to meet virtue! Poor woman! I wonder why she wants to see me! I cannot bear to see *'du malheur, auguste victime'*!" [1]

She came to the end of that well-known aria just as her maid returned.

"Madame," said the maid, "that lady has been taken with a nervous trembling."

"Well, offer her some orange-flower water, or some rum, or some soup!"

"I did, Miss. But she won't take anything; she says it is a nervous complaint she has."

"Where did you take her?"

"Into the big drawing room."

"Hurry up, child! Now, my best slippers, and my flowered dressing gown by Bijou, and as many lace frills as you can find. Do my hair to impress a woman. This woman is on the other side—my opposite! And tell that lady—for she is a really great lady, my girl, which is more than you will ever be!—a woman whose prayers rescue souls from your purgatory!—tell her that I am in bed, that I was singing last night, and that I am getting up."

The Baroness, shown into Josépha's drawing room, did not notice how long she was kept waiting, although, in fact, it was more than half an hour. This drawing room, that had already been redecorated since Josépha had moved into this little villa, was hung with purple and gold silk. The luxury that the nobility formerly lavished on those small houses, whose splendid remains still bear witness to those "follies"[2] from which they were so aptly named, was displayed with all the perfection of modern resources, in these four rooms opening out of each other, warmed by a hot-air system with concealed openings. The Baroness, quite bewildered, examined each object and work of art in complete amazement. Here she found the explanation of fortunes melted away in the melting-pot whose consuming fires are fanned by pleasure and vanity. This woman who, for twenty-six years, had lived among the cold relics of Empire luxury, whose eyes contemplated carpets with faded flowers, tarnished bronzes, silks worn to shreds like her own heart, now realized the power of the seductions of vice, as she beheld its results. It would have been impossible to feel no envy for these beautiful things, these admirable creations to which these great though anonymous artists, whose work makes modern Paris and its contribution to Europe what it is, had all contributed.

Here every object was remarkable for its unique perfection. The ornaments, figurines, and sculptures were all originals, whose models had been destroyed. Here was the last word in modern luxury. To own things that are not vulgarized by two thousand wealthy *bourgeois,* whose notion of luxury is the lavish display of the expensive objects that crowd the shops, is the hallmark of real luxury, the luxury of the aristocracy of today, those ephemeral stars of the Parisian firmament. As she examined the flower-stands filled with the rarest of exotic flowers, adorned with chased bronze and Boulle inlay, the Baroness was alarmed by the thought of the wealth represented by this apartment. And inevitably this sentiment included the person about whom this profusion glittered. Adeline reflected that Josépha Mirah, whose portrait, painted by Joseph Bridau,[3] adorned the adjoining boudoir, was a singer of genius, a Malibran,[4] and she expected to see an overpowering celebrity. She was sorry that she had come. But she was activated by a feeling so natural, by a devotion so unreflecting, that she mustered up her courage to go through with this interview. Besides, she was about to satisfy her curiosity to see what charm such women possessed, in order to extract so much money from the unyielding ore of Paris earth.

The Baroness looked at herself to make sure that she was not a blot on all this luxury; but she looked well in her velvet dress with a cape under which she wore a frill of beautiful lace; her velvet bonnet, to match, suited her. Seeing herself still as dignified as a queen who is still a queen in her eclipse, she reflected that the dignity of suffering is no less than that of talent. She heard doors opening and closing, and at last Josépha appeared. The singer was not unlike Alloris' *Judith,* who must be graven in the memory of all those who have seen that picture in the Pitti palace, near the door of one of the great rooms; she had the same proud bearing, the same haughty expression, black hair, simply knotted, and a yellow dressing gown embroidered with a thousand flowers exactly like the brocade in which the nephew of Bronzino[5] has depicted the immortal homicide.

"Madame la Baronne, you overwhelm me by the honor that you do me in coming here," said the singer, who had made up her mind to play the great lady.

She herself drew up a well-padded easy-chair for the Baroness, and sat down on a folding-chair. She recognized the faded beauty of this lady, and was overcome by deep pity when she saw her shaken by that nervous trembling that became convulsive at the slightest excitement. She read at a glance that saintly life that Hulot and Crevel used in former days to describe; and not only did she abandon the idea of pitting herself against this woman, but she humbled herself before the greatness she recognized in her. The great artist could admire what the courtesan would have scorned.

"Mademoiselle, I am brought here by despair, that drives us to all kinds of means." The Baroness realized from Josépha's expression that she had offended the woman from whom she hoped so much, and she looked at the artist. This look, full of supplication, extinguished the fire of Josépha's eyes, and she smiled back at the Baroness. This silent interchange between the two women was terribly eloquent.

"It is two years and a half since Baron Hulot left home, and I have no idea where he is, although I do know that he is living in Paris," the Baroness continued, with emotion. "I had an absurd idea—just a dream, very likely—that you might have been helping my husband. If you could enable me to see him, Mademoiselle, you should have my prayers, every day, so long as I live."

Two great tears that rolled down the singer's cheeks foretold her answer.

"Madame," she said, in humblest tones, "I have wronged you without knowing you; but now that I have had the privilege of seeing, in your person, the most perfect image of virtue on earth, believe me, I see the greatness of my fault, and deeply repent it; and you may depend upon me to do all I can to remedy it."

She took the Baroness's hand before that lady could prevent her, and kissed it with the deepest respect, even going down on one knee. Then she got up, as proud as when she came on to the stage in the part of Mathilde,[6] and rang the bell.

"Go," she said to her manservant, "go on horseback, kill the horse if necessary, and find little Bijou, of Rue Saint-Maur-du-Temple, and bring her here. See her into a cab and tip the driver so that he will come at a gallop. Don't waste an instant, if you don't want to lose your place. Madame," she said, returning to the Baroness, and speaking to her in tones of the utmost respect, "you must forgive me. When the Duc d'Hérouville became my protector I sent the Baron back to you, when I knew that he was ruining his family for me. What more could I do? In the theater protection is absolutely indispensable at the beginning of our careers. Our salaries do not pay one tenth of our expenses, and we all have temporary husbands. Baron Hulot was nothing to me, but he took me away from a rich man, a conceited ass. Old Crevel would certainly have married me."

"So he told me," said the Baroness, interrupting the singer.

"Well, so you see, Madame, I might have been an honest woman today, with only one lawful husband!"

"You have excuses," said the Baroness, "and God will take them into account. But far from coming here to reproach you, I came to contract a debt of gratitude toward you."

"Madame, I have been looking after the Baron for nearly three years."

"You!" exclaimed the Baroness, with tears in her eyes. "Ah! How can I ever thank you? I have nothing to give but my prayers!"

"The Duc d'Hérouville and I," the singer went on, "a noble soul, a real gentleman ..."

And Josépha gave an account of the settlement and "marriage" of Monsieur Thoul.

"And so, thanks to you," said the Baroness, "my husband has wanted for nothing?"

"We have seen to that."

"And where is he?"

"Nearly six months ago the Duke mentioned to me that the Baron, whom his lawyer knew as Monsieur Thoul, had drawn all the eight thousand francs that were to be paid out to him in regular three-monthly installments," said Josépha. "But neither the Duke nor I have heard a word from the Baron. Our lives are so full and so busy, we artists, that I have not had time to run after old Thoul. And as it happens, Bijou, who does my embroidery, his—what shall I say?"

"His mistress," said Madame Hulot.

"His mistress," Josépha repeated, "has not been here. Mademoiselle Olympe Bijou has perhaps been divorced. Divorces are not uncommon in our part of Paris."[7]

Josépha rose, and despoiled her jardinières of rare flowers to make a charming bouquet for the Baroness, whose expectations, however, had been entirely disappointed. Like all those good folk who imagine that men and women of genius are monsters, who eat, drink, walk, and speak in a way totally different from other people, the Baroness had hoped to see Josépha the opera singer, the fascinator of men, the dazzling and voluptuous courtesan; and instead, she found a woman of calm and poise, with the dignity of her talent, the simplicity of an actress who knows herself to be a queen of the evenings, and besides, better than all that, a courtesan who in her looks, attitude, and behavior paid full and unreserved homage to the *Mater Dolorosa* of the hymn, and who offered flowers to her wounds, as in Italy they crown the Madonna.

"Madame," said the valet, who returned in about half an hour. "Old Madame Bijou is on her way; but you must not count on little Olympe. Your embroideress has become a respectable woman; she is married."

"To all intents and purposes?" asked Josépha.

"No, Madame, really married. She is in charge of a flourishing business; she has married the owner of a fashionable establishment on which thousands have been spent, on the Boulevard des Italiens, and she has left her embroidery business to her sister and her mother. She is Madame Grenouville now. This fat shopkeeper—"

"A Crevel!"

"Yes, Madame," said the valet. "He has settled thirty thousand francs a year on Mademoiselle Bijou as her marriage settlement. Her elder sister, they say, is going to marry a rich butcher."

"Your affair seems to be going badly," said the singer to the Baroness. "Monsieur le Baron is no longer where I installed him."

Ten minutes later Madame Bijou was announced. Josépha prudently made the Baroness go through into her boudoir, and drew the curtain.

"Your presence would frighten her," she said to the Baroness. "She would not give anything away if she thought that you were interested in her confidences, so let me extract her confession! Hide in there; you will hear everything. This scene is acted just as often in real life as in the theater."

"Well, Mother Bijou," said the singer to an old woman swathed in tartan, looking like a porter's wife in her Sunday best. "So now you are all well off! Your daughter has been very lucky!"

"Well off! My daughter gives us a hundred francs a month, and she rides in a coach, and eats off silver; she's a millionaire, she is! Olympe might have saved me from having to work, at my age. Do you call that well off?"

"She ought not to be ungrateful, because you gave her her beauty," said Josépha; "but why has she not been to see me? I saved her from want when I married her to my uncle."

"Yes, Madame, old Thoul! . . . But he is very old, and broken down!"

"What have you done with him? Is he with you? She made a big mistake in leaving him, because now he is worth millions!"

"There!" said old Madame Bijou. "That's just what I told her when she played him up, and he as gentle as anything with her, poor old chap! Oh! Didn't she just wear him out! Olympe was perverted, Madame!"

"How was that?"

"Well, she got to know, if you will excuse my saying so, Madame, a publicity man, the great-nephew of an old mattress-maker in Faubourg Saint-Marceau. This good-for-nothing, like all these good-looking young fellows paid to clap at the plays,[8] you know—he's the cock of the walk in the Boulevard du Temple, where he works up the new shows, and takes care of the reception of the actresses, as he calls it. In the morning he has his breakfast; and before the show he has his dinner, to be up to the mark. In other words, he's all for drinks and billiards. That's no way to live, as I said to Olympe."

"It is a way some men do live, unfortunately," said Josépha.

"Well, Olympe lost her head over that fellow, who kept very bad company, Madame, as you will understand when I tell you he was very nearly arrested in a bar where all the thieves meet. Well, Monsieur Braulard, the head of the publicity, got him out of that. He wears gold earrings, and lives by doing nothing and hanging around women who are crazy about these handsome good-for-nothings! Well, he took all the money off her she got from Monsieur Thoul. The business went to pieces. All that she made on the embroidery business went on the billiards. And then, as I was saying, this young fellow had a pretty sister, who was no better than her brother, a little nobody, over in the students' quarter."

"A Chaumière tart?"[9] said Josépha.

"Yes, Madame," said Bijou's mother. "Well, as I was saying, Idamore—that's what he calls himself, but his real name is Chardin—Idamore always said as how your uncle must have more money than what he said, and he managed, without my daughter knowing anything about it, to send his sister Élodie—that's the fancy stage-name he gave her—to us as a workgirl. And my word, didn't she have things upside down! She got all the workgirls into bad ways, so that you couldn't do anything with them, quite shameless, if you'll pardon my saying so, and she managed somehow or other to get round old Thoul, and she has took him off somewhere we don't know where and left us in a nice fix—what with the bills. We haven't managed to pay them all off yet; but my daughter, who is well up in things, is looking after all that. Well, as I was saying, when Idamore had got hold of the old man, through his sister, he left my poor girl, and he's carrying on now with a young actress in the Funambules. And so you see that was how my daughter came to get married—"

"But do you know where the mattress-maker lives?" asked Josépha.

"Old Père Chardin? As if he lived anywhere! He is drunk by six in the morning. He makes a mattress once a month at most, and spends the day hanging about the bars—he goes in for the pools."

"Goes in for pools? He sounds a fine diver!"

"You don't understand, Madame. I mean billiard pools. He wins three or four every day and he drinks that."

"Drinks the pools!" said Josépha. "But if Idamore hangs about the boulevard, we could find him through my friend Braulard."

"I don't know, Madame, seeing as all this happened six months ago. Idamore is one of the sort that might have gone to jail before now, and from there to Melun,[10] and after that—well—"

"To penal servitude," said Josépha.

"Well, Madame, you know everything," said the old Madame Bijou with a smile. "If my daughter hadn't have known that fellow, she would have been . . . Well, she hasn't done too badly all the same, mind you, because Monsieur Grenouville took such a fancy to her that he's married her."

"And how did that marriage come about?"

"Olympe was desperate, Madame. When she was dropped for that young actress didn't she give her a piece of her mind! My word, didn't she just clean her! Well, and when she had lost old Thoul, who adored her, she decided she'd had enough of men. But then Monsieur Grenouville, who did a lot of business with us—two hundred embroidered Chinese shawls every three months—he wanted to console her. But however that might be, she wouldn't listen to anything without the Mayor and the Church. 'I mean to be respectable,' she said, 'or perish!' And she kept her word. Monsieur Grenouville agreed to marry her, on condition she gave us all up, and we agreed."

"At a price?" said the astute Josépha.

"Yes, Madame, ten thousand francs, and an allowance for my father, who is too old to work."

"I asked your daughter to be kind to old Thoul, and she has thrown him over. That is not good enough! I shall never try to help anybody again. That is what comes of trying to do good! Doing good seems to be a very bad speculation. Olympe might at least have told me about all this in the beginning! If you find old Thoul within a fortnight, I will give you a thousand francs!"

"That's not so easy, lady, but there's a lot of hundred-sou pieces in a thousand francs, so I'll try to earn your money."

"Goodbye, Madame Bijou."

When she went into her boudoir the singer found Madame Hulot in a dead faint; but in spite of her loss of consciousness, her nervous tremor still shook her, as the pieces of a snake still twitch after it has been cut up. Strong smelling salts, cold water, and all the usual methods, brought the Baroness back to life, or, rather, to the consciousness of her sorrow.

"Ah! How low has he fallen!" she said, recognizing the singer, and seeing that she was alone with her.

"Have courage," said Josépha, who had seated herself on a cushion at the Baroness's feet, and who was kissing her hands. "We shall find him! And if he is in the mire—well, he can wash it off. Believe me, for men of breeding it is all a matter of clothes. Allow me to make up for the wrongs I have done you, for I see how much you care for your husband, in spite of his behavior, or you would not have come here! But there it is, poor man! He is too fond of women. But you know, if you had had some of our *chic*, you could have kept him from straying; because then you would have been what we never are—everything to a man. The Government ought to start a school for training honest women! But governments are so strait-laced! They are led by the men who are led by us! I am sorry for nations!... But there, it is a question of helping you, and no laughing matter. Well, do not worry; go home, and set your mind at rest. I will bring you back your Hector just as he was thirty years ago!"

"Oh! Let us go to Madame Grenouville!" said the Baroness. "She will surely know something; perhaps I shall see my husband this very day, and be able to rescue him at once from poverty and shame."

"Madame, I will prove to you at once how deeply I appreciate the honor you have done me, by not allowing the singer Josépha, the Duc d'Hérouville's mistress, to be seen beside the most beautiful and saintly image of virtue. I respect you too much to appear in public with you. I am not affecting humility; it is an honor that I wish to pay you. You make me regret that I cannot be like you, for all the thorns that tear your hands and feet! But there it is—I belong to art, as you do to virtue."

"Poor child!" exclaimed the Baroness, moved, in spite of her own sorrows, by a strange emotion of sympathy and compassion. "I shall pray for you, for you are the victim of a society that must have its entertainment. When you are old, repent. You will be forgiven, if God deigns to hear the prayers of a—"

"Of a martyr!" said Josépha, respectfully kissing the Baroness's skirt.

But Adeline took the singer's hand, drew her to her, and kissed her brow. Blushing with pleasure, the singer saw Adeline to her cab, with every mark of respect.

"It must be some Lady of Charity," said the valet to the maid, "because *she* doesn't treat everybody like that—not even her best friend, Miss Jenny Cadine."

"Just wait a day or two," she said, "and you shall see him, or I shall renounce the God of my fathers; and from a Jewess, you know, that is a promise of success."

While the Baroness was visiting Josépha, Victorin, in his office, was interviewing an old woman of about seventy-five, who, in order to obtain admission to the presence of the distinguished barrister, had mentioned the terrible name of the Chief of the Secret Police.[11] The attendant announced: "Madame de Saint-Estève."

"That is one of my business names," she said, sitting down.

Victorin was struck by a sort of inner chill at the sight of this terrible hag. Although expensively dressed, she was hideous to behold, by reason of the cold malignity written on her dull, wrinkled, pale, strong-featured face. Marat, imagined as a woman, and at that age, might have been, like this Saint-Estève, a personification of the Terror. This sinister old creature's eyes shone with tigerish, bloodthirsty greed. Her squat nose, whose nostrils, opening into two oval cavities, breathed the fires of hell, suggested the beak of some cruel bird of prey. A spirit of intrigue sat enthroned on her low and cruel forehead. Long wiry hairs grew scattered on her wrinkled face, bespeaking the virility of her projects. Anyone seeing this woman would have reflected that all the painters had failed in their representation of Mephistopheles.

"My dear sir," she began in a patronizing tone, "I have given up undertaking any business for a long time. Anything I do for you will be done entirely on account of my dear nephew, whom I love like a son. Now, the Chief of Police, to whom the President of the Council said a word about your affairs, in consultation with Monsieur Chapuzot, thinks that the police ought not to appear in an affair of this kind. He has given my nephew a free hand, but my nephew does not want to be mixed up in it except in an advisory capacity; he cannot afford to be compromised."

"Then your nephew is—"

"That's right, and I am rather proud of it," she replied, interrupting the lawyer, "for he is my pupil, and the pupil has gone one better than his teacher. We have gone into your business, and we have come to our own conclusions about it. Would you give thirty thousand francs to have this matter done with once and for all? I will settle it for you, and you need not pay until the thing is done."

"You know the people concerned?"

"No, my dear sir; you will have to give me that information. I was told 'There is an old idiot who is in the clutches of a widow. The widow is twenty-nine and has played her thieving game so well that she has taken forty thousand francs a year out of the pockets of two heads of families. She is just about to swallow eighty thousand francs a year by marrying an old fellow of sixty-one; she will ruin an entire respectable family and leave this vast fortune to the child of some lover by promptly getting rid of her old husband.' That is the situation."

"That is correct," said Victorin. "My father-in-law, Monsieur Crevel—"

"Formerly a perfumer, a Mayor; I live in his district, under the name of Ma'am Nourrisson," she replied.

"The other person is Madame Marneffe."

"I don't know her," said Madame de Saint-Estève, "but within three days I will be in a position to count her vests."

"Would you be able to prevent the marriage?" asked the lawyer.

"How far has it gone?"

"The banns have been read twice."

"It would mean kidnapping the woman. This is Sunday; there are only three days, because they will be getting married on Wednesday—no, it is impossible! But we could kill her for you!"

Victorin Hulot jumped, as any upright man would, on hearing those six words spoken in cold blood!

"Murder!" he said. "And how would you do it?"

"For forty years now, sir, we have been playing the part of destiny," she replied with grim pride, "and done just what we pleased in Paris. More families than one, in the Faubourg Saint-Germain[12] at that, have told me their secrets, I can tell you. I have made and marred many a marriage, and torn up many a will, and saved many a reputation. I keep here," she said, tapping her brow, "a little flock of secrets that are worth thirty-six thousand francs a year to me. Well, you would be one of my lambs! A woman like myself would not be what I am if I talked about my ways and means! I act! All that will happen, my dear sir, will be an accident, and you need not have the slightest remorse. You will be like a man cured by a hypnotist, who believes by the end of a month that nature did it all."

Victorin was in a cold sweat. The sight of an executioner would have disturbed him less than this sententious and pretentious sister of the hulks:[13] as he looked at her purple dress, he fancied that she was robed in blood.

"I cannot accept the help of your experience and energy, Madame, if that success is to cost a life, or if even the least criminal act is committed."

"You are still a baby, sir!" Madame Saint-Estève replied. "You want to remain innocent in your own eyes, but all the same you want to see your enemy come to a bad end."

Victorin shook his head.

"Yes," she continued, "you want this Madame Marneffe to drop the prey she has in her jaws! And how do you propose to make a tiger drop its piece of meat? Do you expect to do it by stroking it and saying 'Puss-Puss'? You are not logical. You declare war, and you don't want any wounds! Very well, I will make you a present of your innocence that you have so much at heart. I have always found that innocence is the raw material of hypocrisy! One day in the next three months a poor priest will come and ask you for forty thousand francs for a pious work—a ruined convent in the Levant, in the desert! If you are satisfied with the way things have turned out, give the good man the forty thousand francs! You will pay more than that in income tax! It will be a mere trifle, after all, in comparison with what you will gain."

She rose, on her large feet that bulged out of her satin slippers, and took her leave, smiling and bowing.

"The devil has a sister!" said Victorin, rising.

He saw to the door this hideous stranger, called up from the recesses of the Secret Police like a monster from the lower regions of the theater summoned up by the wand of a fairy in a pantomime. When he had finished his work at the Palais de Justice, Victorin went to call on Monsieur Chapuzot, head of one of the most important departments of the Prefecture of Police, to make some inquiries about this stranger. Seeing Monsieur Chapuzot was alone in his office, Victorin Hulot thanked him for his assistance.

"You sent me," he said, "an old woman who is the very incarnation of the criminal side of Paris."

Monsieur Chapuzot laid his spectacles down on his pile of papers, and looked at the lawyer with an expression of great surprise.

"I should certainly not have taken the liberty of sending anyone to see you, without letting you know beforehand, or sending a note of introduction," he replied.

"Then it must have been the Prefect—"

"I should think it most unlikely," said Monsieur Chapuzot. "The last time the Prince de Wissembourg dined with the Minister of the Interior he saw the Prefect and spoke to him of the situation you are in, a deplorable position—and asked him whether he could help you, in a friendly way. The Prefect, who was naturally anxious to help on account of His Excellency's interest in this family matter, did me the honor of discussing the subject with me. Since the Prefect has held the reins of this much-abused but very useful department he has made it a rule that family matters are to be left alone. In principle, and in theory, he is right; but in practice he is wrong. The police—I have been with them for forty-five years—rendered great services to families between seventeen ninety-nine and eighteen fifteen.[14] Since eighteen twenty the Press and constitutional government have totally altered the conditions of our existence. And so my advice was not to interfere in an affair of this kind, and the Prefect did me the honor of accepting my opinion. The chief of the detective branch, in my presence, received orders not to do anything in the matter, and if by any chance he has sent you anyone I shall reprimand him. It might involve his losing his place. People say 'The police will do this or that'! The police! The police—why, my dear sir, the Marshal and the Council of Ministers do not know what the police are. Only the police know the police. The King, to be sure—Napoleon, Louis XVIII, knew their own police; but as for ours, no one except Fouché, Monsieur Lenoir, Monsieur de Sartines,[15] and a few Prefects of exceptional perspicacity, have any notion of it. Everything is changed nowadays! We are reduced, and disarmed! I have seen many private disasters grow up, which I might have prevented if I had had five grains of independence of action! The very men who have crippled us will regret it, if, like yourself, they are brought face to face with some moral abuse that we ought to be able to sweep away like mud! In public affairs the police are expected to foresee everything when it is a matter of public safety; but as for the family—that is sacred! I would do everything in my power to discover and prevent an attack against the King's life! The very walls of a house would become transparent, but as for meddling in domestic affairs, and in private interests? Never, while I sit in this office, because I should be afraid."

"Of whom?"

"Of the Press, Monsieur le Député of the Left Center!"

"Then what ought I to do?" said Hulot, after a pause.

"Well, you call yourself the family!" said the departmental chief. "There is no more to be said—you can do whatever you like; but as to helping you, as to making the police an instrument of private passions and private interests, that is out of the question! There, you see, lies the secret of the inevitable persecution—which the magistrates pronounced illegal—directed against the predecessor of our present Chief of the Secret Police. Bibi-Lupin[16] used the police for private investigations. This might have led to an immense social danger. With the means at his disposal, that man might have been formidable, he might have been a deputy fate!"

"But in my place—" said Hulot.

"What, you are asking me for advice, you who sell it?" replied Monsieur Chapuzot. "Come, come, my dear sir, you are making fun of me!"

Hulot took his leave of the police official, and went away without noticing the almost imperceptible shrug which the latter gave as he rose to see him to the door.

"And he wants to be a statesman!" said Monsieur Chapuzot, as he turned back to his reports.

Victorin returned home still full of perplexities which he could confide to no one. At dinner the Baroness joyfully told her children that within a month their father might be sharing their comfortable circumstances and end his days peacefully in the bosom of the family.

"Ah! I would gladly give my three thousand six hundred francs a year to see the Baron here!" Lisbeth exclaimed. "But, my dear Adeline, do not count on such happiness in advance, I entreat you!"

"Lisbeth is right," said Célestine. "Mother dear, wait until it happens!"

The Baroness, all love and hope, gave an account of her visit to Josépha, and pitied poor girls like her, for all their good fortune, and spoke of Chardin the mattress-maker, the father of the Oran storekeeper, in order to show that she was not indulging in false hopes.

Lisbeth, next morning, was by seven o'clock in a cab and on her way to the Quai de la Tournelle, where she stopped at the corner of the Rue de Poissy.

"Go," she said to the cabby, "to number seven Rue des Bernardins; it is a house with an entry and no porter. Go up to the fourth floor, and knock at the door on the left, on which is a notice, 'Mademoiselle Chardin, Laces and Shawls mended.' She will answer the door. You must ask for *the gentleman.* She will say, 'He's not in,' and you must say, 'I know, but you must find him, because his *maid-of-all-work* is waiting on the Quai in a cab, and wants to speak to him.' "

Twenty minutes later an old man who looked about eighty, with perfectly white hair, a nose reddened by the cold, and a face pale and wrinkled like an old woman's, shuffling along with bent back, in a pair of list slippers, dressed in an overcoat of shiny alpaca, wearing no decoration, the sleeves of his knitted vest showing at his wrists, and his shirt unpleasantly stained, approached timidly, looked at the cab, recognized Lisbeth, and came to the window.

"Ah, my dear Cousin," she said, "what a state you are in!"

"Élodie takes everything for herself!" said Baron Hulot. "These Chardins are beastly low creatures."

"Would you like to come back to us?"

"Oh, no, no," said the old man. "I would rather go to America."

"Adeline is on your track!"

"Ah! If only someone would pay my debts," said the Baron, with a furtive look. "For Samanon is after me."

"We still have not paid off your arrears; your son still owes a hundred thousand francs."

"Poor boy!"

"And your pension will not be free for another seven or eight months. If you will wait, I have two thousand francs here."

The Baron held out his hand with a gesture of terrifying avidity.

"Give it to me, Lisbeth! God bless you for it! I know where I can go!"

"But you will tell me—won't you, you old monster?"

"Yes. I can wait these eight months, because I have found a little angel, a good creature, innocent, not old enough to be depraved yet."

"Don't forget the police court," said Lisbeth, who hoped to see Hulot there one day.

"Eh? It is in the Rue de Charonne!" said the Baron. "A quarter where no one makes a scandal about anything. Why, no one will ever find me there. I am called Père Thorec, Lisbeth; they think I am a retired cabinet-maker. The child loves me, and I will not let them fleece me any more."

"No, that has already been done," said Lisbeth, looking at the overcoat. "Shall I take you there?"

Baron Hulot climbed into the cab, leaving Mademoiselle Élodie without so much as a goodbye, as he might have thrown aside a novel he had finished.

Half an hour later—during which time Baron Hulot could talk to Lisbeth only of little Atala[17] Judici, for he had by degrees become the victim of those terrible obsessive passions that ruin old men—the cousin set him down, provided with two thousand francs, in the Rue de Charonne, in the Faubourg Saint-Antoine, at the door of a house of dubious and sinister exterior.

"Goodbye, Cousin. You are Thorec now. Is that right? Do not send anyone except porters, and always hire them from different places."

"That is agreed. Oh! I am very lucky!" said the Baron, whose face was radiant with the joy of a future and brand-new happiness.

"They will never find him there," Lisbeth thought, as she stopped her cab at Boulevard Beaumarchais, and returned, by omnibus, to the Rue Louis-le-Grand.

Chapter XXXIV

On the following day Crevel was announced after breakfast when all the family were in the drawing room. Célestine ran forward and flung her arms around her father's neck, and behaved just as though she had seen him only yesterday, although in fact this was his first visit for two years.

"Good morning, Father," said Victorin, shaking hands.

"Good morning, children," said the pompous Crevel. "Madame la Baronne, my homage at your feet! Good gracious me, how these children grow up! They are on our heels! 'Grandpa,' they say, 'we want our place in the sunshine.' Madame la Comtesse, still as beautiful as ever!" he added, looking at Hortense. "Ah! And here is the rest of our riches! Cousin Bette, the Wise Virgin! Well, you all seem to be very comfortable here!" he said, after distributing these phrases, interspersed with hearty laughs that moved with difficulty the broad masses of his red and fleshy face.

And he looked around his daughter's drawing room with an air of contempt.

"Célestine, my dear, I will make you a present of all my furniture from the Rue des Saussayes; it would go very nicely in here. Your drawing room looks as if it needs furbishing up. Ah! Here is that young rogue Wenceslas! Well, are we good children, I wonder? You must learn manners, you know!"

"To make up for those who haven't any," said Lisbeth.

"That piece of sarcasm, my dear Lisbeth, no longer affects me. I have come, my children, in order to put an end to the false position in which I have so long been placed; and, like a good father, to tell you, without making any bones about it, that I am about to be married."

"You have a perfect right to marry," said Victorin, "and for my part, I gladly release you from the promise you made me when you gave me the hand of my dear Célestine—"

"What promise?" asked Crevel.

"That you would never marry," said the barrister. "You must do me the justice of admitting that I never asked you to make any such promise, that you made it quite voluntarily, and in spite of my having said, at that time, you will remember, that you would be making a mistake to tie yourself in such a way."

"Yes, I do remember, my dear fellow," said Crevel, embarrassed. "And look here, on my word of honor, if you will only get on with Madame Crevel, my dear children, you will have no cause for regret. I appreciate your fine feelings, Victorin. You won't find that generosity toward me will be unrewarded. Come, now, hang it all! Why don't you make friends with your stepmother, and come to the wedding?"

"You have not told us yet who the lady is, Father!" said Célestine.

"Why, that is an open secret!" said Crevel. "Don't let us play hide-and-seek about it. Lisbeth must have told you!"

"My dear Monsieur Crevel, there are some names that are not spoken in this house."

"All right then, it is Madame Marneffe."

"Monsieur Crevel," said the lawyer severely, "neither I nor my wife can attend this marriage, not from motives of interest, because what I said just now was spoken in all sincerity. Yes, I should be very glad to think that you would find happiness in that union; but I am moved by considerations of honor and delicacy that I am sure you will understand, and which I would rather not explain, since that would involve reopening old wounds that are still painful here."

The Countess at a sign from the Baroness picked up her son, saying, "Come, you must have your bath now, Wenceslas! Good morning, Monsieur Crevel!"

The Baroness bowed goodbye to Crevel without a word, and Crevel could not suppress a smile at the child's astonishment on being threatened with this untimely bath.

"You are about to marry, sir," said the barrister, when he was alone with Lisbeth, his wife, and his father-in-law, "a woman loaded with the spoils of my father, who in cold blood reduced him to his present state, and who is the cause of my sister's suffering. Do you suppose that I shall give countenance to your folly by my presence? My dear Monsieur Crevel, I am sincerely sorry for you! You have no feeling for the family; you know nothing of the solidarity of honor that unites its different members. There is no arguing with passion—that I know, unfortunately, all too well. Men swayed by passion are as deaf as they are blind. Your daughter, Célestine, has too strong a sense of duty to utter a word of reproach—"

"So I should hope!" said Crevel, trying to cut short this harangue.

"Célestine would not be my wife if she made a single protest," the lawyer continued; "but I, for my part, can at least try to stop you when you are about to step over a precipice, especially as I can give you proof of my disinterestedness. It is not your fortune but yourself that I am thinking of. And to make this point clear, I may add, if only to set your mind at rest in the matter of your marriage contract, that I am now in a position that leaves us nothing to wish for."

"Thanks to me!" put in Crevel, who had turned purple in the face.

"Thanks to Célestine's fortune," replied the lawyer, "and if you regret having given your daughter as your own share of her dowry a sum that amounts to less than half of what her mother left her, we are prepared to return it to you."

"Do you realize, my respected son-in-law," said Crevel, taking up his position, "that if I give Madame Marneffe the protection of my name, she is no longer called upon to answer for her conduct, otherwise than as my wife?"

"That is no doubt very chivalrous," said the lawyer, "and as regards matters of the heart, and the vagaries of passion, most generous. But I know of no name, or law, or title, that could cover the theft of three hundred thousand francs, shamelessly extracted from my father. I must tell you plainly, my dear father-in-law, your future wife is unworthy of you; she deceives you, and she is madly in love with my brother-in-law, Steinbock, whose debts she has paid—"

"It was I who paid them!"

"So much the better," said the lawyer. "I am very much relieved on behalf of Count Steinbock, who may one day be able to repay his debts. But he is loved—much loved, and often—"

"Loved!" exclaimed Crevel, whose face showed utter amazement. "It is cowardly, and dirty, and mean, and vulgar, to slander a woman. Those who make statements of that kind, sir, should be in a position to prove them."

"I will give you proofs."

"I shall expect them."

"The day after tomorrow, my dear Monsieur Crevel, I shall tell you the day and the hour—for I shall then be in a position to expose the appalling depravity of your future wife."

"All right, I shall be charmed," said Crevel, recovering his self-control. "Goodbye, my children, *au revoir.* Goodbye, Lisbeth."

"Go after him, Lisbeth," Célestine whispered to Cousin Bette.

"Well, this is a nice way to rush off!" said Lisbeth to Crevel.

"Ah!" said Crevel. "He's coming on, my son-in-law! He's getting above himself altogether! What with the Law Courts, and the Chamber, and legal trickery and political trickery, he's learned a lot! Very fine! He knows that I am getting married next Wednesday, and by Sunday this fine fellow proposes to fix the time—within three days, if you please!—when he will prove that my wife is unworthy of me! That's a good one! I am going back to sign the contract. Why don't you come with me, Lisbeth—yes, do come—they won't know anything about it! I was going to leave forty thousand francs a year to Célestine, but after the way that Hulot behaved just now I'm through with them for good and all!"

"Give me ten minutes—wait for me in your carriage at the gate. I will make an excuse for going out."

"All right, I will."

"My dears," said Lisbeth, going back to the drawing room, where she found all the family reassembled, "I am going with Crevel; the contract is to be signed this evening, and I shall be able to tell you the terms. This will probably be my last visit to that woman. Your father is furious. He is going to disinherit you."

"His vanity will prevent that!" said the barrister. "He has set his heart on owning the Presles estate, and he will hold on to it, I know. And if he were to have children, Célestine would still have half of what he leaves; the law makes it impossible to give away his whole property. But these questions don't concern me; all I am thinking of is our honor. Go, Cousin," he said, pressing Lisbeth's hand, "and listen carefully to the contract."

Twenty minutes later Lisbeth and Crevel entered the house in Rue Barbet, where Madame Marneffe was waiting, a trifle impatiently, to hear the result of the move that she had ordered. Valérie had, in the end, fallen a victim to that all-absorbing love that every woman experiences once in a lifetime. Wenceslas was its object. This unsuccessful artist had become, in Madame Marneffe's hands, a lover so perfect that he was to her what she had been to Baron Hulot. Valérie was holding a pair of slippers in one hand, Steinbock's hand with the other, and her head was resting on his shoulder. There are some conversations, intimate, disconnected, rather like those rambling literary works of our time on whose title page is written "Copyright reserved." Such a masterpiece of intimate poetry had led naturally to an expression of regret that rose to the artist's lips, not without bitterness.

"Oh! Why did I ever marry?" said Wenceslas. "For if I had only waited, as Lisbeth told me to, I might now have married you!"

"Only a Pole would want to make a wife of his devoted mistress!" exclaimed Valérie. "Exchange love for duty? Pleasure for boredom?"

"You are so fickle!" replied Steinbock. "Did I not hear you talking to Lisbeth about Baron Montès, that Brazilian?"

"Will you get rid of him for me?" said Valérie.

"That," replied the ex-sculptor, "would be the only way of preventing you from seeing him."

"Well, you see, darling," said Valérie, "I was keeping him in reserve for a husband—you see, I tell you everything! The promises I have made to that Brazilian! Oh! long before I knew you!" she added, in reply to a movement from Wenceslas. "Well, because of these promises, that he now uses to torment me, I shall have to marry almost in secret; because if he hears that I am marrying Crevel he is quite capable of—well, of killing me!"

"Oh! as to that!" said Steinbock, with an expression of scorn that signified that such a danger was negligible for a woman loved by a Pole.

And indeed, in the matter of bravery this was no idle boast, for Poles are, really and sublimely, brave.

"And that idiot Crevel wants to make a great show, to make the marriage an excuse for indulging his taste for economical ostentation; he has put me in an embarrassing situation that I really don't see any way out of!"

Valérie could hardly confess to the man she adored that Baron Henri Montès had, ever since the fall of Baron Hulot, inherited the privilege of visiting her at any hour of the night, and that for all her cleverness, she had still not managed to find an excuse for breaking with the Brazilian that would throw the blame on him! She knew only too well the Baron's half-primitive nature, not at all unlike Lisbeth's, and she was afraid when she thought about this Moor of Rio de Janeiro. At the sound of wheels Steinbock, whose arm had been around Valérie's waist, left her, and picked up a newspaper in which he appeared to be absorbed. Valérie was embroidering, with elaborate care, a pair of slippers for her future husband.

"How they slander her!" Lisbeth whispered to Crevel at the door, pointing to that tableau. "Look at her hair! Is it disarranged? To hear Victorin anyone would think you were surprising two turtledoves on their nest!"

"My dear Lisbeth," cried Crevel, striking his pose, "the fact is that to turn an Aspasia into a Lucrèce[1] one has only to inspire a passion in her!"

"Haven't I always told you," said Lisbeth, "that women love fat libertines like you?"

"She would be very ungrateful if she did not," said Crevel, "considering the amount of money I have spent on this place! Grindot and I alone know!" he said, with a wave of the hand in the direction of the staircase.

In the decoration of this house, which Crevel looked upon as his own, Grindot had attempted to rival Cleretti, the fashionable architect of the day, whom the Duc d'Hérouville had employed on Josépha's villa. But Crevel, incapable of understanding the arts, had made up his mind, as all *bourgeois* do, to spend a fixed sum, specified in advance. Thus limited, Grindot had been unable to carry out his architectural dream. The difference between Josépha's house and the villa in the Rue Barbet was that between all things with an individual character and vulgarity. Those things that were to be admired in Josépha's house could not be found elsewhere; those that adorned Crevel's could be bought anywhere. These two kinds of luxury are divided from one another by the river of millions. A unique mirror is worth six thousand francs; a mirror made by a manufacturer who commercializes the design can be bought for five hundred. A genuine piece of Boulle luster will fetch as much as three thousand francs at a public auction; the same thing turned out by the dozen can be manufactured for ten or twelve hundred. The one is, in the world of antiques, what a picture by Raphael is in painting; the other is a copy. How much would you give for a copy of a Raphael? Crevel's house was, in fact, a magnificent specimen of the luxury of fools, while Josépha's was a perfect example of an artist's home.

"War is declared," said Crevel, going up to his wife-to-be.

Madame Marneffe rang.

"Go and fetch Monsieur Berthier," she said to the manservant, "and don't come back without him. If you had been successful," she said, embracing Crevel, "it would only have delayed my happiness, because then we would have had to give a brilliant reception. But since the entire family are opposed to the marriage, my dear, decency demands that it should be very quiet, particularly when the bride is a widow."

"On the contrary, I intend to go in for a display after the style of Louis XIV," said Crevel, who for some time past had come to look down on the eighteenth century. "I have ordered new carriages; there is the bridegroom's coach, and the bride's, two smart coupés, a chaise, and a traveling carriage with a superb sprung seat that trembles like Madame Hulot!"

"Oh! *I intend?* So you are not my little lamb any more? Oh, no, my poodle, you will do what *I* want! We will sign the contract, privately, this evening. And then on Wednesday we shall be officially married—as people really do marry—'on the quiet,' as my poor dear mother used to say. We will go to church on foot, simply dressed and there will be a Low Mass. Our witnesses will be Stidmann, Steinbock, Vignon, and Massol—all clever men who will find themselves at the Mairie just by chance, and who will sacrifice themselves, for our sakes, to the extent of hearing a Mass. Your colleague will marry us, as a great concession, at nine in the morning. The Mass will be at ten, and we shall be back here for breakfast by half-past eleven. I have promised our guests that they will not rise from the table before the evening. We shall have Bixiou and your old friend from the Birottery,[2] du Tillet, Lousteau, Vernisset, Léon de Lora, Vernou, the flower of Paris wit, who won't know we have been married; we will mystify them, we will make them all rather tight—and Lisbeth shall be there; I want her to learn about marriage. Bixiou shall make a pass at her and ... and enlighten her ignorance!"

For two hours Madame Marneffe rattled off nonsense of a kind that gave rise, in Crevel, to this judicious reflection: "How can such a lighthearted woman be depraved? Featherbrained, perhaps! But perverse? Nonsense!"

"And what had your children to say about me?" Valérie asked Crevel, when he chanced to sit down beside her on the sofa. "All sorts of horrors?"

"They say," said Crevel, "that you are guilty of an immoral love affair with Wenceslas—you, who are the soul of virtue!"

"Of course I love my little Wenceslas!" Valérie exclaimed, calling the artist to her, taking his head between her hands, and kissing his brow. "Poor boy, with no one to turn to, and not a penny in the world! Scorned by a carroty haired giraffe! What do you expect, Crevel? Wenceslas is my poet, and I love him as if he were my own son, and I don't care who knows it! These virtuous women see evil in everything. Really, couldn't they even sit beside a man without committing a sin? I suppose I am like a spoiled child, who has been given everything she wants: bonbons no longer excite me. Poor things! I am sorry for them! . . . And who said that about me?"

"Victorin," said Crevel.

"Well, why did you not shut him up, that parrot of a lawyer, with the story of his mamma and the two hundred thousand francs?"

"Oh, the Baroness had fled," said Lisbeth.

"They had better look out, Lisbeth!" said Madame Marneffe with a frown. "If they will receive me, and visit their stepmother—the whole lot of them—well and good. Otherwise, I will see them—and you can tell them so from me—lower than the Baron is now; I shall end by turning nasty. Upon my word, I believe that evil is the scythe for cutting down the good!"

At three Monsieur Berthier, Cardot's[3] successor, read the marriage contract, after a short discussion with Crevel, for certain clauses depended on the decision of young Monsieur and Madame Hulot. Crevel settled on his wife a fortune comprising, firstly, an income of forty thousand francs, from specified securities; secondly, the house, with all its furniture, and thirdly, a lump sum of three million francs. In addition, he made over to his future wife all the benefits the law allowed; he left her all the property free of duties, and in the event of their dying without issue they left their property and estate respectively to one another. This contract reduced Crevel's fortune to a capital of two millions. If he had children by his new wife, Célestine's share was to be reduced to five hundred thousand francs, as the life-interest of the remainder would then accrue to Valérie. This would be about a ninth part of his whole fortune.

Lisbeth returned in time for dinner at Rue Louis-le-Grand, despair written on her face. She explained the marriage contract with commentary, but found Célestine as well as Victorin insensible to this disastrous news.

"You have annoyed your father, my dear children! Madame Marneffe has vowed that you shall receive Monsieur Crevel's wife, and that you shall call on her."

"Never!" said Hulot.

"Never!" said Célestine.

"Never!" exclaimed Hortense.

Lisbeth was possessed by the desire to overcome this proud attitude taken up by all the Hulots.

"She seems to have arms that she can use against you!" she replied. "I don't yet know what she meant, but I shall find out. She spoke vaguely about some story of two hundred thousand francs that has something to do with Adeline."

The Baroness fell gently backward on the divan on which she was sitting, and her convulsions became severe.

"Go there, children!" she exclaimed. "Receive—that woman! Monsieur Crevel is an infamous wretch! No torture could be too bad for him! Obey that woman! Ah, he is a monster! *She knows everything!*"

After these words, uttered with tears and sobs, Madame Hulot had barely enough strength left to go up to her room, leaning on the arms of her daughter and Célestine.

"What does all this mean?" exclaimed Lisbeth, who remained alone with Victorin.

The lawyer, rooted to the spot in very understandable astonishment, did not hear Lisbeth speak.

"What is the matter, my dear Victorin?"

"I am appalled!" said the barrister, whose face had become stern and threatening. "Woe betide anyone who lifts a finger against my mother—I have no more scruples! If I could, I would crush that woman, like a viper! Does she dare to attack the life and honor of my mother?"

"She said—but don't repeat this, Victorin—she said that she would see you all lower than your father—she roundly reproached Crevel for not having silenced you with the secret that seems to be such a terror to Adeline."

The doctor was sent for, for the condition of the Baroness grew worse. The doctor ordered a draft containing a large dose of opium, and after taking it Adeline fell into a heavy sleep; but the entire family were the prey of the most lively alarm. On the following day the barrister left early for the Law Courts, and went by way of the police headquarters, where he begged Vautrin, Chief of the Secret Police, to send him Madame de Saint-Estève.

"We have been forbidden, sir, to interfere in your affairs, but Madame de Saint-Estève is in business, and is at your service," replied the celebrated chief detective.

On returning home the unhappy lawyer learned that there were fears for his mother's reason. Doctor Bianchon, Doctor Larabit, and Professor Angard had been in for a consultation, and had just decided to take drastic measures to stop the rush of blood to the head. Just as Victorin was hearing from Doctor Bianchon a detailed account of his reasons for hoping that the crisis would pass, although his colleagues were less hopeful, the footman announced that his client, Madame de Saint-Estève, had called. Victorin left Bianchon in the middle of a sentence and rushed downstairs like a madman.

"Madness seems to be contagious in this house," said Bianchon, turning to Larabit.

The doctors departed, leaving an intern with instructions on Madame Hulot's treatment.

"A lifetime of virtue!" was the only phrase that the sick woman had spoken since the catastrophe.

Lisbeth did not leave Adeline's bedside, and sat up with her all night; she was the admiration of the two younger women.

"Well, my dear Madame de Saint-Estève," exclaimed the lawyer, showing that hideous hag into his study, and carefully closing all the doors, "how far have you got?"

"Well, my good friend," she said, eyeing Victorin with cold irony, "so you have thought matters over?"

"Have you done anything?"

"Will you pay fifty thousand francs?"

"Yes," replied Hulot, "we have got to take action. Do you know that by a single sentence that woman has endangered my mother's life and reason? So carry on!"

"I have carried on!" replied the hag.

"Well?" Victorin gasped.

"Well, you don't jib at the expenses?"

"On the contrary."

"Because they have run up to twenty-three thousand already."

Hulot looked at Madame de Saint-Estève, stupefied.

"Well, you're surely not a simpleton—you, one of the shining lights of the Law Courts!" said the old woman. "For that sum we have purchased a maid's conscience, and a picture by Raphael, and it is not dear at the price."

Hulot was still speechless, and could only stare at her.

"Well, then," went on the hag, "we have purchased Mademoiselle Reine Tousard, from whom Madame Marneffe has no secrets."

"I see."

"But perhaps you would rather back out?"

"I will pay blindfolded," he replied. "Why, my mother herself said that no torture could be too bad for these people."

"They don't use the rack and the wheel any more," said the hag.

"Can you promise success?"

"Leave it to me," said Madame Saint-Estève. "Your vengeance is simmering."

She looked at the clock; it was six.

"Your vengeance is dressing; the furnaces of the Rocher de Cancale are lighted; the horses are pawing the ground; my irons are getting hot. Oh! I know your Madame Marneffe by heart! Everything is ready; and believe me, there are some pellets in the rattrap. I will tell you tomorrow whether the mouse is poisoned. I think she will be. Good afternoon, my son!"

"Good afternoon, Madame!"

"Do you know English?"

"Yes."

"Have you seen *Macbeth* played in English?"

"Yes."

"Well, my son, you shall be king! That is to say, you will inherit!" said that appalling witch, described long ago by Shakespeare,[4] with whose works she seemed to be familiar. She left Hulot, speechless, at the door of his study.

"Don't forget that the consultation will be tomorrow!" she said with all the unction of a client taking leave of her lawyer. She had seen two people coming in, and wished to pass in their eyes for a pinchbeck countess.

"What nerve!" thought Hulot, as he bowed out his alleged client.

Chapter XXXV

Baron Montès de Montejanos was a lion,[1] but a *lion* unaccounted for. Fashionable Paris—the Paris of the turf[2] and of the courtesans—admired the ineffable waistcoats of this foreign gentleman, his impeccable patent-leather boots, his incomparable sticks, his much-coveted horses, and his carriage driven by Negroes, very obviously slaves, and thoroughly beaten at that. His wealth was notorious; he had a credit account of seven hundred thousand francs with du Tillet, the well-known banker; but he was always seen alone. If he went to first nights, he was always in the stalls. He frequented no drawing room. He had never been known to offer his arm to a courtesan, nor could his name be coupled with that of any pretty society woman. To pass the time he played whist at the Jockey Club. The Paris world was reduced to spreading rumors about his morals, or—which was more amusing—making fun of his personal appearance. He went by the name of Combabus![3] Bixiou,[4] Léon de Lora, Lousteau Florine, Mademoiselle Héloise Brisetout, and Nathan, at a supper one evening with the notorious Carabine, and a number of celebrities of both sexes, had invented this highly diverting explanation. Massol, in his capacity of Councilor of State, and Claude Vignon, as a onetime professor of Greek, had related to the ignorant girls the well-known anecdote, preserved in Rollin's *Ancient History,* concerning Combabus, the voluntary Abelard,[5] placed in charge of the wife of a King of Assyria, Persia, Bactria, Mesopotamia, and other geographical regions best known to old Professor du Bocage, the successor to d'Anville, who created the East of antiquity. This nickname, which kept Carabine's guests in fits of laughter for a quarter of an hour, was made the theme for a whole series of very free jokes, a work of wit to which the Academy could certainly not have awarded the Montyon prize of virtue, but in the course of which the name, henceforth to rest on the tufted mane of the handsome Baron—whom Josépha described as a "superb Brazilian" as one might say a "superb Catoxantha"[6]—was prominent.

Carabine, the most dazzling of the girls, whose delicate beauty and ready wit had snatched the scepter of the thirteenth *arrondissement* from the hands of Mademoiselle Turquet, better known as *Malaga*—Mademoiselle Séraphine Sinet (for this was her real name)—was to the banker du Tillet what Josépha Mirah was to the Duc d'Hérouville.

Now, at about seven o'clock on the very morning of the day on which Saint-Estève had prophesied success to Victorin, Carabine had said to du Tillet, "If you want to be really nice, you will give a dinner for me at the Rocher du Cancale, and bring Combabus. We want to find out whether he has a mistress. I have made a bet on it, and I should like to win."

"He is still at the Prince's Hotel. I will look in," said du Tillet. "We will have some fun! Let's ask everybody—Bixiou, and Lora, and all the gang!"

At half-past six, in the best room of the restaurant where everybody in Europe has dined, a magnificent service of plate, made expressly for dinners for which vanity pays the bills in bank-notes, glittered on the table. A stream of light poured in veritable cascades from the edges of the chased metal. Waiters, whom a provincial visitor might have taken for diplomats but for their youth, stood by with all the gravity of men who know themselves to be overpaid.

Five guests had arrived, and nine more were expected. First of all Bixiou arrived, the salt of every intellectual dish, still going strong in 1843, with a battery of wit always new—a phenomenon as rare in Paris as virtue. Then came Léon de Lora, the greatest living seascape painter, who has at least one advantage over all his rivals—that his standard has never fallen below that of his early work. The courtesans could never do without those two kings of wit. A supper, or dinner, or party without them was unthinkable. Séraphine Sinet—known as Carabine—in her role of acknowledged mistress of the Amphitryon[7] of the evening, had arrived early, and was displaying her shoulders—the loveliest in Paris—and her neck, smooth as if it had been turned on a lathe—her amusing little face and her dress of satin brocaded in blue on a blue ground, and enough English lace to feed a whole village for a month—under the floods of light. The beautiful Jenny Cadine, who was not playing that evening, and whose portrait is too well known to need description, arrived in a fabulously expensive dress. For these ladies a party is always a Longchamps of fashion,[8] in which each tries to carry off the prize for her millionaire by saying, in this way, to her rivals: "Look at the price I am worth!"

A third woman, evidently just beginning her career, looked on, almost with shame, at the luxury of her two rich and established companions. She was simply dressed in white cashmere trimmed with blue embroidery, and her hair had been crowned with a wreath of flowers by some obscure hairdresser whose unskilled hand had unconsciously imparted to her wonderful golden hair the charm of ineptitude. Still awkward in her evening dress, she had—to use a hackneyed image—all the shyness associated with a first appearance. She had come up from Valognes to find some market, in Paris, for a youthfulness to make a man despair, a candor fresh enough to stir the desire of a dying man, and a beauty equal to any that Normandy has already supplied to the theaters of the capital. The lines of that unblemished face suggested the ideal of angelic purity. Her milk-white skin reflected the light like a mirror. Her delicate coloring seemed to have been painted on her cheeks. She was called Cydalise; and, as we shall see, she was a necessary pawn in the game that Ma'am Nourrisson was playing against Madame Marneffe.

"Your arms don't match your name, my child," Jenny Cadine had said when Carabine, who had brought her, introduced this seventeen-year-old masterpiece.

And, in fact, Cydalise displayed to public admiration a pair of arms that were fine, firm and marbled, but reddened with healthy country blood.

"How much is she worth?" Jenny Cadine asked Carabine, aside.

"A fortune."

"What are you going to do with her?"

"Madame Combabus, of course!"

"How much do you get for the job?"

"Guess!"

"A silver service?"

"I have three already!"

"Diamonds?"

"I am selling them!"

"A green monkey?"

"No, a picture by Raphael!"

"What put that crazy idea into your head?"

"Josépha makes me sick with her pictures," said Carabine. "I want to have better ones than any she has."

Du Tillet arrived with the Brazilian, the hero of the evening; the Duc d'Hérouville followed with Josépha. The singer wore a simple velvet dress; but she was wearing a necklace worth a hundred thousand francs, of pearls scarcely distinguishable from her skin, white as a camellia. She had placed one red camellia among her black braided hair (a beauty spot!) with dazzling effect, and she had had the amusing idea of wearing eleven rows of pearls on each arm. She shook hands with Jenny Cadine, who said, "Do lend me your mittens!"

Josépha took off her bracelets, and handed them to her friend, on a plate.

"What style!" said Carabine. "Quite the duchess! Did you ever see so many pearls? You must have plundered the sea to dress the Nereid, Monsieur le Duc!" she added, turning to the little Duc d'Hérouville.

The actress took only two of the bracelets, and clasped the other twenty on to the singer's beautiful arms, which she kissed.

Lousteau, the literary sponger, la Palférine and Malaga, Massol and Vauvinet, Theodore Gaillard, one of the proprietors of an important political newspaper, made up the party. The Duc d'Hérouville, who was polite, as members of the aristocracy always are to everyone, greeted la Palférine with that special nod that, without implying either esteem or intimacy, conveys to everybody "we are of the same class, the same breed—equals"! This greeting, the *shibboleth*[9] of the aristocrat, was created to be the despair of intellectuals and the upper middle classes!

Carabine placed Combabus on her left and the Duc d'Hérouville on her right. Cydalise was on the other side of the Brazilian, and Bixiou next to the girl from Normandy. Malaga sat beside the Duke.

At seven they attacked the oysters; by eight, between two courses, they were drinking iced punch. Everyone knows the menu of this kind of party. At nine everyone was talking, as people do talk after drinking forty-two bottles of various wines among fourteen people. The dessert—the wretched dessert of the month of April—was on the table. But of the entire party, the only one who had been affected by this heady atmosphere was the girl from Normandy, who was humming a Christmas carol. With the exception of this poor child, nobody had lost the use of his reason, for the guests, and the women, were the *élite* of Paris diners-out. Wits shone, and eyes, though brilliant, remained full of intelligence, while talk drifted into satire, anecdote, and gossip. Conversation, which had hitherto kept to the vicious circle of racing, horses, the Bourse, the comparative merits of various celebrities, and current scandals, threatened to become intimate, to split up into heart-to-heart conversations between adjacent couples.

This was the moment at which, at looks from Carabine in the direction of Léon de Lora, Bixiou, la Palférine, and du Tillet, the subject of love was introduced.

"It is not good form for doctors to discuss medicine, the nobility never discuss their families, and men of talent never speak of their works," said Josépha. "Why should we talk shop? I had the Opera canceled so as to come, and I certainly don't intend to work here! So let us change the subject, my dears!"

"We were talking about real love, darling!" said Malaga. "The kind of love for which a man will fling everything to the winds—father and mother, wife and children—and end his days in Clichy!"

"Talk away then," said the singer. "I don't know the animal!"

A phrase picked up from the slang of the Paris streets can, with the help of the expression of eyes and face, be an absolute poem on the lips of a courtesan.

"Then don't I love you, Josépha?" said the Duke in a low voice.

"Perhaps you do really love me," the singer whispered in his ear, smiling, "but I don't love you in that way, with the kind of love for which the entire universe is plunged in darkness in the absence of the beloved. I am fond of you, and you are useful to me, but you are not indispensable; and if you were to leave me tomorrow I should have three dukes instead of one!"

"Does love exist in Paris?" asked Léon de Lora. "Nobody has even time to make a fortune, so how can you possibly dedicate yourself to true love, that engulfs you as water dissolves a lump of sugar? A man would have to be extremely rich to fall in love, because love annihilates a man—like our Brazilian friend, for instance. As I said a long time ago, extremes meet! A real lover is like a eunuch; there are no longer any women on earth for him! He is mysterious; he is like the true Christian in his desert solitude! For instance, our noble Brazilian!"

Everyone present looked at Henri Montès de Montejanos, who was embarrassed at finding himself the center of all eyes.

"He has been feeding there for an hour, without noticing any more than an ox that he is sitting beside the most—I dare not in this company say the most beautiful, but certainly the most fresh woman in Paris."

"Everything is fresh here, even the fish," said Carabine. "That is what this restaurant is famous for."

Baron Montès de Montejanos looked at the landscape painter in a friendly way and said, "Very good! Your very good health!"

He bowed to Léon de Lora, lifted his glass of port wine, and drank it with dignity.

"Are you really in love, then?" Carabine asked her neighbor, interpreting the toast in this way.

The Brazilian Baron refilled his glass, bowed to Carabine, and repeated the toast.

"To the lady's health!" replied the courtesan, in such an amusing tone that du Tillet, Bixiou, and the landscape painter burst out laughing.

The Brazilian remained as unmoved as a bronze statue. This composure annoyed Carabine. She knew perfectly well that Montès was in love with Madame Marneffe, but she had not bargained for this blind fidelity, this obstinate silence of conviction. A woman is as often judged by her lover's attitude as a lover by the bearing of his mistress. Proud of loving Valérie, and of being loved by her, the Baron's smile had for these experienced connoisseurs a touch of irony, and he was, moreover, superbly handsome; wine had not flushed him, and his eyes, with their peculiar golden-brown brilliance, did not betray the secrets of his heart. Carabine, therefore, said to herself, "What a woman! How she has sealed up that heart of yours!"

"He is a rock!" said Bixiou in an undertone; he thought the whole thing was merely a practical joke, and had no suspicion of the importance attached by Carabine to the demolition of that fortress.

While this conversation, apparently so frivolous, had been going on, on Carabine's right, the discussion on love was continued on her left between the Duc d'Hérouville, Lousteau, Josépha, Jenny Cadine, and Massol. They were discussing the question of whether this rare phenomenon was a product of infatuation, obstinacy, or love. Josépha, bored by all this theorizing, was eager to change the subject.

"You are talking of something you know nothing about! Which of you has ever loved a woman—and a woman unworthy of you, at that—enough to spend every penny of his fortune, and his children's, to pledge his future, to tarnish his past, to risk going to prison for robbing the State, to kill an uncle and a brother, and to allow himself to be so completely blindfolded that he did not even realize that he was being hoodwinked to prevent him from seeing the abyss into which, as a crowning joke, he was being driven? Du Tillet has a cash-box under his left breast; Léon de Lora keeps his wit there. Bixiou would think himself a fool if he were to love anyone besides himself; Massol has a ministerial portfolio instead of a heart. Lousteau has only a stomach, or he would never have let Madame de la Baudraye[10] walk out on him; Monsieur le Duc is too rich to need to prove his love by his ruin; and Vauvinet does not count, because I do not regard a moneylender as belonging to the human race. So none of you has ever loved, any more than I have, or Jenny, or Carabine. For my own part, I have seen the phenomenon I have just described only once. It was," and she turned to Jenny Cadine, "our poor Baron Hulot, whom I am advertising for like a lost dog, because I must find him."

"It rather looks," thought Carabine, looking hard at Josépha, "as though Madame Nourrisson has two pictures by Raphael, because Josépha is playing my game."

"Poor fellow!" said Vauvinet. "He was a great man, a great personality. He had real style! And a fine figure of a man, too! He looked like Francis the First![11] What a volcano! And he had an absolute genius for getting hold of money! Wherever he is, he is sure to be needing it, and I don't doubt but he will manage to extract it somehow, from those walls built of bones that you see in the Paris suburbs, near the city gates, where he is no doubt hiding."

"And all that," said Bixiou, "for that little Madame Marneffe! There's a hard-boiled bitch for you!"

"She is going to marry my friend Crevel," observed du Tillet.

"And she is madly in love with my friend Steinbock," said Léon de Lora.

These three phrases were three pistol shots that struck Montès full in the chest. He turned white, and the shock was so painful to him that he got up with difficulty.

"You are all swine!" he said. "How dare you name an honest woman in the same breath as all your fallen creatures! Let alone making her a target for your gibes!"

Montès was interrupted by cries of "Bravo" and unanimous applause. Bixiou, Léon de Lora, Vauvinet, du Tillet, and Massol gave the signal; it was a chorus.

"Long live the Emperor!" said Bixiou.

"Crown him!" cried Vauvinet.

"Three groans for a good dog! Three cheers for Brazil!" exclaimed Lousteau.

"Ah, my bronze Baron, so you love our Valérie!" said Léon de Lora. "You're not disgusted then?"

"His remark may not be parliamentary, perhaps, but it is magnificent!" Massol observed.

"But my very dear customer, you were recommended to me; I am your banker—your innocence will reflect on my credit!"

"Tell me, then—for you are a reasonable man—" began the Brazilian, addressing du Tillet.

"Thank you, on behalf of the rest of the company," said Bixiou, saluting.

"Tell me, is any of this true?" Montès continued, without taking any notice of Bixiou's remark.

"Well, if it comes to that," said du Tillet, "I have the honor to tell you that I am invited to Crevel's wedding."

"Ah! Combabus is about to defend Madame Marneffe!" said Josépha, rising solemnly.

She went over to Montès with a tragic air, and gave his head a little friendly pat, looked at him for a moment with an expression of mock-heroic admiration on her face, and shook her head.

"Hulot is the first example of love in spite of everything! Here is the second!" she said. "But he should not really count; he comes from the tropics!"

When Josépha gently touched his forehead Montès dropped down into his chair again, with a pleading look at du Tillet.

"If I am being made the butt of one of your Paris practical jokes," he said, "if you wanted to discover my secret ..." and he looked around the table with flaming eyes, including everyone in a glance in which blazed the sun of Brazil ... "for God's sake say so," he went on, with almost childish supplication, "but do not speak evil of a woman whom I love."

"To be sure! . . . But," Carabine whispered to him, "supposing you were being shamefully deceived, betrayed, tricked by Valérie, and supposing I could prove it to you, within an hour, at my house, what would you do?"

"I could not tell you that here, in front of all these Iagos," said the Brazilian Baron.

Carabine thought he had said *magots*—apes.

"Very well, say no more!" she replied with a smile. "Don't give the wittiest men in Paris anything to laugh at, but come home with me, and we can talk ..."

Montès was crushed.

"Proofs!" he muttered. "Only imagine—"

"You shall have more than enough," said Carabine, "but if the mere suspicion excites you like this, I fear for your reason."

"Is he obstinate, this fellow? He is worse than the late King of Holland![12] Lousteau, Bixiou, Massol—listen, all of you. Aren't you all invited to lunch with Madame Marneffe the day after tomorrow?" asked Léon de Lora.

"*Ja,*" replied du Tillet. "I have the honor of saying to you again, Baron, that if by any chance you were thinking of marrying Madame Marneffe you are voted out, like a bill in Parliament, by a black ball called Crevel. My old colleague Crevel, my friend, has an income of eighty thousand a year, and I don't suppose you have quite as much as that, because otherwise, no doubt, you would have been preferred."

Montès listened with a half-absent air, with a half-smile that alarmed the whole company. The headwaiter at that moment came over and whispered to Carabine that a relation of hers was in the hall and would like to speak to her. The courtesan rose, went out, and found Madame Nourrisson, swathed in black lace.

"Well, am I to go to your house, my child? Has he risen to the bait?"

"Yes, Mother—the pistol is so thoroughly loaded that I am only afraid it may go off too soon," said Carabine.

Chapter XXXVI

An hour later Montès, Cydalise, and Carabine, returning from the Rocher du Cancale, entered Carabine's little drawing room in the Rue Saint-Georges. The courtesan found Madame Nourrisson sitting in an easy-chair by the fire.

"Why, here is Auntie!" she exclaimed.

"Yes, my child, I came myself to fetch my little allowance; you would have forgotten all about me, although I know you have a kind heart, and I have some bills that must be paid tomorrow. A wardrobe dealer is always short of cash. Who have you got with you? This gentleman looks thoroughly upset."

The hideous Madame Nourrisson, at this moment completely transformed so as to look like a respectable old woman, got up to kiss Carabine, one of the hundred-odd courtesans whom she had launched in the horrible career of vice.

"He is an Othello who has made no mistake. I have the honor of introducing to you Monsieur le Baron Montès de Montejanos."

"Oh, I have heard a great deal about him; they call you Combabus, because you love only one woman; in Paris, that comes to the same thing as loving no one at all. Well, is it by any chance about the object of your love? Madame Marneffe, Crevel's kept woman? Why, sir, you should thank your lucky stars, instead of cursing them. She's nothing at all, that little lady! I know all her goings-on!"

"That's all very well," said Carabine, into whose hand Madame Nourrisson had slipped a letter when she kissed her. "But you don't know these Brazilians! They are reckless fellows, who insist on being stabbed through the heart. The more jealous they are, the more jealous they want to be. He is talking of killing everybody off; but he'll never kill anyone, because he's in love. Well, I brought the Baron here to show him proofs of his misfortune that I had from little Steinbock."

Montès was drunk. He listened as if the whole thing were happening to somebody else. Carabine went to take off her velvet cloak, and read the facsimile of the following note:

> My sweet, *he* is dining with Popinot this evening, and calling for me at the Opera at eleven. I will leave at half-past five, and count on finding you at our *paradise,* where you can order dinner to be sent up from the *Maison d'Or.* Dress, so that you can take me on to the Opera. We shall have four hours to ourselves. Give this note back to me; not that your Valérie doesn't trust you—I would give you my life, my fortune, and my honor—but I am afraid of some accident.

"Well, Baron, this is the note sent to Count Steinbock this morning. You can read the address! The original has been burned."

Montès turned the note over and over, recognized the writing, and was struck by a reasonable idea, which proves how completely his brain was deranged.

"If it comes to that, what motive have you for torturing my heart, because you must have paid a good deal to have this note in your possession long enough to get it lithographed?" he said, looking at Carabine.

"You great fool!" said Carabine, at a nod from Madame Nourrisson. "Don't you see poor little Cydalise? She is only sixteen, and she is so much in love with you that she has lost her appetite, and she's heartbroken because you have never even looked at her!"

Cydalise applied a handkerchief to her eyes and pretended to cry.

"She is furious, although she looks as though butter wouldn't melt in her mouth, to see the man she loves the dupe of a bitch like Valérie; she would like to kill her."

"Oh! as to that," said the Brazilian, "that is my business."

"Kill her? You, my lad? We don't do that sort of thing in Paris nowadays!" Madame Nourrisson put in.

"Oh!" said Montès. "This is not my native country! I belong to a part of the world where I can afford to laugh at your laws! And if you will give me proof—"

"Well, is this letter nothing?"

"No," said the Brazilian. "I don't believe in writing. I will trust nothing but my own eyes."

"As to seeing," said Carabine, who understood precisely the meaning of another nod from the supposed aunt, "you can see as much as you like, my dear tiger, but on one condition."

"What is that?"

"Look at Cydalise."

At a hint from Madame Nourrisson, Cydalise looked tenderly at the Brazilian.

"Will you love her? Will you take care of her?" said Carabine. "A girl as beautiful as that is worth a house, and a carriage! It would be a shame to leave her to go about on foot. And she is in debt.... How much do you owe?" Carabine asked, pinching Cydalise's arm.

"What she is worth," said Madame Nourrisson, "is another matter. The point is that she is marketable!"

"Listen!" exclaimed Montès, noticing at last this lovely feminine masterpiece. "Will you let me see Valérie?"

"And Count Steinbock into the bargain!" said Madame Nourrisson.

During the last ten minutes the old creature had been watching the Brazilian, and she saw that in him she had an instrument tuned to the murderous pitch that she required; seeing, besides, that he was blind enough not to notice who was leading him on, she spoke as follows:

"Cydalise is my niece, my beau from Brazil, and so I take some interest in her affairs. This smashup will be a matter of ten minutes; because it is a friend of mine who lets Count Steinbock the furnished room where he and Valérie are at this moment having their coffee—some coffee, for she calls that her coffee. Now listen to me, Brazil! I like Brazil; it is a hot country. What about my niece?"

"Old ostrich!" said Montès, struck by the ostrich feathers in Nourrisson's hat, "you interrupted me. If you will let me see Valérie and that artist together—"

"As you would like to be with her yourself!" said Carabine. "That is agreed."

"Very well, I will take this girl from Normandy and she shall come with me—"

"Where?" asked Carabine.

"To Brazil!" replied the Baron. "I will marry her. My uncle left me ten square leagues of entailed estate; that is why I still have a house there. I have a hundred Negroes there; nothing but Negroes and Negresses, and pickaninnies bought by my uncle."

"A slave dealer's nephew!" said Carabine, making a face. "That needs thinking about. Cydalise, my child, are you fond of Negroes?"

"Now, no more backchat from you, Carabine," said Madame Nourrisson. "A nice thing! This gentleman and I are talking business!"

"If I take another Frenchwoman, I'm going to have her to myself," the Brazilian continued. "I warn you, Mademoiselle, that I am a king, but not a constitutional king; I am a Czar. I buy all my subjects, and nobody can escape from my kingdom, which is a hundred leagues from any human habitation, bordering on the country of the savages of the interior, and separated from the coast by a wilderness as wide as your France—"

"I should prefer a garret here!" said Carabine.

"That is what I thought," replied the Brazilian, "for I sold all my property in Rio de Janeiro to come back to Madame Marneffe."

"No one makes a voyage like that for nothing," said Madame Nourrisson. "You have a right to be loved for yourself, especially being so handsome—he's very handsome, you know!" she said, turning to Carabine.

"Handsome! He is handsomer than the *Postillon de Longjumeau*!"[1] said the courtesan.

Cydalise took the Brazilian's hand, but he let it go again as politely as he could.

"I came back to fetch Madame Marneffe!" said the Brazilian, going back to his story. "And do you know why I was three years in coming back?"

"No, savage!" said Carabine.

"Well, she had so often said to me that she wanted to live, alone with me, in some wild solitude."

"He isn't a savage, after all," said Carabine, with a peal of laughter. "He is just another civilized fool, after all!"

"She said it to me so often," the Baron went on, disregarding the courtesan's teasing, "that I had a delightful house built, in the center of that immense estate. I came back to France to fetch Valérie, and the first night I saw her again—"

"*Saw* is good," said Carabine. "I will remember that word."

"She told me to wait until that miserable Marneffe died, and I agreed, and forgave her for having accepted Hulot's advances. I don't know whether the devil has gone into petticoats, but that woman, from that moment, has fallen in with every whim of mine, all my demands! And never for one moment has she given me cause to suspect her!"

"That takes a lot of believing!" said Carabine to Madame Nourrisson.

Madame Nourrisson nodded her head in agreement.

"My faith in that woman," said Montès, weeping, "was as great as my love. I was ready just now to fight everybody at table."

"I noticed that!" said Carabine.

"If I am deceived, if she marries, if she is in Steinbock's arms at this moment, that woman deserves to die a thousand deaths, and I will kill her as if I were crushing a fly!"

"And what about the police, dearie?" said Madame Nourrisson, with an old crone's leer to make your flesh creep.

"And the detectives, and the judges, and the law courts, and all the rest of the setup?" said Carabine.

"You are a fool, my dear!" said Madame Nourrisson, who was anxious to know the Brazilian's plans for vengeance.

"I will—kill her!" he repeated coldly. "Well, you call me a savage; you surely can't expect me to imitate the stupidity of your countrymen, who go and buy poison at the chemist's? I thought about it on the way here—of my vengeance, in case you were right about Valérie. One of my Negroes carries about with him one of the most deadly of all animal poisons—a terrible disease,[2] more powerful than any vegetable poison, and there is no cure known for it, except in Brazil. I will give it to Cydalise, who will infect me; then, when death is in the veins of Crevel and his wife, I shall be beyond the Azores with your cousin, whom I shall cure, and take for my wife. We savages have our own ways of doing things! Cydalise," he said, looking at the country girl, "is the guinea pig I need. How much does she owe?"

"A hundred thousand francs!" said Cydalise.

"Brief—but to the point," Carabine remarked aside to Madame Nourrisson.

"I am going mad!" the Brazilian exclaimed in a hollow voice, dropping into an easy-chair. "It will kill me! But I want to see for myself—it is impossible! A lithographed note! After all, it might quite well be a forgery! Baron Hulot loved Valérie? But he could not have done—if he had, she would not now be alive! But I will not leave her alive for another man if she is not entirely mine!"

Montès was terrible to see, and still more terrible to hear! He roared, he raged, he broke everything he could lay his hands on; rosewood was as brittle as glass.

"He's very destructive!" said Carabine, looking at Madame Nourrisson. "My lamb," she said, tapping the Brazilian, "Orlando furioso[3] is all very well in a poem; but in a flat, it is prosaic, and expensive."

"My boy," said Nourrisson, getting up and coming over to the dejected Brazilian, "I know exactly how you feel! When one loves like that, when you are united 'unto death,' life must answer for love. Whichever one breaks faith tears everything up by the roots—why, it is universal catastrophe! You have my respect, my admiration—above all, my approval of your plan of action, which goes far toward making me a Negrophile! But you love her! You will relent!"

"I! If she is so false, I—"

"Come, now, you are talking too much, when all is said and done!" said Madame Nourrisson, pulling herself together. "A man who means to be avenged, who claims to be a savage in his conduct, does not go on like this. In order to let you see the object of your love in her paradise, you must take Cydalise and look as if you had gone into the wrong room through an error on the part of the maid with your lady friend on your arm. But don't make a scene! If you want your revenge you must behave like a coward, seem to be in despair, and let your mistress get the better of you. Isn't that the way?" said Madame Nourrisson, seeing the Brazilian's surprise at the subtlety of her plan.

"Come along, ostrich," he said, "let us go. I understand."

"Goodbye, my precious!" said Madame Nourrisson to Carabine. She made a sign to Cydalise to go ahead with Montès, and remained alone with Carabine.

"Now, my lambkin, I am only afraid of one thing—that he will strangle her! I should be in a very nasty position, because we have to do these things quietly. Yes, I think you have earned your Raphael; but they say it's only a Mignard. But never mind, it's much nicer; they told me that Raphaels are all blackened, but this one is as good as a Girodet."

"All I want is to outdo Josépha," said Carabine, "and it is all one to me whether it's a Mignard or a Raphael!... Do you know, that gold digger had on such pearls this evening... you would sell your soul for them!"

Cydalise, Montès, and Madame Nourrisson got into a cab that was standing by Carabine's door. Madame Nourrisson whispered to the driver the number of a house in the same block as the Italian Opera, which they might have reached in a few minutes, for it is only seven or eight minutes away from the Rue Saint-Georges; but Madame Nourrisson had told the driver to drive along the Rue le Peletier, and to go very slowly, so that they could examine the waiting carriages.

"Brazilian!" said the Nourrisson, "look out for your angel's carriage and servants!"

The Baron pointed to Valérie's carriage as the cab drove past it.

"She has told her people to fetch her at ten, and she has gone in a cab to the house where she is now with Count Steinbock; she will have dined there, and in half an hour she will be at the Opera! Neat work!" said Madame Nourrisson. "That explains how she has been able to hoodwink you for so long."

The Brazilian made no reply. He had become a tiger, and had reassumed the imperturbable composure that had been so much admired at dinner. He was as calm as a bankrupt the day after he has stopped payment.

At the door of the fatal house stood a hackney coach with two horses, the kind called a *Compagnie générale* from the company that runs them.

"Stay in the cab," said Madame Nourisson to Montès. "You can't just walk in there, as you would into a café; someone will come and fetch you."

The *paradise* of Madame Marneffe and Wenceslas was very different from Crevel's little villa, which he had sold to Count Maxime de Trailles; for, in his opinion, it had ceased to be necessary. This paradise, a paradise for all and sundry, consisted of a room on the fourth floor, opening on to the staircase of a house situated in the same block as the Italian Opera. On each floor of this house, on every landing, there was a room formerly intended to serve as a kitchen to each flat. But as the house had been turned into a sort of hotel whose rooms were let out for clandestine love affairs at exorbitant rents, the owner, the real Madame Nourrisson, a wardrobe dealer in Rue Neuve-Saint-Marc, had been wise enough to realize the immense value of these kitchens, and had turned them into a sort of dining rooms. Each of these rooms, shut off by two thick partitions, looking out onto the street, was completely cut off, by means of thick double doors that opened onto the landings. Important secrets could, therefore, be discussed over dinner without any risk of being overheard. For greater security, the windows were provided with sun blinds outside and shutters inside. The rent of these rooms was accordingly three hundred francs a month. This house, with its paradises and mysteries, was let out for eighty thousand francs a year by Madame Nourrisson the First, who made a profit of twenty thousand a year on an average, after paying for a manageress (Madame Nourrisson the Second), for she herself had nothing to do with the running of it.

The paradise rented by Count Steinbock had a Persian carpet on the floor. The coldness and hardness of a cheap floor of red tiles could no longer be felt under a soft pile. The furniture consisted of two attractive chairs and a bed in an alcove, just then half concealed by a table covered with the remains of an excellent dinner, where two bottles with long necks and an empty Champagne bottle up to its neck in ice, strewed this field of Mars, tilled by Venus. There was an upholstered easy-chair—no doubt sent by Valérie—drawn up beside a smoking chair, and a pretty rosewood chest of drawers with a mirror in a beautiful frame in the Pompadour style. A hanging lamp shed a subdued light, increased by candles on the table and by others on the mantelpiece.

This sketch will give an idea—*urbi et orbi*[4]—of a clandestine love affair in the squalid style stamped upon it by Paris in 1840. How different indeed from adulterous love as symbolized by Vulcan's nets[5] three thousand years ago!

As Cydalise and the Baron came upstairs, Valérie, standing in front of the fireplace, on which a faggot was blazing, was allowing Wenceslas to lace her stays. At such a moment a woman neither too fat nor too thin, like the fine, elegant Valérie, is divinely beautiful. The soft rosy flesh, the moist skin, invites the sleepiest eyes. The lines of the body are so thinly veiled, so delicately suggested by the dazzling folds of a petticoat and the outline of the stays, that a woman, at such times, is irresistible, like all those things that we must leave. Her face, happy, smiling in the mirror, the impatient foot, the hand lifted to repair the disorder of curls in hair still half unpinned, eyes in which gratitude smiles, and the glow of contentment, which, like a sunset, warms every feature—all these things make such an hour a mine of memories! And indeed, whoever, looking back over his life's early errors, can recall some such exquisite details as these will perhaps understand—without, to be sure, excusing—the follies of a Hulot or a Crevel. Women know so well their power at such a moment that they never fail to reap from it what one might call the aftermath of love.

"Come now! After two years you still don't know how to lace up a woman! And you are too much of a Pole altogether! It's ten o'clock, my Wenceslas!" said Valérie, laughing.

At this moment a treacherous maid adroitly lifted the latch of the double door that constituted the whole security of Adam and Eve with the blade of a knife. She opened the door in a hurry—for those who hire these Edens have seldom very much time to themselves—and revealed one of those charming *genre* tableaus that Gavarni[6] has so often exhibited at the Salon.[7]

"This way, Madame!" said the maid.

And Cydalise entered, followed by Baron Montès.

"But there is someone here! I beg your pardon, Madame," said the girl from Normandy, in alarm.

"What! Why, it is Valérie!" Montès exclaimed, slamming the door violently.

Madame Marneffe, overcome with an emotion too genuine to be concealed, dropped onto a low chair by the fireplace. Two tears came to her eyes, but dried again at once. She looked at Montès, noticed the girl, and broke into a peal of forced laughter. The dignity of an outraged woman covered up the scantiness of her incompleted toilet. She came up to the Brazilian, and gave him a look of such pride that her eyes glittered like weapons.

"So this," she said, standing in front of the Brazilian, and pointing to Cydalise, "is the other side of your fidelity! You, who have made me enough promises to convince an atheist in love! You, for whom I have done so much—even committed crimes! You are right, sir, I cannot compete with a girl of that age, and of such beauty! I know what you are going to say to me," she went on, pointing to Wenceslas, whose state of undress was too clear a proof to be denied, "but that is my own affair. If I could still love you, after such a shameful betrayal—for you have spied on me; you have bought every step up these stairs, the mistress of the house, and the maid, and perhaps Reine even—a fine piece of work, to be sure!—if I could still feel any affection for a man capable of such a cowardly act, I would give you reasons that would redouble your love! But I leave you to your doubts—doubts that will become remorse! Wenceslas, my dress!"

She took her dress, put it on, looked at herself in the mirror, and calmly finished her toilet, without paying any further attention to the Brazilian, exactly as if she were alone.

"Wenceslas, are you ready? You go first."

She had, out of the corner of her eye, and in the mirror, been watching Montès's face, and she thought she could trace in its pallor indications of that weakness that exposes these strong men to the fascination of women; she took his hand, and came so close to him that he could breathe those terrible, loved scents, so intoxicating to lovers, and, feeling his pulse beating high, she looked at him reproachfully.

"You have my permission to give an account of your expedition to Monsieur Crevel; he will never believe you, and besides, I have a perfect right to marry him; he will be my husband the day after tomorrow—and I shall make him very happy . . . Goodbye! Try to forget me!"

"Ah! Valérie!" Henri Montès cried, crushing her in his arms. "It is impossible! Come to Brazil!"

Valérie looked at the Baron, and saw that he was her slave again.

"Ah! If you still loved me, Henri! In two years I should be your wife! But your face at this moment seems to me very suspicious!"

"I swear to you that they made me drunk, that false friends have thrown this woman on my hands, and that the whole thing is the work of chance!" said Montès.

"Must I forgive you, then?" she said, smiling.

"And do you still insist on marrying?" the Baron asked, tormented by a harrowing anxiety.

"Eighty thousand francs a year!" she said, with almost comic enthusiasm. "And Crevel loves me so much that he will die of it!"

"Ah! I understand!" said Montès.

"Very well! In a few days we will talk things over!" she said.

And she went downstairs, triumphant.

"I have no more scruples!" thought the Baron, who remained rooted to the spot for a moment. "What! The woman means to make his love the means of getting rid of that idiot, as she counted on Marneffe's death! I shall be the instrument of divine anger!"

Two days later du Tillet's fellow guests who had torn Madame Marneffe to shreds were sitting around her table, an hour after she had assumed her new personality by changing her name for the glorious one of a mayor of Paris. Such verbal treachery is the most light and everyday affair in Parisian social life. Valérie had had the pleasure of seeing the Brazilian Baron at the church, on the invitation of Crevel, who, being now a complete husband, had asked him out of bravado. Montès's presence at the wedding breakfast surprised no one. All these sophisticated people had been long familiar with the weaknesses of passion, the subterfuges of pleasure. Steinbock, who was beginning to despise the woman whom he had looked upon as an angel, was in a mood of deep melancholy that was considered in excellent taste. The Pole seemed in this way to be indicating that all was over between himself and Valérie. Lisbeth came to embrace her dear Madame Crevel, excusing herself from staying to the wedding breakfast on account of the serious state of Adeline's health.

"Don't worry," she said to Valérie as she left, "they shall receive you, and you shall receive them. The Baroness is at death's door after merely hearing the words *two hundred thousand francs.* Oh! you have a hold over them all with that little story! You're going to tell it to me, aren't you?"

A month after her marriage Valérie had reached her tenth quarrel with Steinbock, who wanted to have an explanation on the subject of Henri Montès; he reminded her of his words during the scene in their paradise, and, not satisfied with lashing Valérie with terms of contempt, kept such a watch over her that she no longer had a free moment, what with Crevel's attentions on the one hand and Wenceslas's jealousy on the other. No longer having Lisbeth with her, to give her good advice, she went so far as to reproach Wenceslas bitterly with the money she had given him. This aroused Steinbock's pride so thoroughly that he did not return to the Crevels' house. Valérie had achieved her object, which was to get rid of Wenceslas for a little while, to recover her freedom. She waited until Crevel had to make a journey into the country—to see Count Popinot, in order to arrange for Madame Crevel's introduction—to make an appointment to see the Baron, whom she wished to have with her for a whole day, in order to give him those reasons that were to redouble the Brazilian's love. On the morning of that day, Reine, judging the magnitude of her crime by the sum she had received, tried to warn her mistress, in whom she naturally took more interest than in strangers; but as she had been threatened with being declared insane and being locked up in the Salpetrière[8] in case of indiscretion, she was cautious.

"Madame is so well off now!" she said. "Why do you want to take up again with that Brazilian? For my part, I don't trust him!"

"That's true, Reine," she said, "so I want to get rid of him."

"Well, Madame, that is a weight off my mind. He frightens me, that blackamoor! He might do anything."

"Don't be silly! It is for him you should be afraid, when he is with me!"

Lisbeth came in at this moment.

"My dear darling nanny, what ages since we have seen each other!" said Valérie. "I am very unhappy . . . Crevel bores me to death, and I haven't Wenceslas any more—we have quarreled."

"I know," said Lisbeth. "It is because of him I came. Victorin met him, about five in the evening, going into a cheap restaurant in the Rue du Valois. He worked on his feelings, and took him back to the Rue Louis-le-Grand . . . Hortense, when she saw Wenceslas thin and unhappy and shabbily dressed, welcomed him with open arms. . . . That is how you let me down."

"Monsieur Henri, Madame!" the manservant whispered to Valérie.

"Leave me, Lisbeth; I will explain everything tomorrow."

But, as we shall see, Valérie was soon in no condition to explain anything to anybody.

Chapter XXXVII

By the end of May Baron Hulot's pension had been freed by the successive payments that Victorin had made to Baron Nucingen. As everyone knows, these six-monthly pensions are only payable on presentation of a certificate stating that the recipient is alive, and as the whereabouts of Baron Hulot were unknown, the installments, earmarked for paying off the debt to Vauvinet, were accumulating in the Treasury. Vauvinet having signed his replevin,[1] it was now urgently necessary to find the recipient in order that the arrears could be drawn. The Baroness had, thanks to Doctor Bianchon's care, recovered her health. Josépha's kindness, in the form of a letter, whose spelling betrayed the collaboration of the Duc d'Hérouville, contributed to her complete recovery. Here is the letter that the singer wrote to the Baroness, after six weeks of active search:

> MADAME LA BARONNE,
>
> Monsieur Hulot was living, two months ago, in the Rue des Bernardins, with Élodie Chardin, the lace mender, who had taken him away from Mademoiselle Bijou; but he has left there, leaving all his things, and without a word of explanation, and no one knows where he has gone. I have not lost hope, and I have put a man on to tracing him, who already thinks that he has seen him in Boulevard Bourdon.
>
> The poor Jewess will keep her promise to the Christian. Will the angel please pray for the demon? That must sometimes happen in heaven!
>
> I am, with the deepest respect, always your humble servant,
>
> JOSÉPHA MIRAH.

The younger Hulot d'Ervy, having heard nothing more from the terrible Madame Nourrisson, seeing that his father-in-law was married, having brought back his brother-in-law into the family fold, having had no trouble from his new stepmother, and seeing his mother recovering from day to day, devoted himself to his legal and political work, and was swept along on the rapid current of Paris life, in which hours are like days. Toward the end of the session he was busy writing up a report of a meeting of the Chamber, and decided to sit up all one night, working on it. He returned to his study at about nine in the evening, and as he waited for his manservant to bring him his candles with shades he thought about his father. He was reproaching himself for leaving the search to the singer, and had just decided to see Monsieur Chapuzot about the matter the very next day, when he saw, at his window, in the twilight, a fine old head, bald and yellow, fringed with white hair.

"Will you ask them, sir, to open the door to a poor hermit from the desert, who is collecting money for the rebuilding of a religious hostel?"

This apparition, whose words suddenly reminded the lawyer of a prophecy made by the terrible Nourrisson, shook him profoundly.

"Let that old man in," he said to his manservant.

"He will make the room stink, sir," said the servant. "He is wearing a brown habit that he cannot have changed since he left Syria, and he has no vest."

"Bring him in," the lawyer repeated.

The old man entered. Victorin examined the supposed hermit on pilgrimage with a suspicious eye, and saw a superb example of those Neapolitan monks whose habits are scarcely distinguishable from beggars' rags, whose sandals are tatters of leather, as the monks themselves are the tatters of humanity. The disguise was so perfect that, while remaining on his guard, the barrister rebuked himself for having believed in Madame Nourrisson's spells.

"What do you want from me?"

"Whatever you feel you ought to give me."

Victorin took a hundred-sou piece from a pile of crowns and held it out to the stranger.

"That is not very much on account for fifty thousand francs," said the mendicant from the desert.

This phrase removed all Victorin's doubts.

"And has heaven kept its promises?" said the lawyer, with a frown.

"The doubt is an offense, my son!" replied the hermit. "If you would prefer not to pay until after the funeral, you are within your rights; I will return in a week's time."

"The funeral!" the lawyer exclaimed, getting up.

"Time passes," said the old man, turning to leave, "and the dead are soon disposed of, in Paris."

When Hulot, who had looked down, was about to reply, the active old man had disappeared.

"I don't understand a word of it," Hulot told himself. "All the same, if we have not found my father by the end of eight days, I will put them on to finding him. Where does Madame Nourrisson—yes, that is her name—find such actors?"

On the following day Doctor Bianchon allowed the Baroness to go down into the garden, and had just examined Lisbeth, who had been confined to her room for a month with a mild attack of bronchitis. This brilliant doctor, who would not venture to give a definite opinion on Lisbeth without seeing decisive symptoms, accompanied the Baroness into the garden, to observe the effect of fresh air on her nervous tremor—which he had under observation—after two months of seclusion. The idea of curing this nervous complaint had stimulated Bianchon's professional genius. Finding this great and eminent doctor sitting with them a few minutes, the Baroness and her children set about making conversation with him.

"You must have a very fully occupied life—and very sadly occupied," said the Baroness. "I know what it is like to spend all one's day seeing scenes of distress and physical suffering."

"Madame," said the doctor, "I know the kind of scenes that charitable work brings you into contact with; but you will get used to them in the end, as we all do. It is the law of society. The confessor, the magistrate, the lawyer, would find life impossible if the sense of duty to society did not triumph over the impulses of common humanity.[2] Life would be impossible if this were not so. Is not the soldier, in time of war, also confronted with spectacles still more cruel than those we see? And all soldiers who have been in action are kind. And we doctors have the pleasure of seeing successful cures, just as you have the satisfaction of saving families from the evils of hunger, depravity, and misery, by giving them work, and bringing them back into social life; but what consolation has the magistrate, the police officer, or the lawyer, who spend their whole lives investigating the most sordid scheming of self-interest, a social monstrosity that may regret not having succeeded but which knows nothing of repentance? One half of society spends its life observing the other half. An old friend of mine, a lawyer who has now retired, used to say to me that for the past fifteen years solicitors and barristers have been as suspicious of their clients as of their clients' opponents. Your son is a lawyer. Has he never found himself compromised by the client whom he was defending?"

"Oh! very often," said Victorin, with a smile.

"What is the cause of this deep-rooted evil?" asked the Baroness.

"Want of religion," replied the doctor, "and the encroachment of money, which is only another name for egoism solidified. Money, in the old days, was not everything; other values took precedence over it. There was nobility, and talent, and services rendered to the State; but today the law makes money the measure of everything—it has made it the basis of public capacity! Certain magistrates are not eligible[3]—Jean-Jacques Rousseau would not have been eligible! The perpetual subdivision of inherited estates means that everyone must think of himself from the age of twenty. Well, between the necessity of making money and crooked scheming there is no longer any obstacle, because the religious sense is lacking in France, in spite of praiseworthy efforts toward a Catholic revival. That is what anyone is bound to conclude, who sees, as I do, life from the inside."[4]

"But surely you have a few pleasures?" said Hortense.

"A true doctor's passion," replied Bianchon, "is for science. This devotion, and the knowledge that he is doing useful work, are what sustain him. Why, at this very moment you see me in a state of scientific enthusiasm, and yet many superficial judges would pronounce me heartless. Tomorrow, at the Academy of Medicine, I am going to announce a discovery. I am studying, at this very moment, a lost disease—a fatal disease, moreover, for we have no cure for it in temperate climates, although it is curable in the West Indies—a malady that was prevalent in the Middle Ages. It is a splendid fight, that of the doctor against an enemy of this kind. I have thought of nothing but my patients—for there are two of them, a husband and wife—for ten days! Are they not connections of yours? For surely, Madame, you are Monsieur Crevel's daughter?" he said, turning to Célestine.

"What! Is your patient my father?" said Célestine. "Does he live in Rue Barbet-de-Jouy?"

"Yes, that is so," replied Bianchon.

"And the disease is fatal?" Victorin repeated, horrified.

"I must go to my father!" exclaimed Célestine, getting up.

"I positively forbid it, Madame," said Bianchon calmly. "This disease is contagious."

"But you go there yourself," said the young woman. "Do you think that a daughter's duty is less compelling than a doctor's?"

"A doctor knows how to protect himself from infection, Madame, and the impulsiveness of your devotion convinces me that you might not be as prudent as I am."

Célestine got up and went into the house, where she dressed to go out.

"Doctor," said Victorin to Bianchon, "have you any hope of saving Monsieur and Madame Crevel?"

"I hope, but I do not believe, that I shall," said Bianchon. "The case seems to me quite inexplicable. This disease is peculiar to Negroes and the American natives, whose skin formation is different from that of the white races. Now, I can trace no contact between Negroes, redskins, or half-castes and Monsieur or Madame Crevel. It may be a very interesting complaint to us, but it is a terrible one to an ordinary person. The poor woman, who was, I am told, very pretty, is well punished for her sins, for at this moment she is revoltingly ugly, if she is still anything at all! Her teeth and her hair are dropping out, and she looks like a leper; she is a horror to herself. Her hands are dreadful to look at, swollen, and covered with greenish pustules; the nails are coming loose, and lie in the midst of sores that she has scratched; in short, all the extremities of the body are decomposing into running ulcers."

"But what is the cause of these symptoms?" asked the barrister.

"Oh," said Bianchon, "the cause is a rapid disintegration of the blood, that breaks down at an alarming rate. I hope to act on the blood—I am having it analyzed. I am going home to pick up the results of the investigation made by my friend Professor Duval, the famous chemist, so as to be able to take drastic measures—the sort of desperate remedy we sometimes attempt in the effort to defeat death."

"The hand of God is in it!" said the Baroness, in tones of deep emotion. "And although that woman has done me wrongs that have made me, at times, pray that Divine judgment might descend upon her head, heaven knows, Doctor, that I hope you will succeed!"

Victorin Hulot turned dizzy. He looked at his mother, the doctor, and his sister in turn, and trembled lest they should read his thoughts. He saw himself as a murderer. Hortense, for her part, thought God very just. Célestine returned, and asked her husband to go with her.

"If you go there, Madame, and you, Monsieur, keep at least a foot away from the patients' beds. That is all that is necessary. And on no account must you or your wife embrace the dying man! I think you ought to go with your wife, Monsieur Hulot, to see that she does not disobey these orders."

Adeline and Hortense, left alone, went to keep Lisbeth company. Hortense's hatred for Valérie was so intense that she could not contain herself.

"Cousin! My mother and I are avenged!" she exclaimed. "That venomous creature is poisoned—she is in a state of decomposition!"

"What are you saying?" said Bette, getting up from her chair. "Do you mean Valérie?"

"Yes," said Adeline. "The doctors have given her up; she is dying of a loathsome disease, whose very description makes one's blood run cold."

Cousin Bette's teeth chattered—she broke out into a cold sweat; the violence of the shock revealed the depth of her passionate attachment to Valérie. "I must go there!" she said.

"But the doctor has forbidden you to go out?"

"That doesn't matter. I must go! Poor Crevel, what a state he must be in, for he adores his wife!"

"He is dying, too," replied Countess Steinbock. "Ah! all our enemies are in the Devil's clutches!"

"In God's hands, my child!"

Lisbeth dressed, put on her famous yellow cashmere shawl, her black velvet bonnet, and her boots; and, in spite of the remonstrances of Adeline and Hortense, she went out, as if impelled by some irresistible force. When she arrived at Rue Barbet, a few minutes after Monsieur and Madame Hulot, Lisbeth found seven doctors whom Bianchon had called in to observe this unique case, and whom he had just joined. These doctors were standing in the drawing room discussing the patients. First one and then another of them went into Valérie's bedroom, or Crevel's, to make an observation, and came back with some argument founded on this rapid examination.

Two widely different views divided these princes of science. One, alone in his opinion, believed that it was a case of poisoning, and spoke of some private vengeance, denying that this was the malady described in the Middle Ages. Three others took the view that it was a disintegration of the lymph and the humors. The other party, agreeing with Bianchon, maintained that this disease was caused by a form of blood poisoning resulting from some unknown morbid infection. Bianchon had just brought the result of the blood analysis carried out by Professor Duval. The treatment, although without hope of a cure, and entirely empirical, depended upon the diagnosis.

Lisbeth stopped, petrified, three paces away from the bed on which Valérie lay dying, on seeing there a priest from Saint Thomas-d'Aquin by her friend's pillow and a Sister of Charity tending her. Religion found a soul to save in a mass of putrefaction which, of all the five senses, retained only that of sight. The Sister of Charity, the only being who had been willing to accept the task of nursing Valérie, stood a little apart. So the Catholic Church, that divine body, always activated by the spirit of sacrifice in all things, had in its double role of the spiritual and the corporal come to the aid of that wicked and foul creature, lavishing on her its infinite compassion and the inexhaustible riches of the Divine mercy.

The servants, horrified, refused to enter the sickrooms; they thought only of themselves, and considered that their master and mistress were rightfully punished. The stench was so foul that, in spite of open windows and the most powerful scents, no one could remain long in Valérie's bedroom. Religion alone watched there. How could a woman with Valérie's great intelligence fail to ask herself from what motive these two representatives of the Church remained there? The dying woman had listened to the words of the priest. Repentance had made inroads into that perverse soul, in proportion as the wasting malady ravaged her beauty. The delicate Valérie had offered less resistance to the progress of the disease than Crevel, and she was to be the first to die, having, indeed, been the first to be attacked.

"If I had not been ill myself, I would have come and nursed you," said Lisbeth at last, after exchanging a look with the suffering eyes of her friend. "I have been confined to my room for two or three weeks; but when I heard from the doctor how ill you were I got up and came."

"Poor Lisbeth, so you still love me at least, I see," said Valérie. "Listen! I have not more than a day or two left to think, for I cannot say to *live.* As you see, I have not a body any more; I am a heap of mud. They won't let me look at myself in a mirror. And it is no more than I deserve. And I only wish, that in order to receive mercy, I could repair all the harm that I have done."

"Oh!" said Lisbeth, "if you talk like that, you must really be dying!"

"Do not prevent this woman from repenting; leave her to her Christian thoughts!" said the priest.

"There is nothing left!" thought Lisbeth, appalled. "I do not recognize her eyes, or her mouth! There is not one feature of her left! And her wits have deserted her! Oh! This is terrifying!"

"You do not know," Valérie continued, "what death is, what it is to be compelled to think of the day after your last day, of what awaits you in the grave—worms for the body, and for the soul . . . What? Oh, Lisbeth, I feel that there is another life! And I am so terrified by that thought that I hardly notice the pain of my rotting flesh! And I said to Crevel in jest, making fun of a saint, that God's vengeance takes every form of misfortune! Well, I was prophetic!

Do not make light of sacred things, Lisbeth! If you love me, do as I am doing, and repent!"

"I!" said the peasant. "I have seen vengeance everywhere in nature. The insects perish in order to satisfy the desire to avenge themselves on their attackers! And these gentlemen," she said, turning to the priest, "tell us, do they not, that God exacts revenge, and that His vengeance is eternal!"

The priest looked at Lisbeth with an expression full of gentleness, and said to her, "You are an atheist, Madame."

"But look what I have come to!" said Valérie.

"And how did you get this gangrene!" asked the spinster, who still clung to her peasant incredulity.

"Oh! Henri sent me a letter that leaves me in no doubt as to my fate.... He has killed me! To die—just when I would like to live honestly—and to die an object of horror! Lisbeth, give up all thoughts of revenge! Be kind to that family, to whom I have already, in a will, left as much of my property as I am free to dispose of as I please. Go, my child, even though you are the only being now who does not keep away from me in horror—I beg you, go away, leave me—I have time only to consign myself to God!"

"She is delirious!" thought Lisbeth, as she turned to go.

Even the strongest affection that there is, friendship between women, has not the heroic constancy of the Church. Lisbeth, stifled with the evil smell, left the room. She saw the doctors still deep in discussion. But Bianchon's opinion had carried the day, and they were now only debating the best way to apply the theory.

"In any case, there will be a splendid post-mortem," said one of the opponents, "and we shall have two specimens, so that we shall be able to make comparisons."

Lisbeth returned with Bianchon, who went up to the patient's bed without seeming to notice the fetid atmosphere that came from it.

"Madame," he said, "we are going to try a powerful drug that may save you."

"If you save me," she said, "shall I be beautiful as I used to be?"

"Possibly!" said the learned doctor.

"I know what that 'possibly' means!" said Valérie. "I should look like those women who have fallen into the fire! No, leave me to the Church! I can please no one now but God! I must try to be reconciled to Him—it will be my last flirtation. Yes, I must try to *make* God!"

"That is my poor Valérie's last joke—that is so like her!" said Lisbeth, in tears.

The peasant felt that it was her duty to go into Crevel's bedroom, where she found Victorin and his wife sitting three feet away from the infected man.

"Lisbeth," he said, "they won't tell me how my wife is. You have just seen her. How is she?"

"She is better; she says she is saved," said Lisbeth, permitting herself this ambiguity in order to quiet Crevel.

"Ah! That's good," said the Mayor. "For I was afraid I had been the cause of her illness. A man is not a commercial traveler in the perfumery business for nothing. I was blaming myself. If I were to lose her, what would become of me? On my word of honor, children, I adore that woman!"

Crevel sat up in bed and tried to strike his attitude.

"Oh! Papa! If only you could be well again, I would receive my stepmother, I give you my word!"

"Poor little Célestine!" said Crevel. "Come here and kiss me!"

Victorin held back his wife, who had jumped up.

"Perhaps you did not know, sir," said the barrister gently, "that your illness is contagious."

"That's true," said Crevel. "The doctors are congratulating themselves on having discovered in me some plague or other, dating from the Middle Ages, which they are trumpeting all over their faculties.[5] ... Very funny, I call it!"

"Papa," said Célestine, "be brave, and you will pull through this illness."

"Don't you worry, children, death thinks twice before carrying off a Mayor of Paris!" he said, with ludicrous composure. "And in any case, if my borough is so unfortunate as to sustain the loss of the man whom it has twice honored with its vote—there! you see how well I express myself!—well, I still know how to pack my bags. I am an old commercial traveler, I am used to departures. Yes, my children, I am a strong-minded man!"

"Papa, promise me to let a priest come and see you."

"Never!" said Crevel. "What are you thinking of? I drank the milk of the Revolution. I may not have Baron d'Holbach's wit,[6] but I have his strength of mind. I was never more Regency, more Musketeer, more Abbé Dubois and Marshal de Richelieu, in my life! I'll be damned if my poor wife, who must be taking leave of her senses, didn't send me a fellow in a soutane—to me, the admirer of Béranger, the friend of Lisette,[7] the child of Voltaire and Rousseau! The doctor said, just to try me, to see whether this illness was getting me down: 'Have you seen Monsieur l'Abbé?' Well, I imitated the great Montesquieu.[8] I just gave the doctor a look, like this," he said, turning three-quarters, as in his portrait, and stretching out his hand authoritatively, "and I said to him:

> *... Cet esclave est venu,*
> *Il a montré son ordre, et n'a rien obtenu.*[9]

"*His order* is a nice pun, that proves that even in his last hours Monsieur le Président de Montesquieu conserved all the grace of his genius, for they had sent him a Jesuit! I like that passage. One cannot say it of his life, but of his death. Oh! what a *passage*!—another pun—the *passage* of Montesquieu!"

Hulot watched his father-in-law sadly, asking himself whether stupidity and vanity did not perhaps possess a power as strong as that of true greatness of soul. The causes that set in motion the springs of the soul seem to bear no relation to the results. Can it be that the strength displayed by a great criminal is the same that upholds a Champcenetz who goes proudly to his death?

By the end of the week Madame Crevel was buried, after terrible sufferings, and Crevel followed his wife two days later to the grave. So the conditions of the marriage contract were annulled, and Crevel inherited Valérie's property.

The day after the funeral the old monk appeared again, and the barrister received him in perfect silence. Without a word, the monk held out his hand, and, also without a word, Victorin Hulot gave him eighty thousand-franc notes, taken from a sum of money found in Crevel's desk. The younger Madame Hulot inherited the estate of Presles and an income of about thirty thousand francs a year. Madame Crevel had left three hundred thousand francs to Baron Hulot. The scrofulous Stanislaus was to inherit, on his majority, Crevel's house, and an income of twenty-four thousand francs.

Chapter XXXVIII

Among the many sublime associations instituted in Paris by Catholic charity, one, founded by Madame de la Chanterie,[1] exists for the purpose of enabling couples of the poorer classes, who are living together, to go through the ceremonies of civil and religious marriage.[2] The civil authorities, who draw a large revenue from registration fees, and the all-powerful section of the middle class that benefits from the notary's fees, feigns to ignore the fact that three-quarters of the working classes cannot afford to pay fifteen francs for their marriage certificate. The Chamber of Notaries is, in this respect, behind that of attorneys. The Paris attorneys—a much-abused body—undertake, free of charge, lawsuits on behalf of persons without means, while the notaries have not yet been able to bring themselves to decide to issue marriage certificates gratis to poor people. As for the tax, the whole machinery of government would have to be shaken to its foundations in order to relax the rigor of this legislation. The Registrar's office is deaf and dumb. The Church, on its side, draws revenues from marriages. The Church, in France, is excessively commercial; she carries on, in the house of God, an ignoble traffic in chairs and kneeling-stools, which shocks foreigners, although she cannot have forgotten Our Lord's anger when he drove the money-changers out of the Temple. But if the Church is unwilling to forgo her dues, we must, however, remember that these dues, so-called pew-rents, today constitute one of her main resources, and the responsibility for the Church's abuses lie with the State. This combination of circumstances, at a time when we are all too much concerned with the Negroes and petty offenders brought before the police courts to trouble about the sufferings of honest people, means that a large number of honest couples remain unmarried, for want of thirty francs, the lowest cost for which the notary, the registrar, the Mayor and the Church, will unite two Paris citizens in marriage. Madame de la Chanterie's foundation, whose object is to bring back poor couples to religious and legal respectability, seeks out such couples, in which it is the more successful because it helps them in their distress before attempting to rectify their irregular union.

When Baroness Hulot had quite recovered she took up her work again. And it was then that the worthy Madame de la Chanterie asked Adeline to add the legalization of natural marriages to the good works in which she was already engaged.

One of the Baroness's first efforts in this work was made in the sinister quarter that used to be called *La Petite Pologne,* that lies between the Rue du Rocher, the Rue de la Pépinière, and the Rue de Miroménil. It exists there as a sort of offshoot of the Faubourg Saint-Marceau. By way of describing this quarter, let it suffice to say that the landlords of certain houses, occupied by workingmen out of work, by dangerous characters, by laborers employed in dangerous occupations, dare not collect their rents, and cannot find any bailiffs who are willing to attempt to expel their insolvent tenants. At the present time speculation, which is changing the face of this corner of Paris and building on the waste ground that lies between the Rue d'Amsterdam and the Rue du Faubourg-du-Roule, will no doubt modify the character of the neighborhood, for the builder's trowel, in Paris, has a more civilizing effect than is generally realized! By building good, attractive-looking houses, with porters' lodges, by laying pavements and opening shops, speculation disperses, by raising the rent, undesirable characters, families with no furniture, and bad tenants generally. In this way districts are cleared of these sinister populations, these dens into which the police never venture unless they are obliged to do so.

In June 1844 the aspect of the Place de Laborde and its environs was still far from reassuring. Any well-dressed pedestrian chancing to go up one of these dreadful side streets would have been astonished to see aristocracy rubbing shoulders there with this sinister underworld. In such places, where ignorant poverty proliferates and misery is driven to bay, one finds the last public letter-writers to be found in Paris. Wherever you see written the words "Public Letter-writer," in large script, on a white sheet of paper in the window of some first-floor or squalid ground-floor premises, you may safely conclude that the quarter is the haunt of many illiterate people, and of the vices and crimes that arise out of misfortune. Ignorance is the mother of all crimes. For a crime is, before everything else, a result of lack of intelligence.

During the Baroness's illness this quarter, to which she was a second Providence, had acquired a public letter-writer, who had set up in the alley known, by one of these antitheses with which Parisians are familiar, as the Passage du Soleil—for this alley was more than usually dark. This writer, who was thought to be a German, was called Vyder, and was living with a young girl, of whom he was so jealous that he never allowed her to go out except to visit a family of honest stove-fitters in the Rue Saint-Lazare, Italians, like all stove-fitters, who had been settled for many years in Paris. This family had been saved from impending bankruptcy, which would have reduced them to misery, by Baroness Hulot, acting on behalf of Madame de la Chanterie. In the course of a few months want had given place to comfort, and religion had entered the hearts that had so lately cursed Providence with the energy peculiar to Italian stove-fitters. One of the Baroness's first visits, therefore, was to that family. She was happy at the scene that met her eyes at the back of the house where these good people lived, in the Rue Saint-Lazare, near the Rue du Rocher. Above the stoves and the workshop, now well fitted out, and positively swarming with workmen and apprentices, all of them Italians from the valley of Domo d'Ossola, the family lived in a little flat, to which labor had brought abundance. The Baroness was welcomed as if she had been the Blessed Virgin in person. After a quarter of an hour's inquiry into the family's circumstances, while she was waiting for the husband in order to learn from him how his affairs were progressing, Adeline embarked upon a little saintly spying by asking whether there were any unfortunate cases known to the stove-fitter's family.

"Kind lady, you would rescue the damned from hell! Yes, indeed," said the Italian woman. "There is a young girl just close by here who is in need of saving!"

"Do you know her well?" asked the Baroness.

"She is the granddaughter of an employer my husband used to work for who came to France at the time of the Revolution, in seventeen ninety-eight, called Judici. Old Judici was one of the first stove-fitters in Paris under Napoleon. He died in eighteen nineteen, leaving his son very well off. But the son squandered it all with bad women, and finally married one, who was cleverer than the others, by whom he had this poor little girl, who has just turned fifteen."

"What became of him?" said the Baroness, struck by the similarity of the character of this Judici with that of her husband.

"Well, Madame, this child—Atala she is called[3]—has left her father and mother to live close by here with an old German who must be eighty if he's a day, called Vyder, who does all their business for people who cannot read or write. But if this old libertine, who, they say, bought the child from her mother for fifteen hundred francs, would at least marry the girl, as he cannot have long to live, and as he very likely has an income of a few thousand francs—well, the poor child, who is a perfect little angel, would be saved from getting into trouble, and above all from poverty, which would force her into bad ways."

"Thank you for having told me of this good work that should be done," said Adeline; "but one must set about it tactfully. What is this old man like?"

"Oh, he is a very decent old fellow, Ma'am. He makes the child very happy, and he has some sense, too; for do you know, I think he left the neighborhood where the Judicis were living to save the child from her mother's clutches. The mother was jealous of her daughter, and it seems as if she had hoped to turn her beauty to profit, to make that child into a young madam! Atala remembered us, and she advised her gentleman to settle near us; and as the old man saw what we were like, he lets her come here. But get them married, Ma'am, and you will have done something worthy of you. Once they are married the child will be free; she will escape from her mother in that way, who spies on her, and who would like, for her own profit, to see her in the theater, or successful in the shameful career that she has started her in."

"Why has the old man not married her?"

"There was no need," said the Italian woman, "and although old Vyder is not exactly bad, I think he had enough cunning to want to keep the upper hand, and if he married her—well! he would be afraid, poor old chap, of the thing that all old men are afraid of!"

"Could you send for the girl?" said the Baroness. "If I could see her here, I should find out if there is anything to be done."

The stove-fitter's wife made a sign to her eldest girl, who went off at once. Ten minutes later that young person returned, leading by the hand a young girl of fifteen and a half, a beauty in the Italian style.

Mademoiselle Judici had inherited from her father's side that skin, olive by daylight, that at night, in artificial light, becomes lily-white; eyes that in size, shape, and brilliance were worthy of the Orient; thick, curling eyelashes like little black feathers; jet-black hair; and that natural dignity of Lombardy that makes a stranger, walking in Milan on a Sunday, fancy that every porter's daughter must be a queen.

Atala, informed by the stove-fitter's daughter of the visit of the great lady, of whom she had heard so much, had hastened to put on a pretty silk dress, neat boots, and an elegant little cape. A bonnet with cherry-colored ribbons set off superbly the beauty of her head. This child stood in an attitude of naïve curiosity, watching the Baroness out of the corner of her eye, much puzzled by her nervous trembling. The Baroness sighed deeply when she saw this masterpiece of womanhood condemned to the mire of prostitution, and inwardly vowed to bring her back to a life of virtue.

"What is your name, my child?"

"Atala, Ma'am."

"Can you read and write?"

"No, Ma'am; but that doesn't matter, because Monsieur can."

"Did your parents ever take you to church? Have you made your first communion? Do you know your catechism?"

"Well, Ma'am, Papa wanted me to do things something like what you say, but Mamma would not hear of it."

"Your mother?" exclaimed the Baroness. "Is she very unkind, then, your mother?"

"She always used to beat me! I don't know why, but my father and mother were always quarreling about me."

"Then no one has ever told you about God?" said the Baroness.

The child opened her eyes wide.

"Oh, Mamma and Papa often used to say 'my God,' and 'for God's sake,' and 'God damn you,'" she replied, with touching naïveté.

"Have you never seen any churches? Did you never think of going inside one?"

"Churches? Oh, you mean Notre Dame and the Pantheon. Yes, I have seen these from a distance, when Papa used to take me about Paris. But he didn't do that very often. There aren't any churches like that in the Faubourg."

"Which Faubourg did you live in?"

"In the Faubourg."

"Yes, but which?"

"Why, Ma'am, in the Rue de Charonne."

The inhabitants of the Faubourg Saint-Antoine never refer to that notorious district otherwise than as "the Faubourg." For them it is the Faubourg *par excellence,* the supreme Faubourg, and even factory owners understand by that word the Faubourg Saint-Antoine in particular.

"Did no one ever teach you the difference between right and wrong?"

"Mamma used to beat me when I did things she didn't like."

"Then you didn't know that you were doing wrong in leaving your father and mother to go and live with an old man?"

Atala Judici looked at the Baroness with an expression of scorn, and did not answer.

"The girl is a perfect heathen," said Adeline.

"Oh, there are plenty more like her in the Faubourg, Ma'am," said the stove-fitter's wife.

"But, good heavens, she knows nothing—not even what is wrong! Why won't you answer me?" she said, trying to take Atala's hand.

Atala, indignant, drew back.

"You are an old fool!" she said. "My father and mother had had scarcely anything to eat for a week! My mother wanted to do something dreadful, I think, because my father beat her, and called her a thief! But then Monsieur Vyder paid all my father's and mother's debts and gave them money—oh, a whole bag of it—and then he took me away, and my poor Papa cried. But we had to say goodbye! Well, was that wrong?" she asked.

"And are you very fond of this Monsieur Vyder?"

"Am I fond of him!" she said. "Why, Ma'am, I should think I am! He tells me beautiful stories every evening! And he has given me lovely dresses, and underclothes, and a shawl. Why, I am rigged up like a princess, and I don't wear sabots any more! And for two months I haven't known what it is to be hungry! I don't live on potatoes now! He brings me bonbons, and burnt almonds—they are simply delicious, chocolate almonds—I do anything he wants me to, for a bag of chocolates! And besides, my old Daddy Vyder is very kind, and he looks after me so well, so nicely, that it makes me realize what my mother ought to have been like. He is going to get an old servant to help me, because he doesn't like me to spoil my hands doing the cooking. He has been making a good bit of money for the last month; he gives me three francs every evening, to put in my money-box! The only thing is, he doesn't like me going out, except to come here! Really, he's ever such a nice man! So he can do whatever he likes with me! He calls me his little kitten! And my mother never used to call me anything but bad names, or thief, or vermin! Don't I know it!"

"Well, then, why don't you marry your Daddy Vyder, my child?"

"But we are married, Ma'am!" said the young girl, looking at the Baroness with an expression full of pride, without a blush, her brow clear, her eyes untroubled. "He said to me that I was his little wife; but it is a bore being a man's wife! I mean, if it wasn't for the chocolate almonds!"

"Good heavens!" the Baroness said to herself, "what kind of monster can it be who has the heart to take advantage of such complete and pure innocence! Surely to bring back this child into the ways of virtue would redeem many sins! For I knew what I was doing!" she thought, remembering the scene with Crevel. "But she knows nothing!"

"Do you know Monsieur Samanon?" Atala asked, with a cunning expression.

"No, my child. Why do you ask me that?"

"Really and truly?" said the innocent creature.

"You need not be afraid of this lady, Atala!" said the stove-fitter's wife. "She is an angel!"

"Only my old man is afraid of being found by this Samanon—that's why he is in hiding. And I do so wish he could be free."

"Why?"

"Why, he would take me to Bobino, perhaps to the Ambigu."

"What an adorable creature!" said the Baroness, kissing the young girl.

"Are you rich?" asked Atala, who was playing with the Baroness's lace cuffs.

"Yes and no," she replied. "I am rich for good little girls like you, when they are willing to be taught their Christian duties by a priest and walk in the right way."

"Walk in what way?"

"In the way of virtue!"

Atala looked at the Baroness with an air of sly amusement.

"Look at Madame—she is happy since she returned to the bosom of the Church," said the Baroness, pointing to the stove-fitter's wife. "You are only married as the animals mate."

"I?" said Atala. "Why, if you will give me all the things that old Vyder gives me, I would be very glad not to be married. It's a nuisance! Do you know what it is like?"

"Once you are united to a man, as you are," said the Baroness, "virtue requires you to remain faithful."

"Until he dies," said Atala, knowingly. "I shall not have long to wait. If you knew how old Vyder coughs and wheezes! Pouh! Pouh!"—and she imitated the old man.

"Virtue and morality demand," the Baroness continued, "that the Church, that represents God, and the Mayor, who represents the law, should consecrate your marriage. Look at Madame—she is properly married."

"Is it nicer?" asked the child.

"You will be happier," said the Baroness, "because no one will be able to blame you for the marriage. You will be pleasing God! Ask Madame whether she married without having received the sacrament of marriage."

Atala looked at the stove-fitter's wife.

"What has she more than I have?" she asked. "I am prettier than she is."

"Yes, but I am an honest woman," retorted the Italian woman, "and you might be called a bad name."

"How can you expect that God will protect you if you ride roughshod over the laws of God and man?" said the Baroness. "Do you know that God has a paradise in store for those who follow the laws of His Church?"

"What is there in paradise? Are there theatres?" said Atala.

"Why, in paradise," said the Baroness, "there are all the joys you can possibly imagine. It is full of angels, with white wings. We see God there in His glory, and partake of His power; we are happy every moment for all eternity!"

Atala Judici listened to the Baroness as she might have listened to music; and seeing that all this was Greek to her, Adeline decided that she would have to approach the matter in a different way, through the old man.

"Go home, my child, and I will come and talk to Monsieur Vyder. Is he French?"

"He is Alsatian. But he will be rich! Why, if you would pay what he owes to that wicked Samanon, he would pay you back! For in a few months, he says, he will be getting six thousand francs a year, and then we will go and live in the country, far away, in the Vosges."

At the word "Vosges" the Baroness became lost in thought. She remembered her own village! She was roused from this melancholy meditation by the voice of the stove-fitter, who now came in to tell her about his prosperity.

"In a year I shall be able to repay you the money you lent us. For it is God's money, it belongs to the poor and the unfortunate! If I grow rich, you can always come to me for money. I will repay to others, through you, the help that you brought us."

"Just now," said the Baroness, "I don't want to ask you for money, but for your help in a good work. I have just seen the little Judici girl who is living with an old man, and I want to persuade them to be married in church, legally."

"Ah! old Vyder—he is a very decent old fellow, and he gives good advice. The poor old chap has already made a number of friends in the neighborhood, since he came here two months ago. He has put my accounts in order for me. He is a brave Colonel,

I believe, who did good service under the Emperor. And how he loves Napoleon! He has a decoration, but he never wears it. He is waiting until he is straight again; for he is in debt, poor old fellow! I shouldn't wonder if he isn't hiding, and the bailiffs on his track!"

"Tell him I will pay his debts if he will marry the child."

"Oh, that will not be difficult! Why not go and see him now? It is just round the corner, in the Passage du Soleil."

The Baroness and the stove-fitter set out for the Passage du Soleil.

"This way, Ma'am," said the stove-fitter, pointing down the Rue de la Pépinière.

The Passage du Soleil runs, in fact, from the bottom of the Rue de la Pépinière through to the Rue du Rocher. Halfway down this passage, recently made, whose shops are let at a very modest rent, the Baroness saw, above a window screened halfway up with green oiled silk to prevent passers-by from staring in, a notice on which was written "Public letter-writer"; and on the door:

BUSINESS AGENCY.
PETITIONS DRAWN UP, ACCOUNTS AUDITED.
ALL WORK CONFIDENTIAL,
AND CARRIED OUT PROMPTLY.

The interior was like one of the waiting rooms where passengers on the Paris omnibuses wait for their connections. A staircase inside led, no doubt, to the first-floor rooms, looking onto the alley, that went with the shop. The Baroness noticed a blackened deal writing table, some boxes, and a shabby secondhand chair. A cap and a green oiled-silk eye-shade fixed with dirty copper wire suggested either precautions for disguise or weakness of the eyes—not unlikely in an old man.

"He is up there," said the stove-fitter. "I will go up and tell him to come down."

The Baroness lowered her veil and sat down. A heavy step made the little wooden staircase creak and Adeline could not restrain a piercing cry when she saw her husband, Baron Hulot, in a gray knitted vest, shabby gray flannel trousers, and slippers.

"What can I do for you, Madame?" said Hulot gallantly.

Adeline rose, seized Hulot, and said to him in a voice broken with emotion, "At last I have found you!"

"Adeline!" the Baron exclaimed in amazement and locked the door of the shop. "Joseph!" he said to the stove-fitter, "go out by the back way!"

"My dear," she said, forgetting everything else in her excess of joy, "you can return to your family. We are rich; your son has an income of a hundred and sixty thousand francs! Your pension is released, and you can draw fifteen thousand francs arrears by simply presenting a certificate stating that you are alive! Valérie is dead and has left you three hundred thousand francs. Everything has been forgotten by now—why, you can return to the world, and you will find a fortune waiting for you in your son's house. Come, and our happiness will be complete. I have been looking for you for nearly three years, and I was so sure that I should find you that I have a room all ready for you. Oh! come away from here, and from the dreadful situation I see you in!"

"I would like nothing better," said the Baron, quite dazed, *"but can I bring the child?"*

"Hector, give her up! Do this for your Adeline, who has never asked you to make any sacrifice! I promise to give the child a dowry, and to marry her well, and see that she is educated. Let it be said that one woman who has made you happy is happy herself, and will not relapse into vice, into the mire!"

"So it is you," said the Baron with a smile, "who wanted to marry me off? Wait there a moment," he added, "and I will go upstairs and dress—I have some presentable clothes in a suitcase."

Left alone, Adeline again looked around that sordid little shop, and burst into tears.

"He has been living here," she thought, "while we were in comfort! Poor man! How he has been punished—and he was always so elegant!"

The stove-fitter came to say goodbye to his benefactress, who asked him to fetch a cab. When he returned, the Baroness asked him to take in little Atala Judici, to take her away there and then.

"Tell her," she added, "that if she will be instructed by the vicar of St. Mary Madeleine, the day she makes her first communion I will give her a dowry of thirty thousand francs and a good husband, some fine young man."

"My eldest son, Ma'am! He is twenty-two and he worships that child!"

The Baron now came down, and there were tears in his eyes.

"You are making me leave," he whispered to his wife, "the only creature whose love has ever been anything like your love for me! The child is in tears! I cannot leave her like this!"

"Don't distress yourself, Hector! She is going to live with a good family, and I can answer for her conduct."

"Then I can come with you," said the Baron, escorting his wife to the cab.

Hector, the Baron d'Ervy once more, had put on a coat and trousers of blue cloth, a white waistcoat, black gloves and cravat. As the Baroness seated herself inside the cab Atala slipped in like an eel.

"Oh, Ma'am!" she pleaded, "let me come with you! I shall be very good, and obedient, I shall do everything you tell me! But don't take Daddy Vyder away from me, who has been so kind to me, and given me such beautiful things! And I shall be beaten!"

"Come, Atala!" said the Baron. "This lady is my wife, and we must part!"

"She! She is so old!" replied the naïve child. "And she trembles like a leaf! Look at her head!"

And she mimicked the Baroness's trembling. The stove-fitter, who had hurried after little Judici, came to the door of the cab.

"Take her away!" said the Baroness.

The stove-fitter took Atala in his arms, and carried her to his house by main force.

"Thank you for that sacrifice, my dear!" said Adeline, taking the

Baron's hand and pressing it in an excess of joy. "How you have altered! You must have suffered! What a surprise for your daughter! And your son!"

Adeline and the Baron talked like lovers who meet after a long absence, pouring out a hundred things at once. Ten minutes later the Baron and his wife reached the Rue Louis-le-Grand, where Adeline found the following letter waiting for her.

> MADAME LA BARONNE,
>
> Monsieur le Baron d'Ervy stayed for a month in the Rue de Charonne, under the name of Thorec, an anagram of Hector. He is now living in the Passage du Soleil, under the name of Vyder. He calls himself an Alsatian, and is a letter-writer; he is living with a young girl called Atala Judici. You must be careful, because there is an active search on foot for the Baron, on whose behalf I do not know.
>
> The actress has kept her word, and remains, always, Madame la Baronne,
>
> YOUR VERY HUMBLE SERVANT,
>
> J. M.

The Baron's return was greeted with transports of joy, which quite reconciled him to family life. He forgot little Atala Judici, for his excesses had reduced him to that state of emotional instability characteristic of childhood. The family's happiness was clouded by the change in the Baron. He had left home still a hale man, and he returned almost a centenarian, broken, bowed, his expression degraded. A splendid dinner, planned by Célestine, reminded the old man of the singer's dinner parties, and he was quite overwhelmed by the splendors of his family.

"You are celebrating the return of the prodigal father!" he whispered to Adeline.

"Hush! That is all forgotten!" she replied.

"And where is Lisbeth?" the Baron asked, noticing that the spinster was not present.

"Unfortunately, she is in bed," replied Hortense. "She will never get up again, and she will not be with us long. But she is hoping to see you after dinner."

On the following morning, at sunrise, the younger Hulot was informed by the porter's wife that men of the Municipal Guard were posted all around his house. The police were searching for Baron Hulot. The bailiff, who had followed the concierge, presented a summons to the barrister, asking him whether he was willing to pay on behalf of his father. It was a matter of ten thousand francs, borrowed on notes-of-hand, from a usurer by the name of Samanon, who had probably lent the Baron two or three thousand. The young man asked the bailiff to send away the guard, and paid.

"Will this be the last?" he wondered, anxiously.

Lisbeth, already miserable enough on account of the good fortune that smiled on the family, could not survive this happy event. She became so much worse that Bianchon gave her only a week to live, defeated at last in that long battle, in which she had won so many victories. She kept the secret of her hate through her painful death from pulmonary consumption. And she had the supreme satisfaction of seeing Adeline, Hortense, Hulot, Victorin, Steinbock, Célestine, and their children, all in tears around her bed, mourning her as the angel of the family. Baron Hulot, on a substantial diet, such as he had not enjoyed for three years, recovered his strength, and was almost himself again. This restoration made Adeline so happy that her nervous tremor greatly improved.

"She will be happy, after all!" thought Lisbeth on the eve of her death, seeing the veneration with which the Baron behaved toward his wife, whose sufferings had been described to him by Hortense and Victorin.

This reflection hastened the end of Cousin Bette, who was followed to the grave by the whole family, all in tears.

Baron and Baroness Hulot, having reached the age for complete rest, gave Count and Countess Steinbock the beautiful rooms on the first floor, and moved into the second. The Baron, through the efforts of his son, obtained early in 1845 a directorship on a railway company, carrying a salary of six thousand francs, which, with his pension and the money left him by Madame Crevel, produced an income amounting to twenty-four thousand francs a year. As Hortense had obtained independent control of her own money during her three years of separation from her husband, Victorin no longer hesitated to make over to his sister the two hundred thousand francs left in trust, and this produced an income of twelve thousand francs a year for Hortense. Wenceslas, now the husband of a rich woman, was entirely faithful to her; but he idled his time away, without ever being able to bring himself to the point of beginning any piece of work, however small. Once more an artist *in partibus*,[4] he was a great social success, and was consulted by a number of amateurs; in other words, he became a critic, like all weak characters who are false to their first promise. Each of these families, therefore, enjoyed its own particular fortune, although living under one roof.

Made wise by so many misfortunes, the Baroness left to her son the management of her affairs, thus leaving the Baron only his salary and pension; the smallness of this income would, they hoped, prevent him from relapsing into his old habits. But, by an unbelievable piece of good fortune, the Baron seemed to have renounced the fair sex. His serenity, which they put down to the course of nature, at last so completely reassured his family that they were able to enjoy to the full Baron d'Ervy's renewed amiability and his many charming qualities. He was attentive and considerate toward his wife and children, accompanied them to the theater, and into society, in which he appeared once more; and did the honors of his son's drawing room with infinite charm. Altogether this reformed prodigal father afforded his family the greatest possible happiness. He was a charming old man, a complete wreck, to be sure, but full of wit, and retained only so much of his old vice as made it into a social virtue. Consequently everyone was completely reassured. His children and his wife praised the father of the family up to the skies, forgetting the death of two uncles! Life cannot go on without a great deal of forgetting!

Madame Victorin, who was an excellent housekeeper—thanks, no doubt, to Lisbeth's training—found it necessary, in such a large household, to employ a man cook. And the cook naturally had to have a kitchenmaid. Kitchenmaids are ambitious creatures nowadays, anxious to discover the chef's secrets and become cooks themselves as soon as they know how to serve up a sauce. Consequently kitchenmaids change very frequently. At the beginning of December 1845, Célestine employed as a kitchenmaid a buxom Normandy wench from Isigny, thick-set, with firm red arms and a common face, as stupid as you please, who could scarcely be induced to abandon the classical cotton bonnet worn by the girls of lower Normandy. Her reddish face, with its firm brown contours, might have been carved out of stone. Naturally no attention was paid in the household to the arrival of this girl—whose name was Agathe—the sort of typical knowing wench that arrives in Paris every day from the provinces. Agathe did not get on too well with the chef, for she was coarse-tongued, having been used to serving carters in the low-class tavern from which she came; so that far from making a conquest of the cook, and persuading him to teach her the noble art of cookery, she was looked down on by him. The chef's attentions were reserved for Louise, Countess Steinbock's maid. So the country wench, thinking herself ill-used, was forever complaining; she was always sent out, on some pretext or other, when the chef was putting the finishing touches on a dish, or making a sauce.

"I am certainly out of luck," she said. "I shall find another place."

But she stayed on, although she had given notice twice.

One night Adeline, awakened by an unusual noise, noticed that Hector was no longer in the bed in which he slept, next to hers—for they slept in twin beds side by side, as befitted an old couple. She lay awake for an hour, and still the Baron did not return. Becoming alarmed, fearing some terrible disaster, perhaps a stroke, she went up to the floor above, where the servants slept. There she was attracted to Agathe's room by seeing a light streaming through the half-open door, and by the murmur of two voices. She stopped in dismay when she recognized the voice of the Baron, who, seduced by Agathe's charms, had been brought by the calculated resistance of this odious slut to the point of saying to her these hateful words:

"My wife has not long to live, and if you like you could be a Baroness."

Adeline gave a cry, dropped her candlestick, and fled.

Three days later the Baroness, who had received the last sacraments on the previous evening, lay dying, her family in tears at her bedside. Just before she died she took her husband's hand, pressed it, and whispered to him, "My dear, I had nothing left to give you but my life; in a few minutes you will be free, and you can make a Baroness Hulot."

And tears trickled from the eyes of the dead woman, a sight that must be rare. The savagery of vice had overcome the patience of the angel, who, on the edge of eternity, uttered the only reproach that she had spoken in her whole life.

Baron Hulot left Paris three days after his wife's funeral. Eleven months later Victorin learned indirectly of his father's marriage with Mademoiselle Agathe Piquetard, celebrated at Isigny, on February 1st, 1846.

"Parents can oppose the marriage of their children, but children cannot prevent the follies of parents in their second childhood," said Councilor Hulot to Councilor Popinot, second son of the onetime Minister of Commerce, who had spoken to him of that marriage.

Notes

Chapter I

1. *milords:* light, four-wheeled carriages with two seats. So named because of their association with British aristocrats.
2. *captain of the National Guard:* Service in the National Guard was compulsory for French men. Balzac enjoyed this obligation rather less than Crevel; he constantly avoided service and once briefly went to prison rather than serve.
3. *The Rue de Bellechasse and the Rue de Bourgogne:* Balzac situated his novels in the Paris he lived in; many of the streets he names, including the two named here, still exist. The contemporary Parisian reader would recognize the neighborhood as the Faubourg Saint-Germain, one of the wealthiest and most aristocratic of Parisian neighborhoods.
4. *an old mansion standing in its own garden:* These *hôtels particuliers* were the urban residences of the great aristocrats. The new house built in the courtyard is symbolic of the decline of the aristocracy and of French society in general.
5. *General Hulot:* The old soldier makes his first appearance in the novel *Les Chouans,* Balzac's first literary success and the first novel in what would become *The Human Comedy.* Many of the characters the reader will encounter in *Cousin Bette* play important roles in other works of *La Comédie humaine.*

6. *this name, so admirably suited to the figure:* The name Crevel suggests the French verb *crever,* which can mean, among other things, "to burst."
7. *Restoration:* The Restoration of the Bourbon monarchy after the fall of Napoleon. The so-called First Restoration lasted from 1814 until Bonaparte's return from Elba in 1815; the Second began after Waterloo in 1815. The Restoration endured until the July Revolution of 1830, which brought Louis-Philippe d'Orléans—cousin to the Bourbons and First Prince of the Royal Blood—to the throne; this government, known as the July Monarchy, lasted until still another revolution in 1848.
8. *Tartuffe* and *Elmire:* In a famous scene in Molière's masterpiece *Tartuffe,* the hypocritical religious swindler Tartuffe attempts to forcefully seduce Elmire, the wife of his rich and gullible benefactor.

Chapter II

1. *"he occupies the best part":* Victorin's house is divided into apartments.
2. *"the Assizes":* the criminal court.
3. *"Regency! Louis XV!":* Crevel likes to show his self-styled sophistication by making frequent allusions to the great eighteenth-century age of aristocratic libertinage. The Regency of the notorious Duc Philippe d'Orléans (1674–1723) marked the beginning of the reign of Louis XV (1715–1774), himself a legendary libertine.
4. *"Birotteau, Popinot's father-in-law":* Crevel is a minor character in *La Grandeur et décadence de César Birotteau* (The Rise and Fall of César Birotteau). Popinot, also a character in *César Birotteau,* like Crevel starts out as one of Birotteau's clerks, and achieves great success in business and politics; he also plays an important role in *Le Cousin Pons,* the companion novel to *La Cousine Bette.* The two novels together are known as *Les Parents pauvres* (The Poor Relations).
5. *"Duprez in petticoats":* The tenor Gilbert Louis Duprez (1806–1896) was one of the most famous opera singers in Paris.
6. *"Mademoiselle de Romans":* one of the mistresses of Louis XV.
7. *"Saint-Simonism":* Among the radical propositions of the Count de Saint-Simon (1760–1825) and his followers was the emancipation of women.

8. *"a Jewess"*: Balzac was fascinated by the figure of the exotic *Juive;* the courtesans Esther in *Splendeurs et misères des courtisanes* (A Harlot High and Low) and Coralie in *Illusions perdues* (Lost Illusions) are Jewish, but are very different from Josépha. In *Louis Lambert,* Pauline de Villenoix, the "spiritual wife" of the mystic Louis Lambert, is descended from converted Jews.
9. *"Madame Schontz, Malaga, and Carabine"*: All notable courtesans within *La Comédie humaine.* Their unusual names are all invented *noms de guerre.*
10. *"one of the Kellers . . . the Marquis d'Esgrignon"*: The Keller brothers are politically active bankers in Balzac's Paris. The Marquis d'Esgrignon is the protagonist of Balzac's *Le Cabinet des antiques.*
11. *"Thirteenth District"*: At the time of the novel, Paris was divided into twelve districts, or arrondissements (there are twenty today); the term *thirteenth arrondissement* was used to describe the demimonde, the world of the grand courtesans and the men who kept them.
12. *"hundred-sou pieces"*: worth five francs. The franc was worth twenty *sous,* one *sou* was worth five *centimes,* or cents. At the time, it was still common to speak of *écus,* translated here as crowns, worth three francs, and *louis,* worth twenty francs.
13. *"an expression from the old days!"*: Crevel is an ex-*parfumeur;* gloves were sold in perfume shops like his.
14. *"moderation in all things, as our King has said"*: King Louis-Philippe was known for preaching political moderation, or the *juste milieu,* the sensible middle ground.

Chapter III

1. *"du Tillet"*: An unscrupulous banker who also started his career working for Crevel's predecessor, Birotteau.
2. *"free lances"*: in French, *condottieri,* after the mercenaries of Renaissance Italy. In *La Comédie humaine,* the term refers to ambitious young men without family wealth or connections, who have only their wits in their quest for success. For Balzac, the image recalled that Parisian society was a battlefield.
3. "lex talionis": The law of revenge, i.e., "an eye for an eye."

4. France was frequently at war after the declaration of the Republic in 1792. Bonaparte owed his initial fame to his successes with the Army of Italy.
5. *Adeline at sixteen ... all daughters of the same salt wave:* Many of the women named in this paragraph are famous beauties of French history: Mme du Barry (1743–1793) was the last mistress of Louis XV; Mme Tallien (1773–1835) was the wife of an important revolutionary politician; Bianca Capella was a sixteenth-century Venetian noblewoman; Diane de Poitiers (1499–1566) was the mistress of King Henri II; the legendary Ninon de Lenclos (1619–1705), often thought of as a courtesan, was a seventeenth-century libertine and woman of letters; the actress Mlle Georges (1787–1867) was a contemporary of Balzac's, as was Juliette Récamier (1777–1849), who was loved by Châteaubriand and Benjamin Constant.
6. *men like d'Orsay, Forbin, and Ouvrard:* Famous *beaux* of the elegant society of the Empire: the d'Orsay brothers, Albert and Alfred, personified male elegance in Paris and London; the Comte de Forbin (1656–1733) was also a painter and archaeologist; Gabriel-Julien Ouvrard (1770–1846) is better remembered for his scandalous success as a financier than for his good looks.
7. *the* Directoire: The Directory was the government of France from 1794—the end of the Terror and the collapse of the Convention—until 1799, when Bonaparte seized power and created the Consulate. High society under the Directory was notoriously libertine.
8. *the Prince de Wissembourg:* Born Cottin (Bonaparte gave his most successful generals grand titles; see note 6, chapter XXVII), the character of Wissembourg is closely modeled on Nicolas Soult, the Napoleonic general who was named duc de Dalmatie. Reconciled to the Bourbons and named a Peer in 1814, Soult rallied to Bonaparte during the Hundred Days. Exiled after the Second Restoration, Soult was called back to the government in 1823. Soult's Imperial colleague, Clarke—named Duc de Feltre by Napoleon—remained loyal to the Bourbons and was Minister of War in 1816.
9. *the war with Spain:* This war was declared in 1823 when the French Bourbons decided to defend the absolute monarchy of their distant

cousin Ferdinand VII against a liberal uprising seeking constitutional rule.

10. *the scene of his exploits in 1799 and 1800:* In the late 1790s, Royalist rebels known as *Chouans* conducted a guerrilla war against the Republic in western France. This uprising is the subject of Balzac's *The Chouans, or Brittany in 1799.* (See note 5, chapter I.)

CHAPTER IV

1. *Ninon:* Ninon de Lenclos (see note 5, chapter III).
2. *Pons Brothers:* These illustrious embroiderers are cousins of the protagonist of *Le Cousin Pons* (see note 4, chapter II).
3. *Bette:* The name "Bette" is a homophone of the French word *bête,* which means "beast" as a noun and "stupid" as an adjective. In the French, she is frequently referred to as "la Bette," which suggests "the Beast." In a letter to his mistress, the Countess Eveline Hanska (see note 10 below) Balzac said that Bette was a composite of his mother, with whom he had a very difficult relationship; of Eveline's aunt Rosalie Rzewuska, who actively opposed Mme Hanska's liaison with the low-born and vulgar novelist; and the Romantic poet Marceline Desbordes-Valmore, who loved and married a much younger, impoverished, and handsome husband. This is one of the few instances of Balzac specifically identifying the real-life models for one of his characters.
4. *the disaster of Fontainebleau:* refers to Napoleon's first abdication in 1814.
5. *the Volunteer Corps of 1815:* Napoleon's army.
6. *foraging business:* i.e., a private contractor who procures food and other supplies for the military.
7. *the Corsicans:* Corsica was considered exotic in the Romantic era, due chiefly to it being the birthplace of Bonaparte. Balzac's short story *The Vendetta* reflects this conception.
8. *Richelieu:* Cardinal de Richelieu (1585–1642) rose to become de facto prime minister under Louis XIII. His descendant (by way of his brother), the Maréchal de Richelieu, is a frequent point of reference in *Cousin Bette.*
9. *Nanny:* the implication is that Bette is as stubborn as a nanny goat.
10. *"He has fought for Poland!":* The Polish revolt against Russian rule in 1830

captured the Romantic imagination. Balzac had a special reason for speaking so well of Poles: the Russo-Ukrainian Countess Eveline Hanska, née Rzewuska, was from an old and politically active family of the Polish nobility. Their relationship began when Mme Hanska wrote Balzac an admiring, anonymous letter in 1832. They met face-to-face only in 1833, in Geneva. After an eighteen-year, mostly epistolary affair, Balzac married Eve only a few months before his death in 1850.

11. *"the Grand Duke Constantine"*: Brother of Czar Alexander I, the Grand Duke Constantine was Viceroy of Poland. Forced to flee Warsaw in 1831, he died of cholera while returning to Saint Petersburg.
12. *"the knout"*: A whip used to torture criminals and rebels in Russia that was symbolic of the oppressive, autocratic rule of the Czars.
13. "idole de mon âme!": Translates as "idol of my soul."
14. "O Mathilde!": An aria from Rossini's *William Tell.*

CHAPTER V

1. *"Charles XII"*: King Charles XII (1607–1718) of Sweden was a great military leader; a General Steinbock did in fact serve under him. Balzac often blurred the line between history and fiction in this way.
2. *"the eighteen-twelve campaign"*: This campaign against Russia was a fatal disaster for Bonaparte and his empire. Many Polish aristocrats threw in their lot with Bonaparte against the Czar.
3. "Fecit": Latin for "made by."
4. "twenty-two": The reader may notice that Balzac is inconsistent with regard to the age of Hortense and Bette. Such disregard for details is not unusual in *La Comédie humaine.* More important to Balzac than specific age is Hortense's youthful innocence and the fact that Bette is a middle-aged spinster.
5. *"Count de Rastignac"*: Rastignac, hero of *Le Père Goriot,* is one of the most recognizable of Balzac's recurring *La Comédic humaine* characters.
6. "Madame la Présidente": i.e., the wife of a presiding judge.
7. *Baron Hector Hulot:* Many critics believe that Balzac based the character of Hector Hulot on his friend Victor Hugo. Beside the assonance between the two names, Hugo was married to Adèle Foucher, while Hulot married Adeline Fischer. Hugo's personal life had become the

subject of scandal in the 1840s (see note 4, chapter XXVII). If Hugo saw any resemblance between himself and Hulot he does not seem to have taken offense. Hugo delivered Balzac's eulogy at Père Lachaise cemetery in 1850.

8. *Brillat-Savarin:* influential gastronomic writer (1755–1826).
9. Robert le Diable: Meyerbeer's opera is a frequent point of reference for Balzac. The French and Italian operas were the two leading companies in Paris.
10. *"bills of exchange":* Essentially an IOU, a bill of exchange (*lettre de change*) was a written recognition of debt. These bills were traded by moneylenders, often at a discount according to the solvency of the debtor.

Chapter VI

1. *the Louvre:* Napoleon had intended to complete the Louvre by extending its two wings to connect with the Palace of the Tuileries, which once stood near today's Place du Caroussel. The project was completed by Napoleon III in the 1860s. The Palace of the Tuileries was badly damaged in the civil unrest that followed the fall of the Second Empire in 1870, and was completely demolished soon after.
2. *three dynasties:* i.e., Bonaparte, the Bourbon kings Louis XVIII (died 1824), Charles X (deposed in 1830), and Louis-Philippe d'Orléans.
3. *Henri III and his minions . . . Marguerite's lovers:* Henri III (1551–1589) was widely criticized for his *mignons*—the source of the English word "minion"—who were his companions in debauchery. Henri's sister, Marguerite de Valois (1553–1615), was the first wife of Henri IV (1553–1610). Known as the Reine Margot, Marguerite was accused of numerous infidelities. Henri had their childless marriage annulled in 1599, and later married Marie de Médici.
4. *the legitimist newspaper:* Balzac is referring to the *Gazette de France,* with offices in the rue du Doyenné; its popularity had steadily declined since 1831.
5. *Cambacérès:* The jurist and politician Jean-Jacques-Régis de Cambacérès (1753–1824) was Napoleon's Grand Chancellor. Much of the Napoleonic Code was based on Cambacérès's work.
6. desiderata: refers to the pieces missing from a collection, such as an

entomologist's. Mme Hanska's son-in-law was a dedicated entomologist.

7. "made": this "phrase borrowed from the slang of the gutters": Balzac's courtesans and prostitutes use the verb *faire* (to make) when they have won a new protector or client.
8. *"The Countess":* The marriage of the rich parvenu Marshal Count de Montcornet and his very aristocratic but impoverished wife, Virginie de Troisville, figures prominently in *Les Paysans* (The Peasants).
9. *Voltaire . . . and Robespierre:* A list of celebrities of eighteenth-century society: Voltaire, the author of *Candide,* was the greatest of the *philosophes;* Pilâtre de Rozier, a physician who experimented with hot-air ballooning, died in 1785 while trying to cross the English Channel; Beaujon was a great financier; Marcel was dancing-master to Louis XV; Molé was an actor; Sophie Arnould was an opera singer and wit of the Ancien Régime; Benjamin Franklin was enormously popular in Paris while acting as emissary of the Continental Congress; Robespierre, the leader of the Convention during the Terror, was himself guillotined in 1794.
10. *"hospital":* At the time, hospitals were chiefly charitable institutions that treated indigents almost exclusively.

Chapter VII

1. *the exile was saved:* The motif of the desperate young suicide rescued by a decidedly equivocal savior is echoed in Vautrin's rescue of Lucien in *Lost Illusions,* and of Esther in *A Harlot High and Low.*
2. *Kosciusko:* The Polish patriot Tadeuz Kosciusko—who also fought for American independence—is said to have cried *"Finis Poloniae!"* ("This is the end of Poland!") when the Russian army captured Warsaw in 1794.
3. *"Clichy":* the debtors' prison in the rue de Clichy.
4. *"Chaumière":* a public ball popular with students and prostitutes. The neighborhood around the church of Notre Dame de Lorette was so heavily frequented by prostitutes that the word "lorette" became a synonym for prostitute. Balzac uses the word frequently.
5. *chlamys:* a cloak worn in ancient Greece.

CHAPTER VIII

1. *"Mademoiselle Héloise Brisetout . . . Monsieur de Stidmann"*: The guests are all members of the demimonde, or thirteenth arrondissement. The men named are all artists and writers.
2. patito: i.e., the tolerated lover.
3. *two pictures by Grueze . . . superbly framed:* This impressive collection reflects Balzac's growing interest in art collecting. Cousin Pons's art collection is even larger and more impressive. Likewise, the interest in frames reflects the taste of both Pons and Balzac.
4. *"a big profit"*: The duke's investment reflects the growing importance of the Paris stock exchange in the nineteenth century. Crevel, as we will see, is an investor in railroad stocks.
5. *d'Esgrignon . . . and la Schontz:* Josépha names not the artists and writers who enliven the thirteenth arrondissement, but the aristocrats and bankers who finance them. All of the people named represent recurring characters of varied importance, and all of the women named are courtesans.
6. *"a deed of endowment"*: The lovestruck duke has given Josépha not merely the income, but the capital that produces 30,000 francs per year. The investment is in *rentes,* government securities that paid a regular income to investors.
7. "On vous appelle Hulot . . .": "Your name is Hulot, I no longer know you!" Josépha mocks Hulot with a parody of a famous line from Corneille's *Horace.*
8. *Bonaparte became Emperor . . . :* One of Bonaparte's early popular triumphs was the *13 vendémiaire* (October 4, 1795), when the artillery officer brutally repressed a royalist insurrection in the heart of Paris. He was credited by his supporters with saving the Republic. M. Sauce was a minor official who stopped King Louis XVI at Varennes when the royal family attempted to flee Paris and the Revolution in 1791. Throughout the Revolution, Louis was extremely reluctant to use force against his own people.
9. *Prince Eugène:* Napoleon's stepson, Prince Eugène de Beauharnais (1781–1824), while viceroy of Italy, established an art museum in Rome.

10. *"entailed mansions or hereditary estates":* The Napoleonic Code, which strictly regulated inheritance, had the effect of breaking up large estates.

Chapter IX

1. *Terborch:* Gerard Terborch was a seventeenth-century Dutch painter.

Chapter X

1. *the Rocher de Cancale:* Very popular with Balzac's sophisticated society, the Rocher de Cancale was one of the most elegant and expensive restaurants in Paris.
2. *"one thousand crowns":* a crown is used for the *écu,* worth three francs (see note 12, chapter II).
3. *"Charenton":* a lunatic asylum on the outskirts of Paris, founded in 1645.

Chapter XI

1. *Parisian Creole:* The stereotype of the Creole woman—meaning here a European born in the tropics—was that of a languid sensualist.
2. *lost soul:* The French, *une âme damnée,* or someone who would risk damnation for another, is more explicit.
3. *Mohican:* Like the Corsicans mentioned earlier, Amerindians were exotic figures to Romantic Europeans. Balzac, in particular, was a great admirer of James Fenimore Cooper's *The Last of the Mohicans.*
4. *"the happy medium":* Or *juste milieu,* was the watchword of the July Monarchy.

Chapter XII

1. *Boulle:* celebrated father-son furniture makers of the mid-eighteenth century.
2. *Zaïre:* In Voltaire's tragedy *Zaïre,* the Frankish princess Zaïre is captured by the Turks as a child; the Sultan Orosmanes subsequently falls in love with her.
3. *Pompadour, Marshal de Richelieu:* Pompadour refers to Jeanne-Antoinette Poisson (1721–1764), or Madame de Pompadour, the famous mistress of Louis XV; the Maréchal de Richelieu (1696–1788)—from the family of the great minister of Louis XIII—was a notorious libertine.

4. *"Monsieur Lebas's son":* The bourgeois Lebas family figures prominently in Balzac's *La Maison du Chat-qui-pelote* (At the Sign of the Cat and Racket).
5. *"an unpublished Déjazet":* The actress Virginie Déjazet was as famous for her wit as for her talents on the stage; "unpublished," i.e., unknown.
6. *Hagar:* Abraham's concubine in the book of Genesis.
7. *"Bohemia":* still another term for the demimonde, the thirteenth arrondissement. See the short story "Un Prince de la bohème" ("A Prince of Bohemia").
8. *"his deer park":* The Parc-aux-Cerfs was a small house in Versailles where Louis XV was said to have raised young orphans to become his mistresses. In his youth, Louis XV was famous for his good looks.
9. *"investments worth ten thousand francs":* i.e., the thousand francs' capital in government *rentes.*
10. *"Dulcinea":* Don Quixote's beloved.
11. *"Mahomet's houris":* According to Muslim beliefs, the houris are beautiful women who surround Mohammed in paradise.
12. *one of the finest wits ...:* The Prince de Ligne (1735–1814), a Belgian aristocrat, was famous for his wit.
13. *"Putting up with Héloise's artist":* Balzac's courtesans typically have two lovers, a rich bourgeois or aristocrat to pay the bills, and a younger man—usually an artist or writer—to enjoy the wages of sin. Héloise's artist is the caricaturist Bixiou.
14. *"just as Henry IV allowed Bellegarde to Gabrielle":* King Henri IV turned a blind eye to his mistress Gabrielle d'Estrées's infidelity with the young duc de Bellegarde.

CHAPTER XIII

1. *Agnes:* unclear; a reference to Saint Agnes, or to a lamb-like Christian?
2. *Jesuitically:* i.e., hypocritically, deviously; following a long-standing stereotype of the Jesuit order.
3. *Clichy Castle:* Stidmann continues his joke with this reference to the debtors' prison in the rue de Clichy.
4. *Léon de Lora:* a minor recurring character.
5. *Bridau:* The artist Joseph Bridau of Balzac's *La Rabouilleuse* (A Bachelor's Establishment).

6. *the Turk:* In French, *Bédouin,* i.e., a barbarian who does not understand the artistic temperament. "English" is used in a similar way.

CHAPTER XIV

1. *forage business:* i.e., Fischer serves as a military supplier (see note 6, chapter IV).
2. *. . . scrutinize a substitute:* "trafficker in human flesh" refers to an agent whose business was to find substitutes for wealthy young men who wanted to avoid conscription.
3. *"the Little Corporal":* Bonaparte, who led an army to Egypt in 1798. Balzac refers to this campaign in the short story "Une passion dans le désert" ("A Passion in the Desert"), and in the novel *Le Médecin de campagne* (The Country Doctor).
4. *". . . on your accounts to us":* This type of embezzlement, which was fairly common among army suppliers, made fortunes for many people.
5. *"we have been there for eight years":* The colonization of Algeria was one of the innovations of the July Monarchy.
6. *Baron de Nucingen:* Throughout *La Comédie humaine,* the ruthless banker Nucingen incarnates the growing force of capitalism in early nineteenth-century France. His story is told in *La Maison Nucingen* (The House of Nucingen).
7. *Peer of France:* i.e., A member of the Chambre des Pairs, the upper house of the bicameral legislature under the July Monarchy. The lower house was the Chambre des Députés.
8. *his inimitable German-Jewish accent:* Raine has resisted the temptation to transcribe this accent here. Balzac greatly amused himself when creating Nucingen's heavily German-accented French (see p. 265 and note 3, chapter XXV).
9. *" 'I, too, have known that sorrow, and withstood it' ":* A very loose paraphrase of a famous verse from *Bérénice* by Jean Racine (1639–1699). The sorrow Nucingen refers to is his own very expensive obsession with the courtesan Esther in *Splendeurs et misères des courtisanes.* Nucingen could better withstand that sorrow due to his immense fortune.
10. *peculation:* embezzlement.

11. *a Jupiter to that middle-class Danaë:* In order to seduce the imprisoned maiden Danaë, Jupiter (Zeus) visited her in the form of a golden rain; their son was Perseus.
12. *"Cinna":* In Corneille's *Cinna,* the young Roman nobleman rebels against the emperor Augustus, who then pardons him. Crevel, not surprisingly, thus casts himself in the role of the generous and forgiving emperor.

CHAPTER XV

1. *a second Fabert:* Abraham de Fabert (1599–1662) was a great general and Marshal of France in the seventeenth century.
2. *amateurs:* In the original sense of the word, connoisseurs who appreciate venal beauty.
3. *Laïs:* a celebrated courtesan of ancient Athens; *Laïs* came to be a general term for courtesan.
4. *Sophie Arnould:* a great soprano in eighteenth-century Paris. In the social world, she was appreciated for her sharp wit (see note 9, chapter VI).
5. *Madame Colleville:* a minor figure in *Les Employés* (The Clerks), she is more adulteress than courtesan. Mme de la Baudraye's passion for the second-rate writer Lousteau is the subject of *La Muse du département* (The Departmental Muse).
6. *the first surgeon of Louis XV:* La Martinière, who counseled the aging monarch to give up his amorous adventures.
7. *Charles X* and the *Royal House:* Charles X, youngest brother of Louis XVI, was the last of the Bourbon kings, deposed by the July Revolution of 1830 (see note 7, chapter 1). For a legitimist like Balzac, Louis-Philippe d'Orléans would be considered a usurper.
8. *This Benjamin:* In the Old Testament, Benjamin is the favorite son of Jacob. There is also a play on words, as *benjamin* in French refers to the youngest son in a family, while this Benjamin is the eldest.
9. *Claude Vignon:* a critic who appears frequently in *La Comédie humaine.*
10. *borough:* again, arrondissement.
11. *Louis XII:* At fifty-two, King Louis XII (1462–1515) married the

sixteen-year-old sister of Henry VIII of England. He died soon after the marriage.

12. *his cross:* that is, his cross of the Legion of Honor.

CHAPTER XVI

1. *Bleeding Nun:* a terrifying figure from the very Gothic and immensely popular English novel *The Monk* (1796), by Matthew Lewis.
2. *since 1838:* Balzac was highly critical of certain socialist pamphlets that appeared in or after 1838.
3. *The Montyon prize:* A sort of French Alfred Nobel, the Baron de Montyon (1733–1820) established cash prizes for industry, science, medicine, virtue, and the arts, including the literary work judged most useful to society. Balzac strongly believed that he should have won the prize for his 1833 novel *Le Médecin de campagne* (The Country Doctor).

CHAPTER XVII

1. *crepe:* Black crepe was the traditional material of mourning clothes.
2. Imitation of Christ: or *Imitatio Christi,* written by Thomas à Kempis in the fifteenth century, was a celebrated devotional work. It figures prominently in Balzac's *L'Envers de l'histoire contemporaine* (The Underside of Contemporary History).

CHAPTER XVIII

1. *Mirabeau:* Honoré-Gabriel Riqueti, or the Comte de Mirabeau (1749–1791), the great orator of the National Assembly in 1789–91, was also a notorious womanizer; Crevel's imitative pose is still another of his pretensions.
2. *"two louis":* the *louis* was worth twenty francs.
3. *the suppression of public gambling:* as of December 31, 1837.

CHAPTER XIX

1. *five sous:* twenty-five centimes.
2. *"Saint-Preux":* The noble, selfless hero of Rousseau's *La Nouvelle Héloïse,* is a very different character from the jealous and ultimately violent Othello.

3. *"Orléans shares"*: i.e., shares in the Paris-Orléans railroad. Balzac's characters have far better luck investing in railroad stocks than did Balzac himself.

Chapter XX

1. Liaisons dangereuses: Choderlos de Laclos's scandalous 1782 novel features the ruthless and brilliant libertines Valmont and Mme de Merteuil.
2. *Crevel's little house*: The *petite maison*—used for assignations—was a prize possession of rich, aristocratic libertines in the eighteenth century.
3. *"Molière . . . in* your *title"*: *Le Cocu imaginaire* (The Imaginary Cuckold) is a farce by Molière.
4. *"Canillac"*: The Marquis de Canillac was one of the libertine companions of the Regent, Louis-Philippe d'Orléans.
5. *"Gubetta"*: A curious allusion, Gubetta is Lucrecia's devoted henchman in Victor Hugo's play *Lucrèce Borgia* (1833).
6. *"Arnal"*: Pierre Arnal (1794–1872) was a famous comic actor of the vaudeville theater.
7. *"an American cousin"*: i.e., not a real cousin.
8. *"Susannah"*: In the Old Testament, Susannah was falsely accused of adultery by two elders whose advances she had refused. Daniel saved her life by exposing her accusers.
9. *"Benjamin"*: See note 8 to chapter XV. Montès will be both the youngest and the most favored of Valérie's lovers.

Chapter XXI

1. *Curtius:* When an earthquake opened a crevice in the Roman forum, the young patrician Marcus Curtius threw himself into the abyss to appease the gods.
2. *Murat:* Joachim Murat (1767–1815), general and brother-in-law of Napoleon, later made king of Naples, was famous for a courage that bordered on recklessness.
3. *Phidias:* great sculptor of ancient Greece, ca. fourth century B.C.E.
4. *Beaumarchais, Richardson, and the Abbé Prévost:* Pierre-Augustin Caron de

Beaumarchais's Figaro—the shrewd and witty valet from *The Barber of Seville* and *The Marriage of Figaro*—was an important figure in the French imagination; *Lovelace* refers to the villainous rake of Samuel Richardson's novel *Clarissa,* which is a very frequent point of reference for Balzac; the Abbé Prévost's novel *Manon Lescaut,* hugely popular, made the tragic prostitute Manon an archetype.

5. *Canova ... Voltaire ... Phidias:* Balzac could have added himself to this list of hard-working artists; he frequently worked all through the night, and referred to himself as a literary galley-slave.
6. *Madame Schontz:* the shrewd courtesan who earns enough money, through her relationship with the Marquis de Rochefide, to make herself an acceptable match for a provincial magistrate; this story is part of the novel *Béatrix.*
7. *"old girl":* a literal interpretation of *vieille fille,* which has the sense of "old maid" in English.
8. *"Calypso":* According to Fénelon's *Télémaque* (see note 11, chapter XXXI), the nymph Calypso mourned the loss of her lover Ulysses until his son Telemachus came to take his place.

Chapter XXII

1. *Austerlitzes:* The Battle of Austerlitz was a huge victory for Bonaparte against Austria in 1805.
2. *the* assassine *of our grandmothers' days:* The *assassine* was a beauty spot (a *mouche*) placed just below the eye, considered very seductive in the eighteenth century.
3. *Madame* de *Marneffe:* Crevel has given his lover an article (de, du, de la, or des) that usually, but not always, denotes aristocratic birth.
4. *"Madame de Maintenon":* (1635–1719), morganatic wife of Louis XIV, became increasingly devout toward the end of her life. The reference to Ninon de Lenclos (see note 5, chapter III) alludes to Valérie's wit.
5. *the generous white eagle ... the two-headed eagle:* The white eagle was the symbol of independent Poland. Poland had been partitioned by Prussia, Russia, and Austria in 1772 and 1795, subjugated by Napoleon, and carved up again at the Congress of Vienna in 1815, with the lion's share going to Russia (see note 10, chapter IV). The two-headed eagle

was the emblem of both the Austrian and Russian empires. It refers here to Russia, which had annexed Poland outright in 1820.

6. *Louis XI:* The shrewd and devious Louis XI (1423–1483), called the Spider King, did much to strengthen the French monarchy left weakened by the Hundred Years' War and the power of the great dukes of Burgundy. The Romantics referred to his legend frequently, including Balzac in *Maître Cornélius* and Victor Hugo in *Notre Dame de Paris.*
7. *Manons as Irises and Chloes:* i.e., they made their mistresses into nymphs and goddesses; *Manon* refers again to Manon Lescaut (see note 4, chapter XXI).
8. *"Célimène":* character from Molière's masterpiece *The Misanthrope,* became the archetype of the unfaithful lover—the *coquette*—in French culture.
9. *"Hercules at the feet of Omphale":* Zeus punished Hercules by making him the slave of Queen Omphale, who forced him to perform humiliating tasks.
10. *"ferocious Judith":* in the Old Testament, the Jewish heroine who seduced and beheaded the general Holofernes.
11. *"Camille Maupin":* the pen name of the aristocratic writer Félicité des Touches, a character based in large measure on George Sand. She is universally admired within *La Comédie humaine.*
12. *odalisque:* a harem slave or concubine.
13. *Phaedra to Hippolytus:* In a famous scene from Racine's *Phèdra,* Phaedra confesses her tortured, forbidden love for Hippolytus, her husband's son. The virtuous Hippolytus is horrified by this (quasi-)incestuous passion.
14. *yellow-faced:* in French, *"ce chinois de Marneffe"* ("that Chinaman Marneffe"), a reference to Marneffe's illness, but implying also a devious nature.

Chapter XXIII

1. *"the Rocher de Cancale":* See note 1, chapter X.
2. *"make":* See note 7, chapter VI.

CHAPTER XXIV

1. *"acting editor":* a pun on Marneffe's legal responsibility for the child that is not his.

CHAPTER XXV

1. *"Versailles* Rive Gauche *railway"*: Crevel has invested in another railroad that runs from the Left Bank in Paris to Versailles.
2. *Madame de Merteuil:* The Marquise de Merteuil is the brilliantly manipulative villainess of Laclos's *Les Liaisons dangereuses.*
3. "Mennesir the Paron Hilotte": A brief example of the Germanic accent Balzac liked to give Nucingen and other German or Alsatian characters (see note 8, chapter XIV).

CHAPTER XXVI

1. *the* Nouvelle Héloise: Rousseau's sentimental epistolary novel was one of the first great works of the Romantic era.
2. *Hymen:* the Greek god of marriage.

CHAPTER XXVII

1. *Jan:* a complimentary nod to Balzac's good friend Laurent-Jan, an artist and writer.
2. *melancholic Englishmen:* a playful swipe at the stereotypical Romantic, such as Lord Byron.
3. *"the cholera":* Nucingen's affliction; another reference to the banker's passion for Esther van Gobseck in *Splendeurs et misères des courtisanes.*
4. *Hulot:* Victor Hugo was discovered *in flagrante* with a mistress on July 5, 1845. As Hugo had just been named a member of the Chamber of Peers, the situation became a national scandal.
5. *Scene of Paris life: Scène de la vie parisienne.* The individual works of *The Human Comedy* were divided into three groups: *The Study of Mores* (*Les études de moeurs*), *The Philosophical Studies* (*Les études philosophiques*), and the *Analytical Studies* (*Les études analytiques*). The first group, by far the largest, was further divided into: *Scenes of Private Life, Scenes of Provin-*

cial Life, Scenes of Parisian Life, Scenes of Political Life, Scenes of Military Life, Scenes of Country Life.

6. *Sub-Lieutenant Cottin:* Cottin is Wissembourg's family name, predating his imperial glory (see note 8, chapter III).
7. *July celebrations:* i.e., the celebrations of the July Revolution and the establishment of the new government.

CHAPTER XXVIII

1. *Gros-René:* Gross-René is a crass character from Molière's farce *Le Délit amoureux* (The Lover's Crime). The line quoted, however, actually comes from *L'école des femmes* (The School for Wives).
2. *Carème:* The famous chef—whose name, ironically, is the French word for the lenten fast—was employed by some of the greatest aristocrats of the time, including Talleyrand and the Prince of Wales.
3. *Marchesa de Pescara ... Diane de Poitiers:* Vittoria Colonna, Marchesa di Pescara (1492–1547), was famous for her beauty and her fidelity to her husband, even after his death. Diane de Poitiers was the mistress of King Henri II (see note 5, chapter III).
4. *Count Popinot:* Crevel's former colleague at Birotteau's shop, who has been far more successful than Crevel (see note 4, chapter II).
5. *Maecenases:* Maecenas was the legendary patron of the arts of classical Rome.
6. *"the vessels of the Danaids":* The Danaids, from Greek mythology, were fifty sisters who killed their husbands and were condemned to carry water in leaking vessels for eternity.
7. *Dubois who gave the Regent three kicks:* As a joke, the Regent Louis-Philippe d'Orléans once disguised himself as the valet of his minister Guillaume Dubois, who took his role too seriously.
8. *"regicides":* this method of execution and torture was carried out on Ravaillac, the assassin of Henri IV, in 1610.

CHAPTER XXIX

1. *"Her Holiness the Bank":* i.e., the Bank of France.
2. *"Racine":* from Racine's *Athalie.* Toward the end of his life, Racine turned from Ancient Greece and Rome to the Bible as a source for his tragedies.

3. *"three-per-cents"*: i.e., government *rentes* paying three percent.
4. *"monstrance"*: the vessel used to present the Eucharist to the congregation in the Catholic Mass.
5. *"Egeria"*: the nymph who, according to legend, advised the Roman king Numa Pompilius.
6. *"present Prime Minister"*: François-Pierre-Guillaume Guizot (1787–1874), whose *égérie* was the Russian princess de Lieven.
7. *(as Rabelais puts it)*: Balzac was a great admirer of the often ribald work of François Rabelais (ca. 1483–1553), author of *Gargantua* and *Pantagruel* and one of the greatest humanists of the French Renaissance.
8. *Montyon*: a contemporary philanthopist (see note 3, chapter XVI).

Chapter XXX

1. *the Invalides*: The Hôtel des Invalides was established by Louis XIV as a hospital and residence for wounded veterans.
2. *"In 1809"*: The 1809 campaign against Austria culminated in the Battle of Wagram, one of Napoleon's last significant victories.
3. *"Marshal Masséna"*: one of the most successful generals of the Republic and the Empire; a great favorite of Bonaparte's.
4. *"Arcoli"*: One of the Italian battles (1796) that made General Bonaparte a hero to the French people.
5. *this rival of Bernadotte*: Jean-Baptiste-Jules Bernadotte (1763–1844) was arguably the most successful general of the era. In 1809, in order to make an ally of Bonaparte, the Swedish Senate named him heir to the childless Charles XIII. Bernadotte turned on his onetime comrade and joined in the alliance against him in 1812. Bernadotte became King Charles XIV of Sweden and Norway; his descendants still hold the Swedish throne.
6. *"piece of crown property"*: The Royal family and the parliament were in a dispute over the ownership of the château at Rambouillet.
7. *"that clerk in the Treasury"*: an allusion to a contemporary scandal; a respected family man embezzled from the Treasury to support his mistress.
8. *"an infernal blackguard"*: in French, *"un j. . . f. . . !"* for *jean-foutre* (roughly,

"son of a bitch"); an example of "the language of Sub-lieutenant Cottin."

9. *"I am at your service!":* The honorable old soldier wants a duel to avenge the insult to his family.
10. *Beresina:* The Beresina River was the site of a disaster for the *Grande Armée* in retreat after the failed Russian campaign. Balzac evokes the crossing of the Beresina in the short story "Adieu."
11. *Sganarelle:* the shifty valet was a stock character in French farce; Molière used the name frequently.
12. *"Come, sir": Venez, monsieur;* the furious marshal uses the formal *vous* form with his disgraced brother.
13. Le fait-Paris . . . : roughly translates as "The news of Paris is not what the common people think." A parody of an anticlerical line from Voltaire's Oedipe:
    Nos prêtres ne sont pas ce qu'un vain peuple pense:
    Notre crédulité fait toute leur science.
    (Our priests are not what the people think them to be,
    Their wisdom comes only from our credulity.)

Chapter XXXI

1. (*See* Les Chouans): title of one of the later works of *La Comédie humaine.* It became increasingly common for Balzac to make references such as this to other parts of his literary whole.
2. *Emperor Alexander . . . Emperor Napoleon's:* Napoleon and Alexander, once great admirers of each other, had become enemies by 1812. The battle of Dresden—during which General Vandamme was taken prisoner—took place in 1813.
3. *Condé of the Republic:* Louis II de Bourbon, Prince de Condé (1621–1686)—called "Le Grand Condé," first Prince of the Royal Blood and cousin to Louis XIV—was one of the greatest generals of seventeenth-century France.
4. Madame: the Duchesse de Berry (1798–1870), widowed daughter-in-law of Charles X and mother to the legitimist heir, Henri de Bourbon (1820–1883), to the throne. In 1832, she attempted to lead

a rebellion against the Orléans monarchy, but was soon captured in Brittany.

5. "sans culotte": literally "without breeches," the name was used to designate first the common people and later the most radical factions during the Revolution. Josépha is playing on Hulot's string of "withouts"; she also makes a sly reference to Hulot's emasculated position.
6. *"as Gourville counted on Ninon"*: Another reference to Ninon de Lenclos, who rescued Gourville—one of her lovers—when he was accused of embezzling from the government of Louis XIV.
7. *"Sardanapalus"*: ancient king of Assyria; that is to say, Hulot's audacious conduct is worthy of a great pagan king.
8. " 'C'est Vénus toute entière . . .' ": "It is Venus relentlessly fixed on her prey," from Racine's *Phèdre,* in which love—Phaedra's passion for her husband's son—is the revenge of the cruel goddess.
9. *"the* Bois*"*: the Bois de Boulogne, the park on the western edge of Paris, where fashionable people, women in their carriages and men on horseback, went to see and to be seen.
10. *"Schontz and Rochefide"*: See note 6, chapter XXI.
11. *"Fénelon"*: churchman, moralist, and writer of the late seventeenth century.
12. *"Ambigu-Comique"*: one of Paris's second-tier theaters.
13. *"on the wrong side of the blanket"*: i.e., a marriage of the thirteenth arrondissement.
14. *"Mabille"*: another of the public, open-air balls frequented by students and prostitutes.
15. *"my friend d'Aiglemont"*: The Marquis d'Aiglemont is a victim of Nucingen's financial genius in Balzac's *La Maison Nucingen* (The House of Nucingen).
16. *Olympe Bijou:* this girl seems to already have a *nom de guerre* for her budding career. Bijou means "jewel," and Olympe, besides its classical connotation, suggests the grand courtesan Olympe Pélissier, whom Balzac knew personally and who later became the wife of Rossini.
17. *"Bartholo"*: the jealous husband of Beaumarchais's *The Barber of Séville.*
18. *"Augustes . . . Victors"*: handsome young seductors of various plays and works of fiction.
19. ors: *Or* is the French word for gold.

CHAPTER XXXII

1. *"Mesdames Popinot . . . and de la Bâtie":* The ladies named are all recurring characters in *La Comédie humaine;* they run the gamut from the oldest nobility (Mmes de Grandlieu and de Navarreins) to the Imperial (Mme de Carigliano) to the ennobled bourgeoise (Mme la Comtesse Popinot).
2. *"Dr. Bianchon":* one of Balzac's the most frequently reappearing characters. According to legend, Balzac called out for Dr. Bianchon on his deathbed.
3. *"an estate I have my eye on":* Certain estates gave their owners the right to an aristocratic name. Note how the social and the political are intertwined in Crevel's ambitions. Mme de Sérizy is a well-known *coquette* of Balzac's high society.
4. *President of the Council:* essentially the prime minister.

CHAPTER XXXIII

1. " 'du malheur, auguste victime' ": literally "of misfortune, the august victim," a then-famous line from Sacchini's opera *Oedipe à Colone.* The verse became famous as a tribute to Louis XVI when the royal family attended the opera soon after the first Restoration.
2. *"follies":* like the *"petites maisons"* (see note 2, chapter XX), they were extravagant houses often meant for the mistresses of the aristocrats or financiers who built them.
3. *Joseph Bridau:* This talented artist is a creation of Balzac's (see note 5, chapter XIII).
4. *Malibran:* Maria-Félicia Malibran (1808–1836) was a famous soprano in the Paris opera.
5. *nephew of Bronzino:* Another sign of Balzac's interest in art, this reference is nonetheless incorrect: Allori (1577–1621), not Alloris, was the great-nephew of the painter Bronzino (1503–1572).
6. *Mathilde:* of Rossini's *William Tell.*
7. *"our part of Paris":* again, a reference to the thirteenth arrondissement (see note 11, chapter II). Divorce had been legalized during the Revolution, and banned again under the Restoration.
8. *"paid to clap at the plays":* The success or failure of a play, playwright, or

actor could be determined by *claques,* groups of spectators paid to cheer or to harass a given play.

9. *"A Chaumière tart":* i.e., a prostitute who works the Chaumière ball (see note 4, chapter VII).
10. *"Melun":* the site of a large prison.
11. *the terrible name of the Chief of the Secret Police:* A reference to Vautrin (see p. 386), alias Jacques Collin. Balzac's arch-criminal (*Old Goriot, Lost Illusions*) obtains this position in 1829, at the end of *Splendeurs et misères des courtisanes.* Readers of that novel will also recognize his ferocious aunt and criminal mentor, Jacqueline Collin, alias Mme de Saint-Estève, alias Mme Nourrisson.
12. *"The Faubourg Saint-Germain":* the most aristocratic neighborhood in Paris (see note 3, chapter I).
13. *sister of the hulks:* "Hulks" refers to galley-ships where the worst criminals were sent, usually for life.
14. *"seventeen ninety-nine and eighteen fifteen":* From the Consulate through Waterloo, these dates measure the whole reign of Napoleon, including the first exile to Elba.
15. *"Fouché, Monsieur Lenoir, Monsieur de Sartines":* Joseph Fouché (1759–1820) was Napoleon's legendary Minister of Police. Jean Lenoir was the last lieutenant general of the Police under the Ancien Régime; Lenoir was preceded by Antoine Sartines (or Sartinez).
16. *"Bibi-Lupin":* a reference to Eugène-François Vidocq (1775–1857), the real-life model for Vautrin. Vidocq was a criminal who was recruited to serve the secret police.
17. *Atala:* Contemporary readers would have immediately recognized the name of the virtuous Amerindian maiden of Chateaubriand's short, sentimental novel of the same name.

Chapter XXXIV

1. *"Aspasia into a Lucrèce":* Aspasia was a famous courtesan of ancient Greece, the witty mistress of Pericles; Lucrèce refers to the virtuous Roman patrician who killed herself rather than submit to being raped.

2. *"the Birottery"*: a reference to Birotteau's perfume shop (see note 4, chapter II).
3. *Cardot's:* A minor recurring character, Cardot is the lawyer for most of Balzac's bourgeoisie.
4. *that appalling witch, described long ago by Shakespeare:* Balzac alludes to Macbeth's encounter with the weird sisters (*Macbeth:* Act I, scene iii):
"... you should be women,
And yet your beards forbid me to interpret
That you are so."
cf. p. 368: Mme de Saint-Estève's facial hair and virile manner.

CHAPTER XXXV

1. *lion:* an ambitious and adventurous young man of Balzac's high society; Rastignac and de Marsay are the archetypal *lions* of *La Comédie humaine.*
2. *turf:* refers to the social scene around horse-racing, which was becoming increasingly popular. The fashionable Jockey-Club was a manifestation of the Anglophilia of high society in Paris of the period.
3. *Combabus:* A legendary figure of antiquity, this favorite of King Seleucide Antiochus of Syria castrated himself to resist the temptation of the queen.
4. *Bixiou:* the caricaturist is a secondary but important character in many of Balzac's works; he enlivens gatherings of the thirteenth arrondissement with his scathing wit. It is interesting to note how Balzac insists on this character's aging: in *La Maison Nucingen,* he is presented as "the Bixiou of 1836," who "alas" has changed greatly from the "Bixiou of 1825"; here we see the "Bixiou of 1843."
5. *Abélard:* Pierre Abélard was the famous twelfth-century monk and scholar, as well known for his scandalous personal life as for his controversial scholarship. Hired as a tutor, he fell in love with and seduced his student Héloïse. When the girl became pregnant, the couple married in secret. Nonetheless, Héloïse's outraged family had Abélard abducted and castrated. Abélard and Héloïse were then sent to separate cloisters, and carried on a famous correspondence in

Latin. The couple became symbolic of star-crossed love in French literature.

6. *"Catoxantha"*: a rare specimen of beetle.
7. *Amphitryon:* i.e., the host of the evening, after an ancient king of Thebes.
8. *a Longchamps of fashion:* Longchamps was an elegant promenade in the Bois de Boulogne.
9. shibboleth: from the Old Testament, a sort of password; Balzac frequently refers to the *shibboleths* of different social groups.
10. *"Lousteau . . . Madame de la Baudraye"*: a reference to Balzac's *La Muse du département* (The Departmental Muse).
11. *"Francis the First"*: traditionally thought of by the French as the ideal Renaissance prince. He also had a reputation as a libertine.
12. *"the late King of Holland"*: William I of Holland lost the provinces that were to become Belgium when he refused to make concessions to the discontented citizens in 1830.

Chapter XXXVI

1. Postillon de Longjumeau: a reference to a popular song of the time.
2. *"a terrible disease"*: a fatal venereal disease will be passed from the slave to Cydalise, from Cydalise to Henri, and finally to Valérie.
3. *"Orlando furioso"*: Ludovico Ariosto's 1516 epic poem portrays the chivalric hero Orlando (Roland) driven mad by love.
4. urbi et orbi: Latin for "to the city and to the world."
5. *Vulcan's nets:* Vulcan captured his wife, Venus, and the war-god Mars in a net in order to prove their infidelity to the other gods.
6. *Gavarni:* the artist Paul Gavarni (1804–1866) was known for his portrayals of courtesans and lorettes.
7. *the Salon:* the biennial exposition of works sponsored by the Académie Royale de Peinture et de Sculpture.
8. *the Salpetrière:* this hospital served as both an asylum and a prison for prostitutes and vagrants.

CHAPTER XXXVII

1. *Vauvinet having signed his replevin:* i.e., Vauvinet having legally demanded the monies due him.
2. *"The confessor ... of common humanity":* Bianchon's speech echoes the famous one made by the lawyer Derville at the end of Balzac's *Le Colonel Chabert* (1832).
3. *"eligible":* i.e., eligible to vote.
4. *"... life from the inside":* Bianchon echos Balzac's political views in this speech.
5. *"their faculties":* i.e., their students and colleagues.
6. *"Baron d'Holbach's wit":* The Baron d'Holbach (1723–1784) was one of the *philosophes.*
7. *"Béranger, the friend of Lisette":* The enormously popular songs of Pierre-Jean de Béranger (1780–1857), including "Lisette," were often subversive, antiroyalist, and anticlerical.
8. *"Montesquieu":* Charles de Secondat, Baron de Montesquieu (1689–1755), author (*The Persian Letters, The Spirit of Laws*), and political theorist, was said to have rejected the priest sent to his deathbed, because the Jesuit was really seeking to censor the writer's papers after his death.
9. *... Cet esclave ... obtenu:* Crevel quotes Racine's *Bajazet* to demonstrate his disdain for the priest:

   "... That slave came
   He showed me his orders, and obtained nothing."

CHAPTER XXXVIII

1. *Madame de la Chanterie:* the heroine of Balzac's *L'Envers de l'histoire contemporaine* (The Underside of Contemporary History); the character incarnates Balzac's ideal of Christian charity (see note 2, chapter XVII).
2. *civil and religious marriage:* Since the Revolution, only civil marriages were legally recognized; it was (and remains) common for couples to have two ceremonies.
3. *"Atala she is called":* Balzac's contemporaries would have seen in this name an echo of Chateaubriand's short novel *Atala* (1826) (see note 17, chapter XXXIII). Chateaubriand's Atala is a virtuous Amerindian

maiden who kills herself when torn between love and a vow of chastity made to God. Balzac's Parisian savage is rather less noble.

4. *artist* in partibus: In the Catholic Church, bishops *in partibus* had the title but no official diocese; i.e., Steinbock is an artist who creates no art.

About the Translator

Kathleen Raine, born in Ilford, England, in 1908, is the author of a number of poetry collections, including *Stone and Flower* (1943) and *Living with Mystery* (1992). A prolific essayist, critic, and editor, she also published a three-volume autobiography, *Farewell Happy Fields* (1973), *The Land Unknown* (1975), and *The Lion's Mouth* (1977). Her many literary accolades include the distinguished title of Commandeur de l'Ordre des Arts et des Lettres, awarded to her by the French government. Dr. Raine has translated works by Denis de Rougemont and Pedro Calderón de la Barca. Her fine translation of Balzac's *Lost Illusions* is available from the Modern Library in both cloth and paper. She lives in London.

A Note on the Type

The principal text of this Modern Library edition was set in a digitized version of Janson, a typeface that dates from about 1690 and was cut by Nicholas Kis, a Hungarian working in Amsterdam. The original matrices have survived and are held by the Stempel foundry in Germany. Hermann Zapf redesigned some of the weights and sizes for Stempel, basing his revisions on the original design.